P9-CMC-766

AUGUSTUS

JOHN WILLIAMS (1922–1994) was born and raised in northeast Texas. Despite a talent for writing and acting, Williams flunked out of a local junior college after his first year. He reluctantly joined the war effort, enlisting in the Army Air Corps, and managed to write a draft of his first novel while there. Once home, Williams found a small publisher for the novel and enrolled at the University of Denver, where he was eventually to receive both his B.A. and M.A., and where he was to return as an instructor in 1954. He remained on the staff of the creative writing program at the University of Denver until his retirement in 1985. During these years, he was an active guest lecturer and writer, editing an anthology of English Renaissance poetry and publishing two volumes of his own poems, as well as three novels, *Butcher's Crossing*, *Stoner*, and the National Book Award–winning *Augustus* (all published as NYRB Classics).

DANIEL MENDELSOHN was born in 1960 and studied classics at the University of Virginia and at Princeton, where he received his doctorate. His essays and reviews appear regularly in *The New York Review of Books*, *The New Yorker*, and *The New York Times Book Review*. His books include *The Lost: A Search for Six of Six Million*; a memoir, *The Elusive Embrace*; and the collection *Waiting for the Barbarians: Essays from the Classics to Pop Culture*, published by New York Review Books. He teaches at Bard College.

AUGUSTUS

JOHN WILLIAMS

Introduction by
DANIEL MENDELSOHN

NEW YORK REVIEW BOOKS

New York

THIS IS A NEW YORK REVIEW BOOK
PUBLISHED BY THE NEW YORK REVIEW OF BOOKS
435 Hudson Street, New York, NY 10014
www.nyrb.com

Library of Congress Cataloging-in-Publication Data
Williams, John Edward, 1922–
  Augustus / John Williams ; introduction by Daniel Mendelsohn.
     pages ; cm. — (New York Review Books Classics)
  ISBN 978-1-59017-821-8 (paperback)
  1. Augustus, Emperor of Rome, 63 B.C.–14 A.D.—Fiction. 2. Rome—
History—Empire, 30 B.C.–284 A.D.—Fiction. 3. Emperors—Fiction.
I. Title.
  PS3545.I5286A94 2014
  813'.54—dc23

                        2014013233

ISBN 978-1-59017-821-8
Available as an electronic book; 978-1-59017-822-5

Printed in the United States of America on acid-free paper.
10 9 8 7 6 5 4 3 2

INTRODUCTION

Compared to John Williams's earlier novels, *Augustus*—the last work to be published by the author, poet, and professor, whose once-neglected *Stoner* has become an international literary sensation in recent years— can seem like an oddity. For one thing, it was the only one of his four novels to win significant acclaim during his lifetime: Published in 1972, *Augustus* won the National Book Award for fiction in the following year. (Williams was born in Texas in 1922 and died in Arkansas in 1994, after a thirty-year career teaching English and creative writing at the University of Denver.) More important, the novel's subject—the eventful life and history-changing career of the first emperor of Rome—seems impossibly remote from the distinctly American preoccupations of the author's other mature works, with their modest protagonists and pared-down narratives. *Butcher's Crossing* (1960) is the story of a young Bostonian who, besotted with Emersonian transcendentalism, goes west in 1876 to explore the "wilderness" where, he believes, "the central meaning he could find in all his life" lies; there he participates in a savage buffalo hunt that suggests the costs of the American dream. *Stoner* (1965) traces the obscure and, to all appearances, unsuccessful life of an assistant professor of English at the University of Missouri in the early and middle years of the last century— a man of desperately humble origins who sees the Academy as an "asylum," a place where he finds at last "the kind of security and warmth that he should have been able to feel as a child in his home." (Williams later repudiated his first novel, *Nothing But the Night*, published in 1948, about a dandy with psychological problems.)

It would be difficult to find a figure ostensibly less like these idealistic and, ultimately, disillusioned minor figures than the real-life world leader known to history as Augustus—a man whose many and elaborate names, given and taken, augmented and elaborated, acquired and discarded over the eight decades of his tumultuous and grandiose life stand in almost comic contrast to the simple disyllables Williams gave those two other protagonists. Both, as readers will notice, share their creator's name—William Andrews, William Stoner: a coincidence that makes it almost impossible not to seek some element of autobiography in the early novels.

No such temptation exists in the case of *Augustus*. The emperor who gave his lofty name to a political and literary era was born Gaius Octavius Thurinus in 63 BC, the year in which the statesman Cicero foiled an aristocrat's attempt to overthrow the Roman Republic (a system of government to which Augustus himself would administer the coup de grâce three decades later). The offspring of one Gaius Octavius, a well-to-do knight of plebeian family origins, he was raised in the provinces about twenty-five miles from Rome. While still a teenager, the sickly but clever and ambitious youth sufficiently impressed his maternal great-uncle Julius Caesar to be adopted by him; he was thereafter known as Gaius Julius Caesar Octavianus ("Octavian").

In 44 BC, following Caesar's assassination and his subsequent deification by decree of the Senate, the canny nineteen-year-old, eager to capitalize on his dead relative's prestige and thereby enhance his standing with Caesar's veterans, referred to himself as Gaius Julius Caesar Divi Filius ("Son of the Divine"). By the time he was twenty-five, having avenged Caesar's murder by vanquishing Brutus and Cassius at Philippi, the new Gaius Julius Caesar had shrewdly maneuvered himself to the center of power in the Roman world as one of three military dictators, or "triumvirs." (Another was Marc Antony, with whom he would eventually quarrel.) At this point the "Gaius" and "Julius" disappeared, to be replaced by "Imperator": a military title used by troops to acclaim successful leaders, and the root of the English word "emperor."

Within another decade this Imperator Caesar Divi Filius had successfully wrested absolute control of the vast Roman dominions from his one remaining rival, Antony, whom he defeated at Actium in 31 BC and who committed suicide a year later, along with his paramour, Cleopatra. (As the imperator gave the order to murder Cleopatra's teenaged son Caesarion—a potential rival, since the youth's father had been Julius Caesar himself—he remarked that "too many Caesars is no good thing.") Master of the world at thirty-three, he then set about consolidating his power, craftily legitimating his autocratic rule under the forms of traditional republican law, and establishing the legal, political, and cultural foundations for empire that would persist, in one form or another, for the next fifteen centuries. And, indeed, beyond: The current structure of the Roman Catholic Church derives directly from Augustus's political creation.

One title that this astonishingly adept figure never used was *rex*, "king"—a word much loathed by the Romans, some of whom killed his great-uncle partly out of fear that he wanted to be one; shrewdly, the master of the world referred to himself as *princeps*, "first citizen." In 27 BC, ostensibly in gratitude to the new Caesar for ending a century of civil bloodshed and establishing political stability at home and abroad, the Roman Senate voted him an unprecedented additional title that had suggestive religious associations: *augustus*, "the one who is to be venerated." It is the name by which he has come to be known by history—one that bore no resemblance whatsoever to the one he was born with.

No resemblance to his former self: It is here that the hidden kinship between *Augustus* and its two predecessors lies. A strong theme in Williams's work is the way that, over time, our sense of who we are can be irrevocably altered by circumstance and accident. In his Augustus novel, Williams took great pains to see past the glittering historical pageant and focus on the elusive man himself, one who, more than most, had to evolve new selves in order to prevail. The surprise of his final novel is that its famous protagonist turns out to be no different in the end from this author's other disappointed heroes—which is to say, neither better nor worse than most of us. The concerns of this spectacular historical saga are intimate and deeply humane.

The life of the first emperor is an ideal vehicle for a historical novel, a genre that is most successful when scholarly adherence to the known facts is balanced by imaginative insights into character and motivation. Augustus is a figure about whom we know at once a great deal and very little, and who therefore invites both description and invention.

The biographies and gossip, recording and conjecturing began in the emperor's own lifetime. One work, the ancient equivalent of an authorized biography, was composed by a contemporary of Augustus's who appears as a character in Williams's novel: the philosopher and historian Nicolaus of Damascus, whose CV included a stint as tutor to the children of Antony and Cleopatra. The emperor himself composed an official autobiography, the *Res Gestae Divi Augusti* ("Deeds Accomplished by the Divine Augustus"), clearly intended as a form of political propaganda: Inscribed on bronze tablets affixed to the portals of his mausoleum, it was reproduced in inscriptions throughout the empire.

If we are to believe Tacitus, writing a century after Augustus's reign, the obscurity of the emperor's nature and motives was already a subject of discussion among his contemporaries. In his *Annals*, that historian paraphrases a debate that took place at the time of the emperor's death, at the age of seventy-six, in 14 AD:

> Some said "that he was forced into to civil war—which one can neither plan nor execute on upstanding moral principles—by the duty owed to a father [i.e., Julius Caesar], and by the necessities imposed by the state, in which at the time the rule of law had no place ... and that there was no other remedy for a country at war with itself than to be ruled by one man. The state he founded

went by the name of neither a kingdom nor a dictatorship, but of a principate [a state presided over by a 'first citizen'] . . . there was law for the citizens and due respect shown to the allies; the capital was made magnificent by his embellishments; only in rare instances did he use force, and then only to effect a larger stability."

And yet:

It was said, on the other hand, "that duty toward a father and the exigencies of state were merely put on as a mask: it was in fact from a lust for domination that he had stirred up the veterans by bribery, had, while still a very young man, raised a private army, tampered with the Consul's legions . . . he wrested the consulate from a reluctant Senate and turned the arms that had been entrusted to him for a war with Antony against the republic itself. Citizens were proscribed and lands divided . . . Undoubtedly there was peace after all this, but it was a peace that dripped blood."

The emperor may, indeed, have cultivated a certain opacity as a means of maintaining control: if his nature and motives were hard to guess, so too would his actions be. Small wonder that his official seal was the enigmatic, riddling Sphinx.

How to write about such a figure? In *Augustus*, the question is slyly put in the mouth of that Nicolaus who was commissioned to write the First Citizen's biography. "Do you see what I mean," the confounded scholar writes after a meeting with Augustus, whose notorious prudence he cannot reconcile with an equally notorious penchant for gambling. "There is so much that is not said. I almost believe that the form has not been devised that will let me say what I need to say." This is an in-joke on Williams's part: The form Nicolaus dreams of—which is of course the one Williams ended up using—is the epistolary novel, a genre that wasn't invented until fifteen centuries after Augustus, when Diego de San Pedro wrote *Prison of Love* (1485), generally regarded as the first example of the genre. And yet its roots go right back to Augustus's reign: The Roman poet Ovid—also a character in *Augustus*, providing gossipy updates on the doings of the imperial court—composed a work called *Heroides* ("Heroines"), a sequence of verse epistles by mythical women to their lovers. (The worldly litterateur's taste for gossip ultimately doomed him: It's likely that his involvement in a scandal involving the emperor's family was the cause of his exile to a bleak settlement on the Black Sea.)

The epistolary form, so long associated with romantic subjects, is in fact ideally suited to Williams's project. The portrait his novel creates, refracted through not only (invented) letters but also journal entries, senatorial decrees, military orders, private notes, and unfinished histories, is at once satisfyingly complex and appropriately impressionistic, subjective. (In his choice of genre Williams was undoubtedly influenced by Thornton Wilder's 1948 novel *The Ides of March*: In it, the events leading up to the assassination of Julius Caesar are presented through fictional letters and documents that are intermixed with citations of actual works by real-life figures, such as the poet Catullus, a contemporary and acquaintance of Caesar, and the first-century AD historian Suetonius.) In *Augustus*, the authors of the invented epistles and documents are, with very few exceptions, real-life characters, and Williams, who was impatient with historical fiction that merely "updated" the past, clearly relished the opportunity to impersonate some well-known figures. He was determined, he wrote in a note while working on *Augustus*, "not [to] have Henry Kissinger in a toga."

Here, then, is the wit and also the preening of Cicero, the orator who, despite his opposition to Julius Caesar, was allied at one point with the young Octavian, whom at first he dangerously underestimates. ("The boy is nothing, and we need have no fear . . . I have been kind to him in the past, and I believe that he admires me . . . I am too much the idealist, I know—even my dearest friends do not deny that.") Here too is the worldly Ovid, his report to his friend Propertius on a day at the races in the emperor's box nicely filigreed with self-conscious poeticisms. "The sun was beginning to struggle up from the east through the forest of buildings that is Rome . . ."

Even those figures who left few traces of their writing style appear fully fleshed and, as far as the historical record permits us to know, true to life. Maecenas, the canny, well-born patron of the arts and intimate of Horace, Vergil, and Augustus—who ridiculed his friend's effete writing style—is presented as an aesthete whose fussing ("much has been said about those eyes, more often than not in bad meter and worse prose") conceals a nice hint of steel; it is hard to imagine the emperor suffering lightweights gladly. Augustus's ambitious third wife, Livia, mother of his eventual successor, Tiberius, comes across as coolly pragmatic and no more excessively conniving than most of the people around her: a far more persuasive character than the Grand Guignol poisoner of Robert Graves's *I, Claudius*. ("Our futures are more important than ourselves," Williams's Livia matter-of-factly writes her son, demanding that he divorce his beloved wife in order to enter into a dynastic match with Augustus's daughter, Julia, whom he loathes.) And Williams invents excerpts from a now-lost memoir by Marcus Agrippa—Augustus's great friend from youth, the author of his military victories, his eventual son-in-law, and the father to his heirs—to give the tersely prosaic, "official" version of events: "And after the triumvirate was formed and the Roman enemies of Julius Caesar and Caesar Augustus were put down, there yet remained in the West the forces of the pirate Sextus Pompeius, and in the East the exiled murderers of the divine Julius..." (Williams knows how to deploy the persuasive stylistic tic: to Agrippa he gives the habit of beginning his sentences with "and.") A possible criticism of the earlier novels is that the author occasionally works so hard to make the writing "beautiful" that it sometimes works against believability; in particular, Andrews in *Butcher's Crossing* often expresses himself in a high style at odds with his callow youth. The ventriloquism imposed by *Augustus*'s epistolary form saves Williams from this vice. It is his most rigorous work.

One particularly shrewd choice he made in writing *Augustus* was the decision to withhold the emperor's own voice until the end, where we get to hear it at last in a long (again: fictional) letter from Augustus to Nicolaus of Damascus, which constitutes the novel's third and final section. Not surprisingly, the emperor's account of his past doesn't square with many of the suppositions and speculations that have preceded it. For instance, it now emerges that what a friend had understood to be the young Octavian's cry of grief and confusion on hearing the news of Caesar's assassination was—at least as the aged emperor would now have his correspondent believe—an expression of "nothing...coldness," followed by a feeling of triumph: "I was suddenly elated...I knew my destiny." As if to underscore the unbridgeable distance between what is perceived and what is true, between the official and unofficial, public and private narratives of our own lives, Williams intersperses this climactic fictional mini-autobiography with italicized excerpts of the *Res Gestae Divi Augusti*. Where does the truth of a life lie? For Williams, whose interest not merely in history but in historiography—the study of how history gets written—distinguishes this novel, the question is rich with irony. After reading Nicolaus's authorized biography (and reflecting on his own official autobiography), Williams's Augustus wryly comments that "when I read those books and wrote my words, I read and wrote of a man who bore my name but a man whom I hardly know."

To the shrewd historical novelist, the challenge posed by that unknowability is also an advantage. Like the best works of historical fiction about the classical world—Marguerite Yourcenar's *Memoirs of Hadrian*, Wilder's *The Ides of March*, Graves's Claudius novels, Mary Renault's evocation of fifth-century Athens in *The Last of the Wine*—*Augustus* suggests the past without presuming to re-create it.

For to have attempted simply to re-create the past would have left no room for the serious literary concern at the heart of *Augustus* and the author's other works. In a 1985 interview, Williams described what he saw as the common theme of both *Stoner* and *Augustus*: "I was dealing with governance in both instances, and individual responsibilities, and enmities and friendship.... Except in scale, the machinations for power are about the same in a university as in the Roman Empire..." The effect of power (and of struggles for power) on individuals is, in fact, a theme of the episode in Augustus's reign that first captured Williams's imagination and would set the novel in motion. Not long after the publication of *Butcher's Crossing*, the author first heard the story of the devastating scandal that had rocked both the empire and the imperial family: In 2 BC the emperor was forced to exile his beloved daughter and only child, Julia, to a tiny island called Pandateria. One of the charges was adultery—a violation of the strict morality laws her father had instituted as part of his campaign to renew old-fashioned Roman virtues in his new state. (By that point the emperor's daughter, trapped in a hateful marriage to Tiberius, was notorious for her flagrant affairs.) Another was treason: There are strong indications that some of the men whom she took as lovers were part of a faction opposed to Tiberius's succession.

In this tale of a spirited woman whose passions brought her into disastrous conflict with her obligations, Williams perceived a compelling theme: what he called "the ambivalence between the public necessity and the private want or need." It is one that his Julia, one of the novel's subtlest and most arresting characters—intelligent, ironic, rebellious, worldly, philosophical—tartly comments upon in the Pandateria journal Williams invents for her. "It is odd to wait in a powerless world, where nothing matters. In the world from which I came, all was power; and everything mattered. One even loved for power; and the end of love became not its own joy, but the myriad joys of power." It is no accident that *Augustus* falls into two main sections: the first recounts the emperor's unlikely, triumphant rise to power, whereas the second, anchored by Julia's journal entries, maps the disintegration of his family and personal happiness, largely as the result of his machinations to perpetuate his power through ill-conceived dynastic marriages that eventually encourage factionalism and, most likely, murder. Which is to say, part one is about success in the public, political sphere and part two about failure in the private, emotional sphere—the latter being a potential cost, Williams suggests, of the former.

The conflict between individuals and institutions is a theme we can also see working in *Stoner*—the book, it's worth remembering, that

Williams wrote immediately after learning of the Julia story, the contours of which *Stoner*'s narrative to some extent inverts. For its thwarted
hero repeatedly, stoically submerges his private wants to the obligations
in which, as happens to us all, he has become enmeshed and which end
up constituting his life. There is an unhappy marriage alleviated too
briefly by an affair with a sympathetic graduate student; there is father-
hood. (Williams is particularly good on the tenderness of father-
daughter relationships, both here and in *Augustus*.) And there is the
middling career, delicately supported by a few cautious allies and open
to threats from one or two enemies he has inevitably made in the course
of things. A remarkable set piece of the novel is a scene that takes place
during a Ph.D. oral examination at which Stoner tries to prevent an
unprepared and cheating protégé of a rival professor from passing: He
succeeds at first, but the rival becomes the head of the English depart-
ment and thereafter works, on the whole successfully, to thwart Stoner's career and happiness over many years. (In *Augustus*, a character
called Salvidienus—a bosom friend of the emperor's youth who ultimately betrayed him—observes that "every success uncovers difficulties that we have not foreseen, and every victory enlarges the magnitude
of our possible defeat.")

    And yet Williams's work cannot be reduced to a series of parables
about individuals struggling with, and within, institutions. For one
thing, to read *Stoner* as an academic genre novel, as many do—a "novel
of university life," as the Irish novelist John McGahern admiringly
wrote—is too limiting; it provides no room for the work's subtle psy-
chology and complex ethics. (Its one significant failure is the represen-
tation of Stoner's harridan of a wife: Engineered to make Stoner
miserable, she is far nastier than she needs to be.) For another, such an
approach can't account for *Butcher's Crossing*, in which the strictures of
society and its institutions are almost wholly absent; it is, if anything,
their absence that creates some of the dreadful outcomes in that novel,
which charts the characters' descent, during and after the buffalo hunt,
into a pre-civilized, asocial stupor ("their food and their sleep were the
only things that had much meaning for them").

The theme at play in all three of John Williams's mature novels is in fact rather larger: it is that, as Stoner puts it to the mistress he must abandon for the sake of his family and his job, "we are of the world, after all." All of Williams's work is preoccupied by the way in which, whatever our characters may be, the lives we end up with are the often unexpected products of the friction between us and the world itself—whether that world is nature or culture, the deceptively Edenic expanses of the Colorado Territory or the narrow halls of a state university, the carnage of a buffalo hunt or the proscriptions of the Roman Senate, a dirt farm in Missouri or the opulent courts of Antioch and Alexandria. At one point in *Augustus* a visitor to Rome asks Octavian's boyhood tutor what the young leader is like, and the elderly Greek sage replies, "He is a man like any other.... He will become what he will become, out of the force of his person and the accident of his fate."

An inescapable and sober conclusion of all three novels is that the friction between "force of person" and "accident of fate" becomes, more often than not, erosion: a process that can blur the image we had of who we are, revealing in its place a stranger. Just before Andrews leaves for the buffalo hunt, a kindly whore he wants but cannot bring himself to bed—his loss of innocence will take another form, during and after the hunt—warns the soft-skinned and handsome young man that he'll change and harden. This prophecy comes quite literally true at the height of the slaughter of the buffalo: "in the darkness Andrews ran his hand over his face; it was rough and strange to his touch...he wondered how he looked; he wondered if Francine would recognize him if she could see him now." Similarly, Stoner understands at the end of his life that whatever his ideals may have been, they have yielded to chance and necessity, which made him other to what he had hoped: "He had dreamed of a kind of integrity, of a kind of purity that was entire; he had found compromise and the assaulting diversion of triviality. He had conceived wisdom, and at the end of the long years he had found ignorance. And what else? he thought. What else?"

So too Williams's Augustus, whose many names, the last one sharing no common element with the first, reflect with particular vividness the processes of unexpected evolution and irreversible erosion so fascinating to this author. In Augustus's concluding letter to Nicolaus, Stoner's word "triviality" tellingly reappears, as the dying emperor ruefully becomes aware of "the triviality into which our lives have finally descended." What occasions this thought is Augustus's weary realization that the peace and stability for which he has long struggled may not, after all, be what the Roman, or indeed any, nation wants: "The possibility has occurred to me that the proper condition of man, which is to say that condition in which he is most admirable, may not be that prosperity, peace, and harmony which I labored to give to Rome." He has founded his empire, in other words, on a misconception.

This painful concluding irony is typical of Williams. It bears a strong resemblance, for instance, to the awful end of *Butcher's Crossing*, when the buffalo hunters return at last to civilization after the slaughter only to find that, during the months of their absence, the bottom has dropped out of the market for buffalo hides—which means that all their labor, all the slaughter, the deprivations and sacrifices have been in vain. In *Augustus*, the irony is painfully underscored in a brief coda that takes the form of the last of the many documents the author so imaginatively invents: a letter written forty years after the emperor's death by the now elderly Greek physician who had attended him on his deathbed. The letter is addressed to the courtier and philosopher Seneca, and in it the writer, having weathered the reigns of the cruel Tiberius and the mad Caligula, celebrates the advent of a new emperor who "will at last fulfill the dream of Octavius Caesar." That emperor is Nero.

And yet Williams didn't see his heroes as failures; nor should we. In the long interview he gave a few years before his death, he remarked that he thought Stoner was "a real hero":

A lot of people who have read the novel think that Stoner had such a sad and bad life. I think he had a very good life. He had a better life than most people do, certainly. He was doing what he wanted to do, he had some feeling for what he was doing, he had

some sense of the importance of the job he was doing. He was a
witness to values that are important...You've got to keep the
faith.

"Keep the faith": These characters may have grown away from the selves
they thought they would be, but what they come to understand is that
the lives they have made *are* "themselves"—the dwellings they must inhabit, and must find the courage to inhabit alone. This knowledge is
tragic, but not necessarily sad. At the end of the affair that threatens
the modest (and largely frustrated) life he has painstakingly, con-
fusedly created, William Stoner gently tells his lover, Katherine, that at
least they haven't compromised themselves: "we have come out of this,
at least, with ourselves. We know that we are—what we are." William
Andrews returns from the buffalo hunt dimly aware that his dream of
oneness with Nature was a glib fantasy, and that the lessons he took
away from his encounter with the wild were different from the ones he
imagined he'd be learning—the latter being the "fancy lies" an older,
seasoned partner contemptuously dismisses: "there's nothing....You
get born, and you nurse on lies, and you get weaned on lies, and you
learn fancier lies in school...and then maybe when you're ready to die,
it comes to you—that there's nothing, nothing but yourself and what
you could have done." As with Greek tragedies, both novels expose the
process by which "what you could have done" is gradually stripped
away from a character, leaving only what he did do—which is to say,
the residue that is "yourself." It comes as no surprise to learn that Williams had considered using a quotation from the Spanish philosopher
Ortega y Gasset as an epigraph for *Stoner*: "A hero is one who wants to
be himself."

In the last pages of Williams's final novel the Imperator Caesar Divi
Filius Augustus becomes that deeper kind of hero. Here, finally, he
stoically embraces the truth that Will Andrews's colleague sourly complained about: that to confront one's self, stripped of pretense and illusion, is the climax to which every life inevitably leads, however great or
humble. "I have come to believe that in the life of every man, late or

soon, there is a moment when he knows beyond whatever else he might understand, and whether he can articulate the knowledge or not, the terrifying fact that he is alone, and separate, and that he can be no other than the poor thing that is himself." This is the conclusion to which many good biographies and some of the best works of fiction also lead. "The poor thing that is himself" is hardly the way that most of us would think about the first Roman emperor. It is the achievement of Williams's novel that we are able to do so by its end, and to think of that end as a satisfying one.

—DANIEL MENDELSOHN

AUGUSTUS

For Nancy

AUTHOR'S NOTE

It is recorded that a famous Latin historian declared he would have made Pompey win the battle of Pharsalia had the effective turn of a sentence required it. Though I have not allowed myself such a liberty, some of the errors of fact in this book are deliberate. I have changed the order of several events; I have invented where the record is incomplete or uncertain; and I have given identities to a few characters whom history has failed to mention. I have sometimes modernized place names and Roman nomenclature, but I have not done so in all instances, preferring certain resonances to a mechanical consistency. With a few exceptions, the documents that constitute this novel are of my own invention—I have paraphrased several sentences from the letters of Cicero, I have stolen brief passages from *The Acts of Augustus*, and I have lifted a fragment from a lost book of Livy's *History* preserved by Seneca the Elder.

But if there are truths in this work, they are the truths of fiction rather than of history. I shall be grateful to those readers who will take it as it is intended—a work of the imagination.

I should like to thank The Rockefeller Foundation for a grant that enabled me to travel and begin this novel; Smith College in Northampton, Massachusetts, for affording me a period of leisure in which to continue it; and the University of Denver for a sometimes bemused but kind understanding which allowed me to complete it.

PROLOGUE

Letter: Julius Caesar to Atia (45 B.C.)

Send the boy to Apollonia.

I begin abruptly, my dear niece, so that you will at once be disarmed, and so that whatever resistance you might raise will be too quick and flimsy for the force of my persuasions.

Your son left my camp at Carthage in good health; you will see him in Rome within the week. I have instructed my men to give him a leisurely journey, so that you might have this letter before his arrival.

Even now, you will have started to raise objections that seem to you to have some weight—you are a mother and a Julian, and thus doubly stubborn. I suspect I know what your objections will be; we have spoken of these matters before. You would raise the issue of his uncertain health—though you will know shortly that Gaius Octavius returns from his campaign with me in Spain more healthy than when he began it. You would question the care he might receive abroad—though a little thought should persuade you that the doctors in Apollonia are more capable of attending his ills than are the perfumed quacks in Rome. I have six legions of soldiers in and around Macedonia; and soldiers must be in good health, though senators may die and the world shall have lost little. And the Macedonian coastal weather is at least as mild as the Roman.

You are a good mother, Atia, but you have that affliction of
hard morality and strictness which has sometimes disturbed our
line. You must loosen your reins a little and let your son become
in fact the man that he is in law. He is nearly eighteen, and you
remember the portents at his birth—portents which, as you are
aware, I have taken pains to augment.

You must understand the importance of the command with
which I began this letter. His Greek is atrocious, and his rhetoric
is weak; his philosophy is fair, but his knowledge of literature is
eccentric, to say the least. Are the tutors of Rome as slothful and
careless as the citizens? In Apollonia he will read philosophy and
improve his Greek with Athenodorus; he will enlarge his knowledge of literature and perfect his rhetoric with Apollodorus. I
have already made the necessary arrangements.

Moreover, at his age he needs to be away from Rome; he is a
youth of wealth, high station, and great beauty. If the admiration
of the boys and girls does not corrupt him, the ambitions of the
flatterers will. (You will notice how skillfully I touch that country morality of yours.) In an atmosphere that is Spartan and dis-
ciplined, he will spend his mornings with the most learned scholars of our day, perfecting the humane art of the mind; and he will
spend his afternoons with the officers of my legions, perfecting
that other art without which no man is complete.

You know something of my feeling for the boy and of my
plans for him; he would be my son in the fact of the law, as he is
in my heart, had not the adoption been blocked by that Marcus
Antonius who dreams that he will succeed me and who maneuvers among my enemies as slyly as an elephant might lumber
through the Temple of the Vestal Virgins. Your Gaius stands at
my right hand; but if he is to remain safely there, and take on my
powers, he must have the chance to learn my strengths. He cannot do this in Rome, for I have left the most important of those
strengths in Macedonia—my legions, which next summer Gaius
and I will lead against the Parthians or the Germans, and which
we may also need against the treasons that rise out of Rome. . . .
By the way, how *is* Marcius Philippus, whom you are pleased to
call your husband? He is so much a fool that I almost cherish
him. Certainly I am grateful to him, for were he not so busily engaged in playing the fop in Rome and so amateurishly plotting

against me with his friend Cicero, he might play at being step-father to your son. At least your late husband, however undistinguished his own family, had the good sense to father a son and to find advancement in the Julian name; now your present husband plots against me, and would destroy that name which is the only advantage over the world that he possesses. Yet I wish all my enemies were so inept. I should admire them less, but I would be safer.

I have asked Gaius to take with him to Apollonia two friends who fought with us in Spain and who return with him now to Rome—Marcus Vipsanius Agrippa and Quintus Salvidienus Rufus, both of whom you know—and another whom you do not know, one Gaius Cilnius Maecenas. Your husband will know at once that the latter is of an old Etruscan line with some tinge of royalty; that should please him, if nothing else about this does.

You will observe, my dear Atia, that at the beginning of this letter your uncle made it appear that you had a choice about the future of your son. Now Caesar must make it clear that you do not. I shall return to Rome within the month; and, as you may have heard rumored, I shall return as dictator for life, by a decree of the Senate that has not yet been made. I have, therefore, the power to appoint a commander of cavalry, who will be second in power only to me. This I have done; and as you may have surmised, it is your son whom I have appointed. The fact is accomplished, and it will not be changed. Thus, if either you or your husband should intervene, there will be upon your house a public wrath of such weight that beside it my private scandals will seem no heavier than a mouse.

I trust that your summer at Puteoli was a pleasant one, and that you are now back in the city for the season. Restless as I am, I long for Italy now. Perhaps when I return, and after my business is done in Rome, we may spend a few quiet days at Tivoli. You may even bring your husband, and Cicero, if he will come. Despite what I say, I am really very fond of them both. As I am, of course, of you.

BOOK ONE

I

I. The Memoirs of Marcus Agrippa:
Fragments (*13 B.C.*)

. . . I was with him at Actium, when the sword struck fire from metal, and the blood of soldiers was awash on deck and stained the blue Ionian Sea, and the javelin whistled in the air, and the burning hulls hissed upon the water, and the day was loud with the screams of men whose flesh roasted in the armor they could not fling off; and earlier I was with him at Mutina, where that same Marcus Antonius overran our camp and the sword was thrust into the empty bed where Caesar Augustus had lain, and where we persevered and earned the first power that was to give us the world; and at Philippi, where he traveled so ill he could not stand and yet made himself to be carried among his troops in a litter, and came near death again by the murderer of his father, and where he fought until the murderers of the mortal Julius, who became a god, were destroyed by their own hands.

I am Marcus Agrippa, sometimes called Vipsanius, tribune to the people and consul to the Senate, soldier and general to the Empire of Rome, and friend of Gaius Octavius Caesar, now Augustus. I write these memories in the fiftieth year of my life so that posterity may record the time when Octavius discovered Rome bleeding in the jaws of faction, when Octavius Caesar slew the factious beast and removed the almost lifeless body, and when Augustus healed the wounds of Rome and made it whole again, to walk with vigor upon the boundaries of the world. Of this triumph I have, within my abilities, been a part; and of that part these memories will be a record, so that the historians of the ages may understand their wonder at Augustus and Rome.

Under the command of Caesar Augustus I performed several functions for the restoration of Rome, for which duty Rome amply rewarded me. I was three times consul, once aedile and tribune, and twice governor of Syria; and twice I received the seal of the Sphinx from Augustus himself during his grave illnesses. Against Lucius Antonius at Perusia I led the victorious Roman legions, and against the Aquitanians at Gaul, and against the German tribes at the Rhine, for which service I refused a Triumph in Rome; and in Spain and Pannonia, too, were rebellious tribes and factions put down. By Augustus I was given title as commander in chief of our navy, and we saved our ships from the pirate Sextus Pompeius by our construction of the harbor west of the Bay of Naples, which ships later defeated and destroyed Pompeius at Mylae and Naulochus on the coast of Sicily; and for that action the Senate awarded me the naval crown. At Actium we defeated the traitor Marcus Antonius, and so restored life to the body of Rome.

In celebration of Rome's delivery from the Egyptian treason, I had erected the Temple now called the Pantheon and other public buildings. As chief administrator of the city under Augustus and the Senate, I had repaired the old aqueducts of the city and installed new ones, so that the citizens and populace of Rome might have water and be free of disease; and when peace came to Rome, I assisted in the survey and mapping of the world, begun during the dictatorship of Julius Caesar and made at last possible by his adopted son.

Of these things, I shall write more at length as these memories progress. But I must now tell of the time when these events were set into motion, the year after Julius Caesar's triumphant return from Spain, of which campaign Gaius Octavius and Salvidienus Rufus and I were members.

For I was with him at Apollonia when the news came of Caesar's death. . . .

II. Letter: Gaius Cilnius Maecenas to Titus Livius
(13 B.C.)

You must forgive me, my dear Livy, for having so long delayed my reply. The usual complaints: retirement seems not to have improved the state of my health at all. The doctors shake their heads wisely, mutter mysteriously, and collect their fees. Nothing seems to help—not the vile medicines I am fed, nor even the abstinence from those pleasures which (as you know) I once enjoyed. The gout has made it impossible for me to hold my pen in hand these last few days, though I know how diligently you pursue your work and what need you have of my assistance in the matter of which you have written me. And along with my other infirmities, I have for the past few weeks been afflicted by an insomnia, so that my days are spent in weariness and lassitude. But my friends do not desert me, and life stays; for those two things I must be grateful.

You ask me about the early days of my association with our Emperor. You ought to know that only three days ago he was good enough to visit my house, inquiring after my illnesses, and I felt it politic to inform him of your request. He smiled and asked me whether or not I felt it proper to aid such an unregenerate Republican as yourself; and then we fell to talking about the old days, as men who feel the encroachment of age will do. He remembers things—little things—even more vividly than I, whose profession it has been to forget nothing. At last I asked him if he would prefer to have sent to you his own account of that time. He looked away into the distance for a moment and smiled again and said, "No—Emperors may let their memories lie even more readily than poets and historians." He asked me to send you his warm regards, and gave me permission to write to you with whatever freedom I could find.

But what freedom can I find to speak to you of those days? We were young; and though Gaius Octavius, as he was called then, knew that he was favored by his destiny and that Julius Caesar intended his adoption, neither he nor I nor Marcus Agrippa nor Salvidienus Rufus, who were his friends, could truly imagine where we would be led. I do not have the freedom of the historian, my friend; you may recount the movements of men and armies, trace the intricate course of state intrigues, balance victories and defeats, relate births and deaths—and yet still be free, in the wise simplicity of your task, from the awful weight of a kind of knowledge that I cannot name but that I more and more nearly apprehend as the years draw on. I know what you want; and you are no doubt impatient with me because I do not get on with it and give you the facts that you need. But you must remember that despite my services to the state, I am a poet, and incapable of approaching anything very directly.

It may surprise you to learn that I had not known Octavius until I met him at Brindisi, where I had been sent to join him and his group of friends on the way to Apollonia. The reasons for my being there remain obscure to me; it was through the intercession of Julius Caesar, I am sure. My father, Lucius, had once done Julius some service; and a few years before, he had visited us at our villa in Arezzo. I argued with him about something (I was, I believe, asserting the superiority of Callimachus's poems to Catullus's), and I became arrogant, abusive, and (I thought) witty. I was very young. At any rate, he seemed amused by me, and we talked for some time. Two years later, he ordered my father to send me to Apollonia in the company of his nephew.

My friend, I must confess to you (though you may not use it) that I was in no profound way impressed with Octavius upon that occasion of our first meeting. I had just come down to Brindisi from Arezzo and after more than ten days of traveling, I was weary to the bone, filthy with the dust of the road, and irritable. I came upon them at the pier from which we were to embark. Agrippa and Salvidienus were talking together, and Octavius stood somewhat apart from them, gazing at a small ship that was anchored nearby. They had given no sign of noticing my approach. I said, somewhat too loudly, I imagine: "I am the Maecenas who was to meet you here. Which of you is which?"

Agrippa and Salvidienus looked at me amusedly and gave me their names; Octavius did not turn; and thinking that I saw arrogance and disdain in his back, I said: "And you must be the other, whom they call Octavius."

Then he turned, and I knew that I was foolish; for there was an almost desperate shyness on his face. He said: "Yes, I am Gaius

Octavius. My uncle has spoken of you." Then he smiled and offered me his hand and raised his eyes and looked at me for the first time.

As you know, much has been said about those eyes, more often than not in bad meter and worse prose; I think by now he must be sick of hearing the metaphors and whatnot describing them, though he may have been vain about them at one time. But they were, even then, extraordinarily clear and piercing and sharp— more blue than gray, perhaps, though one thought of light, not color. . . . There, you see? I have started doing it myself; I have been reading too many of my friends' poems.

I may have stepped back a pace; I do not know. At any rate, I was startled, and so I looked away, and my eyes fell upon the ship at which Octavius had been gazing.

"Is that the scow that's going to take us across?" I asked. I was feeling a little more cheerful. It was a small merchant ship, not more than fifty feet in length, with rotting timbers at the prow and patched sails. A stench rose from it.

Agrippa spoke to me. "We are told that it is the only one available." He was smiling at me a little; I imagine that he thought me fastidious, for I was wearing my toga and had on several rings, while they wore only tunics and carried no ornaments.

"The stench will be unendurable," I said.

Octavius said gravely, "I believe it is going to Apollonia for a load of pickled fish."

I was silent for a moment; and then I laughed, and we all laughed, and we were friends.

Perhaps we are wiser when we are young, though the philosopher would dispute with me. But I swear to you, we were friends from that moment onward; and that moment of foolish laughter was a bond stronger than anything that came between us later —victories or defeats, loyalties or betrayals, griefs or joys. But the days of youth go, and part of us goes with them, not to return.

Thus it was that we crossed to Apollonia, in a stinking fishboat that groaned with the gentlest wave, that listed so perilously to its side that we had to brace ourselves so that we would not tumble across the deck, and that carried us to a destiny we could not then imagine. . . .

I resume the writing of this letter after an interruption of two days; I shall not trouble you with a detailing of the maladies that occasioned that interruption; it is all too depressing.

In any event, I have seen that I do not give you the kind of thing that will be of much use to you, so I have had my secretary go through some of my papers in search of matters more helpful to your task. You may remember that some ten years ago I spoke at the dedication of our friend Marcus Agrippa's Temple of Venus and Mars, now popularly called the Pantheon. In the beginning I had the idea, later discarded, of doing a rather fanciful oration, almost a poem, if I may say so, which made some odd connections between the state of Rome as we had found it as young men and the state of Rome as this temple now represents it. At any rate, as an aid to my own solution to the problem that the form of this projected oration raised, I made some notes about those early days, which I now draw upon in an effort to aid you in the completion of your history of our world.

Picture, if you can, four youths (they are strangers to me now), ignorant of their future and of themselves, ignorant indeed of that very world in which they are beginning to live. One (that is Marcus Agrippa) is tall and heavy-muscled, with the face almost of a peasant—strong nose, big bones, and a skin like new leather; dry, brownish hair, and a coarse red stubble of beard; he is nineteen. He walks heavily, like a bullock, but there is an odd grace about him. He speaks plainly, slowly, and calmly, and does not show what he feels. Except for his beard, one would not know that he is so young.

Another (this is Salvidienus Rufus) is as thin and agile as Agrippa is heavy and stalwart, as quick and volatile as Agrippa is slow and reserved. His face is lean, his skin fair, his eyes dark; he laughs readily, and lightens the gravity which the rest of us affect. He is older than any of us, but we love him as if he were our younger brother.

And a third (is it myself?) whom I see even more dimly than the others. No man may know himself, nor how he must appear even to his friends; but I imagine they must have thought me a bit of a fool, that day, and even for some time afterward. I *was* a bit luxuriant then, and fancied that a poet must play the part. I dressed richly, my manner was affected, and I had brought along with me from Arezzo a servant whose sole duty it was to care for my hair—until my friends derided me so mercilessly that I had him returned to Italy.

And at last he who was then Gaius Octavius. How may I tell you of him? I do not know the truth; only my memories. I can say again that he seemed to me a boy, though I was a scant two years older. You know his appearance now; it has not changed much. But now he is Emperor of the world, and I must look beyond that to see him as he was then; and I swear to you that I, whose service to him has been my knowledge of the hearts of both his friends and enemies, could not have foreseen what he was to become. I thought him a pleasant stripling, no more, with a face too delicate to receive the blows of fate, with a manner too diffident to achieve purpose, and with a voice too gentle to utter the ruthless words that a leader of men must utter. I thought that he might become a scholar of leisure, or a man of letters; I did not think that he had the energy to become even a senator, to which his name and wealth entitled him.

And these were those who came to land that day in early autumn, in the year of the fifth consulship of Julius Caesar, at Apollonia on the Adriatic coast of Macedonia. Fishing boats bobbed in the harbor, and the people waved; nets were stretched upon rocks to dry; and wooden shacks lined the road up to the city, which was set upon high ground before a plain that stretched and abruptly rose to the mountains.

Our mornings were spent in study. We rose before dawn, and heard our first lecture by lamplight; we breakfasted on coarse food when the sun shone above the eastern mountains; we discoursed in Greek on all things (a practice which, I fear, is dying now), and spoke aloud those passages from Homer we had learned the night before, accounted for them, and finally offered brief declamations that we had prepared according to the stipulations of Apollodorus (who was ancient even then, but of even temper and great wisdom).

In the afternoons, we were driven a little beyond the city to the camp where Julius Caesar's legions were training; and there, for a good part of the rest of the day, we shared their exercises. I must say that it was during this time that I first began to suspect that I might have been wrong about Octavius's abilities. As you know, his health has always been poor, though his frailness has been more apparent than mine, whose fate it is, dear Livy, to appear the model of health even in my most extreme illness. I, myself, then, took little part in the actual drills and maneuvers; but Octavius always did, preferring, like his uncle, to spend his time with the centurions, rather than with the more nominal officers of the legion. Once, I remember, in a mock battle his horse stumbled and he was thrown heavily to the ground. Agrippa and Salvidienus were standing nearby, and Salvidienus started at once to run to his aid; but Agrippa held him by the arm and would not let him move. After a few moments Octavius arose, stood stiffly upright, and called for another horse. One was brought him, and he mounted and rode the rest of the afternoon, completing his part in the exercise. That evening in our tent, we heard him breathing heavily, and we called the doctor of the legion to look at him. Two of his ribs were broken. He had the doctor bind his chest tightly, and the next morning he attended classes with us and took an equally active part in a quick-march that afternoon.

Thus it was during those first days and weeks that I came to know the Augustus who now rules the Roman world. Perhaps you will transform this into a few sentences of that marvelous history which I have been privileged to admire. But there is much that cannot go into books, and that is the loss with which I become increasingly concerned.

III. Letter: Julius Caesar to Gaius Octavius at Apollonia, from Rome (*44 B.C.*)

I was remembering this morning, my dear Octavius, the day last winter in Spain when you found me at Munda in the midst of our siege of that fortress where Gnaeus Pompeius had fled with his legions. We were disheartened and fatigued with battle; our food was gone; and we were besieging an enemy who could rest and eat while we pretended to starve them out. In my anger at what seemed certain defeat, I ordered you to return to Rome, whence you had traveled in what seemed to me then such ease and comfort; and said that I could not bother with a boy who wanted to play at war and death. I was angry only at myself, as I am sure you knew even then; for you did not speak, but looked at me out of a great calm. Then I quieted a little, and spoke to you from my heart (as I have spoken to you since), and told you that this Spanish campaign against Pompeius was to settle at last and forever the civil strife and faction that had oppressed our Republic, in one way or another, ever since my youth; and that what I had thought to be victory was now almost certain defeat.

"Then," you said, "we are not fighting for victory; we are fighting for our lives."

And it seemed to me that a great burden was lifted from my shoulders, and I felt myself to be almost young again; for I remembered having said the same thing to myself more than thirty years before when six of Sulla's troops surprised me alone in the mountains, and I fought my way through them to their commander, whom I bribed to take me alive back to Rome. It was then that I knew that I might be what I have become.

Remembering that old time and seeing you before me, I saw myself when I was young; and I took some of your youth into myself and gave you some of my age, and so we had together that odd exhilaration of power against whatever might happen; and we piled the bodies of our fallen comrades and advanced behind them so that our shields would not be weighted with the enemy's hurled javelins, and we advanced upon the walls and took the fortress of Cordova, there on the Mundian plain.

And I remembered too, this morning, our pursuit of Gnaeus Pompeius across Spain, our bellies full and our muscles tired and the campfires at night and the talk that soldiers make when victory is certain. How all the pain and anguish and joy merge together, and even the ugly dead seem beautiful, and even the fear of death and defeat are like the steps of a game! Here in Rome, I long for summer to come, when we will march against the Parthians and the Germans to secure the last of our important borders. . . . You will understand better my nostalgia for past campaigns and my anticipation of campaigns to come if I let you know a little about the morning that occasioned those memories.

At seven o'clock this morning, the Fool (that is, Marcus Aemilius Lepidus—whom, you will be amused to know, I have had to make your nominal coequal in power under my command) was waiting at my door with a complaint about Marcus Antonius. It seems that one of Antonius's treasurers was collecting taxes from those who, according to an ancient law cited at tedious length by Lepidus, ought to have their taxes collected by Lepidus's *own* treasurer. Then for another hour, apparently thinking that allusive loquacity is subtlety, he suggested that Antonius was ambitious—an observation that surprised me as much as if I had been informed that the Vestal Virgins were chaste. I thanked him, and we exchanged platitudes upon the nature of loyalty, and he left me (I am sure) to report to Antonius that he perceived in me some excessive suspicion of even my closest friends. At eight o'clock, three senators came in, one after another, each accusing the other of accepting an identical bribe; I understood at once that all were guilty, that they had been unable to perform the service for which they were bribed, and that the briber was ready to make a public issue of the matter, which would necessitate a trial before the assembly—a trial that they wished to avoid, since it might conceivably lead to exile if they were unable to bribe enough of the jury to insure their safety. I judged that they would be successful in their effort to buy off justice, and so I trebled the reported amount of the bribe and fined each of them that amount, and resolved that I would deal similarly with the briber. They were well-pleased, and I have no fear of them; I know that they are corrupt, and they think that I am. . . . And so the morning went.

How long have we been living the Roman lie? Ever since I can remember, certainly; perhaps for many years before. And from what source does that lie suck its energy, so that it grows stronger than the truth? We have seen murder, theft, and pillage in the name of the Republic—and call it the necessary price we pay for freedom. Cicero deplores the depraved Roman morality that worships wealth—and, himself a millionaire many times over, travels with a hundred slaves from one of his villas to another. A consul speaks of peace and tranquillity—and raises armies that will murder the colleague whose power threatens his self-interest. The Senate speaks of freedom—and thrusts upon me powers that I do not want but must accept and use if Rome is to endure. Is there no answer to the lie?

I have conquered the world, and none of it is secure; I have shown liberty to the people, and they flee it as if it were a disease; I despise those whom I can trust, and love those best who would most quickly betray me. And I do not know where we are going, though I lead a nation to its destiny.

Such, my dear nephew, whom I would call my son, are the doubts that beset the man whom they would make a king. I envy you your winter in Apollonia; I am pleased with the reports of your studies; and I am happy that you get along so well with the officers of my legions there. But I do miss our talks in the evenings. I comfort myself with the thought that we shall resume them this summer on our Eastern campaign. We shall march across the country, feed upon the land, and kill whom we must kill. It is the only life for a man. And things shall be as they will be.

IV. Quintus Salvidienus Rufus: Notes for a Journal,
at Apollonia (March, 44 B.C.)

Afternoon. The sun is bright, hot; ten or twelve officers and ourselves on a hill, looking down at the maneuvers of the cavalry on the field. Dust rises in billows as the horses gallop and turn; shouts, laughter, curses come up to us from the distance, through the thud of hoofbeats. All of us, except Maecenas, have come up from the field and are resting. I have removed my armor and am lying with my head on it; Maecenas, his tunic unspotted and his hair unruffled, sits with his back against the trunk of a small tree; Agrippa stands beside me, sweat drenching his body, his legs like stone pillars; Octavius beside him, his slender body trembling from its recent exertion—one never realizes how slight he is until he stands near someone like Agrippa—his face pale, hair lank and darkened by sweat, plastered to his forehead; Octavius smiling, pointing to something below us; Agrippa nodding. We all have a sense of well-being; it has not rained for a week, the weather has warmed, we are pleased with our skills and with the skills of the soldiers.

I write these words quickly, not knowing what I shall have occasion to use in my leisure. I must get everything down.

The horsemen below us rest; their horses mill around; Octavius sits beside me, pushes my head playfully off the armor; we laugh at nothing in our feeling for the moment. Agrippa smiles at us and stretches his great arms; the leather of his cuirass creaks in the stillness.

From behind us comes Maecenas's voice—high, thin, a little affected, almost effeminate. "Boys who play at being soldier," he says. "How unutterably boring."

Agrippa—his voice deep, slow, deliberate, with that gravity that conceals so much: "If you had it in your power to remove that ample posterior from whatever convenient resting place it might encounter, you would discover that there are pleasures beyond the luxuries you affect."

Octavius: "Perhaps we could persuade the Parthians to accept him as their general. That would make our task easier this summer."

Maecenas sighs heavily, gets up, and walks over to where we are lying. For one so heavy, he is very light on his feet. He says: "While you have been indulging yourselves in your vulgar displays, I have been projecting a poem that examines the active versus the contemplative life. The wisdom of the one I know; I have been observing the foolishness of the other."

Octavius, gravely: "My uncle once told me to read the poets, to love them, and to use them—but never to trust them."

"Your uncle," says Maecenas, "is a wise man."

More banter. We grow quiet. The field below us is almost empty; the horses have been led away to the stables at the edge of the field. Below the field, from the direction of the city, a horseman, galloping at full speed. We watch him idly. He comes to the field, does not pause there, but crosses it wildly, careening in his saddle. I start to say something, but Octavius has stiffened. There is something in his face. We can see the foam flying from the horse's mouth. Octavius says: "I know that man. He is from my mother's household."

He is almost upon us now; the horse slows; he slides from his saddle, stumbles, staggers toward us with something in his hand. Some of the soldiers around us have noticed; they run toward us with their swords half-drawn, but they see that the man is helpless with exhaustion and moves only by his will. He thrusts something toward Octavius and croaks, "This—this—" It is a letter. Octavius takes it and holds it and does not move for several moments. The messenger collapses, then sits and puts his head between his knees. All we can hear is the hoarse rasp of his breathing. I look at the horse and think absently that it is so broken in its wind that it will die before morning. Octavius has not moved. Everyone is still. Slowly he unrolls the letter; he reads; there is no expression on his face. Still he does not speak. After a long while he raises his head and turns to us. His face is like white marble. He puts the letter in my hand; I do not look at it. He says in a dull, flat voice: "My uncle is dead."

We cannot take in his words; we look at him stupidly. His expression does not change, but he speaks again, and the voice that comes out of him is grating and loud and filled with uncomprehending pain, like the bellow of a bullock whose throat has been cut at a sacrifice: "Julius Caesar is dead."

"No," says Agrippa. "No."

Maecenas's face has tightened; he looks at Octavius like a falcon.

My hand is shaking so that I cannot read what is written. I steady myself. My voice is strange to me. I read aloud: "On this Ides of March Julius Caesar is murdered by his enemies in the Senate House. There are no details. The people run wildly through the streets. No one can know what will happen next. You may be in great danger. I can write no more. Your mother beseeches you to care for your person." The letter has been written in great haste; there are blots of ink, and the letters are ill-formed.

I look around me, not knowing what I feel. An emptiness? The officers stand around us in a ring; I look into the eyes of one; his face crumples, I hear a sob: and I remember that this is one of Caesar's prime legions, and that the veterans look upon him as a father.

After a long time Octavius moves; he walks to the messenger who remains seated on the ground, his face slack with exhaustion. Octavius kneels beside him; his voice is gentle. "Do you know anything that is not in this letter?"

The messenger says, "No, sir," and starts to get up but Octavius puts his hand on his shoulder and says, "Rest"; and he rises and speaks to one of the officers. "See that this man is cared for and given comfortable quarters." Then he turns to the three of us, who have moved closer together. "We will talk later. Now I must think of what this will mean." He reaches his hand out toward me, and I understand that he wants the letter. I hand it to him, and he turns away from us. The ring of officers breaks for him, and he walks down the hill. For a long time we watch him, a slight boyish figure walking on the deserted field, moving slowly, this way and that, as if trying to discover a way to go.

Later. Great consternation in camp as word of Caesar's death spreads. Rumors so wild that one can believe none of them. Arguments arise, subside; a few fist fights, quickly broken up. Some of the old professionals, whose lives have been spent in fighting from legion to legion, sometimes against the men who are now their comrades, look with contempt upon the fuss, and go about their business. Still Octavius has not returned from his lonely watch upon the field. The day darkens.

Night. A guard has been placed around our tents by Lugdunius himself, commander of the legion; for no one knows what enemies we have, or what may ensue. The four of us together in Octavius's tent; we sit or recline on pallets around the lanterns flickering in the center of the floor. Sometimes Octavius rises and sits on a campstool, away from the light, so that his face is in shadow. Many have come in from Apollonia, asking for more news, giving advice, offering aid; Lugdunius has put the legion at our disposal, should we want it. Now Octavius has asked that we not be disturbed, and speaks of those who have come to him.

"They know even less than we, and they speak only to their own fortunes. Yesterday—" he pauses and looks at something in the darkness—"yesterday, it seemed they were my friends. Now I may not trust them." He pauses again, comes close to us, and puts his hand on my shoulder. "I shall speak of these matters only with you three, who are truly my friends."

Maecenas speaks; his voice has deepened, and no longer shrills with the effeminacy that he sometimes affects: "Do not trust even us, who love you. From this moment on, put only that faith in us that you have to."

Octavius turns abruptly away from us, his back to the light, and says in a strangled voice: "I know. I know even that."

And so we talk of what we must do.

Agrippa says that we must do nothing, since we know nothing upon which we can reasonably act. In the unsteady light of the lanterns, he might be an old man, with his voice and his gravity. "We are safe here, at least for the time being; this legion will be loyal to us—Lugdunius has given his word. For all we know, this may be a general rebellion, and armies may already have been dispatched for our capture, as Sulla sent troops for the descendants of Marius—among whom was Julius Caesar himself. We may not be as lucky now as he was then. We have behind us the mountains of Macedonia, where they will not follow against this legion. In any event, we shall have time to receive more news; and we shall have made no move to compromise our position, one way or the other. We must wait in the safety of the moment."

Octavius, softly: "My uncle once told me that too much caution may lead to death as certainly as too much rashness."

I suddenly find myself on my feet; a power has come upon me; I speak in a voice that seems not my own: "I call you Caesar, for I know that he would have had you as his son."

Octavius looks at me; the thought had not occurred to him, I believe. "It is too early for that," he says slowly, "but I will remember that it was Salvidienus who first called me by that name."

I say: "And if he would have you as his son, he would have you act as he would have done. Agrippa has said that we have the loyalty of one legion here; the other five in Macedonia will respond as Lugdunius has, if we do not delay in asking their allegiance. For if we know nothing of what will ensue, they know even less. I say that we march on Rome with the legions we have and assume the power that lies there."

Octavius: "And then? We do not know what that power is; we do not know who will oppose us. We do not even know who murdered him."

Myself: "The power shall become what we make it to be. As for who will oppose us, we cannot know. But if Antonius's legions will join with ours, then—"

Octavius, slowly: "We do not even know who murdered him. We do not know his enemies, thus we cannot know our own."

Maecenas sighs, rises, shakes his head. "We have spoken of ac-

tion, of what we shall do; but we have not spoken of the end to
which that action is aimed." He gazes at Octavius. "My friend,
what is it that you wish to accomplish, by whatever action we
take?"

For a moment Octavius does not speak. Then he looks at each
of us in turn, intently. "I swear to you all now, and to the gods,
that if it is my destiny to live, I shall have vengeance upon the
murderers of my uncle, whoever they may be."

Maecenas, nodding: "Then our first purpose is to ensure that
destiny, so that you may fulfill the vow. We must stay alive. To
that end we must move with caution—but we must move." He
is walking about the room, addressing us as if we were school-
children. "Our friend Agrippa recommends that we remain here
safely until we can know which way to move. But to remain
here is to remain in ignorance. News will come from Rome—
but it will be rumor confounded with fact, fact confounded
with self-interest, until self-interest and faction become the source
of all we shall know." He turns to me. "Our impetuous friend
Salvidienus advises that we strike at once, finding advantage in
the confusion that the world may now be in. To run in the dark
against a timid opponent may win you the race; but it is as likely
to plunge you over a cliff you cannot see, or lead you to a mark
you do not wish to find. No. . . . All of Rome will know that
Octavius has received word of his uncle's death. He shall return
quietly, with his friends and his grief—but without the soldiers
that both his friends and enemies might welcome. No army will
attack four boys and a few servants, who return to grieve a relative; and no force will gather around them to warn and stiffen
the will of the enemy. And if it is to be murder, four can run
more swiftly than a legion."

We have had our say; Octavius is silent; and it occurs to me
how odd it is that we will so suddenly defer to his decision, as we
have not done before. Is it a power in him we sense and have not
known earlier? Is it the moment? Is it some lack in ourselves? I
will consider this later.

At last Octavius speaks: "We shall do as Maecenas says. We'll
leave most of our possessions here, as if we intend to return; and
tomorrow we make as much haste as we can to cross to Italy. But

not to Brindisi—there's a legion there, and we cannot know its disposition."

"Otranto," Agrippa says. "It's nearer anyway."

Octavius nods. "And now you must choose. Whoever returns with me commits his fortune to my own. There is no other way, and there can be no turning back. And I can promise you nothing, except my own chance."

Maecenas yawns; he is his old self again. "We came across on that stinking fish-boat with you; if we could endure that, we can endure anything."

Octavius smiles, a little sadly. "That was a long time ago," he says, "that day."

We say nothing more, except our good nights.

I am alone in my tent; the lamp sputters on my table where I write these words, and through the tent door I can see in the east, above the mountains, the first pale light of dawn. I have not been able to sleep.

In this early morning stillness, the events of the day seem far away and unreal. I know that the course of my life—of all our lives—has been changed. How do the others feel? Do they know?

Do they know that before us lies a road at the end of which is either death or greatness? The two words go around in my head, around and around, until it seems they are the same.

2

By the time you receive this letter, my son, you will have arrived at Brindisi and heard the news. It is as I feared: the will is now public, and you have been named Caesar's son and heir. I know that your first impulse will be to accept both the name and the fortune; but your mother implores you to wait, to consider, and to judge the world into which this will of your uncle invites you. It is not the simple country world of Velletri, where you spent your childhood; nor is it the household world of tutors and nurses where you spent your boyhood; nor is it the world of books and philosophy where you spent your youth, nor even the simple world of the battlefield to which Caesar (against my will) introduced you. It is the world of Rome, where no man knows his enemy or his friend, where license is more admired than virtue, and where principle has become servant to self.

Your mother begs you to renounce the terms of the will; you may do so without traducing the name of your uncle, and no one will think the worse of you. For if you accept the name and the fortune, you accept the enmity of both those who killed Caesar and those who now support his memory. You will have only the love of the rabble, as did Caesar; and that was not enough to protect him from his fate.

I pray that you receive this before you have acted rashly. We have removed ourselves from the danger in Rome, and will stay here at your stepfather's place in Puteoli until the chaos has settled into some kind of order. If you do not accept the will, you may travel safely across the country and join us here. It still is possible to lead a decent life in the privacy of one's own heart and mind. Your stepfather wishes to add some words to this.

Your mother speaks to you from the love that is in her heart; I speak to you from my affection, too, but also from my practical knowledge of the world and of the events of the past days.

You know my politics, and you know that there have been occasions in the past when I could not approve of the course that your late uncle pursued. Indeed, I have from time to time found it necessary, as has our friend Cicero, to assert this disapproval on the floor of the Senate. I mention this only to assure you that it is not from political considerations that I urge you upon the course that your mother has advised, but from practical ones.

I do not approve of the assassination, and had I been consulted about it I would most certainly have recoiled with such aversion that I myself might have been in danger. But you must understand that among the tyrranicides (as they call themselves) are some of the most responsible and respected citizens of Rome. They have the support of most of the Senate, and they are in danger only from the rabble; some of them are my friends, and however ill-advised were their actions, they are good men and patriots. Even Marcus Antonius, who has roused the rabble, does not move against them, and will not; for he, too, is a practical man.

Whatever his virtues, your uncle left Rome in a state from which it is not likely soon to recover. All is in doubt: his enemies are powerful but confused in their resolve, and his friends are corrupt and to be trusted by no one. If you accept the name and the inheritance, you will be abandoned by those who matter; you will have a name that is an empty honor, and a fortune that you do not need; and you will be alone.

Come to us at Puteoli. Do not involve yourself in issues whose resolution cannot improve your interest. Keep yourself aloof from all. You will be safe in our affections.

II. The Memoirs of Marcus Agrippa:
Fragments (*13 B.C.*)

. . . and at that news and in our grief we acted. We made haste
to sail and had a stormy crossing to Otranto, where we landed in
the dark of night and did not let our persons be known to any.
We slept at a common inn and made our servants absent themselves, so that no one might suspect us; and before dawn we set
out on foot toward Brindisi, as if we were country folk. At Lecce
we were halted by two soldiers who watched the approach to
Brindisi; and though we did not give our names, we were recognized by one who had been in the Spanish campaign. From him
we learned that the garrison at Brindisi would welcome us, and
that we might go there without danger. One walked with us
while the other went ahead to tell of our coming, and we came
to Brindisi with the full honor of a guard and the soldiers ranked
on either side of us as we came into the city.

There we were shown a copy of Caesar's will which named
Octavius his son and legatee, and gave his gardens to the people
for their recreation and to every citizen of Rome three hundred
pieces of silver from his fortune.

We had what news there was of Rome, which writhed in disorder; we had the names of those who murdered Caesar, and
knew the lawlessness of the Senate that sanctioned the murder
and set the murderers free; and we knew the grief and rage of the
people under that lawless rule.

A messenger from the household of Octavius awaited us, and
gave him letters from his mother and her husband which, out of
their affection and regard, urged upon him that renunciation of
the legacy which he could not make. The uncertainty of the
world and the difficulty of his task strengthened his resolve, and
we called him Caesar then and gave him our allegiance.

Out of their veneration for his murdered father and their love
for his son, the legion at Brindisi and veterans from miles around
thronged about him, urging him to lead them in vengeance
against the murderers; but he put them off with many words of
gratitude, and we went quietly in our mourning across the land,
from Brindisi along the Appian Way to Puteoli, whence we purposed to enter Rome at a propitious time.

III. *Quintus Salvidienus Rufus: Notes for a Journal,* at Brindisi (*44 B.C.*)

We have learned much; we understand little. It is said that there were more than sixty conspirators. Chief among them were Marcus Junius Brutus, Gaius Cassius Longinus, Decimus Brutus Albinus, Gaius Trebonius—all supposed friends of Julius Caesar, some of whose names we have known since childhood. And there are others whom we do not yet know. Marcus Antonius speaks against the murderers, and then entertains them at dinner; Dolabella, who approved the assassination, is made consul for the year by that same Antonius who has denounced the enemies of Julius Caesar.

What game does Antonius play? Where do we go?

IV. *Letter: Marcus Tullius Cicero to Marcius Philippus* (*44 B.C.*)

I have just learned that your stepson, with three of his young friends, is even now on his way from Brindisi, where he landed only a few days ago; I am hastening this letter to you, so that you might have it before his arrival.

It is rumored that despite your letter of advice (a copy of which you were most kind to send to me, and which I acknowledge with much gratitude) he intends now to accept the terms of Caesar's will. I hope that this is not true, but I fear the rashness of youth. I entreat you to use what influence you have to dissuade him from this course, or, if the step has been taken, to persuade him to renounce it. To this end, I shall be glad to lend whatever assistance I can; I shall make preparations to leave my lodge here at Astura in the next few days, so that I may be with you at Puteoli when he arrives. I have been kind to him in the past, and I believe that he admires me.

I know that you bear some affection for the boy, but you must understand that he is, however remotely, a Caesar, and that the enemies of our cause may make use of him if he is allowed to go his own way. In times such as these, loyalty to our Party must take precedence over our natural inclinations; and none of us wants harm to come to the boy. You must speak to your wife about this (I remember that she has great power over her son) as persuasively as you can.

I have had news from Rome. The situation is not good, but neither is it hopeless. Our friends still do not dare show their faces there, and even my dear Brutus must do what he can in the countryside, rather than remain in Rome and repair the Republic. I had hoped that the assassination would at once restore our freedom, return us to the glory of our past, and rid us of the upstarts that now presume to disturb the order that we both love. But the Republic is not repaired; those who should act with fortitude seem incapable of resolution, and Antonius prowls like a beast from one spoil to another, pillaging the treasury and gathering power wherever he can. Had we to endure Antonius, I could almost regret the death of Caesar. But we will not have to endure him long—of that I am convinced. He moves so recklessly that he must destroy himself.

I am too much the idealist, I know—even my dearest friends do not deny that. Yet I most reasonably have faith in the eventual justice of our cause. The wound will heal, the thrashing will cease, the Senate will find that ancient purpose and dignity which Caesar almost extinguished—and you and I, my dear Marcius, will live to see that old virtue of which we have so often spoken once again settle like a wreath upon the brow of Rome.

The events of the past few weeks press upon me. These matters have taken so much of my time that my own affairs suffer. One of the managers of my property, Chrysippus, came to me yesterday and remonstrated seriously with me; two of my shops have fallen down and others are deteriorating so badly that not only the tenants, but even the mice have threatened to migrate! How fortunate I am to have followed Socrates—others would call this a calamity, but I do not even count it a nuisance. How insignificant are such things! In any event, as a result of a long discussion with Chrysippus, I have come up with a plan whereby I can sell a few buildings and repair others, so that I will make my loss a profit.

V. Letter: Marcus Tullius Cicero
to Marcus Junius Brutus (44 B.C.)

I have seen Octavius. He is at his stepfather's villa at Puteoli, which is just next to mine; and since Marcius Philippus and I are friends, I have free access to see him when I wish. And I must tell you at once that he has, indeed, accepted the inheritance and the name of our dead enemy.

But before you despair, let me hasten to assure you that this acceptance is of less moment than either of us might have dreamed. The boy is nothing, and we need have no fear.

With him are three of his young friends: one Marcus Agrippa, a huge bumpkin who would appear more at ease tramping a furrow, either before or after the plough, than walking in a drawing room; one Gaius Cilnius Maecenas, a harsh-featured but oddly effeminate youth who flounces rather than walks, and who flutters his eyelashes in a most repulsive way; and one Salvidienus Rufus, a thin intense boy who laughs a bit too much, but who seems the most tolerable of the lot. So far as I can gather, they are nobodies, with neither families of any import nor fortunes of any account. (If it comes to that, of course, neither is young Octavius's pedigree immaculate; his grandfather, on his father's side, was a mere country moneylender, and beyond that only the gods know where he comes from.)

In any event, the four of them wander about the house as if they had nothing to do, talking to visitors and generally making nuisances of themselves. They seem to know nothing, for you can hardly get an intelligent response from any of them; they ask stupid questions, and then seem not to understand the answers, for they nod vacantly and look somewhere else.

But I do not let either my contempt or my elation become apparent. I put on a grave show with the boy. When he first came, I clucked with sympathy and uttered platitudes about the loss of close relatives. From his response, I became persuaded that his grief was personal rather than political. Then I equivocated a bit, and suggested that however unfortunate the assassination (you will forgive me that hypocrisy, dear Brutus), there were many who thought that the act sprang from unselfish and patriotic motives. At no time did I detect in him any sign that he was distressed by these advances. I believe that he is in some awe of me, and that he may be persuaded to come to our side, if I handle this with sufficient delicacy.

He is a boy, and a rather foolish boy at that; he has no idea of politics, nor is he likely to have. He is activated neither by honor nor ambition but by a rather gentle affection for the memory of one he would had been his father. And his friends look only for the advantage that they can have in his favor. Thus he does not, I believe, constitute a danger for us.

On the other hand, we may be able to put this circumstance to our benefit. For he does have claim to the name of Caesar, and (if he can collect it) the inheritance. There are certain to be some who will follow him merely because of the name he has assumed; others, the veterans and retainers, will follow him because of their memory of the man who gave him that name; and still others will follow out of confusion and whim. But the important thing to remember is that we shall have lost none of our own, for those who might follow him are those who otherwise would have followed Antonius! If we can persuade him to our cause, we shall have doubled our victory; for at the worst, we shall have weakened Antonius's side, and that alone would have been victory enough. We shall use the boy, and then we will cast him aside; and the tyrant's line shall have come to an end.

As you can easily understand, I cannot speak freely of these matters with Marcius Philippus; though he is our friend, he is in an awkward position. After all, he is married to the boy's mother; and no man is wholly free of the weaknesses that marital obligations occasionally raise. Besides, he is not of sufficient importance to entrust with everything.

You may keep this letter for less perilous times, but please do not send a copy to our friend Atticus. Out of admiration for me and out of pride in our friendship, he shows my letters to everyone, even if he does not publish them. And the information here should not be known at large, until the future has proved my observations to be true.

A postscript: Caesar's Egyptian whore, Cleopatra, has fled Rome, whether in fear of her life or in despair at the outcome of her ambitions, I do not know; we are well rid of her. Octavius goes to Rome to claim his inheritance, and he goes in utter safety. I could hardly hide my anger and sorrow when I heard this from him; for this stripling and his loutish friends can go there without risk to their persons, while you, my hero of the Ides of March, and our Cassius, must lurk like hunted animals beyond the precincts of the city you freed.

VI. Letter: Marcus Tullius Cicero to Marcus Junius Brutus (44 B.C.)

The briefest of notes. He is ours—I am sure of it. He has gone to Rome, and he has spoken to the people, but only to claim his inheritance. I am told that he does not speak ill of you, or of Cassius, or of any of the others. He praises Caesar in the gentlest of terms, and lets it be known that he takes the inheritance out of duty and the name out of reverence, and that he intends to retire to private life once he has done with the matter at hand. Can we believe him? We must, we must! I shall court him when I return to Rome; for his name may still have value to us.

VII. Letter: Marcus Antonius to Gaius Sentius Tavus, Military Commander of Macedonia (44 B.C.)

Sentius, you gamesome old cock, Antonius sends you greetings, and a report upon the latest triviality—an example of the kind of thing I am daily faced with, now that the burden of administration is upon me. I don't know how Caesar could endure it, day after day; he was a strange man.

That whey-faced little bastard, Octavius, came around to see me yesterday morning. He has been in Rome for the past week or so, acting like a bereaved widow, calling himself Caesar, all manner of nonsense. It seems that Gnaeus and Lucius, my idiot brothers, without consulting me, gave him permission to address the crowd in the Forum, if he would assure them that the speech would not be political. Did you ever hear of a speech that was not political? Well, at least he didn't try to stir them up; so he's not altogether a fool. He got some sympathy from the crowd, I'm sure, but that's about all.

But if not altogether, he certainly is *something* of a fool; for he gives himself airs that are damned presumptuous in a boy, especially in a boy whose grandfather was a thief and whose only name of any account is a borrowed one. He came to my house late in the morning, without an appointment, while half-a-dozen other people were waiting, and he had three of his retinue with him, as if he were a bloody magistrate and they were his lictors. I guess he supposed I would drop everything and come running out to him, which of course I did not do. I told my secretary to inform him that he had to await his turn; I half-expected and half-wanted him to walk out on me. But he didn't, so I kept him waiting for most of the rest of the morning, and finally let him come in.

I must confess that, despite the game I played with him, I was a little curious. I had only seen him a couple of times before— once, six or seven years ago, when he was about twelve, and Caesar let him give the panegyric at his grandmother Julia's funeral; and again, two years ago, at Caesar's Triumphal March after Africa, when I rode in the carriage with Caesar and the boy rode behind us. At one time, Caesar had talked to me a great deal about him; and I wondered if I had missed something.

Well, I hadn't. I shall never understand how the "great" Caesar could have made this boy the inheritor of his name, his power, and his fortune. I swear to the gods, if the will hadn't first been received and recorded in the Temple of the Vestal Virgins, I would have taken a chance on altering it myself.

I don't think I would have been so annoyed if he had left his airs in the reception room and had come into my office like anybody else. But he didn't. He came in flanked by his three friends, whom he presented to me as if I gave a damn about any of them. He addressed me with the proper amount of civility, and then waited for me to say something. I looked at him for a long time and didn't speak. I'll say this for him: he's a cool one. He didn't break and didn't say anything, and I couldn't even tell whether or not he was angry at having been made to wait. So finally I said:

"Well? What do you want?"

And even then he didn't blink. He said: "I have come to pay my respects to you, who were my father's friend, and to inquire about the steps that may be taken to settle his will."

"Your *uncle*," I said, "left his affairs in a mess. I would advise
you not to wait around in Rome until they're straightened out."

He didn't say anything. I tell you, Sentius, there's something
about that boy that rubs me the wrong way. I can't keep my
temper around him. I said: "I would also advise you not to use
his name quite so freely, as if it were your own. It's not your
own, as you well know, and it won't be until the adoption is
confirmed by the Senate."

He nodded. "I am grateful for the advice. I use the name as a
sign of my reverence, not my ambition. But leaving the question
of my name aside, and even my share of the inheritance, there is
the matter of the bequest that Caesar made to the citizens. I judge
that their temper is such that—"

I laughed at him. "Boy," I said, "this is the *last* bit of advice I'll
give you this morning. Why don't you go back to Apollonia and
read your books? It's much safer there. I'll take care of your uncle's affairs in my own way and in my own time."

You can't insult the fellow. He smiled that cold little smile at
me and said, "I am pleased to know that my uncle's affairs are in
such hands."

I got up from my table and patted him on the shoulder.
"That's the boy," I said. "Now you fellows had better get running. I have a busy afternoon ahead of me."

And that was the end of that. I think he knows where he
stands, and I don't think he's going to make any very large plans.
He's a pompous, unimpressive little fellow, and he would be of
no account at all—if only he didn't have some right to the use
of that *name*. That alone won't get him very far, but it has
proved annoying.

Enough of that. Come to Rome, Sentius, and I promise you
that I'll not give you a word of politics. We'll see a mime at Ae-
melia's house (where, by special permission of a consul who will
not be named here, the actresses are allowed to perform without
the encumbrance of clothing), and we'll drink as much wine as
we can, and contest among the girls which is the better man.

But I do wish the little bastard would leave Rome and take his
friends with him.

VIII. *Quintus Salvidienus Rufus:*
Notes for a Journal (*44 B.C.*)

We have seen Antonius. Apprehensive; enormity of our task. He's against us, clearly; will use whatever means he has to stop us. Clever. Made us feel our youth.

But a most impressive man. Vain, yet boldly so. Cloud-white toga (heavy-muscled brown arms gleaming against it) with bright purple band delicately edged with gold; as big as Agrippa but moves like a cat rather than a bull; big-boned, dark handsome face, tiny white slashes of scars here and there; thin southern nose broken at one time; full lips turned up at corners; large, soft brown eyes that can flash in anger; booming voice that would overwhelm one with affection or force.

Maecenas and Agrippa, each in his way, furious. Maecenas deadly, cold (when he is serious, drops all mannerisms and even his body seems to harden); sees no possibility of conciliation, wants none. Agrippa, usually so stolid, trembles with rage, face flushed, huge fists clenched. But Octavius (we must now call him Caesar in public) seems oddly cheerful, not angry at all. He smiles, talks animatedly, even laughs. (It is the first time he has laughed since Caesar's death.) In his most difficult moment, he seems to have no cares at all. Was his uncle like this in danger? We have heard stories.

Octavius will not talk about our morning. We usually take our baths at one of the public places, but today we go to Octavius's home on the hill; he does not want to talk to strangers about our morning until we have discussed it, he says. We toss a ball among us for a while (note: Agrippa and Maecenas so angry they play badly, dropping the ball, throwing it carelessly, etc. Octavius plays coolly, laughing, with great skill and grace; I catch his mood; we dance around the other two, until they do not know whether they are angry at Antonius or us.) Maecenas flings the ball away and shouts at Octavius:

"Fool! Don't you know what we have to face?"

Octavius stops dancing about, tries to look contrite, laughs again, goes to him and Agrippa, puts his arms around their shoulders. He says: "I'm sorry; but I can't stop thinking of that game we played this morning with Antonius."

Agrippa says: "It was no game. The man was deadly serious."

Octavius, still smiling: "Of course he was serious; but don't you see? He was afraid of us. He was more afraid of us than we are of him, and he doesn't know it. He doesn't even know it. That's the joke."

I start to shake my head, but Agrippa and Maecenas are looking strangely at Octavius. Long silence. Maecenas nods, face softens; shrugs with his old affectation, says negligently, pretending to be cross: "Oh, well, if you're going to be *priestly* about it, divining the hearts of men—" He shrugs again.

We go to bathe. We shall have dinner and talk later.

We are in accord; no precipitate action. We speak of Antonius, knowing that he is our obstacle. Agrippa sees him as the source of power. But how to get at it? We have no force of our own to wrest it from him, even if we dared to do so. We must somehow make him recognize us; that will be the first tiny advantage we have. Too dangerous to raise an army now, even to avenge the murder; Antonius's position in the matter too ambiguous. Does he want to avenge the murder as we do? Does he want only power? It is even possible that he was one of the conspirators. In the Senate, he supported an act that forgave the murderers, and gave Brutus a province.

Maecenas sees him as man of great force and action but unable to conceive the end to which action is directed. "He plots; he doesn't plan," Maecenas says. Unless he has discernible enemy, he will not move. But he must be made to move, otherwise we are at stalemate. Problem: How to make him move without his discovering his own fear of us.

I speak with some hesitation. Will they think me too timid? I say that I see Antonius as committed to same ends as ourselves. Powerful, support of legions, etc. Friend of Caesar. Brusqueness toward us not forgivable but understandable. Wait. Convince him of our loyalty. Offer our services. Work with him, persuade him to use his power to ends we have discussed.

Octavius says slowly: "I do not trust him, because there is a part of him that does not trust himself. Going to him would fix us too firmly in his course, and neither Antonius nor we know

surely enough where that course leads him. If we are to be free
to do what we must do, he must be made to come to us."

There is more talk; a plan emerges. Octavius is to speak to the
people—here and there, small groups, nothing official. Octavius
says: "Antonius has persuaded himself that we are innocents, and
it is to our advantage that he continue that self-deception." So we
will say nothing inflammatory—but we will wonder aloud
why murderers have not been punished, why Caesar's bequest to
the people has not been made, why Rome has forgotten so
quickly.

And then an official speech to the populace in which Octavius
announces that Antonius is unable (unwilling?) to release the
monies to pay them, and that Octavius himself, out of his own
pocket, will give them that which Caesar promised.

More discussion. Agrippa says that Octavius will have depleted
his own fortune if Antonius does not release the funds then, and
that if an army is needed we shall be helpless. Octavius replies
that without the good will of the people, an army will be useless
in any event; that we will buy power without seeming to want
power; and that Antonius will be forced to move, one way or another.

It is settled. Maecenas will draft the speech, Octavius will finish
it, we begin tomorrow. Octavius says to Maecenas: "And remember, my friend, that this is to be a simple speech, not a poem. In
any event, I'm sure I'll have to untangle your inimitably labyrin-
thine prose."

They are wrong. Marcus Antonius has no fear of us or anyone.

IX. Letter: Gaius Cilnius Maecenas
to Titus Livius (13 B.C.)

Some years ago my friend Horace described to me the way he
made a poem. We had had some wine and were talking seriously,
and I believe that his description then was a more accurate one
than that contained more recently in the so-called *Letter to the
Pisos*—a poem upon the art of poetry of which, I must confess,
I am not particularly fond. He said: "I decide to make a poem
when I am compelled by some strong feeling to do so—but I

wait until the feeling hardens into a resolve; then I conceive an end, as simple as I can make it, toward which that feeling might progress, though often I cannot see how it will do so. And then I compose my poem, using whatever means are at my command. I borrow from others if I have to—no matter. I invent if I have to—no matter. I use the language that I know, and I work within its limits. But the point is this: the end that I discover at last is not the end that I conceived at first. For every solution entails new choices, and every choice made poses new problems to which solutions must be found, and so on and on. Deep in his heart, the poet is always surprised at where his poem has gone."

I thought of that conversation this morning when I sat down to write you once again of those early days; and it occurred to me that Horace's description of the making of a poem had certain striking parallels to our own working out of our destinies in the world itself (though if Horace heard this, and recalled what he said, he would no doubt scowl dourly and say that it was all nonsense, that you made a poem by discovering a topic, disposing the topic properly, by playing this figure against that, by this disposition of the meter against that sense of the language, and so forth and so on).

For our feeling—or, rather, Octavius's feeling, in which we were caught up as the reader is caught in a poem—was occasioned by the incredible murder of Julius Caesar, an event which seemed more and more to have simply destroyed the world; and the end that we conceived was to have revenge upon the murderers, for the sake of our honor and the state's. It was as simple as that, or it appeared to be. But the gods of the world and the gods of poetry are wise, indeed; for how often they save us from the ends toward which we think we strive!

My dear Livy, I do not wish to play the father with you; but you did not even come to Rome until our Emperor had fulfilled his destiny and was master of the world. Let me tell you a little of those days, so that you might reconstruct, these many years later, the chaos that we confronted in Rome.

Caesar was dead—by the "will of the people," the murderers said; yet the murderers had to barricade themselves in the Capitol against those very people who had "commanded" the act. Two days later, the Senate gave its thanks to the assassins; and in the next breath approved and made law those very acts of Caesar for the proposal of which he had been killed. However terrible the deed, the conspirators had acted with bravery and force; and then they scattered like frightened women after they had taken their first step. Antonius, as Caesar's friend, roused the people against the assassins; yet the night before the Ides of March he had entertained the murderers at dinner, was seen speaking intimately with one of them (Trebonius) at the instant of the murder, and dined again with those same men two nights later! He aroused the populace again to burn and loot in protest against the murder; and then approved their arrest and execution for that lawlessness. He made Caesar's will to be read publicly; and then opposed its enactment with all his power.

Above all, we knew that we could not trust Antonius, and we knew him to be a formidable foe—not because of his shrewdness and skill, but because of his thoughtlessness and reckless force. For despite the sentimental regard in which some of the young now hold him, he was not a very intelligent man; he had no real purpose beyond the moment of his will; and he was not exceptionally brave. He did not even perform his own suicide well, and he did it long after his situation was hopeless, so that it was too late for it to be done with dignity.

How do you oppose a foe who is wholly irrational and unpredictable—and yet who, out of animal energy and the accident of circumstance, has attained a most frightening power? (Looking back on it, it is odd to remember that at once we construed Antonius to be our foe rather than the Senate, though our most obvious enemies were there; I suppose instinctively we felt that if such a bungler as Antonius could manage them, we should not have that much trouble with him either, when the time came.) I do not know how you oppose him; I only know what we did. Let me tell you of that.

We had seen Antonius and had been brusquely dismissed by him. He was the most powerful personage in Rome; we had nothing except a name. We determined that our first necessity was to get recognition from him. We had not been able to get that by overtures of friendship; thus we had to try the overtures of enmity.

First, we talked—among Antonius's enemies and among his friends. Or, rather, we questioned, innocently, as if we were trying to understand the events of the day. When did they suppose Antonius would give attention to Caesar's will? Where were the tyrannicides—Brutus, Cassius, the others? Had Antonius gone over to the Republicans, or was he still faithful to Caesar's Party of the People? That sort of thing. And we were careful to insure that reports of these conversations got back to Antonius.

At first there was no response from him. We persisted. And then at last we heard descriptions of his annoyance; retellings of insults he gave to Octavius began making the rounds; rumors and accusations against Octavius passed from lip to lip. And then we made the move that had to bring him into the open.

Octavius had, with some small assistance from me, composed a speech (I may have a copy of it somewhere among my papers; if my secretary can discover it, I will send it on to you), in which he sorrowfully announced to the people that despite the will, Antonius would not release Caesar's fortune to him, but that he (Octavius), having taken Caesar's name, would fulfill Caesar's obligations—that the bequest would be paid them out of his own pocket. The speech was made. There was nothing really inflammatory in it; the tone was one of sorrow, regret, and innocent bewilderment.

But Antonius acted precipitately, as we had hoped he would. He at once introduced legislation into the Senate which would prevent the legal adoption of Octavius; he allied himself with Dolabella, who at that time was co-consul with him and who had been close to the conspirators; he enlisted the support of Marcus Aemilius Lepidus, who immediately after the assassination had fled Rome and gone to his legion in Gaul; and he made open threats against Octavius's life.

Now you must understand that the position of many of the soldiers and citizens was extremely difficult—or at least so it seemed to them. The rich and powerful were almost without exception against Julius Caesar, and thus against Octavius; the soldiers and the middle citizenry almost without exception loved Julius Caesar, and hence favored Octavius; yet they knew that Marcus Antonius had been Caesar's friend. And now they were witnessing what they took to be a destructive battle between the only two persons who might take their part against the rich and aristocratic.

Thus it happened that Agrippa, who better than any of us knew the soldiers' life and language and habits of thought, went among those minor officers and centurions and common soldiers whom we knew to be veterans of the campaigns and friends to Caesar, and supplicated them to use their offices and common loyalty to quiet the dispute that had grown needlessly between Marcus Antonius and Octavius (whom he called Caesar to them). Assured of Octavius's love and convinced that Antonius could not look upon their efforts as rebellion or disloyalty, they acted.

They were persuaded (there were several hundred of them, I believe) to march first to Octavius's house on the hill. It was important that they go there first, you will understand. Octavius pretended surprise, listened to their pleas for friendship with Antonius, and made a brief speech to them in which he forgave Antonius the insults and agreed to repair the breach that had grown between them. You may be certain that we made sure Antonius was informed of this deputation; if they had marched upon his house without warning, he might easily have mistaken their intention and thought they were led against him in retaliation for his threats upon Octavius's life.

But he knew of their coming; and I have often tried to imagine his anger as he awaited them alone in that huge mansion where Pompeius once lived and that Antonius had appropriated after Caesar's murder. For Antonius knew that he had no choice but to wait, and he might have had an intimation then of the course his life was to run.

At Agrippa's prompting, the veterans insisted that Octavius come with them—which he did, though he would not walk in a position of honor, but was escorted at the rear of the line of march. I must say that Antonius behaved reasonably well when we marched into his courtyard. One of the veterans hailed him, he came out and saluted them, and listened to the speech that had already been given to Octavius—though he was a little curt and sullen when he agreed to the conciliation. Then Octavius was brought forward; he greeted Antonius, the salutation was returned, and the veterans cheered. We did not linger; but I was standing very near the two of them when they came together, and I shall always believe that there was a small, grudging, but appreciative smile on Antonius's face when they clasped hands.

That, then, was the first small power we had. And it was that upon which we built.

I tire, my dear Livy. I shall write again soon, when my health permits it. For there is more that may be said.

Postscript: I trust that you will be discreet in the use of what I tell you.

X. Letter: Marcus Tullius Cicero to Marcus Junius Brutus (September, 44 B.C.)

The events of the past few months have put me in despair. Octavius quarrels with Antonius; I have hope. Their differences are reconciled, they are seen together; I am fearful. They quarrel again, rumors of plots are in the air; I am puzzled. Once again they mend their disputes; and I am without joy. What does it all mean? Does either of them know where he is going? Meanwhile, their disputes and reconciliations keep all of Rome in a turmoil, and keep the assassination of the tyrant alive in the minds of everyone; and through it all, Octavius's strength and popularity steadily increase. I sometimes almost believe that we may have misjudged the boy—and then I am persuaded that it is the accident of event which makes him appear more capable than he is. I do not know. It is too dark.

I have found it necessary to speak against Antonius in the Senate, though it may have put me in some danger. Octavius gives me his support in private conversation, but he does not speak in public. In any event, Antonius now knows that I am his implacable enemy. He threatened such harm that I dared not give my second address to the Senate; but it will be published, and the world will know it.

XI. Letter: Marcus Tullius Cicero to Marcus Junius Brutus (October, 44 B.C.)

Recklessness, recklessness! Antonius has mobilized the Macedonian legions and goes to meet them at Brindisi; Octavius is enlisting the discharged veterans of Caesar's legions in Campania. Antonius intends to march to Gaul against our friend Decimus, ostensibly to avenge the assassination but in fact to augment his power by gaining the Gallic legions. It is rumored that he will march through Rome, showing his strength against Octavius. Shall we have war again in Italy? Can we trust so young a boy and with such a name as Caesar (as he calls himself) with our cause? Oh, Brutus! Where are you now, when Rome has need of you?

XII. *Consular Order to Gaius Sentius Tavus, Military Commander of Macedonia at Apollonia, with Letter (August, 44 B.C.)*

By authority of Marcus Antonius, Consul to the Senate of Rome, Governor of Macedonia, Pontifex of the Lupercalian College, and Commander in Chief of the Macedonian Legions, Gaius Sentius Tavus is hereby ordered to command the chief officers of the Macedonian Legions to mobilize their forces in preparation for a crossing to Brindisi, to make this crossing at the earliest moment in his power, and to hold the legions in that place against the arrival of their supreme commander.

Sentius: this is important. He spent part of last year at Apollonia. He may have made friends with some of the officers. *Investigate this most carefully.* If there are those who seem inclined toward him, transfer them out of the legion at once, or get rid of them in some other way. But get rid of them.

XIII. *A Libel: Distributed to the Macedonian Legions, at Brindisi (44 B.C.)*

To the followers of the murdered Caesar:
Do you march against Decimus Brutus Albinus in Gaul, or against the son of Caesar in Rome?
Ask Marcus Antonius.
Are you mobilized to destroy the enemies of your dead leader, or to protect his assassins?
Ask Marcus Antonius.

Where is the will of the dead Caesar which bequeathed to every citizen of Rome three hundred pieces of silver coin?
Ask Marcus Antonius.

The murderers and conspirators against Caesar are free by an act of the Senate sanctioned by Marcus Antonius.
The murderer Gaius Cassius Longinus has been given the governorship of Syria by Marcus Antonius.
The murderer Marcus Junius Brutus has been given the governorship of Crete by Marcus Antonius.

Where are the friends of the murdered Caesar among his enemies?
The son of Caesar calls to you.

XIV. *Order of Execution*, at Brindisi (*44 B.C.*)

To: Gaius Sentius Tavus, Military Commander of Macedonia
From: Marcus Antonius, Commander in Chief of the Legions
Subject: Treasonable actions in the Legions IV and Martian

The following officers will be presented at the headquarters of the Commander in Chief of the Legions, at the hour of dawn on the twelfth day of November.

P. Lucius	Cn. Servius
Sex. Portius	M. Flavius
C. Titius	A. Marius

At that hour on that day, these men shall suffer execution by beheading. In addition, there will be selected by lot fifteen soldiers from each of the twenty cohorts of the IV and Martian, who shall be executed with their officers in the same manner.

All the officers and men of all the Macedonian Legions are commanded to be present and witness this execution.

XV. *The Acts of Caesar Augustus* (*A.D. 14*)

At the age of nineteen, on my own initiative and at my own expense, I raised an army by means of which I restored liberty to the Republic, which had been oppressed by the tyranny of a faction.

3

My dear old friend, these letters that you require of me—I
could not have suspected how they would take me back to the
days that are gone, and through what a strange tangle of emotions I must go on that journey! Now in these uneventful years
of my retirement, as my time on earth draws to an end, the days
seem to hasten with unseemly speed; and only the past is real, so
that I go there as if I were reborn, as Pythagoras says we are, into
another time and another body.

So many things whirl around in my head—the disorder of
those days! Can I make sense of them, even to you, who know
more of the history of our world than any mortal? I comfort myself with the certainty that you will make sense of what I tell
you, even if I cannot.

Marcus Antonius went to Brindisi to meet the Macedonian legions that he had called up, and we knew that we must act. We
had no money: Octavius had stripped his fortune and sold much
of his property to discharge Julius's bequests to the people. We
had no authority: according to the law, not for ten years would
Octavius be eligible to become even a member of the Senate, and
of course Antonius had blocked every special privilege that the

Senate would have given him. We had no power: only a few hundred of the veterans of Caesar's army in Rome had unequivocally declared for us. We had a name, and the force of our determination.

So Octavius and Agrippa went immediately to the south, to the Campanian coastal farms where Caesar had settled many of his veterans. We knew what Antonius was offering recruits as an enlistment bounty; we offered five times that amount. We offered money that we did not have; it was a desperate gamble, but it was a necessary one. I remained in Rome and composed letters for distribution among the Macedonian legions that were nominally under Antonius's command. We had had promises from them earlier, and had reason to believe that some would defect to us, if the circumstances were right. As you know, the letters had their effect—though it was not precisely what we had anticipated.

For Antonius then made the first of his many serious blunders. Because of some wavering on the part of two of the legions— the Macedonian IV and the Martian, I believe—he had some three hundred officers and men put to death. More than the letters, I am sure, this action worked to our advantage. During the march to Rome, these two legions simply diverged to Alba Longa, and sent word to Octavius that they would cast their fortunes with his. It was not the cruelty of Antonius's act that outraged them, I think; soldiers are used to cruelty and death. But they could not trust themselves to a man who would act so rashly and unnecessarily.

In the meantime, Octavius and Agrippa had had a small success in raising the beginnings of an army to meet the Antonian threat. Some three thousand men with arms (though we let it be thought that it was double that number) assigned themselves to his command; and the same number without arms pledged themselves to our future. With a sizable portion of this three thousand, Octavius marched toward Rome, leaving Agrippa in command of the rest and charging him to march with them toward Arezzo (the place of my birth, as you will remember), and to raise whatever other troops he could on the way. It was a pitiful force to range against the power of our enemies; but it was more than we had had in the beginning.

Octavius encamped the army a few miles outside of Rome and entered the city with only a small body of men to guard his person, and offered his services to the Senate and the people against Antonius; it was known that Antonius was marching toward Rome, and no one could be sure of his purpose. But in their division and impotence, the Senate refused; and in their confusion and fear, the people did not speak as one. As a result, most of the army that we had raised at so much cost to ourselves dispersed, and we were left with fewer than a thousand men at Rome, and a few hundred more who marched (futilely, we thought) with Agrippa toward Arezzo.

Octavius had sworn to himself, to his friends, and to the people that he would have vengeance upon the murderers of his father. And now Antonius was marching through Rome on his way to Gaul—to punish (he said) Decimus Albinus, one of the conspirators. But we knew (and Rome feared) his real purpose, which was to gain for himself the Gallic legions under Decimus's command. With those legions, he would be invincible; and the world would lie like an unguarded treasure house before his plundering ambition. We simply faced the death of the Rome for which Caesar had given his life.

Do you see the position we were in? We had to prevent the punishment of one of those very criminals we had ourselves sworn to punish. And it became clear to us that, unexpectedly, another end had discovered us—an end larger than revenge and larger than our own ambitions. The world and our task enlarged themselves before us, and we felt that we peered into a bottomless chasm.

Without money, without the support of the people, without the authority of the Senate—we could only wait for what would ensue. Octavius withdrew the remnants of his army from the outskirts of Rome, and began slowly to follow Agrippa's little band to Arezzo—though it seemed now that there was no hope of diverting or even delaying Antonius's progress to Gaul.

And then Antonius made his second serious blunder.

In his vanity and recklessness, he marched into the city of Rome with his legions; and they were fully armed.

Not for forty years—since the butcheries of Marius and Sulla—had Roman citizens seen armed soldiers inside the city walls; and there were people still alive then who could remember the cobbles dark with blood, and there were senators then in the House who as young men had seen the rostrum piled with the heads of the senators of that day, and could remember the bodies left in the Forum to be devoured by dogs.

So Antonius swaggered and drank and whored through the city, and his soldiers plundered the houses of his enemies; and the Senate cowered, and did not dare oppose him.

Then the news came to Antonius from Alba that the Martian legion had deserted him and had declared for us. It is said that he was drunk at the time he got the news; in any event, he acted as if he were. For he precipitately called the Senate to meet (he was still consul, remember), and in a long irrational harangue demanded that Octavius be branded a public enemy. But before the speech was over, another piece of news came into the city, and was whispered among the senators even as Antonius was speaking. The Macedonian IV legion, following the Martian, had declared its allegiance to Octavius and the party of the Caesars.

In his rage, Antonius lost control of what little good sense he had. He had defied the constitution once by entering the city with his armed forces; now he defied law and custom by convening the Senate at night and by threatening his opponents with harm if they attended the meeting. In this illegal assemblage, he accomplished the following: he had Macedonia given to his brother, Gaius; and the provinces of Africa, Crete, Libya, and Asia to his own supporters. And then he hastened to the rest of his army at Tivoli, whence he began his march to Rimini, where he was to prepare his siege of Decimus in Gaul.

Thus, what Octavius could not accomplish by his caution, Antonius accomplished for us by his recklessness. Where there had been despair, I could see hope.

Now, my old friend, I will tell you something that no one knows; and you may use it in your history, if you wish. It is known that during the midst of these events, Octavius was on his slow march with the raggle of his troops to Arezzo; what is not known is that, at the moment of Antonius's open display of contempt toward the Senate and the law, and at the moment I judged the temper of the Senate and the people to be what they were, I sent an urgent message to Octavius to return, in dead secret, to Rome, so that we could make our plans. As Antonius swaggered boisterously out of the city, Octavius came secretly in.

And we laid the plan that would give us the world.

II. Letter: Marcus Tullius Cicero to Marcus Junius Brutus, at Dyrrachium (*January, 43 B.C.*)

My dear Brutus, the news we have in Rome from Athens fills all of us who honor the Republic with joy and hope. Had the others who are our heroes acted so boldly and with such decision as you have, our nation would not now be in such a state of turmoil. To think that, so shortly after the illegal assignment that Marcus Antonius made of Macedonia to his half-witted brother Gaius, now that same Gaius cowers in fear in Apollonia, while your armies grow and gather the strength that will one day be our salvation! Would that your cousin Decimus had had that same resolution and skill nine months ago, after our banquet of the Ides of March!

I am sure that the disturbing news of Antonius's new madness has reached you even in Dyrrachium. Disregarding all law and custom, he has terrorized the city; and now he marches into Gaul against Decimus. And until a few weeks ago, it was clear to all of us that he would be successful in that endeavor.

But young Caesar (I call him that now, despite my aversion to the name) and his young friend, Maecenas, came to me in secret with a plan. The boy has asked my advice before, and has courted me; but only recently have I become persuaded that he may be of serious consequence and help to us. Despite his incredible youth, and his much too diffident manner, he has accomplished remarkable things during these last few months.

Quite correctly, he pointed out to me that he maintains the only force capable of deterring Antonius: one army, under Marcus Agrippa, now marches to Arezzo, which is in the path of Antonius's intended entry into Gaul; and another, which has been discreetly encamped several miles from Rome, follows that; and the gods know how many other veterans and recruits they will pick up on the way. But (and this is what makes me begin to trust the young leader) he will not move illegally; he must have the sanction of the Senate and the people. And he proposes that I use my offices (which are still not inconsiderable, I imagine) to effect this sanction.

This I have consented to do, under conditions that are mutually agreeable. For his part, young Octavius Caesar asked that the Senate sanction his actions in raising the army; that the veterans who had joined him, as well as the IV Macedonian and the Martian legions, be formally given honor and the thanks of the people; that he himself be legally given command of the forces that he had raised and that no man be put in military authority over him; that the state defray the expenses of his army and supply them with the bounty he had promised them for their enlistment; that lands be allotted to the troops after their service; and that the Senate waive the law of age (as it has done before) and upon his successful alleviation of the siege of Decimus at Mutina, that he return to Rome as a senator and be allowed to stand for consul.

In another time and in other circumstances, these might have seemed excessive demands; but if Decimus falls, then we are ruined. I confess to you, my dear Brutus, I would have promised nearly anything; but I put a grave face on, and made some demands of my own.

I stipulated that in no way would he or his men take that revenge upon Decimus which he had earlier threatened; that he not oppose as a senator the decrees that I might pass in behalf of the legality of Decimus's position in Gaul; and that he not use the armies sanctioned by the Senate for an adventure against either you in Macedonia or our friend Cassius in Syria.

To all these conditions he agreed, and said, that so long as the Senate adhered to its part of the bargain, he would take no action on his own authority nor allow those under his command to do so.

Thus our cause advances. I have given the speech which put these proposals before the Senate; but as you know, the real work came before I dared to speak, and still I cannot rest in my labors.

III. Quintus Salvidienus Rufus: Notes for a Journal,
at Rome (*December, 44 B.C.*)

Restless, I await my fate. Gaius Octavius is secretly in Rome;
Agrippa marches to the north; Maecenas intrigues with everyone,
our friends and enemies alike. Yesterday he returned from an afternoon spent with Fulvia herself, that red-faced harridan who is
the wife of that same Antonius against whom we are to march.
The Senate has given Octavius Caesar powers that a month ago
we could not have dreamed: the legions of the next consuls, Hirtius and Pansa, are ours; Octavius has military powers second to
none, he will be allowed into the senatorial ranks upon our return
from the Gallic campaign—and I have been given the command of a legion, by Octavius himself with the sanction of the
Senate. It is an honor that I could not reasonably have expected
for many years.

Yet I am restless, and filled with a foreboding. For the first
time I become unsure of the rightness of our course. Every success uncovers difficulties that we have not foreseen, and every
victory enlarges the magnitude of our possible defeat.

Octavius has changed; he is no longer the friend we had in
Apollonia. He seldom laughs, he takes almost no wine, and he
seems to disdain even the harmless, distracting pleasures that we
took with the girls once. So far as I know, he has not even had a
woman since our return to Rome.

"So far as I know," I realize I have said. Once we knew all
about each other; now he has become contained, withdrawn, almost secretive. I, to whom he once talked with open friendship;
from whom he had no secret of his heart; with whom he shared
the closest dreams—I no longer know him. Is it grief for his
uncle that will not leave him? Is it that grief which has hardened
into ambition? Or is it something else that I cannot name? A cold
sadness has come over him and draws him apart from us.

In my leisure now in Rome, as I wait for the consular armies to
be raised, I can think of these things, and wonder. Perhaps when
I am older and wiser I shall understand them.

Gaius Octavius on Cicero: "Cicero is a hopeless conspirator.
What he does not write to his friends, he tells to his slaves."

When did the distrust begin?—if it is distrust.

The morning that Octavius and Maecenas announced the plan to me?

I said: "We would aid that Decimus who was one of the murderers of Julius Caesar?"

Octavius said: "We would aid ourselves, so that we might survive."

I did not speak. Maecenas had not spoken.

Octavius said: "Do you remember the oath we made—you and I and Agrippa and Maecenas—that night in Apollonia?"

I said: "I have not forgotten."

Octavius smiled. "Nor have I. . . . We shall save Decimus, though we hate him. We shall save Decimus for that oath, and we shall save him for the law." For an instant his eyes were cold upon me, though I think he did not see me. Then he smiled again, as if remembering himself.

Did it begin with that?

Facts: Decimus was one of the murderers; Octavius goes to his aid. Casca was one of the murderers; Octavius has agreed not to oppose his election as tribune of the people. Marcus Antonius was a friend of Caesar; Octavius now opposes him. Cicero rejoices publicly in the murder; Octavius has made an alliance with him.

Marcus Brutus and Gaius Cassius raise armies in the East, plunder the treasuries of the provinces, and daily augment their strength; Marcus Aemilius Lepidus is secure in the West and waits with his legions—to what purpose no one knows; and in the south, Sextus Pompeius roams the seas at will, raising barbarian armies that may destroy us all. The legion that I command—all the legions in Italy—is the task too large?

But Gaius Octavius is my friend.

IV. Letter: Marcus Tullius Cicero
to Marcus Aemilius Lepidus
at Narbonne, from Rome (*43 B.C.*)

My dear Lepidus, Cicero sends you greetings, and begs you to remember your duty to the Senate and the Republic. I would not mention now the many honors I have been privileged to do you, were I not filled with gratitude for the many kindnesses you have done me. As we have assured each other in the past, our differences have always been honorable ones, and have rested upon our mutual love for the Republic.

Though I put little faith in such, the rumors in Rome are that you will join forces with Marcus Antonius against Decimus. I do not seriously entertain such a possibility, and I see the rumor only as a symptom of that disease of instability that now afflicts our poor Republic. But I think you should know that the rumor does persist, so that for your own safety and honor you might take the most urgent measures to prove it baseless.

The young Caesar, with the blessing of the Senate and the Republic, marches toward Mutina against the outlaw, Antonius, who besieges Decimus. It may be that he will need your aid. I know that you will now, as you have in the past, observe the order of the law and refuse the chaos of lawlessness, for the sake of your position and the security of Rome.

V. Letter: Marcus Antonius
to Marcus Aemilius Lepidus
at Narbonne, from Mutina (*43 B.C.*)

Lepidus: I am at Mutina against the hired armies of the murderers of Caesar. Decimus is surrounded; he cannot break out.

I am informed that Cicero and others of his odor have been writing you, urging treason against the memory of our slain Julius. The reports of your intentions are ambiguous.

I am not a subtle man; I am not a flatterer; and you are not a fool.

There are three courses open to you: you can march from your camp to join me in the destruction of Decimus and the enemies of Caesar, and thereby gain my eternal friendship and the power that will come to you from the love of the people; you can remain unconcerned and neutral in the comfort of your encampment, and thereby receive neither my blame nor the hatred of the people—nor their love; you can come to the aid of the traitor Decimus and his "savior," the false son of our leader, and thereby receive my enmity and the lasting despite of the people.

I hope that you have the wisdom to choose the first course; I fear that you will have the caution to choose the second; I implore you, for your own safety, not to choose the third.

VI. *The Memoirs of Marcus Agrippa:*
Fragments (*13* B.C.)

We found the Rome we entered torn by strife and ambition. Marcus Antonius, the pretended friend of the slain Julius Caesar, consorted with the murderers, and would not allow him whom we now called Octavius Caesar to receive the honors and powers bequeathed him by his father. Upon ascertaining the ambition of the usurper Antonius, Octavius Caesar took himself into the countryside where his father's veterans tilled the soil, and we raised those troops loyal to the memory of their dead leader who would oppose with us the plunderers of our nation's dream.

Unlawfully, Marcus Antonius levied the Macedonian troops and marched with them into Rome, and thence to Mutina, where he laid siege to Decimus Brutus Albinus. And though Decimus had been among the murderers of Caesar, for the sake of order and the state, Octavius Caesar agreed to defend his lawful governorship of Gaul against the force of the outlaw Antonius; and with the thanks and sanction of the Senate, we gathered our forces and marched toward Mutina, where Antonius had encamped around the legions of Decimus.

Now I must tell of that campaign at Mutina, which was the first responsibility of war I had under Octavius Caesar and Rome.

The senatorial legions were under the command of the two consuls of the year, Gaius Vibius Pansa and Aulus Hirtius, the latter of whom had been the trusted general of our late Julius Caesar. Octavius Caesar commanded the Martian and Macedonian IV legions, though of the latter I had military leadership. Quintus

Salvidienus Rufus had been given the military command of the new legion of recruits we had levied in the countryside of Campania.

Antonius had made his siege of Decimus complete, and he proposed to lie in wait until Decimus's legions, weakened by hunger, must attempt to break through his encampment. We determined that Decimus had put away enough food within the walls of Mutina to endure, so we made winter quarters at Imola, only a two-hour march from Mutina, so that we might quickly go to the aid of Decimus if he made a sally against the Antonian forces. But he cowered within the safety of the city walls, and would not fight; so that when spring came, we faced the prospect of breaking through Antonius's lines ourselves, to save that Decimus who would not save himself. Early in April we determined to move.

Around Mutina the ground is marshy and uneven, cut by gullies and streams; beyond this marsh Antonius was encamped. In secret we searched the land for a way to cross, and discovered a ravine that was unguarded; and in the dead of night, joined by Pansa and five cohorts of his legion, Octavius Caesar and Salvidienus and I led our Martian legion and other soldiers into this ravine, having wrapped our swords and spears with cloth so that the enemy would not be aware of our approach. The moon was full, but a heavy fog clung to the earth, so that we could not see before us; and in single file, each man's hand upon another's shoulder, we inched blindly through the glowing mist, never sure of where we went or whom we might encounter.

Through the night we crept, and in the morning came up on a high road in the marshes; we waited for the fog to lift, and saw no enemy ahead of us. But a sudden gleam came from the brush, and we heard a muffled voice, and we knew we were surrounded. The horn sounded the order for battle, and the soldiers came to their formation on the high ground. The young recruits were ordered by Pansa to stand aside, so as not to hinder the fighting of the veterans, but to stand in readiness if they were needed.

For these were veterans of the Martian legion, and they remembered the slaughter of their comrades at Brindisi by the Antonius they now opposed.

The space upon which we fought was so small that one side

could not flank another; therefore, man fought man like gladiators in an arena, and the dust rose thick as the fog of the night
before, and swords rang in the air, and no one shouted. We heard
only the cries of the wounded and the deep groans of those who
were dying.

We fought through the morning and through the afternoon,
one line relieving another as it became exhausted. Once Octavius
Caesar himself came near death when he seized the standard that
our eagle-bearer, wounded, had let fall; and the consul, Pansa, in
this engagement suffered a mortal wound. Antonius ordered fresh
troops into the battle, and step by step we gave ground; but
under the command of Salvidienus the recruits fought as bravely
as the veterans, and we were able to enter again into our camp
whence we had come the night before. Antonius did not continue the attack after nightfall, so we went into the marsh that
was littered with the bodies of our comrades, and carried back
the wounded. That night we saw the campfires of Antonius's
army beyond the marsh, and heard the singing of his soldiers in
their victory.

We feared the slaughter that the next day might bring, for we
were weary and our numbers were reduced by half; and we
knew that Antonius had troops that he had not used. But during
that night, the legions of the consul Hirtius had been marching to
our relief; and joining us, made an attack upon Antonius's
camp, which was complacent and disordered in its false certainty
of success. And the battles raged for many days, during which
time the Antonian legions were reduced to half their number; our
losses were very slight. Salvidienus was given the legions of the
dying Pansa, and he led them with bravery and skill. At last, our
armies broke into the very camp of Antonius; and the brave Hirtius was killed by one of Antonius's guards, outside the tent
where Antonius had lately rested and whence he had fled.

Upon this defeat, Antonius lost heart; and gathering what remained of his troops, marched northward toward the Alps, which
he crossed at further cost to his strength, and joined the forces of
Marcus Aemilius Lepidus, who had remained safely at Narbonne.

After the flight of Antonius, Decimus, delivered from the siege,
ventured outside the city walls. He sent messengers to Octavius
Caesar, thanking him for his aid, and declaring that his own part

AUGUSTUS

in the murder of Julius Caesar had been caused by the deceptions of the other conspirators; and he asked that Octavius Caesar converse with him, in the presence of witnesses, so that he might be convinced of the sincerity of his gratitude. But Octavius Caesar declined his thanks, saying: "I did not come to save Decimus; therefore I will not accept his gratitude. I came to save the state; and I will accept its thanks. Nor will I speak to the murderer of my father, nor look upon his face. He may go in safety by the authority of the Senate, not by my own."

Six months later, Decimus was surprised and killed by a chieftain of one of the Gallic tribes. He had the head of Decimus severed, and sent it to Marcus Antonius, who gave him a small reward.

VII. Senatorial Proceedings (April, 43 B.C.)

The third day of this month: the reading to the Senate of the dispatches from the Gallic campaign against the insurgent Marcus Antonius: by Marcus Tullius Cicero.

That the siege of Decimus Brutus Albinus is lifted; that the troops of Marcus Antonius are so reduced that they offer no immediate danger to the Republic; that the remnants of Antonius's army flee northward in disorder; that the consuls Aulus Hirtius and Gaius Vibius Pansa are dead, and that their legions are temporarily under the command of C. Octavius, who waits outside Mutina.

The sixth day of this month: resolutions of Marcus Tullius Cicero.

That fifty days of thanksgiving be declared, in which the citizens of Rome will offer their gratitude to the gods and the senatorial armies for the defeat of Marcus Antonius and the deliverance of Decimus Brutus Albinus.

That the dead consuls Hirtius and Pansa be accorded public funerals, with full honors.

That a public monument be erected to memorialize the glorious deed of the legions of Hirtius and Pansa.

That Decimus Brutus Albinus be given a senatorial triumph for his heroic defeat of the outlaw Marcus Antonius.

That the following directive be sent to Gaius Octavius at Mutina (copy appended):

"The Praetors, Tribunes of the Plebeians, the Senate, the People and Commoners of Rome, send greetings to Gaius Octavius, temporary commander of the Consular Legions:

"You are given the thanks of the Senate for the aid you have rendered Decimus Brutus Albinus in his heroic defeat of the insurgent armies of Marcus Antonius, and you are to know that, by edict of the Senate, Decimus Brutus has been made sole commander of the legions in the furtherance of the pursuit of the Antonian forces. You are therefore ordered to turn over the consular legions of Hirtius and Pansa to Decimus Brutus without delay. You are further ordered to disband those legions that you raised on your own authority, giving them the thanks of the Senate, which has formed a commission to study the advisability of offering them some reward for their services. An envoy from the Senate has been sent to Mutina to deal with these matters; you are to leave the transfer of powers to his offices."

All resolutions of Marcus Tullius Cicero passed by the Senate.

VIII. Letter: Gaius Cilnius Maecenas to Titus Livius (13 B.C.)

We had heard the witticism that Cicero made: "We shall do the boy honor, we shall do him praise, and we shall do him in." But I think that even Octavius did not expect the Senate and Cicero to offer so blatant and contemptuous a dismissal. Poor Cicero. . . . Despite the trouble he caused us and the harm that he intended, we were always rather fond of him. Such a foolish man, though; he acted out of enthusiasm, vanity, and conviction. We had learned early that we could not afford those luxuries; we moved, when we had to move, out of calculation, policy, and necessity.

I was, of course, in Rome during the whole of this affair at Mutina; as you know I have led armies in my time (and not altogether badly, if I may say so), but I have always found the task rather boring—to say nothing of the discomfort. So if you need details about the actual fighting, you will have to go elsewhere. If our friend Marcus Agrippa would complete that autobiography with which he has been threatening us, you might find some helpful information there. But poor fellow, he has such problems now (I am sure you know what I mean) that it is unlikely he will.

Octavius needed someone in Rome a good deal more than he needed an indifferent general—someone whom he could trust to keep him informed of the latest shifts in the senatorial whim, the latest intrigues, marriages, and so forth. And for this task I was admirably suited, I believe. At that time (this was nearly thirty years ago, remember) I fancied myself perfectly cynical, I thought ambition of any kind terribly vulgar, I was an inveterate gossip, and no one took me at all seriously. I posted him a daily newsletter, and he kept me informed of the situation in Gaul.

So the action of Cicero and the Senate did not catch him unprepared.

My dear Livy, I chide you often for your Republican and Pompeian sympathies; and though I tease you out of affection, I am sure that you have understood that there is an edge of seriousness in my scolding. You came to manhood in the northern tranquillity of Padua, which had for generations been untouched by strife; and you did not even set foot in Rome until after Actium and the reform of the Senate. Had the chance occurred, it is most likely that you would even have joined with Marcus Brutus to fight against us, as our friend Horace did in fact do, at Philippi, those many years ago.

What you seem so unwilling to accept, even now, is this: that the ideals which supported the old Republic had no correspondence to the fact of the old Republic; that the glorious word concealed the deed of horror; that the appearance of tradition and order cloaked the reality of corruption and chaos; that the call to liberty and freedom closed the minds, even of those who called, to the facts of privation, suppression, and sanctioned murder. We had learned that we had to do what we did, and we would not be deterred by the forms that deceived the world.

To put it briefly, Octavius defied the Senate. He did not disband the legions he had raised; he did not relinquish the armies of Hirtius and Pansa to Decimus; he did not allow the envoys from Rome access to Decimus. He waited into the summer, and the Senate trembled.

Decimus hesitated to do anything at all; and his own soldiers, revulsed by his weakness, deserted by the thousands to us.

Cicero, fearful of our defiance, caused the Senate to order Marcus Brutus to return from Macedonia to Italy with his armies.

We waited, and learned that Antonius had entered Gaul, and had joined the remnants of his forces with those of Lepidus.

We had eight legions, with sufficient cavalry to support them, and several thousand lightly armed auxiliaries. Octavius left three of these legions and the auxiliaries under the command of Salvidienus at Mutina. He had messages sent to Atia and Octavia, his mother and sister, ordering them to take refuge in the Temple of the Vestal Virgins, where they would be safe from reprisals. And we marched on Rome.

It was a necessary action, you must understand; even had Octavius been willing to relinquish the power we had won and to retire from the public scene, he would have done so at the almost certain expense of his life. For it was clear that the Senate was now embarked upon the inevitable, though delayed, consequence of the assassination: the Caesareans had to be exterminated. Antonius would be crushed by the consular armies that had been augmented by those even larger ones of Brutus and Cassius, which were now (by invitation of the Senate) poised in the East, across the Adriatic Sea, waiting to invade Italy; and Octavius would be destroyed in one way or another, by edict of the Senate, or more likely by private murder. Thus it was that suddenly Antonius's cause became our own. The cause was survival; survival depended upon alliance; and alliance depended upon our strength.

We marched on Rome with our legions armed as if for battle, and the news of our approach raced before us like the wind. Octavius encamped his army outside the city upon the Esquiline hill, so that the people and the senators had but to raise their eyes to the east to know our strength.

It was over in two days, and not a drop of Roman blood was spilled.

Our soldiers had the bounty promised them before the campaign at Mutina; the adoption of Octavius by Julius Caesar was made into law; Octavius was given the vacant consulship of Hirtius; and we had eleven legions under our command.

On the fourth day after the Ides of August (though as you know the month then was called Sextilis), Octavius came into Rome to perform the ritual sacrifice attendant upon his accession to the consulship.

A month later he celebrated his twentieth birthday.

IX. Letter: Marcus Tullius Cicero to Octavius Caesar (August, 43 B.C.)

You are quite right, my dear Caesar; my labors for the state deserve the reward of tranquillity and rest. I shall therefore quit Rome and retire to my beloved Tusculum and devote my remaining years to those studies which I have loved second only to my country. If I have misjudged you in the past, I have done so out of that love which too often imposes on us both the cruel necessity of going against our more humane and natural inclinations.

In any event, I doubly rejoice that you grant leave of absence to Philippus and myself; for it means pardon for the past and indulgence for the future.

X. Letter: Marcus Antonius to Octavius Caesar, from the camp of Marcus Aemilius Lepidus near Avignon (September, 43 B.C.)

Octavius: My friend and lieutenant, Decius, whom you released at Mutina to return to me, tells me that you have treated those soldiers of mine that you captured with kindness and respect. For that, you have my gratitude. He further tells me that you made it apparent to him that you bear me no ill will, that you refused to surrender your troops to Decimus, and so forth.

I see no reason why we should not talk, if you think it might be helpful. Certainly you have more in common with my cause than you have with the cause of those time-servers in the Senate. By the way, is it true (as I fear) that they have now also made a public enemy of our friend Lepidus, whom a few months ago they honored with a statue in the Forum? Nothing surprises me any more.

You may have heard that Decimus is dead. A silly business: a little band of Gallic barbarians surprised him. I should have preferred to have dealt with him myself, at a later date.

We could meet at Bononia next month; I have some business there, mostly with the remnants of Decimus's troops, who have decided to come in with me. I would suggest that we not meet with our forces behind us—just a few cohorts, perhaps, for our personal safety. If we came together in full force, our soldiers might get out of hand. Lepidus will have to figure in this, too; so you can expect him. But our men can work out these details.

XI. Senatorial Proceedings: the Consulships of Quintus Pedius and Octavius Caesar (September, 43 B.C.)

That the sentence of outlawry against Marcus Aemilius Lepidus and Marcus Antonius be annulled and that letters of conciliation and apology be sent to them and the officers of their armies.

Passed by the Senate.

Senatorial Trial: against the murderers and conspirators in the murder of Julius Caesar. Prosecutors: Lucius Cornificius and Marcus Agrippa.

That the absent murderer Marcus Junius Brutus be forbidden the bounties of Rome and be condemned in his exile.

That the absent murderer Gaius Cassius Longinus be forbidden the bounties of Rome and be condemned in his exile.

That the Tribune of the People, P. Servilius Casca, having absented himself from the Senate in his guilty fear, be forbidden the bounties of Rome and condemned.

That the absent conspirator and pirate Sextus Pompeius be forbidden the bounties of Rome and be condemned in his exile.

All conspirators and murderers found guilty by Senatorial Jury and condemned to their fates.

XII. Letter: Gaius Cilnius Maecenas to
Titus Livius (*12 B.C.*)

Of all the memories you have dredged from my soul by your questioning, my dear Livy, now you have found the saddest. I have for several days delayed writing you, knowing that I must confront again that old pain.

We were to meet with Antonius at Bologna, and we marched from Rome with five legions of soldiers at our backs, it having been agreed that Antonius and Lepidus would bring no more troops than we did. The conference was to be held on that little island in the Lavinius, where the river widens toward the sea. Narrow bridges connected the island to both banks, and the country was perfectly flat, so that the armies could halt at some distance from the river, and yet keep each other in view at all times. Each side stationed a guard of perhaps a hundred men at either entrance of the bridge, and the three of us—myself, Agrippa, and Octavius—advanced slowly, while across from us Lepidus and Antonius, each with two attendants, came from the other bank at an equal pace.

It was raining, I remember—a gray day. There was a small hut of unhewn stone a few yards away from the bridge, and we made our way toward that, meeting Antonius and Lepidus at the door. Before we entered, Lepidus looked at us for weapons, and Octavius smiled, saying to him:

"We shall not harm each other. We have come here to destroy the assassins; we have not come to mimic them."

We stooped to enter the low door, and Octavius sat at the rough table in the center of the room, with Antonius and Lepidus on either side of him. You realize, of course, that a general agreement had been made even before we met: Octavius, Antonius, and Lepidus were to form a triumvirate modeled upon that of Julius Caesar, Gnaeus Pompeius, and Crassus, made nearly twenty years before; this triumviral power was to last for five years. This power would give them the rule of Rome, with the right to appoint urban magistrates and command the provincial armies. The provinces of the West (Cassius and Brutus held those of the East) were to be divided among the triumvirs. We had already accepted what was by far the most modest portion—the two Africas, and the islands of Sicily, Sardinia, and Corsica—and the possession of even those was in serious doubt since Sextus Pompeius illegally held Sicily and controlled nearly the whole of the Mediterranean; but land was not what we wanted from the compact. Lepidus retained what he had previously commanded: Narbonensis and the two Spains. And Antonius had the two Gauls, by far the richest and most important of the divisions. Behind it all, of course, was the necessity of our combining forces so that we might conquer Brutus and Cassius in the east and thus punish the murderers of Julius Caesar and bring order to Italy.

It became quickly clear that Lepidus was Antonius's creature. He was a pompous and fatuous man, though if he did not speak he made quite an imposing figure. You know the type—he looked like a senator. Antonius let him drone on for a few minutes, and then he made an impatient gesture.

"We can get to the details later," he said. "We have more important business now." He looked at Octavius. "You know that we have enemies."

"Yes," Octavius said.

"Even though the whole Senate was bowing and scraping when you left, you can be sure they're plotting against you now."

"I know," Octavius said. He was waiting for Antonius to continue.

"And not only in the Senate," Antonius said. He got up and walked restlessly about the room. "All over Rome. I keep remembering your Uncle Julius." He shook his head. "You can't trust anybody."

"No," Octavius said. He smiled softly.

"I keep thinking of them—soft, fat, rich, and getting richer." He pounded his fist on the table, so that some of the papers there were jarred to the clay floor. "And our soldiers are hungry, and will get hungrier before the year's out. Soldiers don't fight on empty stomachs and without something to look forward to after it's all over."

Octavius was watching him.

Antonius said: "I keep remembering Julius. If he had just had a little more resolve in dealing with his enemies." He shook his head again.

There was a long silence.

"How many?" Octavius asked quietly.

Antonius grinned and sat down at the table again. "I have thirty or forty names," he said negligently. "I imagine Lepidus has a few of his own."

"You've discussed this with Lepidus."

"Lepidus agrees," Antonius said.

Lepidus cleared his throat, stretched his arm out so that his hand rested on the table, and leaned back. "It is with much regret that I have come to the conclusion that this is the only course open to us, unpleasant though it may be. I assure you, my dear boy, that—"

"Do not call me your dear boy." Octavius did not raise his voice; like his face, it was totally without expression. "I am the son of Julius Caesar, and I am consul of Rome. You will not call me boy again."

"I assure you—" Lepidus said, and looked at Antonius. Antonius laughed. Lepidus fluttered his hands. "I assure you, I intended no—no—"

Octavius turned away from him and said to Antonius: "So it will be a proscription, as it was with Sulla."

Antonius shrugged. "Call it what you want to. But it's necessary. You know it's necessary."

"I know it," Octavius said slowly. "But I do not like it."

"You'll get used to it," Antonius said cheerfully, "in time."

Octavius nodded absently. He drew his cloak more tightly about his body, and got up from the table and walked to the window. It was raining. I could see his face. The raindrops hit the window casement and splashed on his face. He did not move. It was as if his face were stone. He did not move for a long time. Then he turned to Antonius and said:

"Give me your names."

"You will support this," Antonius said slowly. "Even though you don't like it, you will support it."

"I will support it," Octavius said. "Give me your names."

Antonius snapped his fingers, and one of his attendants handed him a paper. He glanced at it, and then looked up at Octavius, grinning.

"Cicero," Antonius said.

Octavius nodded. He said slowly: "I know that he has caused us some trouble and that he has offended you. But he has given me his word that he will retire."

"Cicero's word," Antonius said, and spat on the floor.

"He is an old man," Octavius said. "He can't have many more years."

"One more year—six months—a month is too long. He has too much power, even in his defeat."

"He has done me harm," Octavius said, as if to himself, "yet I am fond of him."

"We're wasting time," Antonius said. "Any other name—" he tapped the roll of paper "—I'll discuss with you. But Cicero is not negotiable."

Octavius almost smiled, I think. "No," he said, "Cicero is not negotiable."

He seemed to lose interest, then, in what they said. Antonius and Lepidus wrangled over names, and occasionally asked for his assent. He would nod absently. Once Antonius asked him if he did not want to add his own names to the list, and Octavius replied: "I am young. I have not yet lived so long as to acquire that many enemies."

And so, late that night, in the lamplight that flickered with every movement of the air, the list was drawn up. Seventeen of the richest and most powerful senators were to be at once condemned to death and their fortunes confiscated; and a hundred and thirty more were to be proscribed immediately thereafter, and their names published, so that Rome might find limits in which to contain its fear.

Octavius said: "If it is to be done at all, it must be done without delay."

And then we slept, like common soldiers, wrapped in our blankets, on the clay floor of the hut—it having been agreed that none of us would speak to our armies until all the details of the compact were settled.

As you know, my dear Livy, much has been said and written of that proscription, both in blame and praise; and it is true that the prosecution of the affair did get rather badly out of hand. Antonius and Lepidus kept adding names to the list, and a few of the soldiers used the confusion to settle their own enmities and to enrich themselves; but such is to be expected. In the matter of passion, whether of love or war, excess is inevitable.

Yet I have always been bewildered when, in the ease of peace, men raise the questions of praise or blame. It seems to me now that both judgments are inappropriate, and equally so. For those who thus judge do not judge so much out of a concern for right or wrong as out of a protest against the pitiless demands of necessity, or an approval of them. And necessity is simply what has happened; it is the past.

We slept the night, and rose before dawn—and now, my friend, I approach that sorrow of which I spoke at the beginning of this letter. It was dread of that approach, perhaps, which invited me to this easy philosophizing, for which I trust you will forgive me.

The proscriptions made, it now remained for the triumvirs to settle the affairs of Rome for the next five years. It had already been agreed that Octavius would relinquish the consulship that he had so recently received from the Senate; by virtue of their position, each of the triumvirs already had consular powers, and it was felt that it was wiser to make use of lieutenants to perform those senatorial duties, thus enlarging the senatorial base of power and freeing the triumvirs to carry out their military tasks unimpeded. The second day's business was to choose the ten consuls who would have authority over the city for the next five years, and to divide the available legions among the triumvirs.

We breakfasted on coarse bread and dates; Antonius complained of the simplicity of the fare; it was still raining. By noon the armies had been disposed, and in the transaction Octavius gained three legions that we had not had before, in addition to the eleven that we already commanded. The afternoon we were to devote to the choice of consuls.

It was an important negotiation, you understand; it was clear, though unspoken, that beyond the agreements we had made, there remained significant differences between the purposes of Marcus Antonius and Octavius Caesar. The consuls were the men who would represent the interests of the triumvirs, individually and collectively, in Rome; it was essential that we choose those whom we could trust, and yet those who were acceptable to the other parties. It was a rather delicate matter, as you can imagine;

and it was not until late in the afternoon that we had proceeded
to the fourth year.

And Octavius offered the name of Salvidienus Rufus.

I am sure that you have had, as we all have, that mysterious experience of prescience—a moment when, beyond reason and
cause, at a word, or at the flicker of an eyelid, or at anything at
all, one has a sudden foreboding—of what, one does not know.
I am not a religious man; but I am sometimes nearly tempted to
believe that the gods do speak to us, and that only in unguarded
moments will we listen.

"Salvidienus Rufus," Octavius said; and I had within me that
sudden sickening rise, as if I were falling from a great height.

For an instant Antonius did not move; then he yawned, and
said sleepily: "Salvidienus Rufus. . . . Are you sure he's your
choice?"

"He is my choice," Octavius said. "You should have no objec-
tion to him. He would be with me now, as are Agrippa and Maecenas, were he not commanding the legions I left behind before I
came here." Octavius added dryly, "You will remember, I believe, how well he fought against you at Mutina."

Antonius grinned. "I remember. Four years. . . . Don't you
think he might grow impatient in that time?"

"We will need him against Cassius and Brutus," Octavius said
patiently. "We will need him against Sextus Pompeius. If we survive those battles, he shall have earned the office."

Antonius looked at him quizzically for a long moment; then he
nodded, as if he had decided something. "All right," he said.
"You can have him—either for the consulship or the proscription. Take your choice."

Octavius said: "I do not understand your joke."

"It's no joke." Antonius snapped his fingers; one of his attendants handed him a sheet of paper. Antonius dropped it negligently in front of Octavius. "I give him to you."

Octavius picked up the paper, unrolled it, and read. His face
did not change expression. He read for a long time. He handed
the paper to me.

"Is this Salvidienus's handwriting?" he asked quietly.

I read. I heard myself say, "It is Salvidienus's handwriting."

He took the letter from my fingers. He sat for a long time

looking in front of him. I watched his face and heard the dull hiss of the rain as it fell on the thatched roof.

"It's not a great gift," Antonius said. "I have no use for him, now that we have our agreement. Now that you and I are to-gether, I wouldn't be able to trust him. This kind of secret would do neither of us any good." He pointed to the letter. "He sent it to me just after I had joined Lepidus at Avignon. I must say I was tempted, but I decided to wait until I saw what came out of this meeting."

Octavius nodded.

"Shall we put his name on the list?" Antonius asked.

Octavius shook his head. "No," he said in a low voice.

"You have to get used to these things," Antonius said impa-tiently. "He's a danger to us now, or will be. His name goes on the list."

"No," Octavius said. He did not raise his voice, but the word filled the room. His eyes turned to Antonius, and they were like blue fire. "He is not to be proscribed." Then he turned away from Antonius, and his eyes dulled. He said in a whisper: "The matter is not negotiable." He was silent. Then he said to me: "You will write to Salvidienus and inform him that he is no longer a general of my armies, that he is no longer in my service, and—" he paused, "—that he is no longer my friend."

I did not look at the letter again; I did not have to. The words were in my mind, and they still are, after these more than twenty-five years, like an old scar. I give the words to you, as they were written:

"Quintus Salvidienus Rufus sends greetings to Marcus Anto-nius. I command three legions of Roman soldiers, and am con-strained to remain inactive as Decimus Brutus Albinus organizes his forces for a probable pursuit of your army and yourself. Oc-tavius Caesar has been betrayed by the Senate, and returns to Rome on a vain mission. I despair of his resolution, and I despair of our future. Only in you do I discern that purpose and will which may punish the murderers of Julius Caesar and rid Rome of the tyranny of an aristocracy. I will, therefore, put my legions at your disposal, if you will consent to honor me with a com-mand equal to your own, and if you will agree to pursue the cause to which I committed myself with Octavius Caesar and which has been betrayed by ambition and compromise. I am ready to march to you at Avignon."

And so in my sorrow I sent the letter to him who had been our brother, using as messenger that Decimus Carfulenus who had jointly commanded at Mutina with Salvidienus. It was Carfulenus himself who told me of what ensued.

Salvidienus had had rumors of Carfulenus's mission, and waited for him alone in his tent. He was pale, Carfulenus said, but composed. He had been newly shaved, and in accordance with the necessity of the ritual his beard was deposited in the little silver box that lay open on his table.

"I have put away my boyhood," Salvidienus said, pointing to the box. "And now I may receive your message."

Carfulenus, so moved that he could not speak, gave him the letter. Salvidienus read it standing, nodded, and then sat down at his table, still facing Carfulenus.

"Do you wish to reply?" asked Carfulenus at last.

"No," Salvidienus said, and then he said: "Yes. I will reply." Slowly but without hesitation he removed a dagger from the folds of his toga, and with his strength and in Carfulenus's sight, he plunged it into his breast. Carfulenus leaped toward him, but Salvidienus raised his left hand to stay his advance. And in a low voice, only a little breathless, he said: "Tell Octavius that if I cannot remain his friend in life, I may do so in death."

He remained seated at his table until his eyes dulled, and he toppled to the dust.

XIII. Letter: *Anonymous to Marcus Tullius Cicero,* at Rome (*November, 43 B.C.*)

One who cherishes for you the tranquillity and rest that you might have in your retirement, urges you to quit the country that you love. You are in mortal and immediate danger, so long as you stay in Italy. A cruel necessity has forced one to go against his more humane and natural inclinations. You must act at once.

XIV. The History of Rome.
Titus Livius: Fragment (A.D. 13)

Marcus Cicero, shortly before the arrival of the triumvirs, had left the city, rightly convinced that he could no more escape Antonius than Cassius and Brutus could escape Octavius Caesar: at first he had fled to his Tusculan villa, then he set out by cross-country roads to his villa at Formia, intending to take ship from Gaeta. He put out to sea several times, but was driven back by contrary winds: and since there was a heavy ground swell and he could no longer endure the tossing of the ship, he at last became weary of flight and of life, and returned to his villa on the high ground, which was little more than a mile from the sea.

"Let me die," he said, "in my own country, which I have often saved."

It is known that his slaves were ready to fight for him with bravery and loyalty: but he ordered them to set down the litter, and to suffer quietly the hard necessity of fate. As he leaned from the litter and kept his neck still for the purpose, his head was struck off. But that did not satisfy the brutality of the soldiers: they cut off his hands, too, reviling them for having written against Antonius. So the head was brought to Antonius and by his order set between the two hands on the rostrum where he had been heard as consul and as consular, where in that very year his eloquent invectives against Antonius had commanded unprecedented admiration. Men were scarcely able to raise their tearful eyes and look upon the mangled remains of their countryman.

4

My dear Nicolaus, I send you greetings, as does our old friend
and tutor, Tyrannion. I send you greetings from Rome, where I
arrived only last week, after a long and most wearying journey
—from Alexandria, by way of Corinth; by sail and by oar; by
cart, wagon, and horseback; and sometimes even on foot, stagger-
ing beneath the weight of my books. One looks at maps, and does
not truly apprehend the extent and variety of the world. It is a
new sort of education, the gaining of which does not require a
master. Indeed, if one travels enough, the pupil may become the
master; our Tyrannion, so learned in all things, has been at some
pains to question me about what I have seen during my travels.

I am staying with Tyrannion in one of a little group of cottages on a hill overlooking the city. It is a sort of colony, I suppose; several established teachers (one does not call them philosophers in Rome, where philosophy is somewhat suspect) live here,
and a few younger scholars who, like myself, have been invited
to live and study with their former masters.

I was surprised when Tyrannion brought me here, so far away
from the city; and I was even more surprised when he explained
the reason. It seems that the public library in Rome is worse than

useless; an incredibly small collection, often badly copied, and as many books in this dreadful Latin tongue as in our own Greek! But Tyrannion assures me that whatever texts I may need are available, though in private collections. One of his friends, who lives here with us, is that Athenodorus of Tarsus of whom we heard so much at Alexandria; he has, Tyrannion assures me, access to the best private collections in the city, to which we wandering scholars always are welcome.

Of this Athenodorus I must say a few words. He is a most impressive man. He is only a few years older than Tyrannion—perhaps in his middle fifties—but he gives one the impression that he has the wisdom of all the ages somehow within his power. He is aloof and hard, but not unkind; he speaks seldom, and never engages in those playful debates with which the rest of us amuse ourselves; and we seem to follow him, though he does not lead. It is said that he has powerful friends, though he never drops a name; and his personage is such that we hardly dare to discuss such matters, even out of his presence. Yet for all his power in the world and of the mind, there is a sadness within him, the source of which I cannot discover. I have resolved to talk to him, despite my trepidation, and to learn what I may.

Indeed, you will be getting these letters through his auspices; he has access to the diplomatic pouch that goes weekly to Damascus, and he has let me know that he will have these letters included.

Thus, my dear Nicolaus, begins my adventure in the world. According to my promise, I shall write you regularly, sharing whatever new learning I get. I regret that you could not come with me, and I hope that the family affairs that keep you in Damascus soon are solved, and that you can join me in this strange new world.

You must think me a bad friend and a worse philosopher; I am not the former, but I may be on my way to becoming the latter. I had resolved to write you every week—and it is nearly a month since I have put pen to paper.

But this is the most extraordinary of cities, and it threatens to engulf even the strongest of minds. Days tumble after each other in a frenzy such as neither of us could have imagined during our quiet years of study together in the calm of Alexandria. I wonder if, in the balm and somnolence of your beloved Damascus, you can even conceive the quality that I am trying to convey to you.

With some frequency I am struck by the suspicion (perhaps it is only a feeling) that we are too complacent in our Greek pride of history and language, and that we too easily assume a superiority to the "barbarians" of the West who are pleased to call themselves our masters. (I am, you see, becoming somewhat less the philosopher and somewhat more the man of the world.) Our provinces have their charm and culture, no doubt; but there is a kind of vitality here in Rome that a year ago I could not have been persuaded was even remotely attractive. A year ago, I had only heard of Rome; now I have seen it; and at this moment I am not sure that I will ever return to the East, or to my native Pontus.

Imagine, if you will, a city which occupies perhaps half the area of that Alexandria where we studied as boys—and then think of that same city containing within its precincts more than twice the number of people that crowded Alexandria. That is the Rome that I live in now—a city of nearly a million people, I have been told. It is unlike anything I have ever seen. They come here from all over the world—black men from the burning sands of Africa, pale blonds from the frozen north, and every shade between. And such a polyglot of tongues! Yet everyone speaks a little Latin or a little Greek, so that no one need feel a stranger.

And how they crowd themselves together, these Romans. Beyond the walls of the city lies some of the most beautiful countryside that you can imagine; yet the people huddle together here like fish trapped in a net and struggle through narrow, winding little streets that run senselessly, mile after mile, through the city. During the daylight hours, these streets—all of them—are literally choked with people; and the noise and stench are incredible. A few months before his death, the great Julius Caesar decreed that only in the dark hours between dusk and dawn might wagons and carts and beasts of burden be allowed in the city; one wonders what it must have been like before that decree, when horses and oxen and goods-wagons of all descriptions mingled with the people on these impossible streets.

Thus the ordinary Roman who lives in the city proper must never have any sleep. For the noise of the day becomes the din of the night, as drovers curse their horses and oxen, and the great wooden carts groan and clatter over the cobblestones.

No one ventures out alone after dark, except those tradespeople who must and the very rich who can afford a bodyguard; even on moonlit nights the streets are pitch dark, since the rickety tenements are built so high that it is impossible for even a vagrant ray of moonlight to find its way down into the streets. And the streets are filled with the desperate poor who would rob you and cut your throat for the clothes you wear and the little silver you might carry with you.

Yet those who live in these towering ramshackle buildings are little safer than those who would wander the streets at night; for they live in constant danger of fire. At night, in the safety of my hillside cottage, I can see in the distance the fires break out like flowers blooming in the darkness, and hear the distant shouts of fear or agony. There are fire brigades, to be sure; but they are uniformly corrupt and too few to accomplish much good.

And yet in the center of this chaos, this city, there is, as if it were another world, the great Forum. It is like the fora that we have seen in the provincial cities, but much grander—great columns of marble support the official buildings; there are dozens of statues, and as many temples to their borrowed Roman gods; and many more smaller buildings that house the various offices of government. There is a good deal of open space, and somehow the noise and stench and smoke from the surrounding city seem not to penetrate here at all. Here people walk in sunlight in open space, converse easily, exchange rumors, and read the news posted at the various rostra around the Senate House. I come here to the Forum nearly every day, and feel that I am at the center of the world.

I begin to understand this Roman disdain for philosophy. Their world is an immediate one—of cause and consequence, of rumor and fact, of advantage and deprivation. Even I, who have devoted my life to the pursuit of knowledge and truth, can have some sympathy for the state of the world which has occasioned this disdain. They look at learning as if it were a means to an end; at truth as if it were only a thing to be used. Even their gods serve the state, rather than the other way around.

Here is a copy of a poem found this morning on every gate of importance that leads into the city. I shall not attempt a translation; I transcribe it in its Latin:

> Stop, traveler, before you enter this farmhouse,
> and look to yourself. There is a boy lives here
> with the name of a man. You will dine with him
> at your peril. Oh, he'll ask you, never fear;
> he asks everyone. Last month his father died;
> now the boy carouses on the stinking wine
> of his freedom and lets the livestock run wild
> beyond the broken fences—except for one,
> the farrow of a pet pig he has taken
> into his household. Do you have a daughter?
> Look to her, also. This boy once had a taste
> for girls lovely as she. He may change again.

I offer a gloss, in the manner of our old teachers. The "boy with the name of a man" is, of course, Gaius Octavius Caesar; the "father" who gave him the name is Julius Caesar; the "farrow" is one Clodia, daughter of the "pig" (that is the nickname given her by enemies), Fulvia, wife of Marcus Antonius, with whom Octavius alternately battles and reconciles. The "girl" alluded to in the last line is one Servilia, daughter of an ex-consul to whom Octavius was engaged, before (as it is said) under pressure from his own and Antonius's troops, he accepted a marriage agreement with Antonius's stepdaughter. There is, of course, more form than substance to the contract; the girl, I understand, is only thirteen years old. But it apparently has placated those forces that want to see Octavius and Antonius on amicable terms. The poem itself, no doubt, has other local allusions that I do not understand; it was almost certainly commissioned by one of the senatorial party who does not want a conciliation of Octavius and Antonius; it is a vulgar thing. . . . But it does have something of a ring to it, does it not?

I am forever surprised. The name of Octavius Caesar is on everyone's lips. He is in Rome; he is out of Rome. He is the savior of the nation; he will destroy it. He will punish the murderers of Julius Caesar; he will reward them. Whatever the truth, this mysterious youth has captured the imagination of Rome; and I, myself, have not been immune.

So, knowing that our Athenodorus has long lived in and around Rome, I took the occasion yesterday evening, after we had dined, to ask him a few questions. (Gradually, he has unbent toward me, and now we may exchange as many as half a dozen words at a time.)

I asked him what manner of man this was, this Octavius Caesar, as he calls himself. And I showed him a copy of the poem that I sent you earlier.

Athenodorus looked at it, his thin, hooked nose almost touching the paper, his thin cheeks drawn inward, his thin lips pursed. Then he handed it back to me, with the same gesture that he has when he returns a paper I have given him for his emendations.

"The meter is uncertain," he said. "The matter is trivial."

I have learned patience with Athenodorus. Again, I questioned him about this Octavius.

"He is a man like any other," he said. "He will become what he will become, out of the force of his person and the accident of his fate."

I asked Athenodorus if he had ever seen this youth, or talked to him. Athenodorus frowned and growled:

"I was his teacher. I was with him at Apollonia when his uncle was killed and he took the path that has led him where he is today."

For a moment I thought that Athenodorus was speaking in metaphor; and then I saw his eyes and knew he was speaking the truth. I stammered: "You—you know him?"

Athenodorus almost smiled. "I dined with him last week."

But he would not speak more of him, nor answer my questions; he seemed to think them unimportant. He said only that his former student could have become a good scholar, had he chosen to do so.

So I am even more nearly at the center of the world than I imagined.

I have attended a funeral.

Atia, the mother of Octavius Caesar, is dead. A herald came through the streets, announcing that the services would be held the next morning in the Forum. So I have at last set eyes upon that man whose person now is the most powerful in Rome, and hence (I suppose) in the world.

I got to the Forum early, so that I would have a good place to see, and waited at the rostrum where Octavius Caesar was to deliver the oration. By the fifth hour of the morning, the Forum was nearly filled.

And then the procession came—the ushers with their flaming torches, the oboists and the buglers and the clarionists playing the slow march, the bier with the body propped upon it, the mourners—and behind the procession, walking alone, a slight figure, whom I took at first to be a youth, since his toga was bordered with purple; it did not occur to me that he might be a senator. But it soon became clear that it was Octavius himself, for the crowd stirred as he passed, trying to get a better view of him. The bearers set the bier before the rostrum, the chief mourners seated themselves on little chairs in front, and Octavius Caesar walked slowly to the bier and looked for a moment at the body of his mother. Then he mounted the rostrum and looked at the people—a thousand, or more—who had gathered for the occasion.

I was standing very close—not more than fifteen yards away. He seemed very pale, very still, almost as if he himself were the corpse. Only his eyes were alive—they are a most startling blue. The crowd became very quiet; from the distance, I could hear the faint careless rumble of the city that went its way like a dumb beast.

Then he began to speak. He spoke very quietly, but in a voice so clear and distinct that he could be heard by everyone who had gathered.

I send you his words; the scribes with their tablets were there, and the next day copies of the oration were in every bookstall in the city.

He said: "Rome will not again see you, Atia, you who were Rome. It is a loss that only the example of your virtue makes endurable, which tells us that our grief, if held too deeply and too long, offends the very purpose of your living.

"You were a faithful wife to the father of my blood, that Gaius Octavius who was praetor and governor of Macedonia, and whose untimely death intervened between his person and the consulship of Rome. You were a stern and loving mother to your daughter, Octavia, who weeps now before your bier, and to your son, who stands before you for the last time and speaks these poor words. You were the dutiful and proper niece of that man who gave at last to your son the father of whom he had been cheated by fate, that Julius Caesar who was villainously murdered within earshot of this very spot where you so nobly lie.

"Of an honored Roman name, you had in full degree those old virtues of the earth which have nurtured and sustained our nation throughout its history. You spun and wove the cloth that furnished your household its clothing; your servants were as your own children; you honored the gods of your house and of your city. Through your gentleness you had no enemy but time, who takes you now.

"Oh Rome, look upon the one who lies here now, and see the best of your nature and your heritage. Soon we shall take these remains beyond the city walls, and there the funeral pyre will consume the receptacle of all that Atia was. But I charge you, citizens, do not let her virtues be entombed with her ashes. Rather let that virtue become your Roman lives, so that, though Atia's person be but ash, yet the better part of her will live on, entombed in the living souls of all Romans who come after her.

"Atia, may the spirits of the dead keep your rest."

A long silence stayed upon the crowd. Octavius stood for a moment on the rostrum. Then he descended, and they bore the body outside the Forum, and beyond the city walls.

I cannot bring myself to believe what I have seen, or to give credence to what I have heard. In this chaos, there is no official news; nothing is posted on the walls of the Senate House; one cannot even be sure that there is a Senate any more. Octavius Caesar has joined with Antonius and Lepidus in what amounts to

a military dictatorship; and the enemies of Julius Caesar are proscribed. More than a hundred senators—*senators*—have been
executed, their property and wealth confiscated; and many times
that number of wealthy Roman citizens, often of noble name, are
either murdered or fled from the city, their property and wealth
in the hands of the triumvirs. Merciless. Among those proscribed:
Paullus, the blood brother of Lepidus. Lucius Caesar, the uncle of
Antonius. And even the famous Cicero is on the published list.
These three, and others, I imagine, have fled the city, and may escape with their lives.

The bloodiest of the work seems to be in the hands of Antonius's soldiers. With my own eyes I have seen the headless bodies
of Roman senators littering the very Forum which a week ago
was their chief glory; and I have heard, from the safety of my
hill, the screams of the rich who have waited too long to flee
Rome and their riches. All except the poor, those with moderate
wealth, and the friends of Caesar, walk in apprehension of what
the morrow might bring, whether their names have been posted
or not.

It is said that Octavius Caesar sits in his home and will not
show his face nor view the dead bodies of his former colleagues.
It is also said that it is Octavius himself who insists that the proscriptions be carried out ruthlessly, at once, and to the letter. One
does not know what one may with safety believe.

Is this the Rome that I thought I was beginning to know, after
these crowded months? Have I understood these people at all?
Athenodorus will not discuss the matter with me; Tyrannion
shakes his head sadly.

Perhaps I am less the man and more the youth than I had believed.

Cicero did not escape.

Yesterday, on a cool, bright December afternoon, wandering
among the bookstalls in the shop area behind the Forum (it is safe
to be on the streets now), I heard a great commotion; and against
my better judgment, out of that curiosity that will someday lead
me either to fame or death, I made my way inside the Forum
gates. A great crush of people was milling around the rostrum
near the Senate House.

"It's Cicero," someone said, and the name went like a whispering sigh among the people. "Cicero. . . ."

Not knowing what to expect, but dreading what I would see, I pushed my way through the crowd.

There on the Senate rostrum, placed neatly between two severed hands, was the withered and shrunken head of Marcus Tullius Cicero. Someone said that it had been placed there by order of Antonius himself.

It was the same rostrum from which, only three weeks before, Octavius Caesar had spoken so gently of his mother, who had died. Now another death sat upon it; and I could not help, at that moment, being somehow pleased that the mother had died before she had been made witness to what her son had wrought.

II. Letter: Marcus Junius Brutus to Octavius Caesar, from Smyrna (42 B.C.)

I cannot believe that you truly apprehend the gravity of your position. I know that you bear me no love, and I would be foolish if I pretended that I bore you much more; I do not write you out of regard for your person, but out of regard for our nation. I cannot write to Antonius, for he is a madman; I cannot write to Lepidus, for he is a fool. I hope that I may be heard by you, who are neither.

I know that it is through your influence that Cassius and I have been declared outlaws and condemned to exile; but let neither of us believe that such a condemnation has more permanent force of law than can be sustained by a flustered and demoralized Senate. Let neither of us pretend that such an edict has any kind of permanence or validity. Let us speak practically.

All of Syria, all of Macedonia, all of Epirus, all of Greece, all of Asia are ours. All of the East is against you, and the power and wealth of the East is not inconsiderable. We control absolutely the eastern Mediterranean; therefore you can expect no aid from your late uncle's Egyptian mistress, who might otherwise furnish wealth and manpower to your cause. And though I bear him no love, I know that the pirate, Sextus Pompeius, is nipping at your heels from the west. Thus I do not fear for myself or my forces the war that now seems imminent.

But I do fear for Rome, and for the future of the state. The proscriptions that you and your friends have instituted in Rome bear witness to that fear, to which my personal grief must be subordinate.

So let us forget proscriptions and assassinations; if you can forgive me the death of Caesar, perhaps I can forgive you the death of Cicero. We cannot be friends to each other; neither of us needs that. But perhaps we can be friends to Rome.

I implore you, do not march with Marcus Antonius. Another battle between Romans would, I fear, destroy what little virtue remains in our state. And Antonius will not march without you.

If you do not march, I assure you that you will have my respect and my thanks; and your future will be assured. If we cannot work together out of friendship to each other, yet we may work together for the good of Rome.

But let me hasten to add this. If you reject this offer of amity, I shall resist with all my strength; and you will be destroyed. I say this with sadness; but I say it.

III. *The Memoirs of Marcus Agrippa:* Fragments (*13* B.C.)

And after the triumvirate was formed and the Roman enemies of Julius Caesar and Caesar Augustus were put down, there yet remained in the West the forces of the pirate Sextus Pompeius, and in the East the exiled murderers of the divine Julius, that Brutus and Cassius who threatened the safety and order of Rome. True to his oath, Caesar Augustus resolved to punish the murderers of his father and restore order to the state, and deferred the matter of Sextus Pompeius to another time, taking only those actions against Pompeius that were necessary for the safety of the moment.

My energies at this time were devoted to enrolling and equipping in Italy those legions that were to lay siege to Brutus and Cassius in the East, and to organizing the lines of supply that would allow us to do battle on that distant soil. Antonius was to send eight legions to Amphipolis, on the Aegean coast of Macedonia, to harass the troops of Brutus and Cassius, so that they might not find an advantage of terrain in which to fight. But Antonius delayed the departure of his legions, so that they were forced to find an inferior position on the low ground west of Philippi, where the army of Brutus rested in security. It became necessary for Antonius to send other legions in support of those in Macedonia, but the fleets of Brutus and Cassius hovered around the harbor at Brindisi; so Augustus commanded me to insure safe passage for Antonius. And with the ships and legions that I had raised in Italy, we drove through the navy of Marcus Junius Brutus and landed twelve legions of troops upon the Macedonian shore at Dyrrachium.

But at Dyrrachium, Augustus fell gravely ill, and we would have waited in fear of his life; but he bade us continue, knowing that all would be lost if we delayed our attack upon the armies of the outlaws. And eight of our legions marched across the country to join the beleaguered advance troops of Marcus Antonius at Amphipolis.

Our way was hindered by the cavalry of Brutus and Cassius, and we suffered severe losses on our journey, arriving at Amphipolis with our troops weary and demoralized. When it became clear that the armies of Brutus and Cassius were securely entrenched upon the high ground at Philippi, protected on the north by mountains and on the south by a marsh that stretched from the camp to the sea, I resolved to send an urgent message to Caesar Augustus; for our task seemed hopeless to our soldiers, and I knew that their failing spirits must be revived.

And so, though gravely ill, Augustus forced his way across the country to reinforce us, and went among his men on a litter, being too weak to walk; and though his face was that of a corpse, his eyes were fierce and hard, and his voice was strong, so that the men took heart and resolve from his presence.

We determined to strike boldly and at once, for each day of waiting cost us supplies, while Brutus and Cassius had all the lanes of the sea for their support. So while three of the legions of Augustus, under my command, pretended to be intent upon constructing a causeway across the great marsh that protected the enemy's southern flank, thus diverting a large number of Republican troops to attack us, the legions of Marcus Antonius struck boldly and broke through the weakened line of Cassius, and pillaged the camp before Cassius could recover from his surprise. And Cassius, on a slight hill with a few of his officers, looked (it is said) to the north, and there saw the troops of Brutus in what he took to be full flight; knowing that his own army was defeated, and thinking that all was lost, he despaired; and fell upon his sword, ending his life there in the dust and blood at Philippi, taking revenge upon himself, it seemed, for the murder of the divine Julius, two years and seven months before.

What Cassius did not know was that the army of Brutus was not in flight. Divining our plan, and knowing that the army of Augustus was dispersed in its diversionary tactic, he made haste to invest our camp, and overran it, capturing many soldiers and killing many more. Augustus himself, half-conscious in his illness and unable to move, was carried from his tent by his doctor and hidden in the marsh until the battle was over and night fell, and he could be carried stealthily to where the remnants of the army had retreated and had joined with the troops of Marcus Antonius. The doctor swore that he had had a dream telling him to remove the ill Augustus, so that his life might be spared. . . .

IV. *Letter: Quintus Horatius Flaccus to His Father,*
from west of Philippi (*42 B.C.*)

My dear father, if you receive this letter, you will know that your Horace, a day ago a proud soldier in the army of Marcus Junius Brutus, at this moment, on this cold autumn night, sits in his tent, writing these words by the flickering light of a lantern, in disgrace with himself, if not with his friends. Yet he feels curiously free from the obsession that has gripped him these last several months; and if he is not happy, he is at least beginning to know who he is. . . . Today I was in my first battle; and I must tell you at once that at the first moment of serious danger to myself I dropped my shield and sword, and I ran.

Why I ever embarked upon this venture, I do not know; and surely you are too intelligent to know either. When, out of that kindness of yours to which I have grown so used that I sometimes do not think of it, you sent me to study in Athens year before last, I had no thought of engaging myself in anything so foolish as politics. Did I align myself with Brutus and accept a tribuneship in his army in a contemptible effort to rise above my station into the aristocracy? Was Horace ashamed of being the son of a mere freedman? I cannot believe that that is true; even in my youth and arrogance, I have known that you are the best of men, and I could not wish for a more noble and generous and loving father.

It was, I believe, because in my studies I had forgotten the world, and had begun almost to believe that philosophy was true. Liberty. I joined the cause of Brutus for a word; and I do not know what the word means. A man may live like a fool for a year, and become wise in a day.

I must tell you now that I did not drop my shield and run from the battle out of mere cowardice—though that was no doubt part of it. But when I suddenly saw one of Octavius Caesar's soldiers (or maybe Antonius's, I do not know) advancing toward me with naked steel flashing in his hands and in his eyes, it was as if time suddenly stood still; and I remembered you, and all the hopes you had of my future. I remembered that you had been born a slave, and had managed to buy your freedom; that your labor and your life were early turned to your son, so that he might live in an ease and comfort and security that you never had. And I saw that son uselessly slaughtered on an earth he had no love for, for a cause he did not understand—and I had a sense of what your years might have been with the knowledge of your son's discarded life—and I ran. I ran over bodies of fallen soldiers, and saw their empty eyes staring at the sky which they would never see again; and it did not matter to me whether they were friend or foe. I ran.

If the fates are kind to me, I shall return to you in Italy. I shall fight no more. Tomorrow, I shall post this letter to you and make my preparations. If we are not attacked, I shall be in no danger; if we are, I shall run again. In any event, I shall not linger at this massacre that leads to an end I cannot see.

I do not know who will be victorious—the Party of Caesar or the Party of the Republic. I do not know the future of our country, or my own future. Perhaps I shall have to disappoint you, and become a tax collector like yourself. It is a position, however lowly in your eyes, to which you lend dignity and honor by your presence. I am your son, Horace, and proud to be so.

V. *The Memoirs of Marcus Agrippa:* Fragments (*13 B.C.*)

And Brutus withdrew once more to the high ground and entrenchments at Philippi, whence, it became clear, he did not propose to retreat. We knew, perhaps better than Brutus, that each day of waiting cost us dearly, for our supplies were running low; nothing could be transported over the sea controlled by Brutus's navy; behind us were the flat and barren plains of Macedonia, and before us the hostile and barren hills of Greece. Thus we made to be copied sheets of reproaches to the officers of Brutus's army, taunting them with their timidity and cowardice; and at night we shouted challenges across the campfires, so that the soldiers could not even sleep in honor, but dozed fitfully in their shame.

For three weeks Brutus waited, until at last his men, chafing beneath the burden of their inaction, would wait no longer; and Brutus, fearful that his army would be depleted by desertions, ordered his men to descend from the entrenchments that might have saved them, and to attack our camp.

In the late afternoon they came down from the hill like a northern storm; no cries or shouts escaped their lips, and we heard only the clump of hooves and the pad of feet in the dust that came with them like a cloud. I ordered our line to give way before the initial attack; and as the enemy streamed into us, we closed the lines on either side, so that he had to fight on two flanks at once. And we broke the army in two, and each of those parts into two again, so that he could not re-form himself to withstand our attacks. By nightfall, the battle was over; and the stars heard the moans of the wounded, and watched impassively the bodies that did not move.

Brutus escaped with what remained of his legions, and made his way to the wilderness beyond the entrenchments at Philippi, which we had invested. He would have attacked again with what remained of his army, but his officers refused to risk themselves; and in the early dawn, the day after the Ides of November, on a lonely hillock overlooking the carnage of his will and resolve, with a few of his faithful officers, he fell upon his sword; and the army of the Republic was no more.

Thus was the murder of Julius Caesar avenged, and thus did the chaos of treason and faction give way to the years of order and peace, under the Emperor of our state, Gaius Octavius Caesar, now the August.

VI. Letter: Gaius Cilnius Maecenas to Titus Livius (13 B.C.)

After Philippi, slowly, with many stops along the way, more dead than alive, he came back to Rome; he had saved Italy from its enemies abroad, and it remained for him to heal the nation that was shattered within.

My dear Livy, I cannot tell you the shock I had upon seeing him for the first time after those many months, when they carried him in secret to his house on the Palatine. I, of course, had remained in Rome during the fighting, according to Octavius's orders, so that I could keep an eye on things and do what I could to prevent Lepidus, either out of conspiracy or incompetence, from wholly disrupting the internal government of Italy.

He was not quite twenty-two years old that winter when he returned from the fighting, but I swear to you he looked double —treble—that age. His face was waxen, and, slight though he always was, he had lost so much weight that his skin sagged upon his bones. He had the strength to speak only in a hoarse whisper. I looked at him, and I despaired of his life.

"Do not let them know," he said, and paused a long time, as if the uttering of that phrase had exhausted him. "Do not let them know of my illness. Neither the people nor Lepidus."

"I will not, my friend," I told him.

The illness had, in fact, begun the year before, during the time of the proscriptions, and had grown steadily worse; and though the physicians who attended him had been paid handsomely and threatened with their livelihood, if not their lives, for any breach of secrecy, rumors of the illness had crept out. The doctors (a dreadful lot, then as now) might as well not have been called in; they were able to do nothing except prescribe noxious herbs and treatments of heat and cold. He was able to eat almost nothing, and upon more than one occasion he had vomited blood. Yet as his body had weakened, it seemed that his will had hardened, so that he drove himself even more fiercely in his illness than he had in his health.

"Antonius," he said in that terrible voice, "will not return yet to Rome. He has gone into the East to gather booty and to strengthen his position. I agreed to it—I would prefer to have him steal from the Asians and the Egyptians than from the Romans. . . . I believe he expects me to die; and though he hopes for it, I suspect he doesn't want to be in Italy when it happens."

He lay back on his bed, breathing shallowly, his eyes closed. At length he regained his strength, and said:

"Give me the news of the city."

"Rest," I said. "We shall have time when you are stronger."

"The news," he said. "Though my body cannot move, my mind can."

There were bitter things I had to tell him, but I knew that he would not have forgiven me had I sweetened them. I said:

"Lepidus negotiates secretly with the pirate, Sextus Pompeius; he has some notion, I believe, of allying himself with Pompeius against either you or Antonius, whichever proves weaker. I have the evidence; but if we confront him with it, he will swear that he negotiates only to bring peace to Rome. . . . Out of Philippi, Antonius is the hero and you are the coward. Antonius's pig of a wife and his vulture of a brother have spread the stories—while you cowered and quaked in fear in the salt marsh, Antonius bravely punished the enemies of Caesar. Fulvia makes speeches to the soldiers, warning that you will not pay them the bounties that Antonius promised; while Lucius goes about the countryside stirring up the landowner and the farmer with rumors that you will confiscate their properties to settle the veterans. Do you want to hear more?"

He even smiled a little. "If I must," he said.

"The state is very near to being bankrupt. Of the few taxes that Lepidus can collect, a trickle goes into the treasury; the rest goes to Lepidus himself and, it is said, to Fulvia, who, it is also said, is preparing to raise independent legions, in addition to those that rightfully belong to Antonius. I have no proof of this, but I imagine it is true. . . . So it would seem that you got the lesser bargain in Rome."

"I would prefer the weakness of Rome to all the power of the

East," he said, "though I am sure this is not what Antonius had in mind. He expects that if I do not die, I will go under with the problems here. But I will not die, and we will not go under." He raised himself a little. "We have much to do."

And the next day, in his weakness, he arose from his bed, and put his illness aside as if it were of no moment and no account.

We had much to do, he said. . . . My dear Livy, that admirable history of yours—how might it evoke the bustles and delays, the triumphs and defeats, the joys and despairs of the years following Philippi? It cannot do so, and no doubt it should not. But I must not digress, even to praise you; for you will scold me again.

You have asked me to be more particular about the duties I performed for our Emperor, as if I were worthy of a place in your history. You honor me beyond my merits. Yet I am pleased that I am remembered, even in my retirement from public affairs.

The duties that I performed for our Emperor . . . I must confess that some of them seem to me now ludicrous, though of course they did not seem so then. The marriages, for example. Through the influence and by the edicts of our Emperor, it is now possible for a man of substance and ambition to contract a marriage on grounds that are rational—if "rational" is not too contradictory a word to describe such an odd and (I sometimes think) unnatural relationship. Such was not possible in the days of which I speak—in Rome, at least, and to those of public involvement. One married for advantage and political necessity—as, indeed, I myself did, though my Terentia was on occasion an amusing companion.

I must say, I was rather good at such arrangements—and I must also confess that as it turned out none were advantageous or even necessary. I have always suspected that it was that knowledge which led Octavius, some years later, to institute those not altogether successful marriage laws, rather than the kind of "morality" imputed to them. He has often chided me about my advice in those early days. For it was invariably wrong.

For example: The first marriage I contracted for him was in the very early days, before the formation of the triumvirate. The girl was Servilia, the daughter of that P. Servilius Isauricus who, when Cicero opposed Octavius after Mutina, agreed to stand for senior consul with Octavius against Cicero—and the marriage to his daughter was to be our surety that he would be supported by the power of our arms, if that became necessary. As it turned out, Servilius was impotent in his dealings with Cicero and was of no help to us; the marriage never took place.

The second was even more ludicrous than the first. It was to Clodia, daughter of Fulvia and stepdaughter to Marcus Antonius, and it was a part of the compact that formed the triumvirate; the soldiers wanted it, and we saw no reason to deny them their whim, however meaningless it was. The girl was thirteen years old, and as ugly as her mother. Octavius saw her twice, I believe, and she never set foot in his house. As you know, the marriage did nothing to quiet Fulvia or Antonius; they continued their plotting and their treason, so that after Philippi, when Antonius was in the East and Fulvia was openly threatening another civil war against Octavius, we had to make our position clear by effecting a divorce.

It was, however, my responsibility for the third contract which Octavius most nearly resented, I think; it was with Scribonia, and it was accomplished within the year after his divorce from Clodia, during our most desperate months, when it seemed that we would either be crushed by the Antonian uprisings in Italy, or by the encroachment of Sextus Pompeius from the south. In what seems now a too desperate effort at conciliation, I went to Sicily to negotiate with Sextus Pompeius—an impossible task, for Pompeius was an impossible man. He was a bit mad, I think— more like an animal than a human. He *was* an outlaw, and that in more than the legal sense; he is one of the few men with whom I have had converse who so repelled me that I had difficulty in dealing with him. I know, my dear Livy, that you admired his father; but you never met either of them, and you certainly did not know his son. . . . In any event, I talked to Pompeius, and extracted what I thought was an agreement— and sealed the compact with an arrangement of marriage with that Scribonia, who was the younger sister of Pompeius's father-in-law. Scribonia, Scribonia. . . . She has always seemed to me the epitome of womankind: coldly suspicious, politely ill-tempered, and narrowly selfish. It is a wonder that my friend ever *did* forgive me for that arrangement. Perhaps it was because from

that marriage came the one thing that my friend loves as much as
he loves Rome—his daughter, his Julia. He divorced Scribonia
on the day of his daughter's birth, and it is a wonder that he ever
married again. But he did marry again, and it was an arrangement
in which I had no part. . . . As it turned out, the marriage to
Scribonia was fraudulent to begin with; for as I was negotiating
with Pompeius, he himself was already deep in negotiations with
Antonius, and the marriage contract was a mere ruse to lull our
suspicions. Such, my dear Livy, was the nature of politics in
those days. But I must say (though I would not repeat it to our
Emperor), looking back on it all, these affairs did have their humorous side.

For my responsibility in arranging only one marriage have I
ever felt any shame; even now, I cannot take it as lightly as I
ought to be able to do—though I suppose no great harm was
done.

At about the time I was negotiating with Pompeius and arranging the marriage with Scribonia, the barbarian Moors,
aroused by Fulvia and Lucius Antonius, rose up against our governor in Outer Spain; our generals in Africa, again at the instigation of Fulvia and Lucius, began to war with each other; Lucius
pretended that his life had been threatened, and marched with his
(and Fulvia's) legions on Rome. They were repulsed there by our
friend Agrippa, and surrounded in the town of Perusia, whose inhabitants (Pompeians and Republicans, mostly) aided them with
vigor and enthusiasm. We really didn't know how much a part
in all this Marcus Antonius had, though we suspected; therefore
we did not dare destroy his brother, for fear that if he were
guilty, Marcus Antonius would use this as a pretext to attack us
from the east; and that if he were innocent, he would misunder-
stand our action, and take revenge upon us. We did not punish
Lucius, but we showed little mercy to those who had aided him,
putting the most treacherous to death and exiling the less
dangerous—though we let the ordinary citizens go free, and
even recompensed them for the property we destroyed. Among
those exiled (and this, my dear Livy, will appeal to your perhaps
overdeveloped sense of irony) was one Tiberius Claudius Nero,
who was allowed to make his way to Sicily with his newborn
son, Tiberius, and his very young wife, Livia.

During all the months of the turmoil in Italy, we had written often to Antonius, trying to describe the activities of his wife and brother and trying to ascertain his part in the disturbances; and though we received letters from Antonius, none of them replied to those we had sent, as if he had not received them. It was winter, of course, when we wrote most urgently; and few of the sea lanes were open; it is possible that he did not receive them. In any event, the spring and part of the summer passed without clear word from him; and then we got an urgent message from Brindisi that Antonius's fleet was sailing toward the harbor, and that the navy of Pompeius was coming up from the north to join him. And we learned that some months earlier, Fulvia had sailed to Athens to meet her husband.

We did not know what to expect, and yet we had no choice. Weak as we were, with our legions scattered against the various troubles on our borders and in our nation, we marched toward Brindisi, fearful that Antonius had landed and was leading his soldiers to meet us. But we learned that the city of Brindisi had refused to let Antonius through the harbor gates, and so we encamped and awaited what would happen. Had Antonius attacked in full force, we no doubt could not have survived.

But he did not attack, nor did we. Our own soldiers were famished and ill-equipped; the soldiers of Antonius were weary with their travels and wanted only to see their families in Italy. Had either side been foolish enough to press the issue, we probably would have had a mutiny.

And then an agent that we slipped among the Antonian forces returned with some startling news. Antonius and Fulvia had quarreled bitterly at Athens; Antonius had left in a rage; and now Fulvia, suddenly and inexplicably, was dead.

We encouraged some of our trusted soldiers to fraternize with the troops of Antonius; and soon deputations from both sides approached their respective leaders and demanded that Antonius and Octavius once more reconcile their differences, so that not again would Roman be pitted against Roman.

And thus the two leaders met, and another war was averted. Antonius protested that Fulvia and his brother had acted without his authority, and Octavius pointed out that he had taken no revenge on either of them for their actions, out of regard for their relationship to Antonius. A pact was signed; a general amnesty for all previous enemies of Rome was declared; and a marriage was arranged.

The marriage was negotiated by me; and it was between Antonius and Octavia, the older sister of our Emperor, who had been widowed only a few months ago, and left with her infant son, Marcellus.

My dear Livy, you know my tastes—but I almost believe I could have loved women, had many of them been like Octavia. I admired her then as I do now—she was very gentle and without guile, she was quite beautiful, and she was one of the two women I have ever known who had both an extensive knowledge and deep understanding of philosophy and poetry, the other being Octavius's own daughter, Julia. Octavia was not a plaything, you understand. My old friend Athenodorus used to say that had she been a man, and less intelligent, she could have become a great philosopher.

I was with Octavius when he explained the necessity to his sister—of whom he was very fond, as you know. He could not look her in the eye when he spoke. But Octavia merely smiled at him and said: "If it must be done, my brother, it must be done; I shall try to be a good wife to Antonius and remain a good sister to you."

"It is for Rome," Octavius said.

"It is for us all," his sister said.

It was necessary, I suppose; we hoped that such a marriage might lead us to a lasting peace; we knew that it would give us a few years. But I must say, I still feel that twinge of regret and sorrow; Octavia must have had some rather bad times.

Though, as it turned out, Antonius was a rather intermittent husband. That might have made it more endurable for her. Yet she never spoke harshly of Marcus Antonius, even in later years.

5

I. Letter: Marcus Antonius to Octavius Caesar; from Athens (39 B.C.)

Antonius to Octavius, greetings. I do not know what you expect of me. I renounced my late wife and ruined my brother's career, because their actions had displeased you. To cement our joint rule, I married your sister, who, though a good woman, is not to my taste. To assure you of my good faith, I sent Sextus Pompeius and his navy back to his Sicily, though (as you well know) he would have joined me against you. To augment your power, I agreed to strip Lepidus of all the provinces he held, save Africa. I agreed, even, after my marriage to your sister, to be designated Priest to the deified Julius—though it seemed odd to be priest to an old friend, a man with whom I have whored and drunk, and though my acceptance of the priesthood was more advantageous to your name than to mine. Finally, I have absented myself from my homeland, so that I may raise the money in the East that will insure our future authority, and to make some order out of the chaos into which our Eastern provinces have fallen. As I said, I do not know what you expect of me.

If I have allowed the Greeks to pretend to themselves that I am the revived Bacchus (or do you prefer Dionysus?), it is so that their love for me will give me some control over them. You criticize me for "playing the Greek" and for assuming the role of the Incarnate Bacchus at the Festival of Athena; and yet you must know that when I agreed to do so, I insisted that the Celestial Athena bring me a dowry—and that by that insistence, I have enriched our treasury by more than I could have done by levying taxes, and have also escaped the resentment that would have inevitably resulted from such a levy.

As for the Egyptian matters that you so delicately raise: first, it is true that I have accepted certain of the Queen's subjects as my aides. This is both helpful to my task, and necessary to my diplomacy. But even if all this were merely for my own pleasure, I see no reason why you should object: Ammonius you know yourself, for he was a friend of your late uncle (or "father," as you now may call him)—and he serves me as faithfully as he served Julius and as he served his Queen. As for Epimachos, whom you call a mere "soothsayer," such a designation reveals (if you will forgive me) a profound ignorance about these Eastern matters. This "mere soothsayer" is an extraordinarily important man: he is the High Priest of Heliopolis, the Incarnation of Thoth, and the Keeper of the *Book of Magic*. He is a good deal more important than any of our own "priests," and he is useful to me; and besides, he is an amusing fellow.

Second, there was never any secret about my connection with the Queen two years ago in Alexandria. But I recall to you that that was two years ago, before either of us had any notion that I might one day become your brother-in-law. And you need not bring up the matter of the twins with which Cleopatra has presented me; they may or may not be my own; whether they are or not is no matter. I have not made secret, either, that I have left children all over the world; these new ones would mean neither more nor less to me than the others. When I have time from my duties, I take my pleasure, and I take it where I can find it. I shall continue to do so. At least, my dear brother, I do not hide my propensities; I am no hypocrite; and your own affairs, I should point out, are not so well hidden as you imagine.

You should know me better than to think (if, indeed, you do think it, as you pretend) that my liaison with Cleopatra had anything to do with my confirmation of her sovereignty in Egypt. For if this confirmation is to my advantage, so it is to yours.

Egypt is the richest of the Eastern nations, and its treasury will be open to us, if we need it. And it is the only Eastern nation that has any semblance of an army, and at least a part of this army will be at our disposal. Finally, it is easier to deal with a single strong monarch who feels some security in his (or her) position than with half a dozen weak ones who feel none.

These things, and many others, should be clear to you, who are no fool.

I will not accept the terms of whatever game it is you think you are playing.

II. Letter: Marcus Antonius to Gaius Sentius Tavus (38 B.C.)

That bloody and outrageous little hypocrite! I am stretched between laughter and anger—laughter at the hypocrisy, and anger at what his hypocrisy might conceal.

Does he imagine that I am without my sources of information here in Athens? I am not shocked by anything he does, and I do not take that high moral tone that he loves to affect. He may divorce as many a Scribonia as he likes, even on the day that she gives birth to a daughter that (given Scribonia) must be his; he may even take within the week another wife, who is already pregnant by her former husband. He may perform this public scandal (and even the more private ones that you report to me), and he will get no remonstrances from me; he may be as bizarre as he likes in his private preferences.

But I know my recent "brother"; and I know that he does nothing from passion or whim. He is such a cold-blooded fish that I must almost admire him.

It must be clear to everyone that his divorce of Scribonia signifies that we no longer have an understanding with her kinsman, Sextus Pompeius. What can I make of this? Why was I not consulted? Does it mean that we are to make war on Sextus? Or will Octavius go it alone?

And what of his new wife, this Livia? You tell me that Octavius once exiled her husband from Italy, because he was a Republican and opposed him at Perusia. Does the new marriage mean that he is again trying to find favor with the remnants of the Republican Party? I do not know what all of this means. . . . You must write often, Sentius; I must be kept informed, and I can trust few, nowadays. I wish I were in Rome; but I cannot leave my task here.

I have been trying to persuade myself that the kind of life I am now leading is worth the trouble. My present wife is as cold and proper in fact as her brother is in pretense. And though I can find my pleasure here and there, I have to be so discreet that the pleasure is reduced almost to nothing. Daily, I am tempted to send her packing; but I have no cause, she is with child, and to divorce her now would cause a breach with her brother that I cannot afford.

III. Extracts from Reports: Epimachos, High Priest of Heliopolis, to Cleopatra, the Incarnate Isis and Queen of the Worlds of Egypt (40–37 B.C.)

Greetings, Revered Queen. This day, at first for amusement and then from desperation, Marcus Antonius diced with Octavius Caesar. For nearly three hours they played, and Antonius lost consistently, winning perhaps one out of four throws. Octavius is well pleased, Antonius annoyed. I cast the sands, and went into a trance, from which I told the story of Eurystheus and that Heracles who became his servant because of the perfidy of the gods. Suggest that in your next letter to him, you refer to some demeaning task you dreamed he had to perform for someone weaker and less worthy than himself. I was grave and portentous; you must be humorous and light.

My auguries have been to no avail; he is married to Octavia, the sister of his enemy. It is the pledge that will satisfy the populace and the soldiers.

I send you two waxen effigies. You are to find in your palace a remote room which has but one door. You are to place the effigy of Antonius on the side of the room where there is a door, the effigy of Octavia on the side where there is none. You are to do this with your own hands; let no one assist you. Then you are to have built between the figures a heavy wall, extending from the floor to the ceiling; there must be no fissure between the two. Each day, at sun's rising and sun's setting, you are to have my priest, Epiktetas, perform the spell outside the room. He will know what to do.

We go to Athens with Octavia, who is now with child and will deliver within three months. I have presented to Antonius a pair of identical greyhounds, which he has raced and of which he has become inordinately fond. On the day that Octavia's child is born, I shall cause the dogs to disappear. You must write him within the next few weeks of a dream that you had about the twins.

The child that Octavia has delivered is a daughter; thus there is no potential heir to his name. The God of the Sun has bowed to our will and has heeded our demands.

He quarrels with Octavius; they are reconciled by Octavia, who takes the part of her husband against her brother. Antonius's suspicions of her are almost gone, and he seems grudgingly fond of her, though he is still made impatient by her quietness and calm. Does Epiktetas perform faithfully the spell, as you instructed him?

He has had a dream of being bound to a couch while his tent burned around him. The soldiers of his army walked past the burning tent, and did not heed his calls, as if they did not hear him. Finally he burst his bonds, but the fire was around him so fiercely that he could not see which way to turn to escape. He awoke in fear, and called for me.

I fasted for three days, and gave him the portents of the dream. I told him that the fire was the intrigue in Rome, heaped and kindled by Octavius Caesar. That he was in a tent, I said, revealed two things: his position (he has no secure and permanent place in the Roman world), and his nature (that he is a soldier). That he was bound to his couch, I said, signified that by his inactivity he had betrayed his nature and allowed himself to become weak and hence impotent to the intrigues against him and to the circumstance of fate. That his soldiers did not heed his calls revealed that by his betrayal of his nature, he had lost control of his men;

that he is properly a man of action, not of words; that men would bend to his deeds, not his talk.

He has become thoughtful, and he studies maps. I say nothing to him, but I believe he is again considering taking up arms against the Parthians. For this, he will come to know that he needs your aid. Discreetly, let him know that it is at his disposal. Thus, you may draw him again to our cause, and insure the future glory of Egypt.

IV. Letter: Cleopatra to Marcus Antonius, from Alexandria (37 B.C.)

My dear Marcus, you must forgive my long silence, as I have forgiven yours. And you must forgive me, too, if I write you now as a woman, rather than as the Queen who is your faithful ally and whose strength is ever at your disposal. For I have been most gravely ill these last few months, and have not wished to cause you concern for my infirmities; indeed, I should not write you now, had not my frailty and my heart overcome my Queenhood.

Sleep is reluctant to cover my eyes; my strength is stolen by fevers that even the skills of my physician, Olympus, cannot allay; I take little food; and despair is like a serpent that creeps into the emptiness of my spirit.

Oh, Marcus, how weary all this must make you! Yet I know your kindness, and know that you will indulge the weakness of an old friend, who thinks of you often and remembers many things.

Perhaps it is that remembering, rather than the advice of Olympus, which has persuaded me to take the journey from Alexandria to Thebes. Olympus says that in the temple there, the Supreme God, Amen-Ra, will take away my illness and return my strength. You used to tease me about my regard for these Egyptian gods; perhaps you were right in that, as you were in so many things. For I almost refused him; and then I remembered (it seems so long ago) another spring, when you and I floated down the Nile and side by side lay on our couch and watched the fertile banks slip by and felt upon our bodies the cool river breeze; and the farmers and herdsmen knelt, and even the goats and cattle seemed to pause in obeisance to us, raising their heads to watch our passing. And Memphis, where they held the bullfights in our honor, and Hermopolis and Akhetaton, where we were God and Goddess, Osiris and Isis. And then the Thebes of the Hundred Gates, and the drowsy days and gay nights . . .

Remembering this, I felt the beginnings of strength return to me; and I told Olympus that I would make the journey and enter the temple of Amen-Ra. But if I am returned to health, it will be from the nourishment I take from these memories along the way, which I hold as dear as my life.

V. Letter: Marcus Antonius to Octavius Caesar (37 B.C.)

You have broken our treaty with Sextus Pompeius, a treaty to which I pledged my word; it is rumored that you intend war upon him, though you have not consulted me in the matter; you intrigue against my reputation, though I have done neither you nor your sister any harm; you seek to subvert from me the little strength I have in Italy, though I have given you, out of my loyalty, much of the power you now have; in short, you have repaid my loyalty with betrayal, my honor with your treachery, my generosity with your self-interest.

You may do what you want in Rome; I will no longer be concerned. When we agreed to extend the triumvirate earlier this year, I hoped that we might, at last, work together. We cannot.

I send your sister and her children to you. You may inform her upon her arrival that she is not to return to me. Though she is a good woman, I want no tie with your house. As for divorce, that I will leave entirely to your discretion. I know that you will decide that matter in terms of your own interest. I do not care.

I shall not dissemble with you; I have no need to; I fear neither you nor your intrigues.

I shall begin my Parthian campaign this spring, without the legions you promised and did not deliver to me. I have summoned Cleopatra to Antioch. She will supply the troops that I need.

If Rome is dying in the web that you weave around her, Egypt will thrive in the power that I will give her. I bequeath the corpse to you; for myself, I prefer the living body.

AUGUSTUS

VI. Letter: Marcus Antonius to Cleopatra (37 B.C.)

Empress of the Nile, Queen of the Living Suns, and my beloved friend—take this letter from Fonteius Capito; I have
asked him to deliver it into your hands alone. You may trust him
as you have trusted me, and question him about all those matters
upon which this letter does not touch. I am—as you have so
often and wisely observed—a man of action, not of words.

Thus my words cannot tell you of the despair I felt when I
learned you were ill, nor of the joy that overwhelmed sorrow
when I learned that on the journey back from the Thebes that
we both remember, your health was returning, like a bird returning home. You wonder how I know this? I must confess—I
have had my benevolent spies in your midst, who, out of love for
us both and out of respect for my deep solicitude, have kept me
informed of your welfare. For despite the circumstances that
have kept us apart, my concern for you has never wavered; and
if sometimes I have not written, it is for the reason that such a re-
minder of our past happiness would give me a pain of loss I could
not bear.

But as Fonteius will tell you, I have awakened as if from a
dream. Oh, my little kitten, who are a Queen, do you know the
bitter cost to me of our long separation? Of course you do—
and I know you understand. I remember your telling me of
your unhappiness when, as a young girl, for reasons of dynasty,
your father would have wed you to your young brother so that
you might have begotten children to continue the line of the Ptol-
emies. Yet your womanhood prevailed; and even as an Isis must
become a woman, so must a Hercules become a man. It is too
burdensome always to remain God and Goddess, King and
Queen.

Will you let Fonteius bring you to Antioch, where I will be
awaiting you? Even if your love for me has gone, I must see you
again, so that I may see for myself that you are well. And there
are matters of state that we may discuss, even if you are to refuse
the matters of the heart. Come to me, if only out of respect for
what we both must remember.

VII. *The Memoirs of Marcus Agrippa:* Fragments (*13 B.C.*)

After the battle of Philippi, the triumvir Antonius being occupied with his adventures in the Eastern world, it remained for Caesar Augustus to repair the harms of the civil wars, and to bring order into the Italy of Rome. He walked among the treasons of his colleague, Antonius, and did not falter; at Perusia, the armies under my command quieted the insurrection raised by Antonius's brother Lucius; and Caesar Augustus, in his mercy, spared his life, though his crime had been grave.

But of all the impediments that lay between Caesar Augustus and the order that was necessary for the salvation of Rome, the gravest was that raised by the traitor and pirate, Sextus Pompeius, who unlawfully governed the islands of Sicily and Sardinia, and whose ships roamed the seas at will, plundering and destroying those merchant vessels that supplied the grain for Rome's survival. So serious were the depredations of Sextus Pompeius that the city came to be in danger of famine; and in their desperation and fear, the people rioted in the streets, to no end save to relieve themselves of a creeping despair. Caesar Augustus, in his pity for the people, offered Pompeius terms; for we had not the strength to meet him in battle. A treaty was signed, and for a period grain flowed back into Rome; and I was sent by Caesar Augustus to Transalpine Gaul as governor, where I was to organize the Gallic legions against the growing hostility of the barbarian tribes before returning to Rome the following year as consul.

But hardly had the treaty been signed before Sextus Pompeius began conspiring with Antonius, and soon the treaty was broken, and Sextus resumed his piracy and plunder. Caesar Augustus recalled me to Rome before the year was out; for the sake of starving Rome, we had no choice but to prepare for war.

The genius of Rome is in its land, its soil; it has never felt at home upon the sea. And yet we knew that if we were to overcome Sextus Pompeius, we must do so upon the sea; for like all unnatural creatures, that was his habitat, and there he would lurk, even if we drove him off the land he held. Caesar Augustus and the Senate appointed me admiral of the Roman navy, and gave to me the charge of establishing for the first time in our history a formidable Roman fleet. I commissioned to be built some three hundred vessels, to augment those few already under the command of Caesar Augustus; and to man these vessels, Augustus gave freedom to twenty thousand slaves in exchange for their faithful service. And since we could not train upon the open sea —for sometimes the vessels of the pirate Pompeius sailed within easy sight of the Italian shore—I made to be cut a deep channel between the lakes of Lucrine and Avernus at Naples, so that they became one body of water; and by reinforcing the Via Herculeana (said to have been built by Hercules himself) with concrete, and opening it at either end to the sea, I caused to be formed that which is now called the Bay of Julius, in honor of my commander and my friend.

And in that bay, protected by land on all sides from the weather and from unfriendly ships, for the year of my consulship, and into the year beyond, I trained the navy that was to confront the seasoned veterans of the pirate Pompeius. And in the summer we were ready.

On the first day of that month which had recently been named in honor of the Divine Julius, we set sail southward for Sicily, where we were to be joined by the auxiliary fleets of Antonius from the east and those of Lepidus from the north. Unseasonable and violent storms met us, and we suffered losses; and though the fleets of Antonius and Lepidus sought shelter, the Roman fleets of Augustus, under his command and my own, sailed through the storms; and though we were delayed, we met the enemy ships at Mylae, on the northern shore of Sicily, and so severely punished them that they were forced to withdraw to the shallow waters where we could not follow; and we invested the town of Mylae, whence the pirate forces had drawn many of their supplies.

Unprepared for our strength, the ships of Pompeius broke before our assault; with the aid of a grappling hook that I had devised, we were able to board many of the ships, and we captured more than we sank, adding them to our growing fleet. And we captured the coastal fortresses of Hiera and Tyndarus, and it seemed to Pompeius that unless he could conclude a decisive victory, and destroy our ships, all the coastal strongholds from which he drew his supplies would fall into our hands; and he would be lost.

Thus he hazarded his fleet in all its strength, in waters favorable to his own ships, to defend the port city of Naulochus, which we would have to take before we could secure Mylae, a few miles to the south, the first stronghold we had captured.

Skilled as he was, Pompeius was unable to prevail against our heavier ships; though he could outmaneuver us, he was reduced at last to attempting to sweep away the banks of oars by which we were moved, though by this effort he lost more ships than he disabled. Twenty-eight Pompeian vessels were sunk with all their crews; the rest were captured, or suffered such damage as to make them inoperable. Only seventeen ships of the entire fleet escaped our assault, and they sailed eastward, with Sextus Pompeius aboard and in pitiful command.

It is said by some that Pompeius sailed eastward in the hope of joining the absent triumvir Antonius, whom he wished to incite anew against Caesar Augustus; it is said by others that he wished to join with Phraates, the barbarian king of Parthia, who warred against our Eastern provinces. In any event, he made his way to the province of Asia, and resumed his occupation of robbery and pillage. There he was captured by the centurion Titius, whose life Pompeius himself once had spared, and was put to death like a common bandit. Thus was the devastation of piracy at last put down in the seas that surrounded the Italy of Rome.

Weary from battle, our forces yet had to invest the other coastal cities of Sicily which had supplied Pompeius, the chief of which was Messina, where most of Pompeius's land armies were stationed. According to the orders of Caesar Augustus, we were to blockade this city, and await his arrival to meet the battle, if there were to be one. But at this time, and at last, the vessels commanded by the triumvir Lepidus, who had joined in none of the battles at sea, met our ships at Messina; and despite my deliverance to him of the orders of Caesar Augustus, he entered into negotiations with the local commander; and refreshed by his peaceful cruise from Africa, he informed me that by his own authority he relieved me of my command; and he received the surrender of all the Pompeian legions in Messina, requiring pledges of fealty to his own authority, and added those legions to those that he already commanded. In our weariness and pain, we awaited the arrival of Caesar Augustus.

VIII. Military Order (September, 36 B.C.)

To: L. Plinius Rufus, Military Commander of the Pompeian Legions at Messina
From: Marcus Aemilius Lepidus, Imperator and Triumvir of Rome, Ruler of Africa and Commander in Chief of the African Legions, Consular and Pontifex Maximus of the Senate of Rome
Subject: The Surrender of the Pompeian Legions in Sicily

Having this day surrendered to my sole authority the legions of the defeated Sextus Pompeius, you are to inform the officers and soldiers formerly under your command of the following:

(1) That they are granted amnesty for all crimes committed before this day against the legitimate authority of Rome, and will suffer no punishment either from my hands or from the hands of any other.

(2) That they are to have neither negotiation nor converse with the officers or men of any legion not under my command.

(3) That their safety and well-being is assured under my responsibility, and that they are to obey no commands from any other than myself or my appointed officers.

(4) That they are to mingle freely with the legions under my command, and are to consider themselves as brothers-in-arms, not as enemies.

(5) That the city of Messina, as a conquered city, is open to them for their enrichment as equally as it is to my own soldiers.

IX. Letter: Gaius Cilnius Maecenas to Titus Livius (13 B.C.)

My dear Livy, I got the news just this morning—Marcus Aemilius Lepidus is dead at Circeii, where he has been living in his retirement and, I suppose, shame, for the past twenty-four years. He was our enemy—yet after so long, the death of an old enemy is curiously like the death of an old friend. I am saddened, as was our Emperor, who informed me of the death and told me that he will allow a public funeral in Rome, a funeral in the old style, if his descendants wish it. And so, after all these years, Lepidus returns to Rome and to the honor that he forsook that day in Sicily, nearly a quarter of a century ago. . . .

It occurs to me that that is one of the things that I have not written to you about. Had I done so a week ago, I would no doubt have gone about it rather lightly; it would have seemed to me one of those half-humorous memories out of the past. But this death has cast a different light upon that memory, and it seems to me now oddly sad.

After a long and disheartening and bloody struggle, the pirate Sextus Pompeius was defeated—by the fleet and legions under the command of Marcus Agrippa and Octavius, and supposedly with the aid of Lepidus. Lepidus and Agrippa were to blockade the city of Messina on the Sicilian coast, so that the scattered fleet of Sextus Pompeius would have no safe harbor to repair the damages done by Agrippa and Octavius. But the commander of the city, one Plinius, having heard of the defeat suffered by Sextus, and at the behest of Lepidus, surrendered the city and eight Pompeian legions without a fight. Lepidus accepted the surrender, and, despite Agrippa's remonstrances, put the legions under his own command; and he allowed the Pompeian as well as his own fourteen legions to plunder and sack the city which, by its surrender, had put itself under his protection.

You understand, my dear Livy, that war is never pretty, and that one must expect a certain brutality from soldiers. But Agrippa came with Octavius into the city after the night of the plunder; and Agrippa has told me a little, though our Emperor would never speak of it.

The houses of the rich and poor were burned without discrimination or reason; hundreds of innocent townspeople, who had been guilty of nothing save the misfortune of having their town occupied by the Pompeian legions—old men, and women, and even children—were slaughtered and tortured by the troops. Agrippa told me that even in the late morning after the carnage, when he and our Emperor rode into the city, they could hear like a single sound the moan and cry of the wounded and dying.

And when our Emperor confronted Lepidus at last, after having dispatched many of his men to care for the suffering townspeople, he was so moved by sorrow that he could not speak; and poor, ignorant Lepidus, mistaking that silence for weakness and in the hysteria of what he must have conceived to be an invincible power afforded him by his sudden acquisition of the twenty-two rested and well-fed legions under his command, peremptorily ordered his colleague, to whom he spoke in contemptuous and threatening tones, to quit Sicily; and said that if he wished to remain a triumvir, he must be content with only Africa, which he (Lepidus) was willing to relinquish to him. It was an extraordinary speech. . . .

Poor Lepidus, I have said. It was a strange delusion he had. Our Emperor did not speak in reply to Lepidus's preposterous claim.

The next day, accompanied only by Agrippa and six bodyguards, he came into the city, and went to the small Forum, and spoke to the soldiers of Lepidus and the surrendered troops of Sextus Pompeius, and told them that the promises of Lepidus were empty without his assent, and that they were in danger of putting themselves beyond the protection of Rome if they persisted in following a false leader. He had the name of Caesar, and that probably would have been enough to lead the soldiers to reason, even without Lepidus's fatal error. For Lepidus's own guard, in Lepidus's presence, made to attack the person of our Emperor, who might indeed have been gravely wounded or even killed, had not one of his guards interposed himself between the Emperor and a hurled javelin, giving his life.

Agrippa told me that as the guard fell at our Emperor's feet, a strange hush fell upon the crowd, and that even the bodyguards of Lepidus remained still and did not pursue their advantage. Octavius looked with sorrow upon the body of his fallen guard, and then lifted his eyes to the multitude before him.

He said quietly, but in a voice that carried to all the soldiers: "Thus by leave of Marcus Aemilius Lepidus, another brave and loyal Roman soldier, who offered harm to none of his comrades, is dead in a foreign land."

He had his other guards pick up the body and bear it aloft; and in front of the guard, unprotected, as if at a funeral, he walked through the crowd; and the soldiers parted before him like stalks of grain before the wind.

And one by one the legions of Sextus Pompeius deserted Lepidus, and joined our forces outside the city; and then the legions of Lepidus, despising the sluggishness and ineptness of their leader, came to our side; until Lepidus, with only a few who remained loyal to him, was helpless inside the city walls.

Lepidus must have expected to be captured and executed, yet Octavius did not move. One would have thought that in such a position he would have chosen suicide, but Lepidus did not. Rather, he sent a messenger to Octavius, and asked pardon, and asked that his life be spared. Octavius agreed, and set a condition.

Thus, on a bright chill morning in the early fall, Octavius ordered an assembly of all the officers and centurions of the legions of Marcus Aemilius Lepidus and Sextus Pompeius, and the officers and centurions of his own legions, in the Forum of Messina. And Lepidus made a public plea for mercy.

With his sparse gray hair blowing in the wind, in a plain toga with none of the colors of office, without attendants, he walked slowly the length of the Forum and mounted the platform where Octavius stood. There he knelt and asked forgiveness for his crimes, and made public relinquishment of all his powers. Agrippa has said that his face was without color or expression, and that his voice was like the voice of one in a trance.

Octavius said: "This man is pardoned, and he will walk with safety among you. No harm is to come to him. He will be exiled from Rome, but he is under the protection of Rome; and he is stripped of all his titles save that of Pontifex Maximus, which is a title that only the gods can take from him."

Without saying more, Lepidus rose and went to his quarters. And Agrippa told me a curious thing. As he was walking away, Agrippa said to Octavius: "You have given him worse than death."

And Octavius smiled. "Perhaps," he said. "But perhaps I have given him a kind of happiness."

. . . I wonder what his last years were like, in his exile at Circeii. Was he happy? When one has had power in his grasp, and has failed to hold it, and has remained alive—what does one become?

X. *The Memoirs of Marcus Agrippa:* Fragments (*13 B.C.*)

And we returned to Rome and the gratitude of the Roman people, whom we had saved from starvation. In the temples of the cities of Italy, from Arezzo in the north to Vibo in the south, statues of Octavius Caesar were raised, and he was worshiped by the people as a god of the hearth. And the Senate and the people of Rome made to be erected in the Forum a statue of gold, in commemoration of the order that had been restored to sea and land.

To celebrate the occasion, Octavius Caesar remitted the debts and taxes of all the people, and gave them assurance of final peace and freedom when Marcus Antonius had subdued the Parthians in the East. And upon my own head, after giving thanks to Rome for its steadfastness, he placed the crown of gold adorned with images of our ships. It was an honor given to no one before and to no one since.

Thus while Antonius in the distant East hunted the barbarian Parthian tribes, in Italy Caesar Augustus devoted himself to securing the borders of his homeland, neglected by the many years of dissension in which it had suffered. We conquered the Pannonian tribes and drove the tribal invaders from the coast of Dalmatia, so that Italy was secure from any threat from the north. In these campaigns, Octavius Caesar himself led his troops, and received honorable wounds in the battles.

6

My dear Strabo, I have witnessed an event, the significance of which only you, the dearest of all my friends, will apprehend. For on this day Marcus Antonius, triumvir of Rome, has become Imperator of Egypt—a king in fact, though he does not call himself such. He has taken in marriage that Cleopatra who is the Incarnate Isis, Queen of Egypt, and Empress of all the lands of the Nile.

I give you news that, I suspect, none of Rome has heard yet, possibly not even that young ruler of the Roman world of whom you have so often written and whom you so admire; for the marriage was sudden, and known even to this Eastern world only a few days before the actual event. Oh, my old friend, I would almost relinquish some part of that wisdom toward which we both have so laboriously striven, if I could but see the look upon your face at this moment! It must be one of surprise—and a little chagrin? You will forgive one who chides and teases you; I cannot resist provoking what I hope is a friendly envy in one whose good fortune in the world has provoked the same in me. For you must have known that your letters from Rome have raised that envy in me. How often in Damascus did I wish that I was with you there, in the "center of the world," as you have called it, conversing with the great men you mention with such frequency and such intimacy. Now I, too, have come into the world; and by a stroke of good fortune, which I still cannot quite believe, I have secured a most remarkable position. I am tutor to the children of Cleopatra, master of the Royal library, and principal of the schools of the Royal household.

All of this has happened so quickly that I can hardly believe it, and I still do not fully understand the reasons for the appointment. Perhaps it is because I am nominally a Jew yet a philosopher and no fanatic, and because my father has had some small business connection with the court of King Herod, whom Marcus Antonius has recently legitimatized as King of all Judaea and with whom he wants to live in peace. Could politics touch one so unpolitical as myself? I hope that I am being too modest; I would like to think that my reputation as a scholar has had the final weight in the matter.

In any event, I was approached by an emissary of the Queen at Alexandria, where I had gone on some business for my father, in the course of which I took the time to make use of the Royal library; I was approached, and I accepted at once. Aside from the material advantages of the position (which are considerable), the Royal Library is the most remarkable I have ever seen; and I will have continual access to books that few men have used or even seen before.

And now that I am a member of the Royal household, I travel wherever the Queen goes; thus, I arrived in Antioch three days ago, though her children remain in the palace at Alexandria. I do not fully understand why the ceremonies were held here, rather than in the Royal palace at Alexandria; perhaps Antonius does not wish to flout Roman law too openly, even though he seems to have cast his fortunes in the East (what *is* the Roman legality of this matter, I wonder, since, it is said, he has not bothered to obtain a legal divorce from his former wife?); or perhaps he merely wants to make clear to the Egyptians that he does not usurp the authority of their Queen. Perhaps there is no meaning.

However that may be, the ceremonies have been held; and to all the Eastern world, the Queen and Marcus Antonius are man and wife; and whatever Rome may think, they are the joint rulers of this world. Marcus Antonius has announced publicly that Caesarion (known to be the child of his one-time friend, Julius Caesar) is heir to the throne of Cleopatra, and that the twins that the Queen has borne are to be considered his legitimate offspring. He has, moreover, increased the extent of Egypt's possessions many-fold; the Queen now has under her authority all of Arabia, including Petra and the Sinai Peninsula; that part of Jordan which lies between the Dead Sea and Jericho; parts of Galilee and Samaria; the whole of the Phoenician coast; the richest parts of Lebanon, Syria, and Cilicia; the whole of the Island of Cyprus, and a part of Crete. Thus I, who was once a Syrian Roman, might now consider myself a Syrian Egyptian; but I am neither. Like you, my old friend, I am a scholar, who would be a philosopher; and I am no more Roman or Egyptian than was our Aristotle a Greek, who never lost his love and pride for his native Ionia. I shall emulate that greatest of all men, and remain content to be a Damascene.

Yet as you yourself have so often said, the world of affairs is an extraordinarily interesting one; and perhaps neither of us, even in the arrogance of our youth, ought to have so removed ourselves from it in our studies. The way to knowledge is a long journey, and the goal is distant; and one must visit many places along the way, if he is to know that goal when he arrives at it.

Though I have seen her at a distance, I have not yet had an audience with the Queen by whom I am employed. Marcus Antonius is everywhere—jovial, familiar, and not at all forbidding. He is a little like a child, I think—though his hair is graying, and he is getting a bit fat.

I think I shall again be happy in Alexandria, as I was during our student days.

As I believe I mentioned in my last letter to you, I had seen the Queen only at a distance—at the wedding ceremony which united her to Marcus Antonius and the power of Rome, a ceremony which only those attached to the Royal household were allowed to attend.

The palace at Antioch is not so imposing as that in Alexandria, but it is grand enough; and at the wedding, I was crowded to the rear of the long hall, from which vantage I could make out very

little, though an ebony dais had been raised, upon which Cleopatra and Antonius stood. All I could see of the Queen was her
jeweled gown, which sparkled in the torchlight, and the great
disk of gold representing the sun, which was set above her crown
of state. She moved in a slow and grave manner, as if she were indeed the goddess that her title proclaims her to be. It was an extraordinarily elaborate ceremony (though described by some of
my new friends as really rather simple), the significance of which
I do not understand; priests marched about and chanted various
incantations in that ancient form of the language which only
they can speak; anointings with various oils were made; wands
were waved. It was all very mystifying and (I must confess I
thought) rather uncivilized, almost barbaric.

And so I went to my first audience with the Queen with an
odd feeling, as if I were going into the presence of some Medea
or Circe, neither quite goddess nor quite woman, but something
more unnatural than either.

My dear Strabo, I cannot tell you how fortunately I was surprised, and how happy I was at my surprise. I expected to encounter a swarthy and rather hefty woman, such as one sees in
the market place; I met a slender woman of fair skin and soft
brown hair, with enormous eyes, who had poise and dignity and
an extraordinary charm, who put me at ease at once and bade me
sit near her on a couch no less luxurious than her own, as if I
were a guest in a simple and friendly household. And we spoke at
length upon those ordinary topics which constitute any civilized
conversation. She laughs easily and quietly, and seems totally at-
tentive to her audience. Her Greek is impeccable; her Latin is at
least as good as mine; and she speaks casually to her servants in a
dialect I cannot understand. She is widely and intelligently read
—she even shares my admiration for our Aristotle, and assures
me that she knows my own work upon his philosophy, and that
her understanding has been enhanced by that knowledge.

I am not, as you know, a vain man; and even if I were, I believe my vanity would have been overwhelmed by my gratitude
and my admiration for this most extraordinary of women. That
one so charming could also rule one of the richest lands in the
world is almost beyond belief.

I have been back in Alexandria for three weeks now, and I have begun my duties; Marcus Antonius and the Queen remain in Antioch, where Antonius is making preparations for his march, later in the year, against the Parthians. My duties are not heavy; I have as many slaves as I need for the management of the Queen's library, and the children take up little of my time.

The twins—Alexander of the Sun and Cleopatra of the Moon—are only a few months more than three years old, and therefore not capable of taking any instruction; but I have been directed to speak to them each day, for a few moments at least, in Greek and (at the Queen's insistence) even in Latin, so that when they grow older the sounds of the language will not be unfamiliar to their ears.

But Ptolemy Caesar—called Caesarion by the people—who is almost twelve years old, is another matter. I believe I would have guessed that he might be the son of the great Julius Caesar, even had I not known it. He recognizes his destiny, and he is prepared for it; he swears that he remembers his father from his mother's residence in Rome, just before the assassination—though he could hardly have been four years old at the time of that event. He is serious, utterly without humor, and oddly intent on whatever he does. It is as if he never had a childhood, and did not want one; he speaks of the Queen as if she were not his mother at all, but only the powerful sovereign that she is; and he awaits the day of his assumption of the Queen's throne, not impatiently, but with the same certainty that he waits the morning sunrise. He would frighten me a little, I believe, if he were to hold the vast power that his mother now has.

But he is a good student, and it is a pleasure to teach him.

For those who put stock in such things, it has been an ominous winter—almost no rainfall, so that the crops will be sparse this year; and a series of cyclones has swept across the lands of Syria and Egypt from the east, laying waste whole villages before spending themselves in the sea. And Antonius has marched from Antioch against the Parthians with what is said to be the greatest expeditionary army since the time of the Macedonian, Alexander the Great (whose blood, it is said, flows in the veins of Cleopatra)—more than sixty thousand seasoned veterans, ten thousand troops of horse from Gaul and Spain, and thirty thousand auxiliary forces recruited from the kingdoms of the Eastern provinces to support the regulars. My young Caesarion, with the innocent ruthlessness of youth (he has recently become interested in the art of warfare), has said that such an army is wasted against the Eastern barbarians; were he king, he says—as if war were truly the game that it seems to him now—he would turn the army toward the west where there is more than plunder to be gained.

The Queen has returned from Antioch, by way of Damascus, and will remain in Alexandria until Antonius concludes his campaign against the Parthians. Knowing that Damascus was my birthplace, she was kind enough to call me into her chambers and give me the news. It is extraordinary how thoughtful and human the great can be. For in Damascus, she had a meeting with King Herod on some business regarding the rents from some balsam fields; and remembering an earlier conversation with me, she inquired after the health of my father, and asked Herod to have conveyed to him greetings from his son and from the Queen.

I have not heard from him since those greetings were conveyed, but I am sure he is pleased. He is growing old, and is becoming feeble in his age. I suspect that at such a time one looks back upon one's life and wonders at its worth, and needs the kindness of some assurance.

II. *Letter: Marcus Antonius to Cleopatra,* from Armenia (*November, 36 B.C.*)

My dear wife, I now thank my Roman gods and your Egyptian ones that I did not succumb to my own desires and to your determination, and allow you to accompany me on this campaign. It has been even more difficult than I anticipated; and it is clear that what I had hoped would be concluded this fall will now have to wait until spring.

The Parthians have proved to be a wily and resourceful foe, and they have made more intelligent use of their terrain than I might have foreseen. The maps made by Crassus and Ventidius on their campaigns here have proved worse than useless; treasons among some of the provincial legions have harmed our cause; and this abominable countryside does not furnish sufficient food to keep my legions in health through the winter.

Thus I have withdrawn from my siege of Phraaspa, where we could not have endured the cold; and for twenty-seven days we have made our way across the country, nearly all the way from the Caspian Sea, and now rest in the comparative safety of Armenia, though we are tired, and illness pervades the camp.

Yet all in all, the campaign has, I believe, been a successful one, though I fear that many of my weary soldiers would not agree with me. I know the Parthian tricks now; and we have mapped the territory with sufficient accuracy to serve us next year. I have sent to Rome the news of our victory.

But you must understand that, despite the tactical success of the campaign, I am now in most desperate straits. We cannot stay in Armenia; I do not fully trust my host, King Artavasdes, who deserted me at a crucial moment in Parthia—though I cannot now upbraid him, since we are his guests. Therefore I shall march with a few legions to Syria, and the rest of the army will join me after it has recovered from its exhaustion.

To endure the winter, even in Syria, we shall need provisions; for we are like beggars now. We shall need food, and clothing, and the materials necessary to repair our damaged war machines. We shall also need horses to replenish those lost in battle and to the weather, so that we might continue training for the campaign next spring. And I must have money. My soldiers have not been paid for months, and some are threatening revolt. And we shall need these things quickly. I attach to this letter a detailed list of those things that I absolutely require, and a supplementary list of things that may be needed later in the winter. I cannot exaggerate our need.

We shall winter in the little village of Leuke Kome, just south of Beirut. You may not have heard of it. There is sufficient dockage there for the ships that you will send. Be careful. For all I know, the mad Parthians may be roaming the coast lines by the time you receive this. But there should be no danger of blockage at Leuke Kome. I trust that this letter will reach you soon, however rough the winter seas are; we shall not be able to endure for many more weeks without provisions.

Outside my tent the snow is falling, so that the plain on which we are encamped is invisible. I can see no other tent; I can hear no sound. I am cold, and in the silence more aware of my loneliness than you can imagine. I long for the warmth of your arms and for the intimacy of your voice. Come to me in Syria with your ships. I must stay there with my troops, else they will scatter before spring comes, and our sacrifices will have been for naught; and yet I cannot suffer another month without your presence. Come to me, and we shall make of Beirut another Antioch, or Thebes, or Alexandria.

III. Report: Epimachos, High Priest of Heliopolis, to Cleopatra, from Armenia (November, 36 B.C.)

Revered Queen: No man is more courageous than that Marcus Antonius whom you have honored by your presence and raised at your side to overlook the world. He fights more bravely than prudence should allow, and endures privations and hardships which would destroy the most seasoned common soldier. But he is no general, and the campaign has been a disaster.

If what I report to you contradicts what you may have heard from other sources, you must know that I write nevertheless in friendship for your husband, in reverence for you, and in anxiety for Egypt and her future.

In the spring we marched from Antioch to Zeugma on the River Euphrates, and thence northward along that river, where food was plentiful, to the watershed between the Euphrates and the River Araxes, and then southward toward the Parthian citadel of Phraaspa. But before Phraaspa, to save time, Marcus Antonius divided his army, sending our supply train, with our food and baggage, and our battering rams and siege wagons by a more level passage, while the bulk of the army advanced rapidly to its goal.

But while that army advanced in safety, the Parthians descended from the mountain upon the more slowly moving force that we had divided from us. News reached us of the attack, but when we arrived it was too late to save anything. The escort was slain, our supplies were burned, our siege wagons and engines of war were all destroyed; and only a few soldiers remained unharmed behind hastily thrown up fortifications. We then dispersed the attacking Parthians, who, having done their damage, prudently withdrew to the mountains that they knew, and where we dared not follow.

That was the "victory" that Marcus Antonius reported to Rome. We counted eighty Parthian dead.

Despite the destruction of all our instruments of siege, all our replacement supplies, our food—Marcus Antonius persisted in his siege of the Parthian city of Phraaspa. Even if the city had not been prepared for us, the task would have been nearly impossible, since we had only the arms that we bore at our sides. We could not lure them into open battle; when we foraged for food, the detachments were set upon by the Parthian archers who appeared from nowhere to kill, and who disappeared again; and winter drew on. For two months we persisted; and at last Antonius exacted from King Phraates a pledge that we would be allowed to retreat from his country without hindrance. And so in mid-October, hungry and exhausted, we began our return whence we had begun, five months before.

For twenty-seven days, in bitter cold, through drifts of snow and in swirling winds, we struggled over mountains and unprotected plains; and upon eighteen separate occasions we were attacked by the mounted archers of the perfidious Phraates. They swooped from everywhere—upon our rear, our flanks, our fronts; let fly their arrows before we could prepare ourselves; and then were gone back into their barbaric darkness, while the poor blind animal that was their victim lumbered on.

It was in these awful days of retreat that your Marcus Antonius showed himself to be the man that he is. He endured all the hardships of his men; he would take no food other than that taken by his comrades, who were reduced to gnawing roots and foraging for insects in rotting wood; nor would he wear clothing warmer than they wore themselves.

We are in Armenia now, where we cannot stay; the King of this country, nominally our ally but no more trustworthy than our foe, has furnished us with a little food. We leave for Syria soon. But I have made an accounting of our losses, and I give them to you.

In these five months, we have lost nearly forty thousand men, many to Parthian arrows, but more to the cold and disease; of these, twenty-two thousand were Antonius's Roman veterans, the best warriors in the world, it is said; and these cannot be replaced, unless Octavius Caesar consents to replace them—and that is not likely. Virtually all the horse is gone. We have no reserve of supplies. We have no clothing, except the rags we wear. We have no food, save that which is in our bellies.

Thus, Revered Queen, if you wish to save even a remnant of this army, you must accede to your husband's request for supplies. Out of his pride, he may not, I fear, wish you to know how desperate his plight is.

IV. Memorandum: Cleopatra to the Minister of Supplies (36 B.C.)

You are hereby authorized to procure and prepare for shipment to the Imperator Marcus Antonius at the port of Leuke Kome in Syria the following items:

Garlic: 3 tons
Wheat or spelt, according to supply: 30 tons
Salt fish: 10 tons
Cheese (of goat): 45 tons
Honey: 600 casks
Salt: 7 tons
Sheep, ready for slaughter: 600
Sour wine: 600 barrels

In addition to above items: if there is significant surplus of dried vegetables in the silos, you are to include that surplus in your shipment. If there is no surplus, you are to allow the foregoing to suffice.

You are also to procure a sufficient quantity of heavy woolen cloth, of the second quality (240,000 yards of the broad width) to manufacture 60,000 winter cloaks; sufficient coarse linen (120,000 yards of the middle width) for the manufacture of a like number of military tunics; and sufficient cured leather (soft) of horse or bullock (2000 skins) to manufacture a like number of pairs of shoes.

Speed is crucial in this matter. You are to assign a sufficient number of tailors and bootmakers to the appropriate ships so that the manufacture of these items may take place there and be completed in a voyage of eight to ten days.

The ships (twelve in number, waiting in the Royal harbor) will be made ready to sail within three days, at which time all procurement and loading must have been completed. The displeasure of your Queen would attend your failure.

V. *Memorandum: Cleopatra to the Minister of Finance (36 B.C.)*

Despite whatever orders or requests you may receive, either from his representative or from Marcus Antonius himself, you are to disburse no monies from the Royal treasury without the explicit approval and authorization of your Queen. Such approval and authorization is to be honored only if it is delivered by hand by a known representative of the Queen herself, and only if it bears the Royal seal.

VI. *Memoranda: Cleopatra to the Generals of the Egyptian Army (36 B.C.)*

Despite whatever orders or requests you may receive, either from his representatives or from Marcus Antonius himself, you are neither to allocate nor promise any troops from the Egyptian army without the explicit approval and authorization of your Queen. Such approval and authorization is to be honored only if it is delivered by hand by a known representative of the Queen herself, and only if it bears the Royal seal.

VII. *Letter: Cleopatra to Marcus Antonius, from Alexandria (winter, 35 B.C.)*

My dear husband, the Queen has ordered that the needs of your brave army be filled; and your wife like a trembling girl flies to meet you, as rapidly as the uncertain winter sea will carry her. Indeed, even as you read this letter, she is no doubt at the prow of the ship that leads the line of supply, straining her eyes in vain for the Syrian coast where her lover waits, cold in the weather, but warm in the anticipation of her lover's arms.

As a Queen, I rejoice at your success; as a woman, I bewail the necessity that has kept us apart. And yet during these hurried days since I received your letter, I have concluded (can I be wrong?) that at last woman and Queen may become one.

I shall persuade you to return with me to the warmth and comfort of Alexandria, and to leave the completion of your success in Parthia for another day. It will be my pleasure to persuade you as a woman; it is my duty to persuade you as a Queen.

The treasons that you have seen in the East have had their birth in the West. Octavius plots against you still, and libels you to those whose salvation is to love you. I know that he has tried to subvert Herod; and I am persuaded by all the intelligence that I can gather that he is responsible for the defections of the provincial legions that hampered your success in Parthia. I must convince you that there are barbarians in Rome as well as in Parthia; and their use of your loyalty and good nature is more dangerous than any Parthian arrow. In the East there is only plunder; but in the West there is the world, and such power as only the great can imagine.

But even now my mind wanders from what I say. I think of you, the mightiest of men—and I am woman again, and care nothing for kingdoms, for wars, for power. I come to you at last, and count the hours as if they were days.

VIII. Letter: Gaius Cilnius Maecenas to Titus Livius (12 B.C.)

How delicately you put things, my dear Livy; and yet, beneath that delicacy, how clear are your brutal alternatives! Were we "deceived" (and therefore fools), or did we "withhold" some information (and were therefore liars)? I shall reply somewhat less delicately than you question.

No, my old friend, we were not deceived about the matter of Parthia; how could we have been deceived? Even before we got Antonius's account of the campaign, we knew the truth of it. We lied to the Roman people.

I must say that I am a good deal less offended by your question than by what I perceive to lie behind it. You forget that I am an artist myself, and know the necessity of asking what to ordinary people would seem the most insulting and presumptuous things. How could I take offense at that which I myself would do, without the slightest hesitation, for the sake of my art? No, it is what I perceive in the tenor of your question that begins to give me offense; for I think (I hope I am wrong) I detect the odor of a moralist. And it seems to me that the moralist is the most useless and contemptible of creatures. He is useless in that he would expend his energies upon making judgments rather than upon gaining knowledge, for the reason that judgment is easy and knowledge is difficult. He is contemptible in that his judgments reflect a vision of himself which in his ignorance and pride he would impose upon the world. I implore you, do not become a moralist; you will destroy your art and your mind. And it would be a heavy burden for even the deepest friendship to bear.

As I have said, we lied; and if I give the reasons for the lie, I do not explain in order to defend. I explain to enlarge your understanding and your knowledge of the world.

After the Parthian debacle, Antonius sent to the Senate a dispatch describing his "victory" in the most glowing and general terms; and demanded, though in absentia, the ceremony of a triumph. We accepted the lie, allowed it currency, and gave him his triumph.

Italy had been racked by two generations of civil wars; the immediate history of a strong and proud people was a history of defeat, for none is victor in a civil strife; after the defeat of Sextus Pompeius, peace seemed possible; the news of such an overwhelming defeat might have been simply catastrophic, both to the stability of our government and to the soul of the people. For a people may endure an almost incredible series of the darkest failures without breaking; but give them respite and some hope for the future, and they may not endure an unexpected denial of that hope.

And there were more particular reasons for the lie. The defeat of Sextus Pompeius had been accomplished only shortly before we got the news from Parthia; the auxiliary legions had been disbanded and settled on the lands promised them; the prospect that they might be called again would have wholly disrupted all land values outside of Rome, and would have proved disastrous to an already precarious economy.

Finally, and most obviously, we still had some hope that Antonius might be deflected from his Eastern dream of Empire and become once again a Roman. It was a vain hope, but at that time it seemed a reasonable one. To have refused him his triumph— to have told your "truth" to all of Rome—would have made it impossible for him ever to have returned in honor or in peace.

In my account of these events, I have been saying "we"; but you must understand that for nearly three years after the defeat of Sextus Pompeius, Octavius and Agrippa were only occasionally in Rome; most of their time was spent in Illyria, securing our borders and subduing the barbarian tribes that theretofore had ranged freely up and down the Dalmatian shore-lands, and had even pillaged villages on the Adriatic coast of Italy itself. During this time I was entrusted with the official seal of Octavius. These decisions were mine, though in every instance, I am proud to say, they were approved by the Emperor, though often after the fact. I remember once he returned to Rome, briefly, to recuperate from a wound received in a battle against one of the Illyrian tribes; and he said to me, only half-jokingly, I think, that with Agrippa at the head of his army and with me, however unofficially, at the head of his government, he felt that the security of the nation demanded that he relinquish any pretense to either position, and for his own pleasure become the head of my stable of poets.

Marcus Antonius. . . . The charges and countercharges that have come down through the years! But beneath them, the truth was there, though the world may never fully apprehend it. We played no game; we had no need to. Though many senators in Rome, being of the old Party and somehow irrationally reversing allegiances and seeing Antonius as the only hope of recapturing the past, we knew to be against us and for Antonius, yet the people were for us; we had the army; and we had sufficient senatorial power to carry at least the most important of our edicts.

We could have endured Marcus Antonius in the East as an independent satrap or Imperator or whatever he chose to call himself, so long as he remained a Roman, even a plundering Roman; we could have endured him in Rome, even with his recklessness and ambition. But it was being forced upon us that he had caught the dream of the Greek Alexander, and that he was sick from that dream.

We gave him his triumph; it strengthened his senatorial support, but it did not draw him back to Rome. We offered him the consulship; he refused it, and did not return to Rome. And in what was really a last desperate effort to avert what we knew was coming, we returned to him the seventy ships of his fleet that had helped us defeat Sextus Pompeius, and we sent two thousand troops to augment his depleted Roman legions. And Octavia sailed with the fleet and soldiers to Athens, in the hope that Antonius might be dissuaded from his awful ambition and return to his duty as husband, Roman, and triumvir.

He accepted the ships; he enlisted the troops; and he refused to see Octavia, nor even gave her dwelling in Athens, but sent her forthwith back to Rome. And as if to leave no doubt in the minds of any of his contempt, he staged a triumph in Alexandria —in *Alexandria*—and presented a few token captives, not to a Senate, but to Cleopatra, a foreign monarch, who sat above even Antonius himself and upon a golden throne. It is said that a most barbaric ceremony followed the triumph—Antonius robed himself as Osiris, and sat beside Cleopatra, who was gowned as Isis, that most peculiar goddess. He proclaimed his mistress to be Queen of Kings, and proclaimed that her Caesarion was joint monarch over Egypt and Cyprus. He even had struck coins on one side of which was a likeness of himself and on the other a likeness of Cleopatra.

As if it were an afterthought, he had sent to Octavia letters of divorce, and had her evicted without ceremony or warning from his Roman dwelling.

We could not then evade what must ensue. Octavius returned from Illyria, and we began to prepare for whatever madness might come from the East.

IX. *Senatorial Proceedings*, Rome (*33 B.C.*)

On this day Marcus Agrippa, Consular and Admiral of the Roman Fleet, Aedile of the Roman Senate, does declare, for the health and welfare of the Roman people, and for the glory of Rome, the following:

I. From his own funds, and without recourse to the public treasury, Marcus Agrippa will have repaired and restored all public buildings that have fallen into neglect, and will have cleaned and repaired the public sewers that carry the waste of Rome into the Tiber.

II. From his own funds Marcus Agrippa will make available to all free-born inhabitants of Rome sufficient olive oil and salt to suffice their needs for one year.

III. For both men and women, free-born and slave, the public baths will for the period of one year be open for use without fee.

IV. To protect the gullible and ignorant and poor, and to halt the spread of alien superstition, all astrologers and Eastern sooth-sayers and magicians are forbidden within the city walls, and those who now practice their vicious trades are ordered to quit the city of Rome, upon pain of death and forfeiture of all monies and properties.

V. In that Temple known as Serapis and Isis, the trinkets of Egyptian superstition shall no longer be sold or purchased, upon pain of exile for both purchaser and seller; and the Temple itself, built to commemorate the conquest of Egypt by Julius Caesar, is declared to be a monument of history, and not a recognition of the false gods of the East by the Roman people and the Roman Senate.

X. Petition: the Centurion Quintus Appius to Munatius Plancus, Commander of the Asian Legions of the Imperator Marcus Antonius, from Ephesus (32 B.C.)

I, Appius, son of Lucius Appius, am of the Cornelian tribe and of Campanian origin. My father was a farmer, who left me a few acres of land near Velletri, which from the age of eighteen to twenty-three I tilled for a humble livelihood. My cottage is there yet, overseen by the wife I married in my youth, who, though a freedwoman, is chaste and faithful; and the land is tended by the three of my sons who remain alive. Two sons I lost—one to disease, and the eldest to the Spanish campaign against Sextus Pompeius, under Julius Caesar, these many years ago.

For the sake of Italy and my posterity, I became a soldier in the twenty-third year of my life, in the consulship of Tullius Cicero and Gaius Antonius, who was uncle to the Marcus Antonius who is now my master. For two years I was a common soldier in that army under Gaius Antonius which defeated in honorable battle the conspirator Catiline; in my third year as a soldier I was with Julius Caesar in his first Spanish campaign, and though I was a young man, in reward for my bravery in battle, Julius Caesar made me a lesser centurion of the IV Macedonian legion. I have been a soldier for thirty years; I have fought in eighteen campaigns, in fourteen of which I was centurion and in one of which I was acting military tribune; I have fought under the command of six duly elected consuls of the Senate; I have served in Spain, Gaul, Africa, Greece, Egypt, Macedonia, Britain, and Germany; I have marched in three triumphs, I have five times received the laurel crown for saving the life of a fellow soldier; and I have twenty times been decorated for bravery in battle.

The oath I took as a young soldier bound me to the authority of the magistrates, the consuls, and the Senate for the defense of my country. To that oath I have been faithful, and have served Rome with that honor of which I am capable. I am now in my fifty-third year, and I ask release from military service, so that I may return to Velletri and spend my remaining years in privacy and peace.

I know that, in the law, you may refuse this release, despite my age and service, since I volunteered freely for another campaign; and I know, too, that what I shall now say may put me in jeopardy. If it is to do so, I shall accept my fate.

When I was detached from the army of Marcus Agrippa and sent to Athens and thence to Alexandria and finally here to Ephesus and the army of Marcus Antonius, I did not protest; that is the soldier's lot, and I have grown accustomed to it. I had fought the Parthians before, and had no fear of them. But the events of the past few weeks have put me into a deep doubt; and I must turn to you, with whom I fought in Gaul under Julius Caesar, and whose honorable behavior toward me gives me some hope that you may hear me before you judge me too harshly.

It is clear that we shall not fight the Parthians, or the Medians, or anyone else to the East. And yet we arm, and we train, and we build the engines of war.

I have given my oath to the consuls and the Senate of the Roman people; it is an oath that I have not broken.

And yet where is the Senate now? And where is my oath to find its fulfillment?

We know that three hundred senators and the two consuls of the year have quit Rome, and are now here in Ephesus, where the Imperator Marcus Antonius has convened them against the seven hundred senators who have remained in Rome; and new consuls in Rome have replaced those who have come here.

To whom do I owe my oath? Where is the Roman people, whom the Senate must represent?

I do not hate Octavius Caesar, though I would fight him, were that my duty; I do not love Marcus Antonius, though I would die for him were that my duty. It is not the place of the soldier to think of politics, and it is not the business of the soldier to hate or love. It is his duty to fulfill his oath.

A Roman, I have fought against Romans before, though I have done so with sorrow. But I have not fought against Romans under the banner of a foreign queen, and I have not marched against my nation and my countrymen as if they were the painted barbarians of a foreign province, to be plundered and subdued.

I am an old man, and tired, and I ask release to return quietly to my home. But you are my commander, and I shall not move against your authority. If it is your decision that I may not be released, I shall acquit myself with that honor in which I trust I have lived.

XI. Letter: Munatius Plancus, Commander of the Asian Legions, to Octavius Caesar, from Ephesus (32 B.C.)

Though we have differed, I have not been your enemy so much as I have been friend to Marcus Antonius, whom I have known since those days when we were both the trusted generals of your late and divine father, Julius Caesar. Through all the years, I have tried to be loyal to Rome, and yet be loyal to the man whom I have had for friend.

It is no longer possible for me to remain loyal to both. As if in an enchantment, Marcus Antonius follows blindly wherever Cleopatra will lead; and she will lead where her ambition takes her, and that is simply the conquest of the world, the succession of her progeny in kingship over that world, and the establishment of Alexandria as the capital of that world. I have been unable to dissuade Marcus Antonius from this disastrous course. Even now, troops from all the Asian provinces gather at Ephesus to join the sad Roman legions which Antonius will hurl against Rome; the doors of Cleopatra's treasury are open to prosecute the war against Italy; and she will not leave Marcus Antonius's side, but goads him bitterly toward your destruction and the fulfillment of her ambition. It is said that henceforward she will march at his side and command, even in battle. Not only myself, but all of his friends have urged him to send Cleopatra back to Alexandria, where her presence might not provoke the hatred of the Roman troops, but he will not, or cannot, move.

Thus I have been forced to choose between a waning friendship for a man and a steady love for my country. I return to Italy, and I renounce the Eastern adventure. And I will not be alone. I have spent my life with the Roman soldier, and I think I know his heart; many will not fight under the banner of a foreign queen, and those who in their confusion will fight, will do so with sorrow and reluctance, so that their strength and soldierly determination will be lessened.

I come to you in friendship, and I offer you my services; if you cannot accept the former, perhaps you will find use for the latter.

XII. *The Memoirs of Marcus Agrippa:* Fragments (*13 B.C.*)

I come now to the account of those events which led to the battle of Actium and at last to the peace of which Rome had long despaired.

Marcus Antonius and the Queen Cleopatra gathered their strength in the East, and moved their armies from Ephesus to the Island of Samos, and thence to Athens, where they poised in threat to Italy and peace. In the second consulship of Caesar Augustus, I was aedile of Rome; and when the year of those duties was over, we turned ourselves to the task of rebuilding the armies of Italy that would repel the threat of Eastern treason, a task which necessitated our absence from Rome for many months. We returned to discover the Senate subverted by the friends of Antonius who were the enemies of the Roman people; we opposed those enemies, and when it became clear to them that they would not prevail in their designs against the order of Italy, the two consuls of the year, and behind them three hundred senators without faith or love for their homeland, quit Rome and made their way out of Italy to join Antonius; and went without hindrance or threat from Caesar Augustus, who saw them depart with sorrow, but without anger.

And in the East, loyal Roman troops, at first by tens and then by hundreds, refusing the yoke of a foreign queen, made their way to Italy; and from them we knew that there would be no escape from war; and knew also that that war would come soon, for Antonius was weakening from the desertions, and would, if he delayed too long, be wholly dependent upon the caprice and inexperience of his barbarian legions and their Asian commanders.

Thus in the late autumn of the year after his second consulship, Caesar Augustus, with the consent of the Senate and the Roman people, did declare that a state of war existed between the Roman people and Cleopatra, Queen of Egypt; and led by Caesar Augustus, the Senate in solemn march took themselves to the Campus Martius, and at the Temple of Bellona, the herald read the words of war, and the priests made sacrifice of a white heifer to the goddess, and prayed that the army of Rome be made safe in all the battles that were to come.

After the defeat of Sextus Pompeius, Augustus had vowed to the Roman people that the civil wars were ended, and that not again would the soil of Italy suffer to receive the blood of her sons. Throughout the winter we trained our soldiers on land, repaired and augmented our fleet, exercising upon the sea when weather allowed us; and in the spring, learning that Marcus Antonius had gathered his fleet and his army at the seaward opening of the Bay of Corinth, whence he purposed to strike swiftly across the Ionian Sea at the Eastern coast of Italy, we moved against him, to save Italy from the wounds of war.

Against us was arrayed the might of the Eastern world—one hundred thousand troops, of which thirty thousand were Roman, and five hundred ships of war, deployed along the coastal lands of Greece; and eighty thousand reserves of troops that remained in Egypt and Syria. Against this force we brought fifty thousand Roman soldiers, a number of which were veterans of the sea campaign against Pompeius, two hundred fifty ships of war, the latter under my command, and one hundred fifty vessels of supply.

The coast of Greece boasts few harbors that may be defended, and thus we had no trouble landing the troops that would fight Antonius on the land; and the ships under my command blockaded the sea routes of supply from Syria and Egypt, so that the forces of Cleopatra and Marcus Antonius would have to depend upon the land that they had invaded for food and supplies.

Loath to take Roman lives, throughout the spring we skirmished, hoping to accomplish our ends by blockade rather than warfare; and in the summer, we moved in strength to the Bay of Actium, where the largest enemy force was concentrated, hoping to lure there those who would prevent our pretended invasion, in which effort we succeeded. For Antonius and Cleopatra sailed in full complement to rescue the ships and men we did not intend to attack, and we fell back before the advance of their ships, and let them enter into the bay, whence we knew eventually they would have to emerge. We would force them to do battle upon sea, though their strength was upon the land.

The mouth of the Bay of Actium is less than one half a mile in width, though the bay itself widens considerably within, so that the enemy ships had sufficient room to harbor; and while they rested inside with the soldiers encamped ashore, Caesar Augustus sent troops of infantry and cavalry around them, and fortified the encirclement, so that they would have retreated overland at great cost. And we waited; for we knew that the armies of the East suffered from hunger and disease, and could not muster the strength for a retreat by land. They would fight by sea.

The ships of war that we had returned to Antonius after the defeat of Sextus Pompeius were the largest of the fleet, and I had learned that those which Antonius had built to war against us were even larger, some carrying as many as ten banks of oars and girded by bands of iron against ramming; such ships are nearly invincible against smaller ships in direct combat, when there is no room for maneuvering. Therefore I had much earlier resolved to rely upon a preponderance of lighter and more maneuverable craft, with as few as two and as many as six banks of oars, and none larger; and resolved to be so patient as to lure the Eastern fleets into the open sea. For at Naulochus, against Pompeius, we had had to engage the enemy ships at shore, where swiftness meant nothing.

We waited; and on the first day of September we saw the lines of vessels draw up for battle, and saw those burned for which there were no rowers; and we made ready for what must ensue on the morrow.

The morning came bright and clear; the harbor and the sea beyond were smooth like a table of translucent stone. The Eastern fleet raised sail, as if hoping to pursue us when a wind came up; the oarsmen dipped their oars; and the fleet, like a solid wall, moved slowly across the water. Antonius himself commanded the starboard squadron of the three groups, which were so close that often the opposing oars clashed together, and the fleet of Cleopatra followed behind the center squadron at some distance.

My own squadron opposed that of Antonius; and those ships commanded by Caesar Augustus were at the port. We were beyond the mouth of the bay, and spread thinly out in a curving line, so that we had no ships behind us.

As the enemy advanced toward us, we did not move; he paused at the mouth, and no oar was dipped for several hours. He wished us to move upon him; we did not move; we waited.

And at last, out of impatience or an excess of boldness, the commander of the port squadron moved forward; Caesar Augustus made as if to withdraw from danger; the squadron pursued him without thought, and the rest of the Eastern fleet followed. Our center squadron fell back, we lengthened our line, and the enemy fleet rode in like fish into a net, and we surrounded them.

Until nearly dusk the battle raged, though the issue was at no time in serious doubt. We had not raised sail, and we could move swiftly about the heavier ships; and having hoisted sail, the enemy's decks did not afford room for slingers and archers to work effectively; and the sails offered easy targets for the fireballs that we catapulted. Our own decks were clear so that when we grappled a ship, our soldiers in superior numbers could board the enemy and overcome him with some ease.

He would attempt to form a wedge so that he could break our line; we darted upon him and broke his formation, so that he had to fight singly; he tried to form again, and we broke him again, so that at last each ship fought for its own survival, as best it could. And the sea blazed with ships that we fired, and we heard above the roar of the flames the screams of men who burned with their ships, and the sea darkened with blood and was awash with bodies that had thrown off armor and struggled weakly to escape the fire and the sword and the javelin and the arrow. Though they opposed us, they were Roman soldiers; and we were sickened at the waste.

During all the fighting, the ships of Cleopatra had hung back in the harbor; and when at last a breeze sprang up, she had her sails set into the wind, and swung around the ships that were locked in battle and made toward the open sea where we could not follow.

It was one of those curious moments in the confusion of warfare with which all soldiers are familiar. The vessel which carried Caesar Augustus and my own ship had come so close together that we could look into each other's eyes and could even shout to be heard above the furor; not thirty yards away, where it had been pursued and then left, was the ship of Marcus Antonius. I believe that all three of us saw the purple sail of Cleopatra's departing flagship at the same time. None of us moved; Antonius stood at the prow of his ship as if he were a carven figurehead, looking after his departing Queen. And then he turned to us, though whether he recognized either of us I do not know. His face was without expression, as if it were that of a corpse. Then his arm lifted stiffly, and dropped; and the sails were thrust into the wind, and the great ship turned slowly and gathered speed, and Marcus Antonius followed after his Queen. We watched the pitiful remains of his own ships that escaped the slaughter, and we did not attempt to pursue. I did not see Marcus Antonius again.

Deserted by their leaders, the remaining ships surrendered; we cared for our wounded enemies, who were also our brothers, and we burned those ships that remained of the Antonian force; and

Caesar Augustus said that no Roman soldier who had been our enemy should suffer for his bravery, but should be returned to honor and the safety of Rome.

We knew that we had won the world; but there were no songs of victory that night, nor joy among any of us. Late into the night the only sound that could be heard was the lap and hiss of water against the burning hulls and the low moans of the wounded; a glow of burning hung over the harbor, and Caesar Augustus, his face stark and reddened in that glow, stood at the prow of his ship and looked upon the sea that held the bodies of those brave men, both comrade and foe, as if there were no difference between them.

XIII. Letter: Gaius Cilnius Maecenas to Titus Livius (*12 B.C.*)

In reply to your questions:

Did Marcus Antonius plead for his life? Yes. It is a matter best forgotten. I had a copy of the letter once. I have destroyed it. Octavius did not reply to the letter. Antonius was not murdered; he did commit suicide, though he bungled the job and died slowly. Let him remain in peace; do not pursue these matters too far.

The matter of Cleopatra: (1) No, Octavius did not arrange her murder. (2) Yes, he did speak to her in Alexandria before she took her life. (3) Yes, he would have spared her life; he did not want her dead. She was an excellent administrator, and could have retained titular control of Egypt. (4) No, I do not know what went on in the interview at Alexandria; he has never chosen to speak of it.

The matter of Caesarion: (1) Yes, he was only seventeen years old. (2) Yes, it was our decision that he be put to death. (3) Yes, it is my judgment that he was the son of Julius. (4) No, he was not put to death because of his name, but because of his ambition, which was inarguable. I spoke to Octavius about his youth, and Octavius reminded me that he himself had been seventeen once, and ambitious.

The matter of Antyllus, the son of Marcus Antonius. Octavius had him put to death. He also was seventeen years of age. He was much like his father.

The matter of Octavius's return to Rome: (1) He was thirty-three years of age. (2) Yes, he received the triple triumph then, at the beginning of his fifth consulship. (3) Yes, that was the same year he fell ill, and we despaired again of his life.

You must, my dear Livy, forgive the curtness of my replies. I am not offended; I am only tired. I look back upon those days as if they happened to someone else, almost as if they were not real. If the truth were known, I am bored with remembering. Perhaps I shall feel better tomorrow.

BOOK TWO

I

I am Hirtia. My mother, Crispia, was once a slave in the household of Atia, wife to Gaius Octavius the Elder, niece to Julius Caesar the God, and mother to that Octavius whom the world knows now as Augustus. I cannot write, so I speak these words to my son Quintus, who manages the estates of Atius Sabinus in Velletri. He writes these words so that our posterity may know of the time before them, and of the part their ancestors had in that time. I am in my seventy-second year, and the end of my life comes toward me; I wish to say these words before the gods close my eyes forever.

Three days ago my son took me into Rome, so that before my eyes dimmed beyond sight I might look again upon the city that I remembered from my youth; and there an event befell me which raised memories of a past so distant that I thought I could never return to it. After more than fifty years, I saw again that one who is now master of the world and who has more titles than my poor mind can remember. But once I called him "my Tavius," and held him in my arms as if he were my own. I shall speak later of that; now I must say my memories of an earlier time.

My mother was born a slave in the Julian household. She was

given to Atia first as a playmate, and then as a servant. But even when she was young, she was granted her freedom for faithful service, so that she might, in the law, marry the freedman Hirtius, who became my father. My father was overseer of all the olive groves on the Octavian estate at Velletri; and it was in a cottage near the villa, on the hill above the groves, that I was born, and where I lived in the kindness of that household for the first nineteen years of my life. Now I have returned to Velletri; and if the gods are willing, I shall die in that cottage in the contentment of my childhood.

My mistress and her husband did not stay often at the villa; they lived in Rome, for Gaius Octavius the Elder was a man of importance in the government of those days. When I was ten years old, my mother informed me that Atia had given birth to a son; and because he was sickly, she decided that he would spend his infancy in the country air, away from the stench and smoke of the city. My mother had recently given birth to a stillborn child, and could nurse her mistress's son. And as my mother took a child to her breast as if it were her own, so did my young heart, which was beginning to stir toward the dream of motherhood.

As young as I was, I washed his body; swaddled him; held his tiny hand when he took his first steps; saw him grow. In my childhood game of motherhood, he was my Tavius.

When that one whom I then called Tavius was five years old, his father returned from a long stay in the land of Macedonia and visited with his family for a few days; he planned to move southward to another of his residences in Nola, where we were to join him for the winter season. But he became suddenly ill, and died before we could take the journey; and my Tavius lost the father whom he had never known. I held him in my arms to comfort him. I remember that his little body quivered; he did not cry.

For four more years he remained in our care, though a teacher was sent from Rome to attend him; and occasionally his mother visited. When I was in my nineteenth year, my mother died; and my mistress Atia—who after her time of mourning and in her duty had married again—decided that her son must return to Rome so that he might begin to prepare himself for manhood. And in her kindness and for the safety of my future, Atia gave into my keeping a portion of land sufficient to keep me from ever living in want; and for the well-being of my person, she gave me in marriage to a freedman of her family, who had a modest but safe prosperity in a flock of sheep that grazed in the mountain country near Mutina, north of Rome.

Thus I went from my youth and became a woman, and in the way of things had to say good-by to the child I had pretended was mine. The days of play were over for me; yet it was I who wept when I had to take leave of Tavius. As if I were the child who needed comfort, he embraced me, and told me he would not forget me. We vowed that we would see each other again; we did not believe that we would. And so the child that had been my Tavius went his way to become the ruler of the world, and I found the happiness and purpose for which the gods had destined me.

How might an ignorant old woman understand greatness in one whom she has known as an infant, as a toddling child, as a boy who ran and shouted with his playmates? Now everywhere outside of Rome, in the villages and towns of the countryside, he is a god; there is a temple in his name in my own town of Mutina, and I have heard that there are others elsewhere. His image is on the hearths of the country folk throughout the land.

I do not know the ways of the world or of the gods; I remember a child who was almost my own, though not born of my body; and I must say what I remember. He was a child with hair paler than the autumn grain; a fair skin that would not take the sun. At times he was quick and gay; at other times quiet and withdrawn. He could be made quickly angry, and as easily removed from that anger. Though I loved him, he was a child like any other.

It must be that even then the gods had given him the greatness that all the world has learned; but if they had, I swear he did not know it. His playmates were his equals, even the children of the lowest slaves; he gave as he received in his tasks or his play. Yes, the gods must have touched him, and yet in their wisdom prevented him from knowing; for I heard in later years that there were many portents at his birth. It is said that his mother dreamed that a god in the form of a serpent entered her, and that she conceived; that his father dreamed that the sun rose from the loins of his wife; and that miracles beyond understanding took place all over Italy at the moment of his birth. I say only what I have heard, and speak of the memories of those days.

And now I must tell of that meeting which raised these thoughts in my head.

My son Quintus wanted me to see the great Forum where he often went to take care of business matters for his employer; and so he aroused me at the first hour of the day, so that we could walk the streets before they were crowded. We had seen the new Senate House, and were walking up the Via Sacra toward the Temple of Julius Caesar, which was white as mountain snow in the morning sunlight. I remembered that once when I was a child I had seen this man who has become a god; and I wondered at the greatness of that world of which I had been a part.

We paused for a moment to rest beside the temple. In my age I tire easily. And as we rested, I saw walking up the street toward us a group of men whom I knew to be senators; they wore the togas with the purple stripes. In their midst was a slight figure, bowed as I am bowed, wearing a broad-brimmed hat and with a staff in one hand. The others seemed to be directing their words toward him. My eyes are weak; I could not make out his features; but some power of knowledge came upon me, and I said to Quintus:

"It is he."

Quintus smiled at me, and asked: "It is who, Mother?"

"It is he," I said, and my voice trembled. "It is that master of whom I have spoken, who once was in my care."

Quintus looked at him again, and took my arm, and we went closer to the street so that we could watch his passing. Other citizens had noticed his approach, and we crowded among them.

I did not intend to speak; but as he passed, those memories of my childhood came up within me, and the word was spoken.

"Tavius," I said.

The word was hardly more than a whisper, but it was said as he passed me; and the one whom I had not intended to address paused and looked at me as if he were puzzled. Then he gestured to the men around him to remain where they were, and he came up to me.

"Did you speak, old mother?" he asked.

"Yes, Master," I said. "Forgive me."

"You said a name by which I was known as a child."

"I am Hirtia," I said. "My mother was your foster nurse when you were a child in Velletri. Perhaps you do not remember."

"Hirtia," he said, and he smiled. He came a step nearer, and looked at me; his face was lined and his cheeks sunken, but I could see that boy I had known. "Hirtia," he said again, and touched my hand. "I remember. How many years . . ."

"More than fifty," I said.

Some of his friends approached him; he waved them away.

"Fifty," he said. "Have they been kind to you?"

"I have raised five children, of whom three live and prosper. My husband was a good man, and we lived in comfort. The gods have taken my husband, and now I am content that my own life draws to an end."

He looked at me. "Among your children," he said, "were there daughters?"

I thought it a strange question. I said: "I was blessed only with sons."

"And they have honored you?"

"They have honored me," I said.

"Then your life has been a good one," he said. "Perhaps it has been better than you know."

"I am content to go when the gods call me," I said.

He nodded, and a somberness came upon his face. He said with a bitterness I could not understand: "Then you are more fortunate than I, my sister."

"But you—" I said, "—you are not like other men. In the countryside your image protects the hearth. And at the crossroads, and in the temples. Are you not happy in the honor of the world?"

He looked at me for a moment, and did not answer. Then he turned to Quintus, who stood beside me. "This is your son," he said. "He has your features."

"It is Quintus," I said. "He is manager of all the estates of Atius Sabinus at Velletri. Since I was widowed, I have been living with Quintus and his family there. They are good people."

He looked at Quintus for a long time without speaking. "I did not have a son," he said. "I had only a daughter, and Rome."

I said, "All the people are your children."

He smiled. "I think now I would have preferred to have had three sons, and to have lived in their honor."

I did not know what to say; I did not speak.

"Sir," my son said; his voice was unsteady. "We are humble people. Our lives are what they have been. I have heard that today you speak to the Senate, and thus give to the world your wisdom and your counsel. Beside yours, our fortune is nothing."

"Is it Quintus?" he said. My son nodded. He said: "Quintus, today in my wisdom, I must counsel—I must order the Senate to take from me that which I have loved most in this life." For a moment his eyes blazed, and then his face softened, and he said: "I have given to Rome a freedom that only I cannot enjoy."

"You have not found happiness," I said, "though you have given it."

"It is the way my life has been," he said.

"I hope that you become happy," I said.

"I thank you, my sister," he said. "There is nothing that I can do for you?"

"I am content," I said. "My sons are content."

He nodded. "I must perform this duty now," he said; but for a long while he was silent, and did not turn away. "We did see each other again, as we promised long ago."

"Yes, Master," I said.

He smiled. "Once you called me Tavius."

"Tavius," I said.

"Good-by, Hirtia," he said. "This time, perhaps we shall—"

"We shall not meet again," I said. "I go to Velletri, and I shall not return to Rome."

He nodded, and he put his lips to my cheek, and he turned away. He walked slowly down the Via Sacra to join those who waited for him.

These words I have spoken to my son, Quintus, on the third day before the Ides of September. I have spoken them for my sons and for their children, now and to come, so that for as long as this family endures it might know something of its place in the world that was Rome, in the days that are gone.

II. *The Journal of Julia,* Pandateria (*A.D. 4*)

Outside my window, the rocks, gray and somber in the brilliance of the afternoon sun, descend in a huge profusion toward the sea. This rock, like all the rock on this island of Pandateria, is volcanic in origin, rather porous and light in weight, upon which one must walk with some caution, lest one's feet be slashed by hidden sharpnesses. There are others on this island, but I am not allowed to see them. Unaccompanied and unwatched, I am permitted to walk a distance of one hundred yards to the sea, as far as the thin strip of black-sand beach; and to walk a like distance in any direction from this small stone hut that has been my abode for five years. I know the body of this barren earth more intimately than I have known the contours of any other, even that of my native Rome, upon which I lavished an intimacy of almost forty years. It is likely that I shall never know another place.

On clear days, when the sun or the wind has dispersed the mists that often rise from the sea, I look to the east; and I think that I can sometimes see the mainland of Italy, perhaps even the city of Naples that nestles in the safety of her gentle bay; but I cannot be sure. It may be only a dark cloud that upon occasion smudges the horizon. It does not matter. Cloud or land, I shall not approach closer to it than I am now.

Below me, in the kitchen, my mother shouts at the one servant we are allowed. I hear the banging of pots and pans, and the shouting again; it is a futile repetition of every afternoon of these years. Our servant is mute; and though not deaf, it is unlikely that she even understands our Latin tongue. Yet indefatigably my mother shouts at her, in the unflagging optimism that her displeasure will be felt and will somehow matter. My mother, Scribonia, is a remarkable woman; she is nearly seventy-five, yet she has the energy and the will of a young woman, as she goes about setting in some peculiar order a world that has never pleased her, and berating it for not arranging itself according to some principle that has evaded them both. She came with me here to Pandateria, not, I am sure, out of any maternal regard, but out of a desperate pursuit of a condition that would confirm once again her displeasure with existence. And I allowed her to accompany me out of what I believe was an appropriate indifference.

I scarcely know my mother. I saw her upon few occasions when I was a child, even less frequently when I was a girl, and we met only at more or less formal social gatherings when I was a woman. I was never fond of her; and it gives me now some assurance to know, after these five years of enforced intimacy, that my feeling for her has not changed.

I am Julia, daughter of Octavius Caesar, the August; and I write these words in the forty-third year of my life. I write them for a purpose of which the friend of my father and my old tutor, Athenodorus, would never have approved; I write them for myself and my own perusal. Even if I wished it otherwise, it is unlikely that any eyes save my own shall see them. But I do not wish it otherwise. I would not explain myself to the world, and I would not have the world understand me; I have become indifferent to us both. For however long I may live in this body, which I have served with much care and art for so many years, that part of my life which matters is over; thus I may view it with the detached interest of the scholar that Athenodorus once said I might have become, had I been born a man and not the daughter of an Emperor and god.

—Yet how strong is the force of old habit! For even now, as I write these first words in this journal, and as I know that they are written to be read only by that strangest of all readers, myself, I find myself pausing in deliberation as I seek the proper topic upon which to found my argument, the appropriate argument itself, the constitution of the argument, the effective arrangement of its parts, and even the style in which those parts are to be delivered. It is myself whom I would persuade to truth by the force of my discourse, and myself whom I would dissuade. It is a foolishness, yet I believe not a harmful one. It occupies my day at least as fully as does the counting of the waves that break over the sand upon the rocky coast of this island where I must remain.

Yes: it is likely that my life is over, though I believe I did not fully apprehend the extent to which I knew the truth of that until yesterday, when I was allowed to receive for the first time in nearly two years a letter from Rome. My sons Gaius and Lucius are dead, the former of a wound received in Armenia and the latter of an illness whose nature no one knows on his way to Spain, in the city of Marseilles. When I read the letter, a numbness came upon me, which in a removed way I judged to have resulted from the shock of the news; and I waited for the grief which I imagined would ensue. But no grief came; and I began to look upon my life, and to remember the moments that had spaced it out, as if I were not concerned. And I knew that it was over. To care not for one's self is of little moment, but to care not for those whom one has loved is another matter. All has become the object of an indifferent curiosity, and nothing is of consequence. Perhaps I write these words and employ the devices that I have learned so that I may discover whether I may rouse myself from this great indifference into which I have descended. I doubt that I shall be able to do so, any more than I should be able to push these massive rocks down the slope into the dark concern of the sea. I am indifferent even to my doubt.

I am Julia, daughter of Gaius Octavius Caesar, the August, and I was born on the third day of September in the year of the consulship of Lucius Marcius and Gaius Sabinus, in the city of Rome. My mother was that Scribonia whose brother was father-in-law to Sextus Pompeius, the pirate whom my father destroyed for the safety of Rome two years after my birth. . . .

That is a beginning of which even Athenodorus, my poor Athenodorus, would have approved.

III. Letter: Lucius Varius Rufus to Publius Vergilius Maro, from Rome (39 B.C.)

My dear Vergil, I trust that your illness does not progress, and that the warmth of the Neapolitan sun has indeed bettered the state of your health. Your friends send their best wishes, and have charged me to assure you that our well-being depends upon your own; if you are well, so are we. Your friends also have charged me to convey to you our regrets that you could not attend the banquet at the home of Claudius Nero last night, a celebration from whose effects I am just this afternoon beginning to recover. It was an extraordinary evening, and it may beguile you from your discomfort if I give you some account of it.

Do you know Claudius Nero, your would-be host? He speaks of you with some familiarity, so I suspect that you have at least met him. If you do know him, you may remember that only two years ago he was in exile in Sicily for having opposed our Octavius Caesar at Perusia; now he has apparently renounced politics, and he and Octavius seem to be the best of friends. He is quite old, and his wife, Livia, seems more nearly his daughter than his spouse—a fortunate circumstance, as you shall shortly understand.

It turned out to be a literary evening, though I doubt that Claudius planned it that way. He is a good fellow, but he has little learning. It soon became clear that Octavius was really behind it all, and that Claudius was, as it were, the pseudo-host. The occasion was designed to honor our friend Pollio, who will at last give to the Roman people that library he has been promising, so that learning may flourish even among the common people.

It was a mixed gathering, but, as it turned out, a rather fortunate one. Most were our friends—Pollio, Octavius and (alas!) Scribonia, Maecenas, Agrippa, myself, Aemilius Macer; your "admirer" Mevius, who no doubt wangled the invitation from Claudius, who knew no better than to invite him; one whom none of us knew, an odd little Pontene from Amasia called Strabo, a sort of philosopher, I believe; for embellishment, several ladies of quality, whose names I cannot recall; and to my surprise (and I suspect to your pleasure) that rather blunt but appealing young man whose work you have been kind enough to admire, your Horace. I believe that Maecenas was responsible for his invitation, despite the rudeness he suffered at Horace's hands several months ago.

I must say that Octavius was in extraordinary good spirits, almost loquacious, despite the usual long face that Scribonia wore. He has just returned from Gaul, you know, and perhaps the rather severe months there have made him hungry for civilized company; moreover, it seems now that the difficulties with both Marcus Antonius and Sextus Pompeius are in abeyance, if not finally settled. Or perhaps his gaiety had its source in the presence of Claudius's wife, Livia, to whom he seems to have taken a strong fancy.

In any event, Octavius insisted upon playing the part of the wine-master, and mixed the wine much more strongly than he usually does, with nearly equal parts of water, so that even before the first course arrived most of us were a little tipsy. He insisted that Pollio, rather than himself, be placed at the position of honor beside Claudius; while he chose to recline at the inferior position at the table, with Livia beside him.

I must say that Octavius and Claudius were exceedingly civilized toward each other, given the circumstances; one would almost think that they had reached an understanding. Scribonia sat at the other table, gossiping with the ladies and glowering at the table where we sat—though the gods know why she should glower. She dislikes the marriage as much as Octavius does, and there is no secret about the fact that a divorce will be effected as soon as Octavius's child is born. . . . What games they must play, those who have power in the world! And how ludicrous must they seem to the Muses! It must be that those who are nearest to the gods are most at their mercy. We are most fortunate, my dear Vergil, that we need not marry to ensure our posterity, but can make the children of our souls march beautifully into the future, where they will not change or die.

Claudius serves a good table, I must say—a very decent Campanian wine before the meal, and a good Falernian afterwards. The meal was neither ostentatiously elaborate nor affectedly simple: oysters, eggs, and tiny onions to begin; roast kid, broiled chicken, and grilled bream; and a variety of fresh fruits.

After the meal, Octavius proposed that we toast the Muses, and that we converse upon their separate functions; and argued briefly with himself as to whether we should drink individual toasts to the ancient three or to the more recent nine; and finally, after pretending a great struggle, decided upon the latter.

"But," he said, and glanced, smiling, at Claudius, "we must honor the Muses to this extent; we must not allow them to be soiled by any mention of politics. It is a subject that might embarrass us all."

There was general, if nervous, laughter; and I suddenly realized how many enemies, past and potential, were in the room. Claudius, whom Octavius had exiled from Italy less than two years before; Pollio himself, our guest of honor, who was an old friend of Marcus Antonius; our young Horace, who only three years ago had fought on the side of the traitor Brutus; and Mevius, poor Mevius, whose envy ran so deep that no man might be spared from the treachery of his flattery, or vice versa.

Pollio, being the guest of honor, began. With an apologetic

bow to Octavius, he chose to extol the ancient Muse of Memory, Mneme; and likening all mankind to a single body, he went on to compare the collective experience of mankind to the mind of that body; and thence rather neatly (though obviously) he spoke of the library which he was establishing in Rome as if it were the most important quality of the mind, memory; and concluded that the Muse of Memory presided over all the others in a beneficent reign.

Mevius gave a tremulous sigh and said to someone in a loud whisper: "Beautiful. Oh, how beautiful!" Horace glanced at him, and raised a dubious eyebrow.

Agrippa addressed himself to Clio, the Muse of History; Mevius whispered loudly something about manliness and bravery; and Horace glowered at Mevius. Upon my turn, I spoke of Calliope —rather badly, I fear, since I could not allude to my own work upon the slain Julius Caesar, even though it is a poem, without trespassing upon Octavius's interdiction against politics.

It was all rather dull, I fear, though Octavius, reclining with Livia seated beside him in the torchlight, seemed pleased; it was his animation and gaiety that made possible what otherwise would have been impossible.

He assigned to Mevius (rather obviously, I thought, though Mevius was too full of himself to notice) that Thalia who is the Muse of Comedy; and Mevius, delighted to be singled out, launched into a long, farcical account (stolen, I believe, from Antiphanes of Athens) about the upstarts of old Athens—slaves, freedmen, and tradespeople—who presumed to set themselves upon a level with their social betters; who wangled invitations to the homes of the great, and gorged themselves at their tables, abusing the kindness and generosity of their noble hosts; and how Thalia, the goddess of the comic spirit, to punish such interlopers, called down upon them certain afflictions, so that their class might be distinguished, and so that the nobility might be protected. Some, Mevius said, she made dwarfs, and gave thatches of hair like the hay in which they were born, and afflicted with the manners of the stable. And so on, and so on.

It became quickly clear that Mevius was attacking your young friend Horace, though for what reason none was quite sure. And no one knew precisely how to behave; we looked at Octavius, but his face was impassive; we looked at Maecenas, who seemed unconcerned. None would look at Horace, except myself, who was seated next to him. His face was pale in the flickering light.

Mevius finished and sat back, satisfied that he had flattered a patron and destroyed a possible rival. There was a murmur. Octavius thanked him, and said:

"Now who shall speak for that Erato who is the Muse of Poetry?"

And Mevius, raised by what he thought was his success, said: "Oh, Maecenas, of course; for he has courted the Muse and won her. It must be Maecenas."

Maecenas waved languidly. "I must decline," he said. "These last months, she has wandered from my gardens. . . . Perhaps my young friend Horace will speak for her."

Octavius laughed, and turned toward Horace with perfect civility. "I have met our guest only this evening, but I will presume upon that slight acquaintance. Will you speak, Horace?"

"I will speak," Horace said; but for a long time he was silent. Without waiting for a servant, he poured himself a measure of unmixed wine, and drank it at once. And he spoke. I give you his words as I remember them.

"You all know the story of the Greek Orpheus of whom our absent Vergil has written so beautifully—son of Apollo and the Muse Calliope, whom the god honored by the presence of his manhood, and inheritor of the golden lyre which sent forth light into the world, making even the stones and trees glimmer in a beauty not apprehended before by man. And you know of his love for Eurydice, of which he sang with such purity and grace that Eurydice thought herself to be part of the singer's own soul and came to him in marriage, at which Hymen wept, as if at a fate no one could imagine. And you know, too, how Eurydice at last, wandering foolishly beyond the precincts of her husband's magic, was touched by a serpent that came out of the bowels of the earth, and dragged from the light of life into the darkness of the underground—where Orpheus in his despair followed, having bound his eyes against a dark that no man can imagine. And there he sang so beautifully and gave such light to the darkness, that the very ghosts shed tears, the wheel upon which Ixion whirled in terror stilled; and the demons of the night relented,

and said that Eurydice might return with her husband to the
world of light, upon the condition that Orpheus remain blind-
folded and not look back upon the wife who followed him. . . .

"The legend does not tell us why Orpheus broke the vow; it
tells us only that he did, that he saw where he had been, and saw
Eurydice drawn back into the earth, and saw the earth close
around her so that he could not follow. And legend tells of how
thereafter Orpheus sang his sorrow, and how the maidens who
had lived in light only and could not imagine where he had been,
came to him and offered themselves to beguile him from his
knowledge; and how he refused them, and how in their anger
then they shouted down his song, so that its magic could not stay
them, and in their mania tore his body apart, and cast it in the
River Hebrus, where his severed head continued to sing its word-
less song; and the very shores parted and widened so that the
singing head might be borne in safety out to the landless sea. . . .
This is the story of the Greek Orpheus which Vergil has told us,
and to which we have listened."

A silence had come upon the room; Horace dipped his cup
into the jar of wine and drank again.

"The gods in their wisdom," he said, "tell us all of our lives, if
we will but listen. I speak to you now of another Orpheus—
not the son of a god and goddess, but an Italian Orpheus whose
father was a slave, and whose mother had no name. Some, no
doubt, would scoff at such an Orpheus; but they would scoff
who have forgotten that all Romans are descended from a god,
and bear the name of his son; and from a mortal woman, and
wear her humanity. Thus even a dwarf who wears upon his head a
thatch of hay may have been touched by a god, if he springs
from the earth that Mars loved. . . . This Orpheus of whom I
speak received no golden lyre, but only a poor torch from a
humble father who would have given his life that his son might
be worthy of his dream. Thus was this young Orpheus in his
childhood shown the light of Rome, equally with the sons of the
rich and mighty; and in his young manhood, at the cost of his father's substance was shown too the source of what was said to be
the light of all mankind that came from the mother city of all
knowledge, Athens. Thus his love was no woman; his Eurydice
was knowledge, a dream of the world, to which he sang his song.

But the world of light that was his dream of knowledge became eclipsed by a civil war; and forsaking the light, this young Orpheus went into the darkness to retrieve his dream; and at Philippi, almost forgetting his song, he fought against one whom he thought to represent the powers of darkness. And then the gods, or the demons—he knows not which, even now—granted him the gift of cowardice, and bade him flee the field with the power of his dream and knowledge intact, and bade him not to look back upon what he fled. But like the other Orpheus, just as he was safely escaped, he did look back; and his dream vanished, as if a vapor, into the darkness of time and circumstance. He saw the world, and knew he was alone—without father, without property, without hope, without dreams. . . . It was only then that the gods gave to him their golden lyre, and bade him play not as they but as he wished. The gods are wise in their cruelty; for now he sings, who would not have sung before. No Thracian maidens blandish him, nor offer him their charms; he makes do with the honest whore, and for a fair price. It is the dogs of the world that yap at him as he sings, trying to drown his voice. They grow in number as more he sings; and no doubt he, too, will suffer to have his limbs torn from his body, even though he sing against the yapping, and sing as he is carried to that sea of oblivion which will receive us all. . . . Thus, my masters and my betters, I have told you a tedious story of a local Orpheus; and I wish you well with his remains."

My dear Vergil, I cannot tell you how long the silence lasted; and I cannot tell you the source of that silence, whether it was shock or fear, or whether all (like myself) had been entranced as if by a true Orphic lyre. The torches, burning low, flickered; and for a moment I had the odd feeling that we all, had, indeed, been in that underground of which Horace had been speaking, and were emerging from it, and dared not look back. Mevius stirred, and whispered fiercely, knowing that he would be heard by whom he intended:

"Philippi," he said. "Power of darkness, indeed! Is this not treason against the triumvir? Is this not treason?"

Octavius had not moved during Horace's recital. He raised himself on his couch and sat beside Livia. "Treason?" he said gently. "It is not treason, Mevius. You will not speak so again in

my presence." He rose from his couch and crossed over to where Horace sat. "Horace, will you permit me to join you?" he asked.
Our young friend nodded dumbly. Octavius sat beside him, and they spoke quietly. Mevius said no more that night.

Thus, my dear Vergil, did our Horace, who has already endeared himself to us, find the friendship of Octavius Caesar. All in all, it was a successful evening.

IV. Letter: Mevius to Furius Bibaculus,
from Rome (January, 38 B.C.)

My dear Furius, I really have not the heart to write you at any length about that disastrous evening at the home of Claudius Nero last September, the only pleasant aspect of which was the absence of our "friend" Vergil. But perhaps it is just as well; for certain events have transpired since that evening that make the whole affair even more ludicrous than it seemed then.

I don't really remember all who were there—Octavius, of course, and those odd friends of his: the Etruscan Maecenas, bejeweled and perfumed, and Agrippa, smelling of sweat and leather. It was ostensibly a literary evening, but my dear, to what low state have our letters fallen! Beside these, even that whining little fraud, Catullus, would have seemed almost a poet. There was Pollio, the pompous ass, to whom one must be pleasant because of his wealth and political power, and to whose works one must listen endlessly if one is foolish enough to attend his parties, stifling laughter at his tragedies and feigning emotion at his verses; Maecenas again, who writes lugubrious poems in a Latin that seems almost like a foreign tongue; Macer, who has discovered a Tenth Muse, that of Dullness; and that extraordinary little upstart, Horace, whom, you will be happy to hear, I rather effectively disposed of during the course of the evening. Garrulous politicians, luxuriant magpies, and illiterate peasants deface the garden of the Muses. It's a wonder that you and I can find the courage to persist!

But the social intrigues that evening were a good deal more interesting than the literary ones, and it is about that which I really want to write you.

We all have heard of Octavius's proclivities toward women. I really had not given the reports so much credence before that evening—he is such a pallid little fellow that one might think a glass of unmixed wine and a fervent embrace would send him lifeless to join his ancestors (whoever *they* might be)—but now I begin to suspect that there may be truth in them.

The wife of our host was one Livia, of an old and conservative Republican family (I have heard that her own father was slain by the Octavian army at Philippi). An extraordinarily beautiful girl, if you like the type—a modest and proper figure, blonde, perfectly regular features, rather thin lips, softly spoken, and so forth; very much the "patrician ideal," as they say. She is quite young—perhaps eighteen—yet she has already given her husband, who must be thrice her age, one son; and she was again rather visibly pregnant.

I must say, we all *had* had a great deal to drink; nevertheless, Octavius's conduct was really extraordinary. He mooned over her like a love-sick Catullus, stroking her hand, whispering in her ear, laughing like a boy (though of course he is really little more, despite the importance he has assigned to himself), all manner of nonsense; and all this wholly in view of his own wife (not that *that* really mattered, though she too is pregnant), and of Livia's husband, who seemed either not to notice or to smile benignly, like an ambitious father rather than a husband whose honor ought to have been offended. At any rate, at the time I thought little of it; I considered it rather vulgar behavior, but what (I asked myself) might one expect from the grandson of an ordinary small-town moneylender. If having filled one cart he wanted to ride in another that was full too, that was his business.

But now, four months after that evening, such an extraordinary scandal is buzzing over Rome that I am sure you would not forgive me if I failed to inform you of it.

Less than two weeks ago, his erstwhile wife, Scribonia, gave birth to a girl child—though it would seem that even the *adoptive* son of a god should have been able to manage a boy. On the same day of the birth, Octavius delivered to Scribonia a letter of divorce—which in itself was not surprising, the whole affair having been negotiated in advance, it is said.

But—and here is the scandal—in the week following, Tiberius Claudius Nero gave Livia a divorce; and the next day gave her (though pregnant still). and with a substantial dowry, to Octavius as wife; the whole affair was sanctioned by the Senate, priests made sacrifices, the whole foolish business.

How *can* anyone take such a man seriously? And yet they do.

V. *The Journal of Julia,* Pandateria (*A.D. 4*)

The circumstances of my birth were known to all the world long before they were known to me; and when at last I had the age to comprehend them, my father was the ruler of the world, and a god; and the world has long understood that the behavior of a god, however odd to mortals, is natural to himself, and comes at last to seem inevitable to those who must worship him.

Thus it was not strange to me that Livia should be my mother, and Scribonia merely an infrequent visitor to my home—a distant but necessary relative whom everyone endured out of an obscure sense of obligation. My memories of that time are dim, and I do not fully trust them; but it seems to me now that those years were ordinarily pleasant. Livia was firm, majestic, and coldly affectionate; it was what I grew to expect.

Unlike most men of his station, my father insisted that I be brought up in the old way, in his own household, in the care of Livia rather than a nurse; that I learn the ways of the household —to weave and sew and cook—in the ancient manner; and yet that I be educated in the degree that would befit the daughter of an Emperor. So in my early years I wove with the slaves of the household, and I learned my letters, Latin and Greek, from my father's slave Phaedrus; and later I studied at wisdom under his old friend and tutor Athenodorus. Though I did not know it at the time, the most significant circumstance of my life was the fact that my father had no other children of his own. It was a fault of the Julian line.

Though I must have seen him seldom in those years, his presence was the strongest of any in my life. I learned my geography from his letters, which were read to me daily; they were sent in packets from wherever he had to be—in Gaul, or Sicily, or Spain; Dalmatia, Greece, Asia, or Egypt.

As I said, I must have seen him seldom; yet even now it seems that he was always there. I can close my eyes, and almost feel myself thrown into the air, and hear the ecstatic laughter of a child's safe terror, and feel the hands catch me from the nothingness into which I had been tossed. I can hear the deep voice, comforting and warm; I can feel the caresses upon my head; I can remember the games of handball and pebbles; and I can feel my legs strain up the little hills in the garden behind our house on the Palatine, as we walked to a point where we could see the city spread out like a gigantic toy beneath us. Yet I cannot remember the face, then. He called me Rome, his "Little Rome."

My first clear visual memory of my father came when I was nine years old; it was in his fifth consulship, and upon the occasion of his triple triumph for his victories in Dalmatia, Actium, and Egypt.

Since that time, there have been no such celebrations of military exploits in Rome; later my father explained to me that he had thought even the one in which he took part was vulgar and barbaric, but that it was politically necessary at the time. Thus, I do not now know whether the grandeur I saw then has been enhanced by its uniquity and its subsequent absence, or whether it was the true grandeur of my memory.

I had not seen my father for more than a year, and he had no chance to visit Rome before the ceremonial march into the city. It was arranged that Livia and I and the other children of the household should meet him at the city gates, where we were escorted by the senatorial procession and placed in chairs of honor to await his coming. It was a game to me; Livia had told me that we were going to be in a parade, and that I must remain calm. But I could not restrain myself from jumping from my chair, and straining my eyes to find the approach of my father down the winding road. And when at last I saw him, I laughed and clapped my hands, and would have run toward him; but I was restrained by Livia. And when he came near enough to recognize us, he spurred his horse ahead of the soldiers he was leading, and caught me in his arms, laughing, and then embraced Livia; and he was my father. It was, perhaps, the last time that I was able to think of him as if he were a father like any other.

For quickly he was moved away by the praetors of the Senate, who fastened about him a cloak of purple and gold and led him into the turreted chariot, and led Livia and me to stand beside him there; and the slow procession toward the Forum began. I remember my fear and disappointment; my father beside me, though he steadied me gently with his hand upon my shoulder, was a stranger. The horns and trumpets at the head of the procession sounded their battle calls; the lictors with their laureled axes moved slowly ahead; and we went into the city. The people crowded the squares where we passed and shouted so loudly that even the sound of the horns was muted; and the Forum where we halted at last swarmed with Romans, so that not a stone upon the ground could be seen.

For three days the ceremonies lasted. I spoke to my father when I could; and though Livia and I were at his side nearly all the time, during his speeches and the sacrifices and the presentations, I felt him drawn away from me into the world that I was beginning to see for the first time.

Yet he was gentle toward me all the time, and answered me when I spoke as if I mattered to him as much as I ever had. I remember once I saw drawn in one of the processions, on a cart gleaming with gold and bronze, the carven figure of a woman, larger than life, upon a couch of ebony and ivory, with two children lying on either side of her; their eyes were closed, as if in sleep. I asked my father who the lady was supposed to be, and he looked at me a long time before he answered.

"That was Cleopatra," he said. "She was Queen of a great country. She was an enemy to Rome; but she was a brave woman, and she loved her country as much as any Roman might love his; she gave her life so that she might not have to look upon its defeat."

Even now, after all these years, I remember the strange feeling that came over me upon hearing that name in those circumstances. It was, of course, a familiar name; I had heard it often before. I thought then of my Aunt Octavia, who in fact shared the responsibility of the household with Livia, and whom I knew had once been married to this dead Queen's husband, that Marcus Antonius who was also dead. And I thought of the children for whom Octavia cared and with whom I daily played and worked and studied: Marcellus and his two sisters, the fruit of her first marriage; the two Antonias who were the issue of her marriage to Marcus Antonius; Jullus, who was the son of Marcus Antonius by an earlier marriage; and at last of that little girl who was the new pet of the household, the little Cleopatra, daughter of Marcus Antonius and his Queen.

But it was not the strangeness of that knowledge that caused my heart to come up in my throat. Though I did not have the words to say it then, I believe it occurred to me for the first time that even a woman might be caught up in the world of events, and be destroyed by that world.

2

To her husband, Livia sends greetings and prayers for his safety;
and according to his instructions, an account of those matters for
which he has evidenced concern.

The works which you set into motion before your departure
northward proceed as you ordered. The repairs upon the Via
Flaminia are completed, two weeks before the scheduled date that
you gave to Marcus Agrippa, who will send you a full accounting of the work in the next packet of mail. Both Maecenas and
Agrippa, who confer with me daily, ask me to assure you that
the census will be completed before your return; and Maecenas
projects that the increase in revenue from this revised tax base
will be even more considerable than he had anticipated.

Maecenas also has asked me to convey to you his pleasure in
your decision not to invade Britain; he is confident that negotiation will accomplish as much; and even if the negotiation does
not, the possible cost of the conquest would outweigh the recovery of the defaulted tribute. I, too, am happy at your decision;
but for the more affectionate reason of regard for your safety.

I slight these reports, knowing that you will get fuller accounts
from those who have the details more firmly in hand, and know-

ing that your interest in hearing from me lies elsewhere. Your daughter is in good health, and she sends you her love. Yes: your letters are read to her daily, and she speaks of you often.

You will be pleased to learn that the last week has seen a decided improvement in her behavior toward the household servants; I am sure that your letter upon the subject had a great effect. This morning she spent nearly two hours at the spinning wheel, and not once did she complain or speak disrespectfully to any who worked with her. She is at last, I believe, beginning to accustom herself to the notion that she may be both a woman and the daughter of an Emperor. Her health is excellent; and she will have grown so that upon your return, you may hardly know her.

The account of that other part of her education, upon which you have insisted and to which with some reluctance I have acquiesced, I shall leave to others, whose reports you will find included in these packets.

There is a bit of gossip that will both please and amuse you. Maecenas has asked me to convey to you the information that he is at last acceding to your wishes and taking a wife; he asked me to give you the news because (he said) the subject was too painful for him to broach himself. As you might expect, he is making a great show of his misery; but I think he is rather enjoying the idea. His wife to be is one Terentia, of a family of no particular importance; Maecenas sniffs, and says that he has nobility enough for them both. She is a pretty little thing, and seems content with the marriage; it appears that she perfectly understands Maecenas's propensities, and is willing to accept them. I believe that she will please you.

Your sister sends you her affectionate greetings, and asks you to give the same to her Marcellus, whom she trusts has been a pleasant companion to his uncle. And I send you my love, and ask you to give to my Tiberius the same. Your family in Rome awaits your return.

Gaius Octavius Caesar, at Narbonne in Gaul, from his servant and devoted friend, Phaedrus. I address you Gaius, for I speak on a household matter.

Your daughter Julia is fast approaching that point in her education at which I can no longer adequately perform as you would wish. I say this with reluctance, for you know my fatherly fondness of her. You have proved me wrong. I doubted that any girl might progress in her studies as rapidly and as ably as might a boy of the same station, equally capable of diligence and understanding. Indeed, of the many of your relatives' children of like age whom you have been kind enough to put under my tutelage, both boys and girls, she has made the most rapid progress, so that even at the age of eleven, she is rapidly approaching the point at which she should be put in another's care. She composes easily in Greek; she has mastered those more fundamental elements of rhetoric which I have exposed her to, though my teaching her such an unladylike subject has occasioned a minor scandal among her fellow pupils; and your friend Horace intermittently aids her with that poetry in his own tongue, a literature of which my command is adequate but not sufficient for your daughter. I gather that the more feminine parts of her curriculum are not so much to her liking—her musicianship is barely adequate, and though she has a natural physical grace, she does not really take to the more formal elements of her dancing lessons; but I also gather that such fashionable accomplishments lie outside your own interest as well. Were I so foolish to think that you might be pleased by flattery, I should pretend no surprise and affect some such nonsense as expecting so much from the daughter of the son of a god, Emperor of all the world, and so forth. But we both know that her character is her own, and that it is a strong one.

I propose, therefore, that in the near future her education be turned over to one more wise and learned than myself, that Athenodorus who was once your own teacher and who is now your friend. He knows her mind, they get on well, and he has consented to the task which I have had the presumption to suggest. I understand that he is to write you regarding another matter, and that in that letter he will also give you his thoughts upon this.

I trust that your journey in Gaul will not keep you away from your daughter longer than is necessary. The only serious distraction in her studies with me is her longing for your presence. I am, Gaius, your faithful servant and, I trust, your friend, Phaedrus of Corinth.

Athenodorus to Octavius, greetings. As you knew I would, I applaud your decision to establish a system of schools in Gaul. You are quite right; if the people there are to become a part of Rome, they must have the Roman tongue, whereby they may know that history and that culture in which they are to thrive. I would to the gods that the fashionable riffraff here in Rome, some of whom you are pleased to call your friends, had so much concern for the education of their own children as you have for your subjects in distant lands. It may be that those in other lands shall become more Roman than we who remain in the heart of our country.

There will be no difficulty in finding teachers to staff the schools; I shall, if you wish, make specific recommendations. Since you have brought peace and some measure of prosperity to our nation, learning has begun to flourish among those classes from whom you must draw your teachers, though perhaps flourish is too strong a word. In general, I would suggest: (1) that you not depend upon the easy idealism of the well-to-do young, whose enthusiasm is almost certain to disappear in the isolation of the provinces; (2) that so far as possible you choose your teachers from native stock and not depend upon the Greeks or Egyptians or whatever, since their students must at least know what a Roman looks like if he is to really apprehend Roman culture; and (3) that you *not* depend upon slaves or even too heavily upon freedmen to fill those pedagogic ranks of which you speak. I think you must understand my reasons for this advice. I know that it has been the tradition in Rome to raise even a slave above a gentleman, if he is learned enough. In Rome he is content to remain a slave, if he can become rich; but in Gaul there will not be the opportunity for the kind of fiscal corruption that he can find in Rome, and he will be discontented. You know yourself that many slaves, especially the learned and rich (our friend Phaedrus excepted, of course), are contemptuous of Rome and its ways, and resentful even of that condition out of which they have not chosen to purchase themselves. In short, in Gaul there will not be the complex of forces that operate here to subject them to some kind of order. I assure you that there are sufficient Italians, from both the countryside and the city, who for a decent wage and some honor, would be happy to fulfill your purposes.

As for the matter of your daughter: Phaedrus has spoken to me, and I have consented. I assume that you will approve. I have now educated so many of the Octavian clan that it would seem inappropriate to me for you to look elsewhere. You may call yourself Emperor of the world; that is not my concern. In this matter, I insist that I remain your master; and I should not like to see the final education of Julia in the hands of anyone other than myself.

II. *The Journal of Julia*, Pandateria (*A.D. 4*)

For the past several years, since shortly after my arrival upon this island of Pandateria, it has been my habit to arise before dawn and to observe the first glimmer of light in the east. It has become nearly a ritual, this early vigil; I sit without moving at an eastern window, and measure the light as it grows from gray to yellow to orange and red, and becomes at last no color but an unimaginable illumination upon the world. After the light has filled my room, I spend the morning hours reading one or another of those books from the library that I was allowed to bring with me here from Rome. The indulgence of my library was one of the few allowed me; yet of all that might have been, it is the one that has made this exile the most nearly endurable. For I have returned to that learning which I abandoned many years ago, and it is likely that I should not have done so had not I been condemned to this loneliness; I sometimes can almost believe that the world in seeking to punish me has done me a service it cannot imagine.

It has occurred to me that this early vigil and this study is a regimen that I became used to many years ago, when I was little more than a child.

When I was twelve years old, my father decided that it was time for me to forgo my childhood studies, and put myself in the care of his old teacher, Athenodorus. Before that, I had, in addition to the kind of education imposed upon my sex by Livia, merely been exercised in the reading and composition of Greek and Latin, which I found remarkably easy, and in arithmetic, which I found easy but dull. It was a leisurely kind of learning, and my tutor was at my disposal at any hour of the day, with no very rigid schedule that I had to follow.

But Athenodorus, who gave me my first vision of a world outside myself, my family, and even of Rome, was a stern and unrelenting master. His students were few—the sons of Octavia, both adopted and natural; Livia's sons, Drusus and Tiberius; and the sons of various relatives of my father. I was the only girl among them, and I was the youngest. It was made clear to all of us by my father that Athenodorus was the master; and despite whatever name and power the parents of his students might have, Athenodorus's word in all matters was final, and that there was no recourse beyond him.

We were made to arise before dawn and to assemble at the first hour at Athenodorus's home, where we recited the lines from Homer or Hesiod or Aeschylus that we had been assigned the day before; we attempted compositions of our own in the styles of those poets; and at noon we had a light lunch. In the afternoon, the boys devoted themselves to exercises in rhetoric and declamation, and to the study of law; such subjects being deemed inappropriate for me, I was allowed to use my time other-wise, in the study of philosophy, and in the elucidation of what-ever poems, Latin or Greek, that I chose, and in composition upon whatever matters struck my fancy. Late in the afternoon, I was allowed to return to my home, so that I might perform my household duties under the tutelage of Livia. It was a release that became increasingly irksome to me.

For as within my body there had begun to work the changes that led me to womanhood, there began to work also in my mind the beginnings of a vision that I had not suspected before. Later, when we became friends, Athenodorus and I used to talk about the Roman distaste for any learning that did not lead to a prac-tical end; and he told me that once, more than a hundred years before my birth, all teachers of literature and philosophy were, by a decree of the Senate, expelled from Rome, though it was a decree that could not be enforced.

It seems to me that I was happy, then, perhaps as happy as I have been in my life; but within three years that life was over, and it became necessary for me to become a woman. It was an exile from a world that I had just begun to see.

*III. Letter: Quintus Horatius Flaccus
to Albius Tibullus (25 B.C.)*

My dear Tibullus, you are a good poet and my friend, but you are a fool.

I will say it as plainly as possible: you are *not* to write a poem celebrating the marriage of young Marcellus and the Emperor's daughter. You have asked me for my advice, I have given it as strongly as I might give a command, and for the several reasons that I shall proceed to enumerate.

First: Octavius Caesar has made it clear, even to me and Vergil, who are among his closest friends, that he would be most unhappy if we ever alluded, directly or indirectly, to the personal affairs of any member of his family in one of our own poems. It is a principle upon which he stands firm, and it is a principle which I understand. Despite your hints to the contrary, he is deeply attached both to his wife and his daughter; he does not wish to condemn the bad poem which offers them praise, nor does he wish to praise the good poem which might offer them offense. Moreover, his life with his family is nearly his only respite from the burdensome and difficult task he has in attempting to run this chaotic world that he has inherited. He does not wish that respite endangered.

Second: your natural talent does not lie in the direction that you describe, and you are unlikely to write a good poem upon this subject. I have admired your poems upon your lady friends; I have not admired your poems upon your friend and commander in chief, Messalla. To write an indifferent poem upon a dangerous topic is to choose to behave foolishly.

And third: even if you were able to somehow turn the natural bent of your talent in another direction, the few attitudes you hint at in your letter convince me that you had better not try what you propose. For no man may write a good poem the worth of whose subject he doubts; and no poet can will away his misgivings. I say this not in recrimination of your uncertainties, my friend; I say it merely as a fact. Were I to engage myself in the composition of such a poem as you propose, I might discover that I had the same ones.

And yet I believe that I would not. You hint that you suspect a coldness in the Emperor's feelings toward his daughter, and that in the marriage he is "using" her for purposes of state. The latter may be true; the former is not.

I have known Octavius Caesar for more than ten years; he is my friend, and we are on truly equal terms. As any friend might do, I have praised him when in my judgment he deserved praise, I have doubted him when I judged he merited doubt, and I have criticized him when I believed that he deserved criticism. I have done these publicly, and with utter freedom. Our friendship has not suffered.

Thus, when I speak to you now of this matter, you will understand that I speak as freely as I ever have, and as I ever will.

Octavius Caesar loves his daughter more than you understand; if he has a fault, it is that his feeling for her is too deep. He has overseen her education with more care than many a less busy father has given to that of a son; nor has he been content to limit her learning to the weaving and sewing and singing and lute-playing and the usual smattering of letters that most women get in school. Julia's Greek is now better than her father's; her knowledge of literature is impressive; and she has studied both rhetoric and philosophy with Athenodorus, a man whose wisdom and learning could augment even our own, my dear Tibullus.

During these years when he so often has had to be absent from Rome, not a week has gone by that his daughter has not received in the mail a packet of letters from her father; I have seen some of them, and they display a concern and kindness that is indeed touching.

And upon those welcome occasions when his duties allowed him the freedom of his family and his home, he spent what might seem to some an inordinate amount of time with his daughter, behaving with the utmost simplicity and joy in her presence. I have seen him roll hoops with her as if he, too, were a child, and let her ride upon his shoulders as if he were a horse, and play blind-man's buff; I have seen them fish together from the banks of the Tiber, laughing in delight when their hooks snagged a tiny sun-fish; and I have seen them walk in perfect companionship in the fields beyond their home, picking wild flowers for the dinner table.

But if you have doubts in that part of your soul which is the poet's, I know that I cannot allay them, though I might erase them from that part of your mind that is a man's. You know that if another father chose for his daughter a husband as rich and promising as young Marcellus, you would applaud his foresight and his concern. You know, too, that the "youth" of Julia in this matter would, in another instance, be cause for another kind of concern. How old was that lady (whom you have chosen to disguise as Delia) when first *you* began your campaign against her virtue? Sixteen? Seventeen? Younger?

No, my dear Tibullus, you are well advised not to write this poem. There are many other subjects, and many other places to find them. If you wish to retain the admiration of your Emperor, stick to those poems about your Delias, which you do so well. I assure you that Octavius reads them and admires them; hard as it may be for you to believe, when he reads a poem he admires good writing more than praise.

IV. *The Journal of Julia*, Pandateria (*A.D. 4*)

In my life, I had three husbands, none of whom I loved. . . .

Yesterday morning, not knowing what I wished to say, I wrote those words; and I have been pondering what they might mean. I do not know what they mean. I only know that the question occurred to me late in my life, at a time when it no longer mattered.

The poets say that youth is the day of the fevered blood, the hour of love, the moment of passion; and that with age come the cooling baths of wisdom, whereby the fever is cured. The poets are wrong. I did not know love until late in my life, when I could no longer grasp it. Youth is ignorant, and its passion is abstract.

I was betrothed first when I was fourteen years of age to my cousin, Marcellus, who was the son of my father's sister Octavia. It was perhaps a measure of my ignorance, and the ignorance of all women, that such a marriage seemed to me perfectly ordinary at the time. Ever since I could remember, Marcellus had been a familiar part of our household, along with the other children of Octavia and Livia; I had grown up with him, but I did not know him. Now, after nearly thirty years, I have hardly a memory of what he was like or even of his physical appearance. He was tall, I believe, and blond in the Octavian way.

But I remember the letter my father sent informing me of the betrothal. I remember the tone of it. It was almost as if he were writing to a stranger; his tone was pompous and stiff, and that was unlike him. He wrote from Spain, where for nearly a year he had been engaged in putting down the border insurrections, a mission upon which Marcellus, though only seventeen years of age, had accompanied him. Persuaded (he said) by Marcellus's fortitude and loyalty, and concerned that his daughter be placed in the care of one whose worth was beyond dispute, he had determined that this marriage was in the best interests of myself and of our family. He wished me happiness, regretted that he would not be in Rome to take his proper part in the ceremony, and said that he was asking his friend Marcus Agrippa to take his place; and told me that Livia would inform me further upon what was expected of me.

At the age of fourteen, I believed myself to be a woman; I had been taught to believe so. I had studied with Athenodorus; I was the daughter of an Emperor; and I was to be married. I believe I behaved in a most urbane and languid fashion, until the urbanity and languidness became almost real; I had no apprehension of the world that I was beginning to enter.

And Marcellus remained a stranger. He returned from Spain, and we spoke distantly, as we always had done. The arrangements for the wedding proceeded as if neither of us was involved in our fates. I know now, of course, that we were not.

It was a ceremony in the old fashion. Marcellus gave me a gift, before witnesses, of an ivory box inlaid with pearls from Spain, and I received it with the ritual words; the night before the wedding, in the presence of Livia and Octavia and Marcus Agrippa, I bade farewell to the toys of my childhood, and gave those that would burn to the household gods; and late that night Livia, acting as my mother, braided my hair into the six plaits that signified my womanhood, and fastened them with the bands of white wool.

I went through the ceremony as if through a dream. The guests and relatives gathered in the courtyard; the priests said the things that priests say; the documents were signed, witnessed, and exchanged; and I spoke the words that bound me to my husband. And in the evening, after the banquet, Livia and Octavia, according to ceremony, dressed me in the bridal tunic and led me to Marcellus's chamber. I do not know what I expected.

Marcellus sat upon the edge of the bed, yawning; the bridal flowers were strewn carelessly upon the floor.

"It is late," Marcellus said, and added in the voice he had used toward me as a child; "get to bed."

I lay beside him; I imagine I must have been trembling. He yawned once more, turned upon his side away from me, and in a few moments was asleep.

Thus did my wifehood begin; and it did not change substantially during the two years of my marriage to Marcellus. As I wrote earlier, I hardly remember him now; there is little reason why I should.

V. Letter: Livia to Octavius Caesar in Spain (25 B.C.)

To her husband, Livia sends affectionate greetings. I have followed your instructions; your daughter is married; she is well. I hasten over this bare information so that I might write of the matter that is of more immediate concern to me: the state of your health. For I have heard (do not ask the source of my information) that it is more precarious than you have let me know; and thus I begin to apprehend the urgency you have felt in seeing your daughter safely married, and am therefore more ashamed than I might have been of my opposition to the marriage, and I sorrow at the unhappiness that that opposition must have caused you. Please be assured now that my resentment is gone, and that at last my pride in our marriage and our duty has laid to rest my maternal ambitions for my own son. You are right; Marcellus carries the name of the Claudian, the Julian, and the Octavian tribes, whereas my Tiberius carries the name only of the Claudian. Your decision is, as usual, the intelligent one. I forget sometimes that our authority is more precarious than it seems.

I implore you to return from Spain. It is clear that the climate there encourages those fevers to which you are subject, and that in such a barbaric place you cannot receive proper care. In this your physician agrees with me, and adds his professional supplication to my affectionate one.

Marcellus returns to you within the week. Octavia sends her love, and asks that you guard the safety of her son; your wife also sends her love, and her prayers for your recovery, and for the well-being of her son Tiberius. Please return to Rome.

VI. Letter: Quintus Horatius Flaccus to Publius Vergilius Maro, at Naples (23 B.C.)

My dear Vergil, I urge you to come to Rome with all possible speed. Ever since his return from Spain, our friend's health has declined; and now his condition is exceedingly grave. The fever is constant; he cannot rise from his bed; and his body has shrunken so that his skin seems like cloth upon frail sticks. Though we all put on cheerful countenances, we have come to despair of his life. We do not deceive him; he, too, feels that his life draws to a close; he has given to his co-consul his records of the army and of revenue, and has given to Marcus Agrippa his seal, so that there might be an adequate succession of his authority. Only his physician, his intimate friends, and his immediate family are allowed in his presence. A great calm has come upon him; it is as if he wishes to savor for the last time all that he has held dearest to his heart.

Both Maecenas and I have been staying here at his private house on the Palatine, so that we might be near him when he wishes aid or comfort. Livia attends him meticulously and with the dutifulness that he so admires in her; Julia laughs and teases him, as he so enjoys, when she is in his presence, and weeps most pitifully when she is out of his sight; he and Maecenas speak fondly of the days of their youth; and Agrippa, strong as he is, can hardly keep his composure when he speaks to him.

Though he would not impose himself and though he does not say so, I know that he wants you here. Sometimes, when he is too weary to converse with his family, he asks me to read to him some of those poems of ours that he has most admired; and yesterday he recalled that happy and triumphant autumn, only a few years ago, when he returned from Samos, after the defeat of the Egyptian armies, and we were all together, and you read to him the completed *Georgics.* And he said to me, quite calmly and without pity of self: "If I should die, one of the things that I shall most regret is not having been able to attend the completion of our old friend's poem upon the founding of our city. Do you think it would please him to know this?"

Though I was hardly able to speak, I said, "I am sure it would, my friend."

He said, "Then you must tell him so when you see him."

"I shall tell him when you have recovered," I said.

He smiled. I could not endure it longer. I made some apology, and went from his room.

As you can see, the time may be short. He is in no pain; he retains his faculties; but his will is dying with his body.

Within the week, if his condition does not improve, his physician (one Antonius Musa, whose abilities, despite his fame, I do not trust) is prepared to put into effect a final and drastic remedy. I urge you to attend him before that desperation is performed.

VII. Medical Directive of Antonius Musa, the Physician, to His Assistants (23 B.C.)

The Preparation of the Baths. Three hundred pounds of ice, to be delivered to the residence of the Emperor Octavius Caesar, at the designated hour. This may be obtained from the storehouse of Asinius Pollio on the Via Campana. The ice is to be broken into pieces of the size of a tightly closed fist, and only those pieces that can be seen to be free of sediment are to be used. Twenty-five of these pieces are to be put into the bath, which will contain water to the depth of eight inches, where they shall be let to remain until all are melted.

The Preparation of the Ointment. One pint of my own powder, to which has been added two spoonfuls of finely ground mustard seed; which mixture is to be added to two quarts of the finest olive oil, which is to be heated just below the point of boiling, and then allowed to cool to the exact degree of body warmth.

The Treatment of the Patient. The patient is to be immersed fully, with the water covering every part of his body except the head, into the cold bath, where he is to remain for the length of time required to count slowly to one hundred. He is then to be removed and wrapped in the undyed blankets of wool, which have been heated over hot stones. He is to remain wrapped until he sweats freely, at which point the entirety of his body is to be anointed with the prepared oil. He is then to be returned to the cold bath, to which has been added sufficient ice to return it to its original coldness.

This treatment is to be repeated four times; then the patient will be allowed to rest for two hours. This routine of treatment shall be continued until the patient's fever subsides.

VIII. The Journal of Julia, Pandateria (A.D. 4)

When my father returned home from Spain, I knew at once the reason for my marriage. He had not expected to survive even the journey to his family, so grave had been his illness in Spain; to insure my future, he gave me to Marcellus; and to insure the future of what he often called his "other daughter," he gave Rome to Marcus Agrippa. My marriage to Marcellus was largely a ritual affair; technically I became nonvirginal; but I was hardly touched by the union and I remained a girl, or nearly so. It was during the illness of my father that I became a woman, for I saw the inevitability of death and knew its smell and felt its presence.

I remember that I wept, knowing that my father would die, whom I had known only as a child; and I came to know that loss was the condition of our living. It is a knowledge that one cannot give to another.

Yet I tried to give it to Marcellus, since he was my husband and I had been taught my proper behavior. He looked at me in bewilderment, and then said that however unfortunate, Rome would endure the loss, since our Emperor had had the foresight to leave his affairs in order. I was angry then, for I felt that my husband was cold and I knew that he thought himself to be the heir to my father's power, and foresaw the day when he too would be an Emperor; now I know that if he were cold and ambitious, it was the only way he knew; it was the life to which he had been reared.

My father's recovery from the illness that should have led to his death was regarded by the world as a miracle emanating from his divinity, and thus in the normal order of things. When the physician Antonius Musa at last performed his desperate treatment, which in later years came to bear his name, the arrangements for my father's funeral were already being made. Yet he survived the treatment, and slowly began to recover, so that by late summer he had regained some of his weight and was able to stroll for a few minutes each day in the garden behind our house. Marcus Agrippa returned the seal of the Sphinx that had been entrusted to him, and the Senate decreed a week of thanksgiving and prayer in Rome, and the people in the countryside all over Italy erected images of him on the crossroads, in celebration of his health and to protect travelers on their journeys.

When it was clear that my father would regain his health, my husband, Marcellus, fell ill with the same fever. For two weeks the fever worsened, and at last the physician Antonius Musa prescribed the same treatment that had saved my father. In another week, in the midst of the rejoicing over the recovery of the Emperor, Marcellus was dead; and I was a widow in my seventeenth year.

IX. Letter: Publius Vergilius Maro to Quintus Horatius Flaccus (22 B.C.)

The sister of our friend Octavius still grieves for her son; time does not bring her that gradual diminution of pain, which is time's only gift; and I fear that my poor efforts to give her heart some solace may have had an effect I did not intend.

Last week, Octavius, knowing that I had been moved to compose a poem upon the death of his nephew, urged me to come again to Rome so that he might hear what I had done; and when I informed him that the poem I had written I intended to incorporate in that long work upon Aeneas, the completed parts of which he has rather extravagantly admired, he suggested that it might give some comfort to his sister to know that her son was so admired by the Roman people that he would live in their memories for so long as they had them. Thus he invited her to be present at the reading, informing her of the nature of the occasion.

Only a few were present at Octavius's house—Octavius himself, of course, and Livia; his daughter Julia (it is difficult to think of one so young and beautiful as a widow); Maecenas and Terentia; and Octavia, who came into the room as if she were a walking corpse, dreadfully pale, with deep shadows under her eyes. Yet she seemed composed, as always, and behaved with graciousness and consideration to those who could comfort her.

We talked quietly for a while, remembering Marcellus; once or twice, Octavia almost smiled, as if charmed by a pleasant memory of her son. And then Octavius asked me to read to them what I had written.

You know the poem and its place in my book; I shall not repeat it. But whatever faults the poem may have in its present state, it was a moving occasion; for a moment we saw Marcellus walking once more among the living, vital in the memories of his friends and his countrymen.

When I finished, there was a quietness in the room, and then a gentle murmuring. I looked at Octavia, hoping that I might see in her face, beyond the sadness, some comfort in the knowledge of our concern and pride. But I saw no comfort there. What I saw I cannot truly describe; her eyes blazed darkly, as if they burned deep in her skull, and her lips were drawn in the awful semblance of a grin that bared her teeth. It was a look, it seemed to me, almost of pure hatred. Then she gave a high toneless little scream, swayed sideways, and fell upon her couch in a dead faint.

We rushed to her; Octavius massaged her hands; she gradually revived, and the ladies took her away.

"I am sorry," I said at last. "If I had known— I only intended her some comfort."

"Do not reproach yourself, my friend," Octavius said quietly. "Perhaps you have given her a comfort, after all—one that none of us can see. We cannot know at last the effects of what we do, whether for good or ill."

I have returned to Naples; tomorrow I shall resume my labors. But I am troubled by what I have done, and I cannot but fear for the future happiness of that great lady who has given so much to her country.

X. Letter: Octavia to Octavius Caesar, from Velletri (22 B.C.)

My dear brother, I arrived, safe but weary, in Velletri yesterday afternoon, and have been resting since. Below my window is the garden where we used to play as children. It is somewhat overgrown now, or at least it seems so to me; most of the shrubs have succumbed to the winter weather, the beeches need pruning, and one of the old chestnut trees has died. Nevertheless, it is pleasant to gaze upon this spot and recall those days when we were free from the cares and sorrows of the world, so many years ago.

I write you upon two matters: first, to extend my long overdue apologies for my behavior on that awful night when our friend Vergil read to us of my late son; and second, to make a request.

When next you have occasion to write or speak to Vergil, will you explicitly ask his forgiveness for me? I did not intend my action, and I would be regretful if he took it as an unkindness. He is a good and gentle man, and I would not have him believe that I thought otherwise.

But it is the request that I make to you with which I am more concerned.

I wish to have your permission to retire from that world of affairs in which I have lived for as long as I can remember, so that I may spend the years that remain to me in the quiet and solitude of the country.

All my life I have done the duty required of me by my family and my country. I have performed this duty willingly, even when it went against the inclinations of my person.

In my childhood and early youth, under the tutelage of our mother, I performed the duties of the household with willing pleasure; and after her death, I more fully performed them for you. When it became necessary to our cause to conciliate the enemies of Julius Caesar, I gave myself in marriage to Gaius Claudius Marcellus, and upon his death I became wife to Marcus Antonius. To the best of my abilities, I was a good wife to Marcus, while remaining your sister and dutiful to our family. After Marcus Antonius divorced me and cast his fortunes in the East, I raised the children of his other marriages as if they were my own, indeed, even that Jullus Antonius of whom you now are so fond; after his death, I took under my protection those children of his by Cleopatra that survived the war.

Both of your wives I have treated as my sisters, though the first was too ill-tempered to receive my kindness and the second too ambitious for herself to trust my duty to our common cause. And from my own body I have given five children to our family and to the future of Rome.

Now my first-born and only son, my Marcellus, is dead in your service; and the happiness of his sister, Marcella, my beloved second-born, is threatened by the necessity of your policy. Fifteen years ago—perhaps even ten years ago—I should have been proud that you had chosen one of my children to shape in the succession of your destiny. But now I believe that my pride is vain, and I do not persuade myself that the possession of fame and power is worth the price of it. My daughter is happy in her marriage to Marcus Agrippa; I believe she loves him; I trust that he is fond of her. The divorce that you propose between them will not make her unhappy because she shall have lost the power and prestige that have accreted to her by the marriage; she shall be unhappy because she shall have lost a man for whom she feels respect and affection.

You must understand me, my dear brother; I do not quarrel with your decision; you are right. It is both fitting and necessary that your successor be one with your daughter, either through marriage or parentage. And Marcus Agrippa is the most able man of all your friends and associates. He is my friend, as well as my son-in-law; despite whatever may happen I trust that he shall remain the former.

And thus without resentment let me ask that the permission that I must give for this divorce be the last public act that I shall have to commit. I grant the permission. Now I wish to remove myself from the household in Rome, and remain with my books here in Velletri for as long as I may. I do not renounce your love; I do not renounce my children; I do not renounce my friends.

But the feeling that I had that awful evening, when Vergil read to us of Marcellus, remains with me, and shall remain for as long as I live; it was as if suddenly, and for the first time, I truly saw that world in which you must live, and saw the world in which I had lived without seeing for so long. There are other ways and other worlds in which one might live, humbler and more obscure, perhaps—though what is that in the eyes of the indifferent gods?

I have not done so yet, but within a few years I shall have reached the age when it will no longer be seemly for me to marry again. Give me these few years; for I do not wish to marry, and I shall not regret not having done so, even when I am old. That which we call our world of marriage is, as you know, a world of necessary bondage; and I sometimes think that the meanest slave has had more freedom than we women have known. I wish to spend the remainder of my life here; I shall welcome my children and grandchildren to visit me. There may be a kind of wisdom somewhere in myself, or in my books, that I shall find in the quiet years that lie ahead.

3

Of all the women I have known, I have admired Livia the most. I was never fond of her, nor she of me; yet she behaved toward me always with honesty and civility; we got along well, despite the fact that my mere existence thwarted her ambitions, and despite the fact that she made no secret of her impersonal animosity toward me. Livia knew herself thoroughly, and had no illusions about her own nature; she was beautiful, and used her beauty without vanity; she was cold, and thus could feign warmth with utter success; she was ambitious, and employed her considerable intelligence exclusively to further her ambition's end. Had she been a man, I do not doubt that she would have been more ruthless than my father, and would have been troubled by fewer compunctions. Within her nature she was an altogether admirable woman.

Though I was only fourteen years of age at the time and could not understand the reason for it, I knew that Livia opposed my marriage to Marcellus, seeing it as a nearly absolute impediment to her son Tiberius's succession to power. And when Marcellus died so quickly after our marriage, she must have felt the possibility of her ambition urgently renewed. For even before the obligatory months of mourning had elapsed, Livia approached me. My father, having been offered the dictatorship of Italy in the wake of a famine, and having refused, had some weeks before prudently removed himself from Rome upon the pretext of business in Syria, so that he might not have further to exacerbate the frustrations of the Senate and the people by the presence of his refusal. It was a tactic that he employed often in his life.

As was her habit, Livia came at once to the point.

"Your time of mourning will be ended soon," she said.

"Yes," I replied.

"And you will be free to marry again."

"Yes."

"It is not appropriate that a young widow should remain long unmarried," she said. "It is not the custom."

I believe I did not reply. I must have thought even then that my widowhood was as much a matter of form as my marriage had been.

Livia continued. "Is your grief such that the prospect of marriage offends you?"

I remembered that I was my father's daughter. "I shall do my duty," I said.

Livia nodded as if she had expected the answer. "Of course," she said. "It is the way. . . . Did your father speak to you of this matter? Or has he written?"

"No," I said.

"I am sure that he has been considering it." She paused. "You must understand that I speak now for myself, not your father. But were he here, I would have his permission."

"Yes," I said.

"I have behaved toward you as if you were my daughter," Livia said. "Insofar as it has been possible, I have not acted against your interests."

I waited.

She said slowly, "Do you find my son at all to your liking?"

I still did not understand. "Your son?"

She made a little impatient gesture. "Tiberius, of course."

I did not find Tiberius to my liking, and I never had; I did not know why. Later I came to understand that it was because he discovered in all others those vices he would not recognize in himself. I said: "He has never been fond of me. He thinks me flighty and unstable."

"That is no matter, even if it is true," Livia said.

"And he is betrothed to Vipsania," I said. Vipsania was the daughter of Marcus Agrippa; and though younger than I, she was almost my friend.

"Nor does that matter," Livia said, still impatiently. "You understand such things."

"Yes," I said, and did not speak further. I did not know what to say.

"You know that your father is fond of you," Livia said. "Some have thought him too fond of you, but that is of no substance here. At issue is the fact, which you know, that he will listen to you more attentively than most fathers will listen to their daughters, and that he would hesitate to go against your wishes. Your wishes carry great weight with him. Therefore, if you find the idea of marriage to Tiberius not disagreeable to you, it would be appropriate for you to let your father know that."

I did not speak.

"On the other hand," Livia said, "if you find the idea wholly disagreeable, you would do me a service now to let me know. I have never dissembled with you."

My head was whirling. I did not know what to say. I said: "I must obey my father. I do not wish to displease you. I do not know."

Livia nodded. "I understand your position. I am grateful to you. I shall not trouble you more with this."

. . . Poor Livia. I believe that she thought then that everything was arranged, and that her will would prevail. But it did not, on that occasion. It was perhaps the bitterest blow of her life.

II. Letter: Livia to Octavius Caesar, at Samos (21 B.C.)

I have been in all things obedient to your will. I have been your wife, and faithful to my duty; I have been your friend, and faithful to your interests. So far as I can determine, I have failed you in only one regard, and I grant that that is an important one:

I have not been able to give you a son, or even a child. If that is a fault, it is one which is beyond my control; I have offered divorce, which, out of what I believed to be affection for my person, you have often refused. Now I cannot be sure of that affection, and I am bitterly troubled.

Though I had reasonable cause to believe that you should have thought my Tiberius to be more nearly your own son than was Marcellus, who was only your nephew, I forgave your choice upon the grounds of your illness and upon the grounds of your plea that Marcellus carried the blood of the Claudian, the Octavian, and the Julian lines, while Tiberius carried only the Claudian. I even forgave what I must see now as your insults to my son; if in the extreme youth in which you judged him he displayed what appeared to be some instability of character and excess of behavior, I might suggest that the character of a boy is not the character of a man.

But now your course is clear, and I cannot conceal from you my bitterness. You have refused my son, and thus you have refused a part of me. And you have given your daughter a father rather than a husband.

Marcus Agrippa is a good man, and I know that he has been your friend; I bear no ill will for his person. But he bears no name, and whatever virtues he may possess are merely his own. It may have been amusing to the world that a man with such a lack of breeding might hold so much power as a subordinate of the Emperor; it will not be amusing to the world that now he is the designated successor, and thus nearly equal to the Emperor himself.

I trust you understand that my position has become nearly impossible; all Rome expected that Tiberius should become betrothed to your daughter, and that in the normal course of affairs he should have had some part in your life. Now you have refused him that.

And you remain abroad upon the occasion of this marriage of your daughter, as you did upon the first—whether out of necessity or choice, I do not know. And I do not care.

I shall continue in my duty toward you. My house will remain your house, and open to you and your friends. We have been too close in our common endeavors for it to be otherwise. I shall, indeed, attempt to continue to remain your friend; I have not been false to you, in thought or word or deed; and I shall not be in the future. But you must know the distance that this has put between us; it is farther than even the Samos where you now sojourn. It shall remain so.

Your daughter is married to Marcus Agrippa, and has removed herself to his house; she is now mother to that Vipsania Agrippa, who once was her playmate. Your niece, Marcella, bereft of a husband, is with your sister at Velletri. Your daughter seems content with her marriage. I trust that you are the same.

III. Broadsheet: Timagenes of Athens (21 B.C.)

Now who is mightier in the house of Caesar—
the one whom all call Emperor and the August,
or that one who, by all custom, should have been
his loving helpmate, dutiful to both bed
and banquet hall? See now how ruler is ruled:
the torches flicker, the company is gay,
and laughter flows more quickly than wine. He speaks
to his Livia, and will not be heard by her;
he speaks again, and is frozen by a smile.
It is said that he refused her a bauble;
you'd think the *Tiber* was *agrip* in winter ice!

But, ruled or ruler, it is no great matter.
There, from a corner, some Lesbia gives a glance
that darkens the torches; bright Delias languish
on couches, their shoulders bare in the dim light;
but he disdains them all. For boldly there comes
to him the wife of a friend (who does not see,
his eyes being filled with the vision of a boy
dancing to the torchlight). Why not? he thinks,
this ruler of men. Of his time, Maecenas
has given freely; this other little thing
he never uses, surely he'd not begrudge.

IV. *Letter: Quintus Horatius Flaccus to Gaius Cilnius Maecenas,*
at Arezzo (*21 B.C.*)

The author of the libel is, indeed, as you suspected, that same Timagenes whom you have encouraged and aided, to whom you unwisely gave your friendship, and whom you introduced into the household of our friend. Besides being an ungrateful guest and uncertain in his meter, he is most foolishly indiscreet; he has bragged about his accomplishment to those who he imagines will admire him, while attempting secrecy among those who will not. He would have at once the responsibility of fame and the pleasure of anonymity, a condition which is clearly impossible.

Octavius knows his identity. He will take no action, though (needless to say) Timagenes is no longer welcome in his house. He has asked me to assure you that he holds you in no way responsible for the betrayal; indeed, he is as much concerned for your feelings in the matter as he is for his own, and hopes that you have not suffered an undue embarrassment. His regard for you is as warm as ever; he regrets your absence from Rome, and is affectionately jealous of the time you have decided to spend at the feet of the Muses.

I, too, regret not seeing you more often; but I believe that I understand even more fully than our friend the contentment you must feel in the quiet and beauty of your Arezzo, away from the bustle and stench of this most extraordinary city. Tomorrow I return to my little place above the Digentia, whose murmur will soothe my ears and at length return me from noise to language. How trivial all these matters will seem there, as they must seem to you in your retreat.

V. *Letter: Nicolaus of Damascus to Strabo of Amasia,*
from Rome (*21 B.C.*)

My dear old friend, you have been eminently correct in your descriptions and enthusiasms over the years—this is the most extraordinary of cities in the most extraordinary of times. Being here now, I think that this is where my destiny has aimed me all my life, though I cannot bewail the long chain of circumstances that has delayed my discovery.

As you may know, I have in recent years become of increasing use to Herod, who knows that he rules Judaea only by the protection of Octavius Caesar; now I am in Rome upon another service to Herod, the extraordinary nature of which I shall reveal to you in due course. At the moment I shall content myself with saying that necessary to that service was the somewhat intimidating duty of presenting myself to Octavius Caesar himself. For despite the fact that you have written me so often of your familiarity with him, his fame and power are such as to overwhelm even your assurances. And I had, after all, once been tutor to the children of his enemy, Cleopatra of Egypt.

But again you were, as you are in all things, right; he put me at my ease at once, greeting me with even more warmth than I might have expected as an envoy from Herod, and recalled his friendship with you, remarking upon how often you had mentioned my name. I did not wish, upon such slight acquaintance, to bring up to him the matter which I had been sent to accomplish; and thus I was particularly pleased when he invited me the next evening to dine with him at his private residence—I had, of course, presented myself to him at the Imperial Palace, which I understand he uses only during his official day.

I must not really have believed you when you wrote me of the modesty of his home. The simple luxury of my own quarters in Jerusalem would put this house to shame; I have seen moderately successful tradespeople live in more elegance! And it is not, I believe, merely an affectation of that austerity toward which he urges others; in this charming and comfortable little house, he seems a friendly host eager to please his guests, rather than the ruler of the world.

Let me set the scene for you and recapture the essence of that evening, in the manner of our master, Aristotle, in those marvelous *Conversations* that we used to study.

The meal—three excellent courses, served in a comfortable style between the austere and elegant—is over. The wine is mixed and poured, the servants moving noiselessly among the guests. It is a small gathering, of Octavius Caesar's relatives and friends. Reclining beside Octavius is Terentia, the wife of Maecenas, who (to my regret, for I should have liked to meet him) is out of the city for the season, devoting himself to his literary studies in the north; upon another couch are Julia, the Emperor's young and beautiful and vivacious daughter, and her new husband, Marcus Agrippa, a large and solid man, who, despite his distinction and importance, seems oddly out of place in this company; the great Horace, short and somewhat stout with graying hair around a young face, has pulled down beside him the Syrian dancing girl who earlier entertained us, and (to her nervous yet exultant delight) is teasing her to laughter; the young Tibullus (who languishes in the absence of his mistress) sits with his wine and observes the company with benevolent sadness; nearby sits his patron Messalla (who once, it is said, was proscribed by the triumvirs, who fought with Marcus Antonius against Octavius Caesar, and who now sits in easy friendship with his host and one-time enemy!) and that Livy, whom you have mentioned so often, and whose first books of that long history of Rome which he has projected, have begun to appear regularly in the bookstalls. Messalla proposes a toast to Octavius Caesar, who in turn proposes a toast to Terentia, whom he attends with courtesy and regard. We drink, and the conversation begins. Our host speaks first.

OCTAVIUS CAESAR: My dear and old friends, I take this occasion to present our guest. From our friend and ally in the East, that Herod who governs Judaea, comes the emissary Nicolaus of Damascus, who also is a scholar and philosopher of much distinction, and therefore doubly welcome in the company which graces my home upon this happy occasion. I am sure that he would wish to give you the greetings of Herod himself.

NICOLAUS: Great Caesar, I am humbled by your hospitality and honored beyond my merits to be included in the company of your renowned and intimate friends. Herod does, indeed, wish me to convey to you and your colleagues in the destiny of Rome his respectful greetings. The kindness and mutual affection which I have observed this evening persuade me that I shall be allowed to speak to you openly of that mission I have come to fulfill from the ancient land of Judaea. As a token of the boundless respect in which he holds Octavius Caesar, my friend and master Herod has given me leave to travel to Rome in order to speak to that man who has led Rome into the light of order and prosperity, and who has united the world. In honor of that Caesar, who is my host, I propose to write a Life, which will celebrate his fame to all the world.

OCTAVIUS CAESAR: As flattered as I am by this gesture of my good friend Herod, I must protest that my accomplishments do not merit such attention. I cannot persuade myself that the considerable talents which you, our new friend Nicolaus, possess should be put to so unimportant a purpose. Therefore, for the sake of those more significant tasks of learning which you might perform, and for the sake of my own sense of propriety and yet with all my gratitude and friendship, I must attempt to dissuade you from this unworthy task.

NICOLAUS: Your modesty, great Caesar, does honor to your person. But my master Herod would have me protest that modesty, and remind you that, great as your fame is, yet there are those in distant lands who have heard of your great accomplishments only by word of mouth. Even in Judaea, where the Latin tongue is used only by the educated few, there are those who do not know of your greatness. Thus were a record of your deeds put into that Greek language which all know, then would Judaea and much of the Eastern world be cognizant even more deeply of their dependence upon your beneficent power; and therefore might Herod more firmly rule, under your auspices and wisdom.

AGRIPPA: Great Caesar and dear friend, you have heeded my counsel before; I beseech you to do so again. Be persuaded by Nicolaus's eloquent request, and forsake your modesty in the interest of that which you must love more than your own person —that Rome, and the order which you have bequeathed her. The admiration which men in distant lands will give to you, will become love for the Rome that you have built.

LIVY: I shall make bold to add my voice to the persuasions you have heard. I know the reputation of this Nicolaus who stands before us now, and you could not put your fame in more trustworthy hands. Let mankind repay in some small measure that which you have given in such abundance.

OCTAVIUS CAESAR: I am at last persuaded. Nicolaus, you have the freedom of my house and you have my friendship. But I would beg you to confine your labors to those matters which have to do only with my acts in regard to Rome, and do not trouble your readers with those unimportant things that might have to do with my person.

NICOLAUS: I accede to your wishes, great Caesar, and shall endeavor by my poor efforts to do justice to your leadership of the Roman world.

. . . And thus, my dear Strabo, was the matter accomplished; Herod will be pleased, and I flatter myself by imagining that Octavius (he insists that I use the familiar address to him, in the intimacy of his house) has full confidence in my abilities to perform this work. You understand, of course, that the foregoing account has been submitted to the formal necessities of the dialogue in which I have cast it; the actual conversation was a good deal more informal and more lengthy; there was much bantering, all quite good-natured; Horace made jokes about Greeks who bore gifts, and asked if I intended to compose my work in prose or in verses; the vivacious Julia, who teases her father constantly, informed me that I could write anything I wanted, since her father's Greek was such that he could easily take an insult as a compliment. But I have, I believe, captured in my account the essence of the matter; for however these people make jokes with each other, there is a kind of seriousness going on—or at least, so it seems to me.

Besides, in order to take further advantage of my stay here (which promises to be a lengthy one), I have projected a new work beyond the *Life of Octavius Caesar*, which Herod has commissioned. It shall be called "Conversations with Notable Romans," and I expect that what you have read will be a part of it. Does it strike you as a feasible idea? Do you think that the dialogue is a suitable form in which to cast it? I shall await your advice, which I treasure as much as always.

VI. Letter: Terentia to Octavius Caesar, in Asia (*20 B.C.*)

Tavius, dear Tavius—I say our name for you, but you do not appear. Can you know how cruel your absence is? I rail against your greatness, which calls you away and keeps you in a country that is strange and detestable to me, because it holds you as I cannot. I know that you have told me that rage against ne-

cessity is the rage of a child; but your wisdom has fled from me
with your body, and I am a restless child until you return.

How could I have been persuaded to let you go from me,
who could not be happy for even a day outside your presence,
once you had loved me? The scandal, you said, if I followed
you—but there can be no scandal where there is common
knowledge. Your enemies whisper; your friends are silent; and
both know you are above the customs that others find necessary
to lead orderly lives. Nor would there have been harm to anyone.
My husband, who is my friend as well as yours, does not have
that pride of possession that a lesser man might have; from the
beginning it was known between us that I would have lovers,
and that Maecenas would go where his tastes led him. He was
not a hypocrite then, nor is he now. And Livia seems content
with things as they are; I see her at readings, and she speaks to
me civilly; we are not friends, but we are pleasant to each other.
On my part, I am almost fond of her; for she chose to relinquish
you, and thus you became mine.

Are you mine? I know that you are when you are with me,
but when you are so far away—where is your touch, that tells
me more than I have known before? Does my unhappiness please
you? I hope it does. Lovers are cruel; I would almost be happy, if
I could know that you are as unhappy as I am. Tell me that you
are unhappy, so that I may have some comfort.

For I find no comfort in Rome; all things seem trivial to me
now. I attend those festivals required of me by my position, the
rituals seem empty; I go to the Circus, I cannot care who wins
the races; I go to readings, my mind wanders from the poems
read—even those of our friend Horace. And I have been faithful to you, all these weeks—I would tell you so, even if it were
not true. But it is true; I have been. Does that matter to you?

Your daughter is well and is pleased with her new life. I visit
with her and Marcus Agrippa once or twice a week. Julia seems
pleased to see me; we have become friends, I believe. She is very
heavy with child now, and seems proud of her impending motherhood. Would I want a child by you? I do not know. What
would Maecenas say? It would be another scandal, but such an
amusing one! . . . You see how I chatter on to your memory, as
I used to do to your presence.

There is no gossip amusing enough to pass on to you. The marriages that you encouraged before you left Rome have at last taken place. Tiberius, it seems, has given up his ambitions, and is wed to Vipsania; and Jullus Antonius is wed to Marcella. Jullus seems happy that he is now officially your nephew and a member of the Octavian family, and even Tiberius seems grumpily content—even though he knows that Jullus's union with your niece is more advantageous than his own marriage to one of Agrippa's daughters.

Will you return to me this autumn, before the winter storms make your voyage impossible? Or will you wait until spring? It seems to me that I shall not be able to endure your absence for so long. You must tell me how I may endure.

VII. Letter: Quintus Horatius Flaccus to Gaius Cilnius Maecenas, at Arezzo (*19 B.C.*)

Our Vergil is dead.

I have just received the news, and I write you of it before grief overwhelms the numbness that I feel now, a numbness that must be a foretaste of that inexorable fate that has overtaken our friend, and which pursues us all. His remains are in Brindisi, attended by Octavius. The details are sketchy; I shall pass on to you what I have learned, for I have no doubt that Octavius's grief will delay his writing to you for some time.

Apparently the work of revision upon his poem, for the sake of which he had absented himself from Italy, had been going badly. Thus when Octavius, returning to Rome from Asia, stopped off at Athens, he had little difficulty persuading Vergil to accompany him back to Italy, for which he was already homesick, though he had been away for less than six months. Or perhaps he had some intimation of his death, and did not want his body to waste in a foreign soil. In any event, before setting out on the final journey, he persuaded Octavius to visit Megara with him; perhaps he wished to see that valley of rocks where the young Theseus is said to have slain the murderer Sciron. Whatever the reason, Vergil remained too long in the sun, and became ill. However, he insisted upon continuing the voyage; aboard ship, his condition worsened, and an old malaria returned upon him.

Three days after landing at Brindisi, he died. Octavius was at his bedside, and accompanied him as far as any can on that journey from which there is no return.

I understand that he was delirious much of the time during his last days—though I have no doubt that Vergil delirious was more reasonable than most men lucid. At the end he spoke your name, and mine, and that of Varius. And he elicted from Octavius the promise that the unperfected manuscript of his *Aeneid* be destroyed. I trust that the promise will not be kept.

I wrote once that Vergil was half my soul. I feel now that I understated what I thought then was an exaggeration. For at Brindisi lies half the soul of Rome; we are diminished more than we know. —And yet my mind returns to smaller things, to things that only you and I, perhaps, can ever understand. At Brindisi, he lies. When was it that the three of us traveled so happily across Italy, from Rome to Brindisi? Twenty years. . . . It seems yesterday. I can still feel my eyes smart from the smoke of the green wood that the innkeepers burned in their fireplaces, and hear our laughter like that of boys released from school. And the farm girl we picked up at Trivicus, who promised to come to my room, and did not; I hear Vergil mocking me, and remember the horseplay. And the quiet talk. And the luxuriant comfort of Brindisi, after the countryside.

I shall not return to Brindisi again. Grief comes upon me now, and I cannot write more.

VIII. The Journal of Julia, Pandateria (*A.D. 4*)

In my youth, when I first knew her, I thought Terentia to be a trivial, foolish, and amusing woman, and I could not understand my father's fondness for her. She chattered like a magpie, flirted outrageously with everyone, and it seemed to me that her mind had never been violated by a serious thought. Though he was my father's friend, I did not like her husband, Gaius Maecenas; and I was never able to understand Terentia's agreement to that union with him. Looking back upon it, I can see that my marriage to Marcus Agrippa was nearly as strange; but then I was young and ignorant, and so filled with myself that I could see nothing.

I have come to understand Terentia, I believe. In her own way, she may have been wiser than any of us. I do not know what has become of her. What does become of people who slip quietly out of your life?

I believe now that she loved my father, perhaps in a way that even he did not understand. Or perhaps he did. She was reasonably faithful to him, taking casual lovers only during his protracted absences. And perhaps, too, his fondness for her was more serious than his appearance of amused toleration led me then to believe. They were together for more than ten years, and seemed happy to be so. I see now—perhaps I dimly saw even then—that my judgments were those of youth and position. My husband, who could have been my father, was the most important man in Rome and its provinces during my father's absence; and I imagined myself to be another Livia, as proud and grave as she, at the side of one who might as well have been the true Emperor. Thus it did not seem appropriate to me that my father should love one so unlike Livia (and, as I foolishly thought, myself) as Terentia. But I remember things now that I did not recognize then.

I remember when my father returned alone from Asia, having only a few days before, at Brindisi, held in his arms his dying friend Vergil, and watched the breath go out of his body. Terentia was the only one who gave him comfort. Livia did not; I did not. I knew the idea of loss, but not its self. Livia spoke to him the ritual words that were meant to be comfort: Vergil had done his duty to his country, he would live in the memories of his countrymen, and the gods would receive him as one of their favored sons. And she hinted that too much grief was unseemly from the person of the Emperor.

My father looked at her gravely, and said: "Then the Emperor will show that grief that befits an Emperor. But how shall the man show the grief that befits him?"

It was Terentia who gave him comfort. She wept at the loss of their friend, recalled old memories, until my father became the man and wept too, at last had to comfort Terentia, and thus was comforted himself.

. . . I do not know why I thought of Terentia today, or of the death of Vergil. The morning is bright; the sky is clear; and far beyond my window, to the east, I see that point of land that juts into the sea above Naples. Perhaps I remembered that Vergil lived there when he was not in Rome, and remembered that he had been fond of Terentia in that dour way of his that concealed so much sentiment. And Terentia is a woman, even as I once was.

Even as I once was. . . . Was Terentia content to be a woman, as I was not? When I lived in the world, I believed that she was content, and had a secret contempt for her. Now I do not know. I do not know the human heart of another; I do not even know my own.

IX. Letter: Nicolaus of Damascus to Strabo of Amasia (*18 B.C.*)

Herod is in Rome. He is well pleased with my life of Octavius Caesar, which has been published abroad, and wishes me to remain here in the city for an indefinite period, so that he might have a trustworthy liaison with the Emperor. It is rather a delicate position, as you might imagine; but I feel confident that I can acquit my duties. Herod knows that I have the confidence and friendship of the Emperor, and I believe he has the wisdom to understand that I will betray neither; he is practical enough, at least, to know that if I do so, I should be of no further use to either of them.

Despite your kind praise, I have at last come to the conclusion that I would be wise to abandon the projected work that was to be called "Conversations with Notable Romans." As I have come to know these people, I have been forced to acknowledge that the Aristotelian mode in which we have both been schooled simply is not one in whose terms they may be defined. It is a difficult decision for me to make, for it must signify one of two things: either those modes in which we were schooled are incomplete, or I am not so finished a scholar of the master as I had led myself to believe. The former is too nearly inconceivable and the latter too humiliating to contemplate; and I would make this admission to none save you, who are the friend of my youth.

Let me try to demonstrate what I mean by an example.

All Rome is aflutter with the news of the latest law enacted by the Senate, which by a recent edict of Octavius Caesar has been reduced to some six hundred members. It is, in short, an effort to codify the marriage customs of this odd country, customs which have in recent times been more nearly acknowledged by abandonment than adherence. Among other things it gives to freed slaves more rights of marriage and property than they have had before, and that has caused some grumbling in certain quarters; but such grumblings are drowned by the cries of outrage at the more startling parts of the law, of which there are two. The first forbids any man who is or will be eligible by reason of his wealth to become a senator, to marry a freedwoman, an actress, or the daughter of an actor or actress. Nor shall the daughter or granddaughter of one of senatorial rank marry a freedman, an actor, or the son of one of those in the acting profession. No freeborn man, regardless of rank, shall marry a prostitute, a procuress, anyone convicted of a criminal act, one who has been an actress—or any woman who has been apprehended and convicted of adultery, regardless of her rank.

But the second part of the law is even more drastic than the first; for it provides that any father who apprehends an adulterer of his daughter in his own home, or the home of his son-in-law, is permitted (though not required) to kill the adulterer without fear of reprisal, and is permitted to do the same to his daughter. A husband is permitted to kill the offending man, but not his wife; in any event, he is required to denounce the offending wife and divorce her, else he may be prosecuted himself as a procurer.

As I say, all Rome is aflutter. Lampoons are circulated wildly; rumors abound; and each citizen has his own notion of what the whole thing means. Some take it seriously; some do not. Some say that it ought to be called the Livian rather than the Julian Law, and suspect that somehow Livia managed to insinuate it behind Octavius Caesar's back, in revenge for his own liaison with a certain lady who is also the wife of his friend. Others attribute it to Octavius himself; and of those, his enemies pretend outrage at his hypocrisy, others are heartened by what they see as the re-establishment of the "old virtues," and yet others see it as some obscure plot on the part of either Octavius Caesar or his enemies.

Through all the uproar, the Emperor himself walks calmly, as if he had no notion of what anyone was saying or thinking. But he does know. He always knows.

That is one side of the man.

Yet there is another. It is one that I, and a few of his friends know. It is unlike the one that I have shown you.

Upon formal occasions, I have been guest in his home on the Palatine, where Livia reigns. These occasions have been pleasant and not at all strained; Octavius and Livia behave toward each other with perfect civility, if not warmth. Upon other occasions I have been guest at the home of Marcus Agrippa and Julia while Octavius was present, usually in the company of Terentia, the wife of Gaius Maecenas. And upon several intimate and casual occasions I have been guest at the home of Maecenas himself, also in the presence of Octavius and Terentia. The three of them behave toward each other with the ease of old friendship.

Yet his liaison with Terentia is known to all, and has been for several years.

And there is more. Almost like a philosopher, he is without faith in the old gods of his countrymen; yet almost like a peasant, he is extraordinarily superstitious. He will use the auguries of his priests to any purpose that seems convenient to him, and be convinced of their truth because of his successful use of them; he will scoff (in a friendly fashion) at what he calls the "transcendent pomposity" of the God of my countrymen, and wonder at the sloth of a race that can invent only one god. "It is more fitting," he said once, "for the gods to be many, and to strive among themselves, as men do. . . . No. I do not believe that the strange God of your Jews would do for us Romans." And once I chided him (we have become that friendly) for his faith in portents and dreams, and he replied: "Upon more than one occasion my life has been saved by my believing what my dreams told me. Once it is not saved, I shall cease believing in them."

In all things, he is the most prudent and cautious man, and will leave nothing to chance that may be gained by careful planning; yet he loves nothing more than to play at dice, and will willingly do so for hours upon end. Several times he has sent a messenger to me, inquiring of my leisure; and I have played with him, though I take more pleasure in observing my friend than I do in the silly game of chance we play. He is utterly serious when he plays, as if his Empire depended upon the turn of the pieces of bone; and when, after two or three hours of play, he has won a few pieces of silver, he is as pleased as if he had conquered Germany.

He confessed to me once that in his youth he had aspired to be a man of letters, and had written poems in competition with his friend Maecenas.

"Where are the poems now?" I asked him.

"Lost," he said. "I lost them at Philippi." He seemed almost sad. Then he smiled. "I even wrote a play, once, in the Greek fashion."

I chided him a little. "Upon one of your strange gods?"

He laughed. "A man," he said, "only a foolish man who was too proud, that Ajax who took his life with his sword."

"And is that, too, lost?"

He nodded. "In my modesty, I took his life again—with my eraser. . . . It wasn't a very good play. My friend Vergil assured me that it was not."

We were both silent for a moment. A sadness had come over Octavius's face. Then he said almost roughly: "Come. Let's have another game." And he shook the dice and threw them on the table.

Do you see what I mean, my dear Strabo? There is so much that is not said. I almost believe that the form has not been devised that will let me say what I need to say.

X. Letter: Quintus Horatius Flaccus to Octavius Caesar (17 B.C.)

You must forgive me for returning your messenger without reply to your invitation. He made it clear that you had bidden him wait upon me; I returned him to you upon my own responsibility.

You ask me to compose the choral hymn for the centennial festival that you have decreed this May. You know that I am flattered that you should think me worthy; we both know that the man who should have had the honor is dead; and I know how deeply important you consider this celebration to be.

Thus, you are no doubt puzzled at my uncertainty about accepting the commission, an uncertainty that has given me a sleepless night. I have at last concluded that it is my duty and my pleasure to accede to your wish; but I think you ought to know the considerations which occasioned my hesitation.

Please know that I understand the difficulty of your task in running this extraordinary nation that I love and hate, and this more extraordinary Empire at which I am horrified and filled with pride. I know, better than most, how much of your own happiness you have exchanged for the survival of our country; and I know the contempt you have had for that power which has been thrust upon you—only one with contempt for power could have used it so well. I know all these things, and more. Thus, when I venture a disagreement with you, I do so in the full knowledge of the wisdom which I confront.

Yet I cannot persuade myself that your new laws will bring anything but grief to yourself and your country.

I know the corruption of our city which you would stem, and I know the intent of the laws, I believe. In the circles in which you move, and which I observe, copulation has become an act designed to obtain power, either social or political; an adulterer may be more dangerous than a conspirator, both to your person and his country; and that act whose natural end is affectionate pleasure has become a dangerous means toward ambition. The slave may gain power over a senator, thus over the ordinary citizen, and at last justice is subverted. I know these things, which your laws would hope to prevent.

Yet you, yourself, could not wish to have these laws enforced universally, with the rigor that law must be enforced. Such an enforcement would be disastrous to yourself, and to many of your most loyal friends. And though those who know your purpose understand that you intend to define a spirit and an ideal, the mass of your enemies will not understand this; and you may discover that your laws against adultery may be put to even more corrupt use than that which they were designed against.

For no law may adequately determine a spirit, nor fulfill a desire for virtue. That is the function of the poet or the philosopher, who may persuade because he has no power; the power you have (which, as I have said, you have used so wisely in the past) cannot legislate against the passions of the human heart, however disruptive to order those passions may be.

Nevertheless, I shall write the choral hymn for the celebration, and I shall take pride in the task. I share your concern and your hope, though I fear the means you have taken to fulfill them. I have been wrong in the past; I hope that I am wrong now.

XI. *The Journal of Julia*, Pandateria (*A.D. 4*)

In this island prison, my life over, I wonder without caring at things I might not have wondered at, had that life not come to an end.

Downstairs in her little bedroom, my mother is asleep; our servant does not stir; even the ocean, which usually whispers against the sand, is still. The midday sun burns upon the rocks, which absorb the heat and throw it back into the air, so that nothing —not even a vagrant gull—will move in its heaviness. It is a powerless world, and I wait in it.

It is odd to wait in a powerless world, where nothing matters. In the world from which I came, all was power; and everything mattered. One even loved for power; and the end of love became not its own joy, but the myriad joys of power.

I was married to Marcus Vipsanius Agrippa for nine years; and according to the world's understanding of such matters, I was a good wife. During his lifetime I gave four children into his hands, and gave one more after his death. They were all his children, and three of them—since they were male—might have mattered to the world. As it turned out, none of them did.

It was, I believe, the birth of my two sons, Gaius and Lucius, that gave me the first real taste of that most irresistible of all passions, the passion for power. For Gaius and Lucius were immediately adopted by my father, it being understood that in the event of his death, first my husband and then one or the other of my sons would succeed as Emperor and First Citizen of the Empire of Rome. At the age of twenty-one I discovered that I was, except for Livia herself, the most powerful woman in the world.

It is empty, the philosophers say; but they have not known power, as a eunuch has not known a woman, and thus can look upon her unmoved. In my life I could never understand my father not apprehending that joy of power by which I learned to live, and which made me happy with Marcus Agrippa, who (as

Livia often said in her bitterness) might as well have been my father.

I have often wondered how I might have managed the power I had, had I not been a woman. It was the custom for even the most powerful of women, such as Livia, to efface themselves and to assume a docility that in many instances went against their natures. I knew early that such a course was not possible for me.

I remember once that my father upbraided me for speaking in what he thought to be an unwomanly and arrogant tone to one of his friends, and I replied that though he might forget that he was the Emperor, I would not forget that I was the Emperor's daughter. It was a retort that gathered some currency in Rome. My father seemed amused by it, for he repeated it often. I do not believe he understood what I meant.

I was the Emperor's daughter. I was wife to Marcus Agrippa, who was my father's friend; but before and after that, I was the Emperor's daughter. It was accepted by all that my duty was to Rome.

Yet there was a part of me which, as year followed year, I came to know with increasing intimacy; it was a part that refused that duty, knowing it was a duty without reward. . . .

A moment ago I wrote of power, and of the joy of power. I think now of the devious ways in which a woman must discover power, exert it, and enjoy it. Unlike a man, she cannot seize it by force of strength or mind or desire; nor can she glory in it with a man's open pride, which is the reward and sustenance of power. She must contain within her such personages that will disguise her seizure and her glory. Thus I conceived within myself, and let forth upon the world, a series of personages that would deceive whoever might look too closely; the innocent girl who did not know the world, upon whom a doting father lavished a love he could not give elsewhere; the virtuous wife, whose only pleasure was in her duty toward her husband; the imperious young matron, whose whim became the public's wish; the idle scholar, who dreamed of a virtue beyond Roman duty, and fondly pretended that philosophy might be true; the woman who, late in life, discovered pleasure, and used men's bodies as if they were the luxurious ointments of the gods; and who herself at last was used, to the intensest pleasure she had ever known. . . .

I was twenty-one years of age when my father decreed the centennial festival to commemorate the founding of Rome, and I had given birth to my second son. My father and my husband were the chief worshipers at the festival, and made many sacrifices to those gods whose descendants are said to have established our city. It fell to me and Livia to preside equally at the banquet of the hundred matrons; I sat on the throne of Diana, and Livia across from me on the throne of Juno; and we received the ritual worship. I saw the faces of the richest and most influential women in Rome look up at me; I knew that many of them were married to enemies of my father who would have murdered him, were they not afraid. They looked at me with that odd expression that goes with the recognition of power; it was not love, nor respect, nor hatred, nor even fear. It was something that I had not seen before, and I felt for a moment that I had just been born.

Within a few weeks after the festival, my husband was to travel upon a variety of missions to the East—to the provinces of Asia Minor; to Macedonia, where my own father had spent his boyhood; to Greece; to Pontus and Syria, and wherever necessity might take him. It was, of course, contrary to all custom that I should accompany him; and until the festival, it had not occurred to me that I might do so, in defiance of custom.

But I did accompany him, despite the anger and persuasions of my father. I remember that my father said: "No wife has ever followed a proconsul and his soldiers into foreign lands; that is a task for freedwomen and prostitutes."

And I replied: "I would know, then, if you prefer me to appear a prostitute before my husband, or be a prostitute in Rome."

I intended the remark flippantly, and my father received it so; but I remember that it occurred to me afterward that it might not have been a joke; and I wondered if I had not been more serious than I had thought. In any event, my father relented; I joined my husband's retinue, and for the first time in my life, with my children and my servants, I crossed the borders of my native land.

From Brindisi to Apollonia, we crossed that little stretch of sea where the Adriatic empties into the Mediterranean; landing at Apollonia, we visited the sites where my husband and my father had companioned when they were boys. It was an easy and pleasant time, but I was eager to go onward, to places more strange and untrodden by Roman feet. From Apollonia we traveled northward through Macedonia to the new territories of Moesia, as far as the River Danube; and I saw strange people, who upon the approach of our carriages and horses, dodged like animals back into the forest, and would not be enticed into the open; they spoke in strange tongues, and many were dressed in the furs of wild animals. And I saw the bleak lives of the soldiers who had the misfortune to be stationed at this outpost of the Empire. They seemed strangely contented, and my husband spoke to them as if theirs were the most natural way of life that he could imagine. I had difficulty remembering that much of his life had been spent thus, in the days before I was born.

After the inspection of the Danube stations, we turned southward, somewhat hurriedly; for the autumn was upon us, and we wished to escape the rigors of a northern winter. I was beginning to regret my decision to accompany Marcus Agrippa, and to long for the comforts of Rome.

But we rested at Philippi, and my spirits raised. My husband showed me the places where he had done battle with the forces of Brutus and Cassius, and told me the tales of those days; and then we made our way leisurely to the shores of the Aegean, and sailed upon that blue water among the islands; and the weather warmed as we went southward.

And I began to know why the gods had sent me upon this journey, far from the city of my birth.

4

For the past three years, I have, in my letters to you, wondered why our friend Octavius Caesar insisted that I accompany Marcus Agrippa and his wife on this long Eastern tour; for it is clear that my connection with Herod is, in itself, not sufficient to justify my long absence from Rome. I now begin to understand his reasons; and before you know them, you shall wonder at my writing to you, in your retirement, rather than to Octavius Caesar himself. But if you will attend me, you will gradually begin to understand.

I write you from Jerusalem, where a few months ago Marcus Agrippa and Julia came with me, upon the invitation of Herod, who offered us a rest from our travels. Agrippa's stay in Jerusalem was limited, however; for no sooner had he arrived than word came of serious disturbances in the Bosporus. The old King, faithful to Rome, is dead; and his young wife, Dynamis, imagining herself no doubt a northern Cleopatra, but perhaps unmindful of that unhappy lady's fate, has allied herself with a barbarian named Scribonius; and in defiance of Roman policy, has declared herself, with her lover, to be the ruler of her husband's kingdom. Indeed, it is rumored that she, at the instigation of her lover, had a hand in her own husband's death. In any event, Marcus Agrippa, knowing that this kingdom is the last bulwark against the northern barbarians, determined to go there and put down the revolt; this he is now in the process of doing, with ships and men provided by Herod.

It was, of course, impossible for Julia to accompany him. She showed no real desire to do so; but neither would she accept Herod's plea that she remain in Jerusalem until her husband rejoined her, nor did she show any inclination to return to Rome. Rather, despite our entreaties, she gathered her retinue, and upon departure of her husband northward, she herself departed for Greece, and for those islands to the north from which she and her husband were recently returned. I have received some alarming news from that part of the world, where she now is; and that news, my dear Maecenas, is the occasion for this letter.

For the past two years, during their leisurely journey southward among the Aegean islands and the coastal cities of Greece and Asia, both Marcus Agrippa and Julia have been received with the honors due the representatives of the Emperor Octavius Caesar and Rome. But in especial Julia, since she is the daughter of the Emperor, has been the recipient of that sort of adulation of which only the island and Eastern Greeks are capable.

The adulation began in an ordinary enough way. At Andros, in honor of her visit, a statue in her likeness was erected; the inhabitants of Mytilene, on the Island of Lesbos, hearing of the homage given by the inhabitants of Andros, constructed a larger statue, in the twin likeness of Julia and the goddess Aphrodite; and thereafter, as island and city learned of the approach of Julia and Agrippa, the ceremonies became more and more extravagant, until at last Julia came to be regarded as the goddess Aphrodite herself, returned to earth, and came to be worshiped (at least ritually) by the people.

I am sure that you will agree that in all this extravagancy, ludicrous as it may appear to civilized men, there is nothing really very harmful; for in these public demonstrations, the Greeks were witty enough to have modified these odd ceremonies so that they might offend no one, and so that they might appear almost Romanized.

But in the midst of all this, something rather extraordinary has begun to happen to the person of Julia, of whom I have been (as you know) rather fond. It is almost as if she has begun to take on some of the attributes of that personage to whom she has been ritually likened; she has become imperious and indifferently arrogant, as if she indeed were not truly mortal.

This has for some time been my impression of her character; but I have just received news from Asia which sadly confirms what had been uncertain.

The report is that Julia, having spent the day in Ilium wandering among the ruins of the ancient site of Troy, attempted to cross the Scamander River by night. By some circumstance that is not clear, the raft bearing Julia and her attendants was overturned, and all were swept downstream. It was, no doubt, a near thing for all of them. In any event, she was finally rescued (by whom, it is not clear); but in her anger at the villagers who, she charges, did not attempt to rescue her, and in the name of her husband, Marcus Agrippa, she imposed upon the village a fine of one hundred thousand drachmas, which would amount to nearly a thousand drachmas for each of them. It is a heavy fine, indeed, for poor people, many of whom would not see a thousand drachmas in a lifetime of labor.

It is said that these villagers, though they heard the cries for help, came to the bank of the river, and watched, and would not attempt the rescue. I believe that this is probably a true account of the incident. Nevertheless, despite what might seem the obvious guilt of the villagers, I shall intercede. I shall ask a favor of Herod (who owes me several), and request that he persuade Marcus Agrippa to remit the fine. I shall do so, not out of pity for the villagers, but out of apprehension for the safety of the house of Octavius Caesar.

For Julia had not spent the day as an innocent tourist at Ilium; and her crossing the Scamander was not an innocent return to her quarters.

I spoke earlier of those public ceremonies—part religious, part political, and part social—in which Julia was elevated upon the throne of Aphrodite. By dwelling upon them, I suppose I have been putting off speaking of another kind of ceremony that is not public, but which is secret and unknown and somewhat frightening to this age of enlightenment.

There is a secret cult among these island and Eastern Greeks which worships a goddess whose name (at least to all those who are not initiates) is unknown. She is said to be the goddess of all gods and goddesses; her power is beyond the power of all the other gods conceived by mankind. Upon certain occasions, the power of this goddess is celebrated by rituals—though what they are no one knows, since the cult is shrouded in the secrecy of its fervor or its shame. But no secret is absolute; and in my travels I have heard enough of this cult to fill me with a revulsion at its nature and an apprehension of its consequences.

It is a female cult; and though there are priests, they are castrates who at one time allowed themselves to be used as sacrificial victims to the goddess. These victims are chosen by the priestesses—it is said that sometimes the priestesses choose their own sons as victims, since within their peculiar doctrine such a victim is the most honored and fortunate of men. He must be under the age of twenty; he must be virginal; and he must be a willing victim.

I do not know the precise nature of the rite; but I have heard, myself, from afar, the flute music and the chants in the sacred groves where the rites are performed. It is said that for three days the initiates and the members of the cult "purify" themselves by abstinence from all fleshly things; it is said, further, that when the rites begin the celebrants intoxicate themselves by dancing, by singing, and the drinking of certain libations—whether of wine or some more mysterious substance, no one knows. Then, when the celebrants are in a frenzy induced by their music and dancing and strange drink, the ceremony begins. One of several sacrificial victims is brought before the woman who has been chosen as the ritual incarnation of the Great Goddess. Save for the fur of some wild animal tied loosely about his waist, he is naked; he is bound to a cross made of some sacred wood from the trees by the grove, by wrist and foot, with lengths of laurel wreath. After he has been placed before the goddess, the celebrants dance about him; it is said that they fling their own clothing from their bodies in their frenzy as they dance. Then the goddess approaches the boy and with the sacred knife loosens the fur that hides his nakedness; and when she finds a victim that pleases her, she cuts the laurel that constrains him, and leads him to a cave in the sacred grove, which has been prepared for the "marriage" of the goddess and the mortal.

The marriage is supposed to be a ritual marriage; but it is a female cult, and secret, and sanctioned neither by law nor public custom. The goddess and her victim remain unseen in the cave for three days; it is said that the goddess uses her victim in whatever way pleases her; food and drink are put at the entrance of the cave, and those celebrants on the outside indulge in whatever lust or perversity that their frenzy leads them to.

After three days, the goddess and her mortal lover emerge from the cave, and cross a body of water to another sacred grove, which becomes the Island of the Blessed; and there the mortal lover becomes immortal, at least in the barbaric minds of the celebrants.

It is known to all that from Ilium to Lesbos this cult prevails, and that it numbers among its members those who belong to the richest and most cultivated families in that part of the world. When Julia's raft was upset, she was returning from such a rite as I have described, completing the prescribed ritual, crossing to the Island of the Blessed. She had been the incarnation of the goddess. And the villagers, in their abhorrence of such dark practices, could not overcome their fear of these strange beings, who (they thought) lived in a world beyond their comprehension and experience. I cannot allow the fine levied upon them to stand; for if I do, the secrecy (which now protects Julia, the unknowing Marcus Agrippa, Octavius Caesar, and even Rome itself) may be broken.

And beyond the vile practices which are rumored, there is another that is even more serious; the members of the cult are required to abjure all authority beyond the dictates of their own desires, and have no allegiance to any man, or law, or mortal custom. Thus, not only is the license of immorality encouraged— but murder, treason, and all other conceivable unlawful acts.

My dear Maecenas, I trust that now you understand why I could not write the Emperor; why I cannot speak to Marcus Agrippa; why I must burden you with this problem, even in your retirement from public affairs. You must find a way to persuade your friend and master to force Julia to return to Rome. If she is not now corrupted beyond retrieval, she will be soon, if she remains in this strange land that she has discovered.

II. *The Journal of Julia*, Pandateria (*A.D. 4*)

I have never known why my father ordered me, in terms that I could not disobey, to return to Rome. He never gave me a reason sufficient to justify the strength of his command; he merely said that it was unseemly that the wife of the Second Citizen be so long absent from the people who loved her, and that there were certain social and religious duties that only I and Livia could perform. I did not believe that that was the true reason for my recall, but he did not allow me to question him further. But he could not fail to know that I had resented my return; it seemed to me then that I was being exiled from the only life in which I had ever been myself, and that I was to spend my days performing a kind of duty in which I no longer could see any meaning.

In any event, it was Nicolaus—that odd little Syrian Jew, of whom my father was unaccountably fond and whom he trusted —who delivered the message to me, traveling all the way from Jerusalem to find me at Mytilene on Lesbos.

I was angry, and I said to him: "I will not go. He cannot force me to return."

Nicolaus shrugged. "He is your father," he said.

"My husband," I said. "I am with my husband."

"Your husband," Nicolaus said; "your husband is in the Bosporus. Your husband is your father's friend. Your father is the Emperor. He misses you, I suspect. And Rome—it will be spring when we return."

And so we set sail from Lesbos, and I watched the islands slip by, like clouds in a dream. It was my life, I thought, that slipped behind me; it was the life in which I had been a queen, and more than a queen. And as the days passed, and as we drew nearer to Rome, I knew that she who returned was not the same woman who had left, three years before.

And I knew that the life to which I returned would be different. I did not know how it would be so, but I knew that it would be. Not even Rome could awe me now, I thought. And I remember that I wondered if I would still feel like a child when I saw my father.

I returned to Rome in the year of the consulship of Tiberius Claudius Nero, the son of Livia and the husband of my husband's daughter, Vipsania. I was twenty-five years of age. Who had been a goddess returned to Rome a mere woman, and in bitterness.

III. *Letter: Publius Ovidius Naso to Sextus Propertius,* in Assisi (*13 B.C.*)

Dear Sextus, my friend and my master—how do you thrive in that melancholy exile you have imposed upon yourself? Your Ovid beseeches you to return to Rome, where you are sorely missed. Things here are not nearly so gloomy as you may have been led to believe; a new star is in the Roman sky, and once again those who have the wit to do so may live in gaiety and pleasure. Indeed, during the past few months, I have concluded that I would be in no other time and in no other place.

You are the master of my art, and older than I—yet can you be sure that you are wiser? Your melancholy may be of your own constitution, rather than Rome's making. Do return to us; there is pleasure yet, before the night comes down upon us.

But forgive me; you know that I am not suited for weighty talk, and once having begun cannot sustain it. I intended at the outset of this letter merely to tell you of a delightful day, hoping that I could persuade you by that to return to us.

Yesterday was the anniversary of the Emperor Octavius Caesar's birth, and thus a Roman holiday; yet it began for me unpropitiously enough. I was in my office disgracefully early—at the first hour, no less, just as the sun was beginning to struggle up from the east through the forest of buildings that is Rome, bringing the city to its feet—for though one may not plead a case on such a holiday as this, one may have to do so the next day; and I had a particularly difficult brief to prepare. It seems that Cornelius Apronius, who has retained me, is suing Fabius Creticus for nonpayment for some lands, while Creticus is countersuing, claiming that the title to the lands is faulty. Both are thieves;

neither has a case; thus the skill of the brief and the persuasion of the pleading are most important—as, of course, is the chance of magistrate.

In any event, I had been working all morning; marvelous lines kept popping into my head, as they always do when I am laboring at something that bores me; my secretary was particularly slow and fumbling; and the noise that came from the Forum grated against my ears much more fiercely than it should have done. I was becoming increasingly irritable, and for the hundredth time swore that I should give up this foolish career that in the long run will only give me riches I do not need and the dull distinction of senatorial office.

Then, in the midst of my boredom, a remarkable thing happened. I heard a clatter outside my door, and laughter; and though I heard no knock, my door burst open, and there stood before me the most remarkable eunuch I have ever seen—coiffed and perfumed, dressed in elegant silks, with emeralds and rubies on his fingers, he stood before me as if he were better than a freedman, better even than a citizen.

"This is not the Saturnalia," I said angrily. "Who has given you leave to burst in upon me?"

"My mistress," he said in a shrill, effeminate voice; "my mistress bids you attend me."

"Your mistress," I said, "may rot, for all I care. . . . Who is she?"

He smiled as if I were a slug at his feet. "My mistress is Julia, daughter of Octavius Caesar, the August, Emperor of Rome and First Citizen. Do you wish to know more, lawyer?"

I suppose I gaped at him; I did not speak.

"You will attend me, I presume?" he said haughtily.

In an instant my irritation was gone. I laughed, and tossed the sheaf of papers I had been clutching toward my secretary. "Do the best you can with these," I said. Then I turned to the slave who waited for me. "I will attend you," I said, "wherever your mistress would have you lead me." And I followed him out the door.

As is my wont, dear Sextus, I shall digress for a moment. In a casual way, I had met the lady in question a few weeks before, at a huge party given by that Sempronius Gracchus whom we both

AUGUSTUS

know. The Emperor's daughter had returned only a month or so before from a long journey in the East, where she had accompanied her husband, Marcus Agrippa, on some business of his, and where Agrippa remains yet. I was anxious to meet her, of course; since her return, the fashionable people of Rome have been talking of nothing else. So when Gracchus, who seems to be on rather friendly terms with her, invited me, I of course quickly accepted.

There were literally hundreds of people at the party at Sempronius Gracchus's villa—really too large a gathering to be very amusing, I suppose, but it was pleasurable in its own way. Despite the numbers of people, I had the chance to meet Julia, and we bantered for a few moments. She is an utterly charming woman, exquisitely beautiful, and really quite intelligent and well-read. She was kind enough to indicate that she had read some of my poems. Knowing her father's reputation for rectitude (as do you, my poor Sextus), I tried to make a sort of rueful apology for the "naughtiness" of my verse. But she smiled at me in that devastating way she has, and said: "My dear Ovid, if you try to convince me that though your verse is naughty, your life is chaste, I shall not speak to you again."

And I said, "My dear lady, if that is the condition, I shall attempt to convince you otherwise."

And she laughed and moved away from me. Though it was a pleasant interlude, it did not occur to me that she would give me another thought, let alone remember my existence for two whole weeks. And yet she did; and yesterday I found myself in her company once more, following the circumstance which I have described.

Outside my door, attended by bearers, there were perhaps half a dozen litters, canopied with silk of purple and gold; they teemed with the movements of their occupants, and laughter shook the street. I stood, not knowing where to turn; my castrate chaperon had wandered away and was haranguing some of the lesser slaves. Then someone stepped from a litter, and I saw at once that it was she, the Julia who had so kindly interrupted my tedious morning. Then another stepped from the litter and joined her. It was Sempronius Gracchus. He smiled at me. I went toward them.

"You have saved me from a death by boredom," I said to Julia. "What now will you do with that life which belongs to you?"

"I shall use it frivolously," she said. "Today is my father's birthday, and he has given me permission to invite some of my friends to sit with him in his box at the Circus. We shall watch the games, and gamble away our money."

"The games," I said. "How charming." I intended my remark to be neutral, but Julia took it as irony. She laughed.

"One does not have that much concern for the games," she said. "One goes to see, and to be seen, and to discover less common amusements." She glanced at Sempronius. "You will learn, perhaps." She turned from me then, and called to the others, some of whom had stepped out of their litters to stretch their legs. "Who would share his seat with Ovid, the poet of love, who writes of those things to which you have dedicated your lives?"

Arms waved from litters, my name was shouted: "Here, Ovid, ride with us—my girl needs your advice!" "No, *I* need your advice!" And there was much laughter. I finally chose a litter in which there was room for me, the bearers hoisted their burdens, and we made our way slowly through the crowded streets toward the Circus Maximus.

We arrived at noon, just as the hordes of people were streaming out of the stands for a hasty lunch before the resumption of the games. I must say, it gave me an odd feeling to see those masses, recognizing the colors of our litters, part before our advance, as the earth parts before the advance of a plow. Yet they were gay, and waved to us and shouted in the most friendly manner.

We debarked from our litters; and with Julia, Sempronius Gracchus, and another whom I did not know leading our band, we made our way among those arcades that honeycomb the Circus toward the stairs. Occasionally from the doorway of one of these arcades, an astrologer would beckon and call to us, whereupon someone in our party would shout: "We know our future, old man!" and throw him a coin. Or a prostitute would show herself and beckon enticingly to one who seemed unattached, whereupon one of the ladies might call to her in mock terror, "Oh, no! Don't steal him from us. He might never return!"

We mounted the stairs; and as we approached the Imperial box there were shushings and calls for quiet, out of deference for the presence of Octavius Caesar. But he was not in the box when we arrived; and I must say that, despite the pleasure I was having in the company of this most delightful troop, I found myself a little disappointed.

For as you know, Sextus, unlike you—not being an intimate of Maecenas, as you are, nor needing that intimacy—I have never met Octavius Caesar. I have seen him from afar, of course, as has everyone in Rome: but I know of him only that which you have told me.

"The Emperor is not here?" I asked.

Julia said, "There are certain kinds of bloodshed that my father does not enjoy." She pointed down at the open space of the course. "He usually comes late, after the animal hunt is over."

I looked to where she was pointing; the attendants were dragging away the slain animals and raking over the earth that was spotted with blood. I saw several tigers, a lion, and even an elephant being dragged across the ground. I had attended one of these hunts before, when I first came to Rome, and had found it extremely dull and common. I suggested as much to Julia.

She smiled, "My father says that either a fool is killed, or a dumb beast, and he cannot bring himself to care which. And besides, there are no wagers to be made on these contests between hunters and beasts. My father enjoys the wagering."

"It's late," I said. "He will be here, won't he?"

"He must," she said. "The games honor his birthday; and he would not be discourteous to anyone who so honors him."

I nodded, and recalled that the games were being presented to him by one of the new praetors, Jullus Antonius. I started to say something to Julia; but I remembered who Jullus Antonius was, and I checked my speech.

But Julia must have noticed my intention, for she smiled. "Yes," she said. "In particular, my father would not be discourteous to the son of an old enemy, whom he has forgiven, and whose son he has preferred to some who are his own kin."

Wisely (I think), I nodded, and did not speak more of the matter. But I wondered about this son of Marcus Antonius, whose name, even these many years after his death, still is honored by many of the citizens of Rome.

Yet there is little time to wonder about things of that sort in such gay comapny. The servants brought tidbits of food on golden plates, and poured wine into golden cups; and we ate, and drank, and chattered as we watched the crowd straggle back to their seats for the afternoon races.

By the sixth hour, the stands were filled, and it seemed to me overflowing with a good part of the population of Rome. Then suddenly, above the natural noise of the crowd, a great roar went up; many of the populace were standing, and were pointing toward the box where we reclined. I turned around, glancing over my shoulder. At the rear of the box, in the shadows, stood two figures, one rather tall, the other short. The tall one was dressed in the richly embroidered tunic and the purple-bordered toga of a consul; the shorter wore the plain white tunic and toga of the common citizen.

The taller of the two was Tiberius, stepson of the Emperor and consul of Rome; and the shorter was, of course, the Emperor Octavius Caesar himself.

They came into the box; we rose; the Emperor smiled and nodded to us, and indicated that we should seat ourselves. He sat beside his daughter, while Tiberius (a dour-faced young man, who seemed not to want to be where he was) found a seat somewhat removed from the rest of the party, and spoke to no one. For several moments the Emperor and Julia talked together, their heads close; the Emperor glanced at me, and said something to Julia, who smiled, nodded, and then beckoned me to join them.

I approached, and Julia presented me to her father.

"I am pleased to meet you," the Emperor said; his face was lined and weary, his light hair shot with white—but his eyes were bright and piercing and alert. "My friend Horace has spoken of your work."

"I hope kindly," I said, "but I cannot pretend to compete with him. My Muse is smaller and more trivial, I fear."

He nodded. "We all obey whatever Muse chooses us. . . . Do you have any favorites today?"

"What?" I said blankly.

"The races," he said. "Do you have any favorite drivers?"

"Sir," I said, "I must confess that I come to the races more nearly for the society than for the horses. I really know very little about them."

"Then you don't wager," he said. He seemed a little disappointed.

"On everything but the races," I said. He nodded and smiled a little, and turned to someone behind him.

"Which do you pick in the first?"

But whoever it was to whom he spoke did not have time to answer. At the far end of the race course, gates opened, trumpets sounded, and the procession entered. It was led by Jullus Antonius, the praetor who had financed the games; he was dressed in a scarlet tunic, over which he wore the purple-bordered toga, and carried in his right hand the golden eagle, which seemed almost ready to take flight from the ivory rod which supported it; and upon his head was the golden wreath of laurel. In his chariot drawn by his magnificent white horse, I must say he was an impressive figure, even at the distance from which I saw him.

Slowly the procession went round the track. Behind Jullus Antonius walked the priests of the rites, who attended the statues, thought by the ignorant to be the literal embodiments of the gods; then came the drivers who were to race, resplendent in their whites and reds, and greens and blues; and at last a crew of dancers and mimes and clowns, who cavorted and tumbled upon the track while the priests relinquished their effigies to the platform around which the racers would drive their chariots.

And then the procession made its way to the Emperor's box. Jullus Antonius halted, saluted the Emperor, and gave him the games in dedication of his birthday. I must say, I looked at Jullus with some curiosity. He is an extraordinarily handsome man—his muscular arms brown from the sun, his face dark and slightly heavy, with very white teeth and curling black hair. It is said that he closely resembles his father, though he is less inclined to fat.

The dedication over, Jullus Antonius came closer to the box and called up to the Emperor:

"I'll join you later, when I get them started."

The Emperor nodded; he seemed pleased. He turned to me. "Antonius knows the horses, and the riders. Listen to him. You'll learn a bit about racing."

I must confess, Sextus, that the ways of the great are beyond me. The Emperor Octavius Caesar, master of the world, seemed concerned only with the impending races; to the son of a father whom he had defeated in battle and whom he forced to commit suicide, he was warm and friendly and natural; and he spoke to me as if we both were the most common of citizens. I remember that I thought briefly of the possibility of a poem upon the subject; but just as quickly I rejected the idea. I am sure that Horace could have done one, but that is not my (or our) sort of thing.

Jullus Antonius disappeared into a gate at the far end of the course, and a few moments later reappeared in his enclosure above the starting gate. A roar went up from the crowd; Jullus Antonius waved, and looked down at the racers lined up beneath him. Then he threw down the white flag, the barriers dropped, and in a cloud of dust the chariots set off.

I stole a glance at the Emperor, and was surprised to see that he seemed hardly interested in the race, now that it had begun. He discerned my glance, and said to me: "One does not bet on the first race, if one is wise. The horses are made so nervous by the procession that they seldom run according to their natures."

I nodded, as if what he said made sense to me.

Before the chariots had completed four of their seven laps, Jullus Antonius joined us. He seemed to know most of the people in the box, for he nodded to them in a friendly manner, and spoke a few of their names. He sat between the Emperor and Julia, and soon the three of them were exchanging wagers and laughing among themselves.

And so the afternoon went. Servants came with more food and wine, and with damp towels so that we could wipe the dust of the track from our faces. The Emperor wagered on every race, sometimes betting with several persons at once; he lost carelessly, and won with great glee. Just before the beginning of the last race, Jullus Antonius rose to leave, saying that he had some last duties at the starting gate. He bade me good-by, and expressed the hope that we might meet again; he bade good-by to the Emperor; and then bowed with what I took to be an elaborate and private irony to Julia, who threw back her head and laughed.

The Emperor frowned, but said nothing. Shortly thereafter, when the crowd had streamed out of the Circus, we took our leave. A few of us gathered at Sempronius Gracchus's home for a while in the evening; and I learned what may have been the source of the little byplay between Jullus Antonius and the Emperor's daughter. It was Julia herself who told me.

Julia's husband, Marcus Agrippa, had once been married to the younger Marcella, daughter of the Emperor's sister, Octavia; early in Julia's widowhood, he had been persuaded by the Emperor to divorce Marcella and marry Julia. And only recently had Jullus Antonius married that Marcella who had been Agrippa's wife.

"It's rather confusing," I said lamely.

"Not really," said Julia. And then she laughed. "My father has it all written down, so that one might always know to whom one is married."

And that, my dear Sextus, was my afternoon and evening. I saw the new, and I saw the old; and Rome is again becoming a place where one can live.

IV. *The Journal of Julia*, Pandateria (*A.D. 4*)

I am allowed no wine, and my food is the coarse fare of the peasant—black bread, dried vegetables, and pickled fish. I have even taken on the habits of the poor; at the end of my day, I bathe and take a frugal meal. Sometimes I take this meal with my mother, but I prefer to dine alone at the table before my window, where I can watch the sea roll in on the evening tide.

I have learned to savor the simple taste of this coarse bread, indifferently baked by my mute servant. There is a grainy taste of earth to it, enhanced by the cold spring water that serves as my wine. Eating it, I think of the hundreds upon hundreds of thousands of the poor and the enslaved who have lived before me— did they learn to savor their simple fare, as I have? Or was the taste of their food spoiled in their mouths by their dreams of the foods they might have eaten? Perhaps one must come to taste as I have done—from the richest and most exotic viands to those of the utmost simplicity. Yesterday evening, sitting at this table where I now write these words, I tried to recall the taste and texture of those foods, and I could not. And in that general effort to recall what I shall never experience again, I remembered an evening at the villa of Sempronius Gracchus.

I do not know why I remembered that particular evening; but suddenly, in this Pandaterian twilight, the scene sprang before me, as if it were being re-enacted upon the stage of a theater, and the remembering caught me before I could fend it off.

Marcus Agrippa had returned from the East and joined me in Rome, where he stayed for three months; and I became pregnant with my fourth child. Shortly thereafter, at the beginning of the year, my father sent Agrippa north to Pannonia, where the barbarian tribes were again threatening the Danube frontier. And Sempronius Gracchus, to celebrate my freedom and to herald the arrival of spring, gave a party, the like of which (he promised everyone) Rome had not seen before; all of my friends, from whom I had been separated while my husband was in Rome, would be there.

Despite the libels that were circulated later, Sempronius Gracchus was not my lover then. He was a libertine, and he treated me (as he treated many women) with an easy familiarity that might give rise to rumors, however false. At that time I was still conscious of the position which my father imagined I ought to occupy; and the time that I had been a goddess at Ilium was like a dream that waited to be fulfilled. I had, for a while, become someone other than myself.

Early in March, my father assumed the office of pontifex maximus, which had been vacated by the death of Lepidus; and he decreed a day of games to celebrate the event. Sempronious Gracchus said that if the old Rome must have a high priest, the new Rome demanded a high priestess; so Sempronius had his party at the end of March, and the city chattered with reports of what the guests were to expect. Some said that the guests would be transported from place to place on tamed elephants; some said that a thousand musicians had been brought from the East, and as many dancers; fancy fed upon expectation, and expectation nourished fancy.

But a week before the date of the party, news reached Rome that Agrippa, having more quickly settled the border uprising than anyone expected, had returned to Italy by way of Brindisi. He proposed to travel across country to our villa near Puteoli, where I was to meet him.

I did not meet him. Despite the annoyance of my father, I pro-

posed that I join my husband the following week, after he had
rested from his journey.

When I made this proposal, my father looked at me coldly. "I
take it that you wish instead to attend that party which Gracchus
is giving."

"Yes," I said. "I am to be the guest of honor. It would be rude
to refuse, so late."

"Your duty is to your husband," he said.

"And to you, and to your cause, and to Rome," I said.

"These young people that you spend your time with," he
said. "Has it occurred to you to compare their behavior with that
of your husband and his friends?"

"These young people," I said, "are friends of mine. You may
be assured that when I grow old, they will be old, too."

He smiled a little then. "You are right," he said. "One forgets.
We all grow old, and we once were young. . . . I will explain to
your husband that you have duties that keep you in Rome. But
you will join him the week after."

"Yes," I said. "I will join him then."

Thus it was that I did not join my husband in the South, and
thus it was that I attended Sempronius Gracchus's party. It became, indeed, the most famous party in Rome for many years,
but for reasons that no one could have foreseen.

There were no tame elephants to transport the guests from
place to place, or any of the other wonders that had been rumored; it was simply a gathering of a few more than a hundred
guests, attended by nearly as many servants and musicians and
dancers. We ate, we drank, we laughed. We watched the dancers
dance, and joined them, to their delight and confusion; and to the
sound of tambourines and harps and oboes we wandered through
the gardens where fountains augmented the music and the torchlight played upon the water in another dance beyond the skill of
human bodies.

Toward the end of the evening there was to be a special performance of the musicians and dancers, and the poet Ovid was to
read a new poem, composed in my honor. Sempronius Gracchus
had constructed for me a special chair of ebony, and secured it
on a slight rise of the earth in the garden, so that all the guests

could (as Gracchus said, with that irony he always had) pay me homage. . . .

I sat upon the chair, and saw them beneath me; a breeze came up, and I could hear it rustle among the cypresses and plane trees as it touched my silken tunic like a caress. The dancers danced, and the oiled flesh of the men rippled in the torchlight; and I remembered Ilium and Lesbos, where once I had been more than a mortal. Sempronius reclined beside my throne, on the grass; and for a moment I was as happy as I had been, and was myself.

But in this happiness, I became aware of someone standing beside me, bowing, attempting to get my attention; I recognized him as a servant from my father's household, and motioned for him to wait until the dance was over.

When the dancers had finished, and after the languorous applause of the guests, I allowed the servant to approach me.

"What does my father require of me?" I asked him.

"I am Priscus," he said. "It is your husband. He is ill. Your father leaves within the hour for Puteoli, and asks you to follow."

"Is it a serious matter, do you think?"

Priscus nodded. "Your father leaves this night. He is concerned."

I turned away from him, and looked at my friends who lounged in their ease and gaiety on the grassy slopes of Sempronius Gracchus's garden. The sound of their laughter, more charming and delicate than the music that had moved the dancers, floated up to me on the warm spring breeze. I said to Priscus:

"Return to my father. Tell him that I shall join my husband. Tell him not to wait for me. Tell him that I will leave here shortly, and will join my husband by my own means."

Priscus hesitated. I said:

"You may speak."

"Your father wishes you to return with me."

"Tell my father that I have always done my duty to my husband. I cannot leave now. I will see my husband later."

Priscus left then, and I started to speak to Sempronius Gracchus about the news I had received; but Ovid had taken his place before me, and had begun to speak the poem that he had written in my honor; I could not interrupt him.

At one time I knew that poem by memory; now I cannot recall a word of it. It is strange that I cannot, for it was a remarkable poem. I believe he never included it in one of his books; he
said that it was my own, and should belong to no one else.

I did not see my husband again. He was dead by the time my
father reached Puteoli; the illness, which the doctors never really
discovered, was rapid and, I hope, merciful. He was a good man,
and kind to me; I'm afraid he never realized I knew that. And I
believe my father never forgave me for not joining him that
night.

. . . It was the truffles. We had a delicacy of truffles that evening at the villa of Sempronius Gracchus. The earthy taste of
those truffles was brought back by the earthy taste of this black
bread, and that reminded me of the evening when I became a
widow for the second time.

V. Poem to Julia:
Attributed to Ovid (circa *13* B.C.)

Restless, and wandering aimlessly, I pass temples and groves where
　　Gods live—Gods who invite passers to worship as they
Pause in the ancient groves where no ax has, in our memory's
　　Mortal endurance, bit hungrily branches or shrubs.
Where might I pause? Janus watches unmoving as I approach him,
　　And as I pass him by—quicker than any discerns
Save he. Now: here is Vesta—reliable, nice in her own way,
　　I think; so I call out. She does not answer me, though.
Vesta is tending her flame—no doubt she is cooking for someone.
　　She waves carelessly, still bending above her hot stove.
Sadly, I shake my head and move on. And now Jupiter thunders,
　　Eyes crackling light at me. What? Does he insist that I swear
Something that might change my ways? "Ovid," he thunders,
　　　　"is there no
End to this love-making life? trivial versing? your vain
Posturing?" I try answering; no pause comes in the thunder.
　　"Look to the years, poor poet; put on the senator's robes,
Think of the state—or at least try to." Deafened by thunder,
　　　　I cannot
Hear more. Sadly, I pass. Now at the Temple of Mars,
Weary, I halt; and I see, more fearsome than any—his left hand
　　Sowing a field and his right slashing a sword through the air—

Ultimate Mars! old father of living and dying! I call him
  Joyfully, hoping at last I will be welcomed. But no.
He who protects and gives name to this March, to this month of my
    own birth,
  Will not receive me. I sigh; is there no place for me, Gods?

Now in despair, and ignored by the most ancient Gods of my an-
    cient
  Country, I wander beyond all of their precincts, and let
Various breezes carry me where they will. And at last—soft,
  Distant, and sweet—sounds come: oboe and tambour and flute;
Music of laughter; the wind; bird songs; leaves rustling in twilight.
  Now it's my hearing that leads; I have to follow, so that
Eyes may glimpse what the music has promised. And suddenly,
  Open before me, a stream, gushing with springs that invade
Cavern and grotto, and idly meander through lilies that tremble
  As if suspended in air; surely, I say to myself,
Surely there dwells here divinity—one that I haven't before known.
  Nymphs in their gossamer gowns celebrate spring and the night;
Yet, above all, high, radiant in beauty, a Goddess, to whom turn
  All eyes. Worshiped in joy, prayed to by gaiety, she smiles,
Brightening the twilight, more gently than does our Aurora; her
    beauty
  Outshines that of the high Juno. I think: It's a new
Venus come down from her high place; no one has seen her before,
    yet all
  Know they must worship her. Hail, Goddess! we leave the old
    Gods
Safe in their groves. Let them scowl at the world, let them scold who
    will listen;
  Here a new season is born; here a new country is found,
Deep in the soul of that Rome we loved of old. We must welcome
    the new, and
  Live in its joy, and be gay; soon will the night come on; soon,
Soon we will rest. But for now we are granted this beauty around us,
  Granted this Goddess who gives life to this sacred grove.

VI. *The Journal of Julia*, Pandateria (*A.D. 4*)

My husband died on the evening of Sempronius Gracchus's
party; I would not have seen him, even if I had left as my father
wanted. My father traveled all night without pausing, and arrived

at Puteoli the next day to find his oldest friend dead. It is said that he looked at the body of my husband almost coldly, and did not speak for a long time. And then with that cold efficiency of his he spoke to Marcus Agrippa's aides, who were putting on their shows of grief. He ordered the body prepared for the procession that would return to Rome; he had word sent back to the Senate to direct the procession; and—still without rest—he accompanied the body of Marcus Agrippa on its slow and solemn journey back to Rome. Those who saw him enter the city said that his face was like stone as he limped at the head of the procession.

I was, of course, present at the ceremonies in the Forum, where my father delivered the funeral oration; and I can attest to his coldness there. He spoke before the body of Marcus Agrippa as if it were a monument, rather than what remained of a friend.

But I can also attest to what the world did not know. After the ceremony was over, my father retired to his room in his private house on the Palatine, and he saw no one for three days, during which time he took no food. When he emerged, he appeared to be years older; and he spoke with an indifferent gentleness that he had never had before. With the death of Marcus Agrippa, there was a death within him. He was never quite the same again.

To the citizens of Rome, my husband left in perpetuity the gardens he had acquired during the years of his power, the baths he had built, and a sufficient amount of capital to maintain them; in addition, he left to every citizen one hundred pieces of silver; to my father he left the rest of his fortune, with the understanding that it was to be used for the benefit of his countrymen.

I thought myself cold, for I did not grieve for my husband. Beneath the ritual show of grief demanded by custom, I felt—I felt almost nothing. Marcus Agrippa was a good man; I never disliked him; I was, I suppose, fond of him. But I did not grieve.

I was in my twenty-seventh year. I had given birth to four children, and was pregnant with a fifth. I was a widow for the second time. I had been a wife, a goddess, and the second woman of Rome.

If I felt anything upon the occasion of my husband's death, it was relief.

Four months after the death of Marcus Agrippa, I gave birth to my fifth child. It was a boy. My father named the child Agrippa, after its father. He would, he said, adopt the child when it came of an age. It was a matter of indifference to me. I was happy to be free of a life that I had found to be a prison.

I was not to be free. One year and four months after the death of Marcus Agrippa, my father betrothed me to Tiberius Claudius Nero. He was the only one of my husbands whom I ever hated.

VII. Letter: *Livia to Tiberius Claudius Nero,* in Pannonia (*12 B.C.*)

You are, my dear son, to follow my advice in this matter.

You are to divorce Vipsania, as my husband has ordered; and you are to marry Julia. It has been arranged, and I have had no small part in the arrangement. If you wish to be angry at any for this turn of events, I must receive a part of that anger.

It is true that my husband has not honored you by adoption; it is true that he does not like you; it is true that he has sent you to replace Agrippa in Pannonia only because there is no one else readily available whom he can trust with the power; it is true that he has no intention of allowing you to succeed him; it is true that you are, as you have said, being used.

It does not matter. For if you refuse to allow yourself to be used, you will have no future; and all my years of dreaming of your eventual greatness will have been wasted. You will live out your life obscurely, in disfavor and contempt.

I know that my husband wishes only for you to act as nominal father to his grandsons, and that he hopes that one or the other of them may be made ready to succeed him, when they are old enough. But my husband's health has never been robust; one cannot know how much longer the gods will allow him to live. It is possible that you may succeed him, beyond his wishes. You have the name; you are my son; and I shall inevitably inherit some power, in the unhappy event of my husband's death.

You dislike Julia; it does not matter. Julia dislikes you; it does not matter. You have a duty to yourself, to your country, and to our name.

You will know in time that I am correct in this; and in time your anger will abate. Do not put yourself in the danger that your impetuosity might invite. Our futures are more important than our selves.

5

I. The Journal of Julia, Pandateria (*A.D. 4*)

I knew Livia's strength, and I knew the necessity of my father's policy. Livia's ambition for her son was the most steadfast and remarkable one that I have ever known; I have never understood it, and I suspect that I never shall. She was a Claudian; her husband before my father, whose name Tiberius retained, had been a Claudian. Perhaps it was the pride in that ancient name that persuaded her of Tiberius's destiny. I have thought, even, that she might have been more fond of her former husband than she pretended, and saw the memory of him in her son. She was a proud woman; and I have suspected from time to time that she felt that in some indefinable way she had been demeaned by taking to her bed my father, whose name at that time certainly was not so distinguished as her own.

My father had dreamed that Marcellus, his sister's son, would succeed him; thus, he betrothed me to him. Marcellus died. And then he dreamed that Agrippa would succeed him, or at least would bring one of my sons (whom my father had adopted) to a point of sufficient maturity to adequately carry on his duties. Agrippa died, and my sons were still children. No male of the Octavian line remained, and there was no one else whom he could trust or over whom he had sufficient power. There was only Tiberius, whom he detested, though he was his stepson.

Shortly after the death of Marcus Agrippa, the inevitability of what I had to do began to work inside me like an infected wound whose existence I would not admit. Livia smiled at me complacently, as if we shared a secret. And it was not until I was near the end of my year of mourning that my father summoned me to tell me what I already knew.

He met me himself at the door, and dismissed the servants who had accompanied me. I remember the quietness of the house; it was late in the afternoon, but no one seemed about, except my father.

He led me across the courtyard to the little cubicle off his bedroom that he used as an office. It was very sparsely furnished, with a table and a stool and a single couch. We sat and talked for a while. He asked about the health of my sons, and complained that I did not bring them to visit him often enough. We talked of Marcus Agrippa; he asked me if I still grieved for him. I did not answer. There was a silence. I asked:

"It is to be Tiberius, isn't it?"

He looked at me. He breathed deeply, and let his breath out, and looked at the floor. He nodded.

"It is to be Tiberius."

I knew it was to be, and had known; yet a shock like fear went through me. I said:

"I have obeyed you in all things since I can remember. It has been my duty. But in this I find myself near to disobedience."

My father was silent. I said:

"You once made me compare Marcus Agrippa to some of my friends of whom you disapproved. I joked, but I did compare; and you must know the outcome of that comparison. I ask you now to compare Tiberius to my late husband, and ask yourself how I might endure such a marriage."

He lifted his hands, as if to fend off a blow; still he did not speak. I said:

"My life has been at the service of your policy, of our family, and of Rome. I do not know what I might have become. Perhaps I might have become nothing. Perhaps I might—" I did not know what to say. "Must I go on? Will you not give me rest? Must I give my life?"

"Yes," my father said. He still did not look at me. "You must."

"Then it is to be Tiberius."

"It is to be Tiberius."

"You know his cruelty," I said.

"I know," my father said. "But I know too that you are my daughter, and that Tiberius would not dare to harm you. You will find a life beyond your marriage. In time, you will grow used to it. We all grow used to our lives."

"There is no other way?"

My father rose from the stool upon which he had been seated and paced restlessly across the floor. I noticed that his limp had grown more pronounced.

"If there was another way," he said at last, "I would take it. There have been three plots against my life since the death of Marcus Agrippa. They were foolishly conceived and ill managed, and therefore easy to discover and deal with. I have been able to keep them secret. But there will be others." His clenched fist struck his open palm softly, three times. "There will be others. The old ones will not forget that an upstart rules them. They will forgive neither his name nor his power. And Tiberius—"

"Tiberius is a Claudian," I said.

"Yes. Your marriage will not guarantee the safety of my authority, but it will help it. The nobility will be a little less dangerous if they believe that one of their own, one who has the Claudian blood, might succeed me. At least it will give them the possibility of patience."

"Will they believe that you would make Tiberius your successor?"

"No," my father said in a low voice. "But they would believe that I might make a Claudian grandson my successor."

Until that moment, although I had accepted the idea of the marriage as inevitable, I had not accepted its actuality.

I said: "So I am once again to be the brood sow for the pleasure of Rome."

"If it were only myself," my father said. He turned his back to me. I could not see his face. "If it were only myself, I would not ask this of you. I would not allow you to marry such a man. But it is not only myself. You have known that from the beginning."

"Yes," I said. "I have known that."

My father spoke as if he were talking to himself. "You have

your children by a good man. That will comfort you. You will remember your husband through the children that you have."

We talked longer that afternoon, but I cannot remember what was said. I believe that a numbness must have come over me, for I remember feeling nothing after the first rush of bitterness. Yet I did not dislike my father for doing what he had to do; I should no doubt have done the same thing, had I been in his position.

Nevertheless, when the time came for me to leave, I asked my father a question. I did not ask it angrily, or in bitterness, or even in what might have seemed pity for myself.

"Father," I asked, "has it been worth it? Your authority, this Rome that you have saved, this Rome that you have built? Has it been worth all that you have had to do?"

My father looked at me for a long time, and then he looked away. "I must believe that it has," he said. "We both must believe that it has."

I was in my twenty-eighth year when I was married to Tiberius Claudius Nero. Within the year I had performed my duty, and delivered a child that bore the Claudian and Julian blood. It was a duty that both Tiberius and I found difficult to fulfill; and even that difficulty, it turned out, was in vain. For the child, a boy, died within a week after its birth. Thereafter, Tiberius and I lived apart; he was abroad much of the time, and I discovered again a way of life in Rome.

II. Letter: Publius Ovidius Naso to Sextus Propertius (10 B.C.)

Why do I write you the news of this place to which, you have made clear, you intend never to return? In which, you assure me, you no longer have the slightest interest? Is it that I distrust your resolve? Or do I hope merely (and in vain, no doubt) to shake it? In the five or six years that you have absented yourself from our city, you have written exactly nothing; and though you profess to be content with the rural charms of Assisi, and with your books, I cannot easily believe that you have forsaken the Muse whom once you served so well. She waits for you in Rome, I am sure; and I hope that you will return to her.

It has been a quiet season. A lovely lady (whose name you

know, but which I shall not mention) has been absent from our circles for more than a year now, which absence has diminished our joy and our humanity. Widowed young, she was persuaded to remarry; and we all know that her new marriage has caused her great unhappiness. Though an important man, her husband is the dourest and least affable man you can imagine; he has no taste for happiness, and cannot endure it in another. He is relatively young—perhaps thirty-two or three—yet except for his appearance, one might take him for a graybeard, he is so irascible and disapproving. He is, I suppose, the kind of man that was common in Rome some fifty or sixty years ago; and he is admired by many of the "older families" simply because of that. No doubt he is a man of principle; yet I have observed that strong principle, coupled with a sour disposition, can be a cruel and inhuman virtue. For with that one can justify nearly anything to which the disposition leads him.

But we hope for the future. The lady of whom I have spoken, recently gave birth to a son who died within the week of his birth; the husband, it is understood, will absent himself from Rome on some business on the northern frontiers; and perhaps once again we shall have in our midst her whose wit, gaiety, and humanity may lead Rome out of the dull hypocrisy of its past.

I shall not subject you, my dear Sextus, to one of my disquisitions; but it seems to me more nearly true, as the years pass, that those old "virtues," of which the Roman professes himself to be so proud, and upon which, he insists, the greatness of the Empire is founded—it seems to me more and more that those "virtues" of rank, prestige, honor, duty, and piety have simply denuded man of his humanity. Through the labors of the great Octavius Caesar, Rome is now the most beautiful city in the world. May not its citizens now have the leisure to indulge their souls, and thus lead themselves, like the city in which they live, toward a kind of beauty and grace they have not known before?

III. Letter: Gnaeus Calpurnius Piso to Tiberius Claudius Nero, in Pannonia (9 B.C.)

My dear friend, I include herewith those reports you have asked me to gather. They come from a variety of sources, which for the time being I shall not name, in the unlikely event that eyes other than your own might see this. In some cases I have transcribed the reports verbatim; in others I have summarized. But the pertinent information is here; and you may be assured that the original documents are safe in my possession, in the event that you might, at a later time, wish to use them.

These reports cover the period of one month, November.

On the third day of this month, between the tenth and eleventh hours of the day, a litter borne by the slaves of Sempronius Gracchus arrived at the lady's residence. The litter was evidently expected, for the lady emerged quickly from her house, and was borne across the city to the villa of Sempronius Gracchus, where a large party was assembled. During the banquet, the lady shared Gracchus's couch; they were observed to carry on a long and intimate conversation. No report of the substance of this conversation is available. A good deal of wine was consumed, so that by the end of the banquet many of the guests were inordinately gay. The poet Ovid read for their entertainment a poem of his that fit the occasion, which is to say one that was suggestive and improper. After this reading, a troupe of mimes performed *The Adulterous Wife*, but more brazenly than is usual. There was music afterward. At some time during the musical performance, people began to drift out of the hall; among these were the lady in question and Sempronius Gracchus. The lady was not seen again until near dawn, when she was observed entering the litter that had waited for her outside Sempronius Gracchus's residence. Thence she was transported to her home.

Two days before the Ides of this month, the lady entertained a group of her friends on her own responsibility. Among the male visitors were Sempronius Gracchus, Quinctius Crispinus, Appius Claudius Pulcher, and Cornelius Scipio; among the lesser guests were the poet Ovid and the Greek Demosthenes, the son of the actor and recently a citizen of Rome. The drinking of wine began early, shortly before the tenth hour, and continued late into the night. Though some of the guests left after the first watch, a larger number remained; and these late stayers, led by the lady, quit the rooms and the gardens, and made their way into the city, coming to a halt in their litters among the walks and buildings of the Forum. Though the Forum was nearly deserted at that hour, yet a small number of townspeople and tradesmen and police observed the party, and may be persuaded to testify, if the need arises. The drinking of wine continued, and that Demosthenes, the son of the actor, for the entertainment of the partygoers, delivered a mock oration from the rostrum beside the Senate House. It was extempore, and no copy could be made; but it seemed to burlesque the kind of speech that the Emperor has often delivered from the same spot. After the speech, the party disbanded; and the lady returned to her home, accompanied by Sempronius Gracchus. It was nearing dawn.

For the next six days nothing untoward occurred in the lady's activities. She attended an official banquet at the home of her parents; with her mother, she sat with the four elder Vestal Virgins at the theater; she attended the Plebeian Games, and remained circumspectly in the box with her father and his friends, among whom were the consul of the year, Quinctius Crispinus, and the proconsul Jullus Antonius.

On the fourth day after the Ides, she was guest of honor at the villa of Quinctius Crispinus at Tivoli. She was accompanied on her journey to Tivoli by Sempronius Gracchus and Appius Claudius Pulcher and a retinue of servants. The weather being mild, the entertainment was held out-of-doors; and it continued far into the night. There was much wine, there were male and female dancers (who did not confine their performances to the theater on the grounds, but danced, nearly naked, among the guests, who wandered about the grounds), and musicians who played Greek and Eastern music. At one time, a number of guests (the lady in question among them), both male and female, plunged into the swimming pool; and though the torchlight was dim, it could be seen that they had divested themselves of their clothing, and were swimming freely together. After the swimming, the lady was seen to retreat into the wooded part of the garden with the Greekling Demosthenes; they did not return for several hours. The lady stayed at the villa of Quinctius Crispinus for three days, and each evening was much the same as the other.

I trust, my dear Tiberius, that these reports will be of use to you. I shall continue to gather the information that you require, in as discreet a manner as I can. And you may depend upon me in any eventuality.

IV. Letter: Livia to Tiberius Claudius Nero, in Pannonia (9 B.C.)

You are to obey me in this, and you are to obey me at once. You are to destroy all the "evidence" that you have so painstakingly gathered, and you are to inform your friend Calpurnius that he is to do nothing more of this nature in your behalf.

What, may I ask, did you propose to do with this "evidence" you think you have? Do you propose to use it for a divorce? And if so, is the cause that your "honor" has been sullied? or do you dream that you will advance our cause by means of this divorce? In any of these fancies you are in error, and seriously so. Your "honor" will not be sullied as long as you remain abroad, for it will be clear to everyone that your wife is not under your control in such a circumstance, especially since you are serving your country and your Emperor; if on the other hand it comes to light that you have been gathering "evidence" and withholding it until a propitious time, then you will seem a fool, and all the honor that you may have gained shall have been lost. And if you dream that you advance yourself by insisting upon a divorce, you shall be mistaken again. Once such a step is taken, you will have no connection to that power we both have dreamed of; your wife may be "disgraced," but you will have gained nothing from that; you shall have lost the beginning that we have made.

It is true that at the moment it seems you have no chance to fulfill our mutual ambition; at the moment, even Jullus Antonius, the son of my husband's old enemy, has been advanced beyond you, and is as close to the accession of power as you are. Except for your name. My husband is old, and we cannot be sure of what the future will bring. Our weapon must be patience.

I know that your wife is adulterous; it is likely that my husband knows it also. Yet if you invoke those laws which he has made, and force him to punish his daughter by them, he will never forgive you; you might as well never have sacrificed your personal life in the first place.

We must bide our time. If Julia is to bring disgrace upon herself, she must do it herself; you must not be involved in any way, and you will be able to remain uninvolved only if you are careful to stay abroad. I urge you to lengthen your business in Pannonia as long as you reasonably can. So long as you remain away from your household, and away from Rome, our cause remains alive.

V. Letter: Marcella to Julia (8 B.C.)

Julia, dear, please come to our house next Wednesday for dinner, and a simple entertainment afterward. Some of your friends (who are also *our* friends, I might add) will be there—certainly Quinctius Crispinus, perhaps others. And of course you are to bring anyone you wish.

I'm so *glad* that we've become friends again, after all these years. I often remember our childhoods, with such fondness— all those children! And the games we played! You, and poor Marcellus, and Drusus, and Tiberius (sorry!) and my sisters—I can't even *remember* them all now. . . . Do you remember that even Jullus Antonius lived with us for a while, after his father's death? My mother cared for him when he was little, even though he was not her own. And now Jullus is my husband. It's a strange world. We have so many things to reminisce about.

Oh, my dear, I know it was I who caused the estrangement between us. But I did feel awkward when my uncle (your father!) forced Marcus Agrippa to divorce me so that he could marry you. I *know* you had nothing to do with it—but I was young, and felt that *never* would I have a husband so important as Marcus was. And I *did* resent you, though I knew that you were not at fault. But things work out for the best, I've always believed; and perhaps Uncle Octavius is wiser than we know. I am well pleased with Jullus. Oh, to tell the truth, Julia, I am more pleased with him than I was with Marcus Agrippa. He is younger and more handsome, and nearly as important as Marcus was. Or he will be, I'm sure. My uncle seems very fond of him.

Oh, I do chatter on, don't I? I'm still the chatterbox. We don't change very much, do we, over the years? I *do* hope I haven't offended you by anything I've said. I may not be any wiser than I used to be, but I'm older; and I *have* learned that it's foolish for women to hold their marriages against each other. They have nothing to do with us, really, have they? At least, so it seems to me.

Oh, you *must* come to our party. Everyone will be devastated if you do not. Shall I have some of my servants call for you? Or had you rather come by your own means? Do let me know.

And bring *whomever* you like—though there will be some very interesting people here. We understand your situation perfectly.

VI. Letter: Gnaeus Calpurnius Piso to Tiberius Claudius Nero, in Germany (8 B.C.)

I hasten to write you, my friend, before you get the news elsewhere and move without the knowledge that ought to determine any action. I have spoken to your mother; and despite our recent disagreement about the "reports" I have been sending you, we are, I believe, in full agreement about what you should do now. You must understand that she cannot speak directly; she will in no way betray the trust of her husband, nor will she recommend in secret what she could not do openly.

Within a few days you will receive a message from your stepfather in which you will be offered the consulship for next year. You may be pleased to know that I will be offered the co-consulship. In ordinary times, and under ordinary circumstances, this might have been thought of as a triumph; but neither the times nor the circumstances are ordinary, and it is essential that you act with the utmost caution.

You must, of course, accept the consulship; it would be unthinkable to refuse it, and disastrous to any future ambition you might have.

But you must not stay in Rome. Your stepfather's aim, of course, is to see that you do. But you must not. Before you leave Germany for the inauguration here, you must arrange your affairs so that it will become absolutely necessary for you to return there as soon as you possibly can. If you have no one you can trust, you must deliberately put your armies in a dangerous position, so that you must return to remedy the danger. I am sure you will be able to arrange something.

I shall now attempt to explain the reasons to justify this seemingly strange course that you must take.

Your wife continues to live as she has done for more than a year. She is openly contemptuous of your marriage contract, and careless of your reputation. Her father must know something of her conduct, yet he does nothing to prevent it—whether out of policy, or affection, or blindness, I do not know. Despite the marriage laws (or perhaps because the Emperor himself inaugurated them), no one quite dares to be the public informer. Everyone knows that the laws are not enforced, and knows it would be inexpedient to insist upon their enforcement now, especially when they would be enforced against one so powerful and popular as your wife.

For she is powerful; and she is popular. Whether by design or accident (and I suspect the former), she has gathered into her circle some of the most powerful younger people in Rome. And it is here that the danger lies.

Those with whom she now regularly and most intimately consorts are your most dangerous enemies, and that they may also oppose the Emperor does not diminish the threat to your position. It does, in fact, enhance that threat.

As you well know, the power that you have is in your following, which is largely made up of families such as mine, who are (in your stepfather's words) the "old Republicans." We are rich, we are ancient, and we are closely knit; but it has been the policy for nearly thirty years to see to it that our public power is limited.

I fear that the Emperor wants you to return as a kind of buffer between the factions—his own, and that of the younger people, of whom Julia is an especial favorite.

If you return and allow yourself to be placed between them, you will, quite simply, be chewed up. And then you will be spit out. And your stepfather will have eliminated a dangerous rival, without having appeared to have lifted a hand. More importantly, he will have discredited an entire faction, without having elevated another. For as long as the faction of the young is fond of his daughter, he trusts that the danger that confronts him is negligible.

But you will be destroyed.

Consider the possibilities.

First: The Claudians and their followers may, under our leadership, gain enough power to turn the Empire back to the course it once followed, and to reinstitute the values and ideals of the old days. This is highly unlikely, but I grant that it is possible. But even if we are able to do so, then we will in all likelihood have united against us both the New People of your stepfather, and the New Young. I think we both would shudder at the consequences of such a unification.

Second: If you remain in Rome, your wife will continue to work against your interests—whether out of design or whim does not matter. She will do so. It is clear that she considers that her power comes from the Emperor, not from your name or station. She is the Emperor's daughter. You would be powerless against her will, and would be made to seem foolish if you set yourself against that will and did not prevail.

Third: Her continued life of dissipation and self-indulgence will, among both your friends and your enemies, offer continued occasion for gossip. Were you to act against this life of hers and insist upon a divorce, it would bring a scandal upon the Octavian house, it is true; it would also gain you the eternal despite of the Emperor and those who support him. If you do *not* act against her behavior, you will seem a weakling; you may even be accused of complicity in her law-breaking.

No, my dear Tiberius, you must not return to Rome with any intention of remaining here, while things are as they are. It is fortunate that I have been made co-consul with you. While you are away, you may be sure that I will protect your interests. It is ironic that I, unworthy as I am, shall be able to do so with more safety and more effectiveness than you might be able to do. It is a most depressing commentary upon the course that our lives have taken us.

Your mother sends her love to you. She will not write until you have received the message from the Emperor. Though she does not say so, I have good reason to believe that she supports me in this most urgent advice that I have given you.

VII. Letter: Nicolaus of Damascus to Strabo of Amasia (7 B.C.)

For the past fourteen years, I have been content to live in Rome, first in the service of Herod and Octavius Caesar, and then in the service and friendship of Octavius Caesar alone; as you may have inferred from my letters, I had begun to think of this city as my home. I have broken most of my ties abroad; and since the deaths of my parents, I have felt no desire or necessity to return to the land of my birth.

But in a few days I shall be entering my fifty-seventh year; and during the last few months—perhaps it is longer—I have come to feel less and less that this is my homeland. I have come to feel that I am a stranger in this city that has been so kind to me, and in which I have been on the most intimate terms with some of the greatest men of our time.

Perhaps I am mistaken, but there seems to me an air of ugly unrest in Rome; it is not that uncertain restlessness that you must have known in the early days of Octavius Caesar's power, nor the restless excitement that infected me when I first came here fourteen years ago.

Octavius Caesar has brought peace to this land; not since Actium has Roman raised sword against Roman. He has brought prosperity to the city and the countryside; not even the poorest of the people wants for food in the city, and those in the provinces prosper from the beneficences of Rome and Octavius Caesar. Octavius Caesar has brought liberty to the people; no longer need the slave live in fear of the arbitrary cruelty of his master, nor the poor man fear the venality of the rich, nor the responsible speaker fear the consequences of his words.

And yet there is an ugliness in the air which, I fear, bodes ill for the future of the city, the Empire, and the reign of Octavius Caesar himself. Faction is ranged against faction; rumors abound; and no one seems content to live in the comfort and dignity which their Emperor has made possible. These are extraordinary people. . . . It is as if they cannot endure safety and peace and comfort.

So I shall leave Rome, this city that has been my home for so many rich years. I shall return to Damascus, and live out the days that remain to me among my books and whatever words I may write. I shall leave Rome in sorrow and love—without anger or recrimination or disappointment. And I realize as I write these words that I really am saying that I shall leave my friend, Octavius Caesar, with these feelings within me. For Octavius Caesar is Rome; and that, perhaps, is the tragedy of his life.

Oh, Strabo, if the truth were known, I feel that his life is over; in these past few years he has endured more than any man ought to endure. His face has upon it the inhuman composure of one who knows his life is over, and who waits only upon the decay of the flesh which signifies that end.

I have never known a man to whom friendship meant so much; and I mean a friendship of a particular kind. His true friends were those whom he knew when he was young, before he gained the power that he now has. I suppose that one with power can trust only those whom he knew and could trust before he had power; or it may be something else. . . . And now he is alone. He has no one.

Five years ago his friend, Marcus Agrippa, whom he had made his son-in-law, died in the loneliness of his return to Italy from a foreign land; and Octavius Caesar could not even bid him farewell. The year following, that good lady, his sister Octavia, died in the bitter isolation she had chosen away from the city and her brother, on a simple farm at Velletri. And now the last of his old friends, Maecenas, is dead; and Octavius Caesar is alone. No one from his youth remains alive, and therefore there is no one whom he feels that he can trust, no one to whom he can talk about those things that are nearest to him.

I saw the Emperor the week after Maecenas died; I had been in the country during the unhappy event, and I hurried back as soon as I learned of it. I tried to offer him my condolences.

He looked at me with those clear blue eyes that are so startlingly young in his lined face. There was a little smile on his lips.

"Well, our comedy is almost over," he said. "But there can be much sadness in a comedy."

I did not know what to say. "Maecenas," I began. "Maecenas—"

"Did you know him well?" Octavius asked.

"I knew him," I said, "but I do not think I knew him well."

"Few people knew him well," he said. "Not many liked him. But there was a time when we were young—Marcus Agrippa was young, too—there was a time when we were friends, and knew that we would be friends for as long as we lived. Agrippa; Maecenas; myself; Salvidienus Rufus. Salvidienus is dead too, but he died long ago. Perhaps we all died then, when we were young."

I became alarmed, for I had never heard my friend talk disconnectedly before. I said: "You are distraught. It is a heavy loss."

He said: "I was with him when he died. And our friend Horace was there. He died very quietly; he was conscious until the end. We talked about the old times together. He asked me to look out for Horace's welfare; he said that poets had more important things to do than to care for themselves. I believe Horace sobbed and turned away. Then Maecenas said that he was tired. And he died."

"Perhaps he was tired."

He said: "Yes, he was tired."

There was a silence between us. And then Octavius said:

"And there will be another soon. Another who is tired."

"My friend—" I said.

He shook his head, still smiling. "I do not mean myself; the gods will not be so kind. It is Horace. I saw the look on his face afterward. Vergil, and then Maecenas, Horace said. He reminded me later that once, many years ago, in a poem—he was making a little fun of one of Maecenas's illnesses—and in the poem he said to Maecenas—can I remember it?—'On the same day shall the earth be heaped upon us both. I make the soldier's vow —you lead, and we shall go together, both ready to slog the road that ends all roads, inseparable friends.' . . . I don't think that Horace will outlive him by many months. He does not wish to."

"Horace," I said.

"Maecenas wrote badly," Octavius said. "I always told him that he wrote badly."

. . . I could not comfort him. Two months later Horace was dead. He was discovered one morning by his servant, in his little house above the Digentia. His face was quiet, as if he were simply asleep. Octavius had his ashes interred beside those of Maecenas, at the farther end of the Esquiline hill.

The only one alive now whom he loves is his daughter. And I fear for that love; I fear most desperately. For his daughter seems to grow more careless of her position month by month; her husband will not live with her, but remains abroad, though he is consul for the year.

I do not believe that Rome can endure the death of Octavius Caesar, and I do not believe that Octavius Caesar can endure the death of his soul.

VIII. *The Journal of Julia*, Pandateria (*A.D. 4*)

The way of life that I had in Rome, then, was a way of almost utter freedom. Tiberius was abroad, spending even the year of his consulship in Germany, organizing the outposts there against the encroachments of the barbarian tribes. Upon the few occasions that he had to return to Rome, he made a ritual visit, and quickly found business elsewhere.

The year after his consulship, my father, upon his own initiative, ordered a replacement for him on the German frontier, and ordered my husband to return to his duties in Rome. And Tiberius refused. It was, I thought, the most admirable thing he had ever done; and I almost respected him for his courage.

He wrote to my father indicating his refusal to pursue a public life, and expressing a desire to retire to the Island of Rhodes, where his family had extensive holdings, to devote the rest of his years to his private studies of literature and philosophy. My father pretended anger; I think that he was pleased. He imagined that Tiberius Claudius Nero had served his purpose.

I have often wondered what my life would have been like, had my husband meant what he wrote to my father.

6

My dear Tiberius, your absence is regretted by your friends in Rome, which seems content in its own stagnation. Yet for the present, perhaps that stagnation is fortunate. There is no news of the past year that might profoundly affect our futures—and that, I suppose, in these days, is the best we can hope for.

Herod the Jew is dead at last, and that is perhaps best for all of us. During the last few years of his life, he was no doubt mad, and growing madder; I know the Emperor had become profoundly distrustful of him, and perhaps was considering to effect his overthrow; and that, of course, if it came to war, would have united the people behind the Emperor as nothing else might have done. Just a few days before he died, Herod had put to death one of his sons, whom he suspected of having plotted against him—which gave the Emperor occasion for another of his witticisms. "I had rather," he said, "be Herod's pig than his son." In any event, he is succeeded by another of his sons, who has made sincere overtures to Rome; so the possibility of an armed excursion seems remote at this time.

Incidental to Herod's death, and preceding it by some time was the departure from Rome of the unpleasant little Nicolaus of Damascus, of whom the Emperor has always been so fond. This may seem a trivial thing to record, yet it has some bearing on our futures, I believe; for this departure has saddened the Emperor more than one might reasonably expect. For now none of his old close friends remain—and he seems to grow more bitter and more private as the months succeed one another. And of course as one grows so, one's grasp upon power and authority progressively must weaken.

And that grasp does seem to be weakening, though in ways that are not yet significant enough to raise uncautious hopes. For example: this year, he refused the clamor of the Senate to accept his thirteenth consulship, pleading age and weariness. When it became clear that he was firm in his decision, the Senate demanded to know whom he would have to serve in his place— and he named Gaius Calvisius Sabinus! Do you remember the name? He is an old Caesarean, older even than the Emperor himself, and was consul once under the triumvirate, some thirty-five years ago, and served under the Emperor and Marcus Agrippa in the naval battles against Sextus Pompeius! The other consul is one Lucius Passienus Rufus (if you can imagine one of such an undistinguished name serving as consul), of whom you may or may not have heard. He is one of the new men, and I really have no idea of his allegiance to the family of the Emperor. I suspect that he will support the government, no matter who might be in power. So the consulship of this year promises no real consolidation that might be ranged against your eventual assumption of power. One who is senile, and one who has no name!

Somewhat more depressing (though we knew it had to come, eventually) were the rites of manhood conferred by the Emperor upon your stepsons. Gaius and Lucius (though neither is sixteen yet) are now citizens of Rome, they wear the togas of manhood, and no doubt as soon as he dares, the Emperor will give each of them at least nominal command of an army. Fortunately, he would not dare do more than that at the moment; and none of us knows what the future may bring. He will see that his old friend, Marcus Agrippa, though dead, is somehow in the center of things, even if it is only through his sons.

None of this, my dear Tiberius, need disturb us, I think; we have expected much of it, and that which we did not expect certainly has done us no harm.

But I fear that my concluding observations, tentative though they may be, offer some cause for apprehension. As you may have suspected, these observations have to do with the recent activities of your wife.

The scandals surrounding your wife have to some degree subsided, and they have done so for several reasons. First, the public is growing used to her behavior; second, what is often described as her infectious charm and gaiety have gone a long way toward softening opinion about her; third, her popularity among the young seems to be growing rather than diminishing; and last (and this is, for reasons that I shall shortly explain, the most ominous) her more blatant disregard of the proprieties seems to have diminished, and to have diminished substantially. It is to this last that I shall address myself.

Her rather indiscriminate and promiscuous choice of lovers seems to be a thing of the past. Sempronius Gracchus, as far as I can gather, is no longer her lover, but remains a friend; the same may be said for Appius Claudius Pulcher, and several others of note. The rather despicable toys with which she once amused herself (such as that Demosthenes, who was little better than a freedman, though technically a citizen) have been discarded; she seems, in a curious way, to have become more serious, though she retains sufficient wit and humor and abandon to still be a favorite of the frivolous young.

This is not to say that she is no longer adulterous; she is. But she seems to have chosen a lover of somewhat more substance than the riffraff she once favored, and one of more danger. It is Jullus Antonius, whose wife (once the intimate of Julia) has conveniently begun to travel abroad a good deal more than she is accustomed to doing.

There still are gatherings of her old friends, of course; but Jullus is always with her, and the discussions are reported to be of a much less frivolous nature than they had been before—though they remain, in my eyes, frivolous enough. At least, I trust that my reports are accurate in this respect. They discuss philosophy, literature, politics, and the theater—all such matters.

I do not know what to make of it, nor does Rome. I do not know whether her father is aware of this new affair, or not; if he is, he condones it; if he is not, he is a fool; for he therefore knows less than any of his fellow citizens. I do not know whether her recent behavior will help us or harm us. But you may be assured that I shall make it my business to keep myself fully informed upon this new development, and that I shall impart what I learn to you. I do have certain sources of information in the household of Jullus Antonius, and I shall develop more—discreetly, you may be sure. I shall not develop these sources in your wife's household. That would be altogether too dangerous to me, to you, and to our cause.

I trust that you will destroy this letter—or if you do not, be sure that it is secreted so that it cannot fall into unfriendly hands.

II. *The Journal of Julia*, Pandateria (*A.D. 4*)

My old friend and tutor Athenodorus once told me that our ancient Roman ancestors thought it unhealthy to bathe more than once or twice a month, that their daily ablutions consisted only of washing from their arms and legs the dirt that had been gathered in the day's labor. It was the Greeks, he said (with a kind of ironic pride), who had introduced to Rome the habit of the daily bath, and who had taught their barbaric conquerors the elaborate possibilities to be discovered in this ritual. . . . Though I have discovered the excellent simplicity of peasant food, and hence, no doubt, in that respect returned to the ways of my ancestors, I have not yet persuaded myself to adopt their habits of the bath. I bathe nearly every day, though I have no retinue to serve me with oils and perfumes, and my bath has but one wall —the rock cliff that rises above the shore of this island that is my home.

In the second year of my marriage to Marcus Agrippa, he opened in Rome, for the comfort of the people, what was said to be the most opulent bathhouse in the history of our city. Before that, I had not often attended the public baths; I believe that when I was young, Livia, fancying herself the model of the ancient virtues, disapproved of the luxuries offered at such places; and I must have caught the infection of her virtue. But my hus-

band had read in a work by a Greek physician that bathing
ought not to be looked upon merely as a luxury, that it might indeed contribute toward the prevention of mysterious illnesses that
periodically swept through any crowded city; he wished to encourage as many of the common people as he might to avail
themselves of such hygienic measures, and he persuaded me to
occasionally forsake the privacy of my own bath and go among
the people, so that all would see that it was fashionable to fre-
quent the public baths. I went as if it were a duty; but I had to
admit to myself that it became a joy.

I had never known the people before. I had seen them in the
city, of course; they had waited on me in the shops; I had spoken
to them, and they had spoken to me. But they had known always
who I was: I was the Emperor's daughter. And I had known (or
thought I had known) that their lives were so distant from my
life that they might as well belong to another species. But naked
in the bath, surrounded by hundreds of women who shout and
scream and laugh, an Emperor's daughter is indistinguishable
from the sausagemaker's wife. And an Emperor's daughter, vain
though she might be, discovered an odd pleasure in such an indis-
tinguishability. So I became a connoisseur of baths, and remained
one for the rest of my life; and after the death of Marcus
Agrippa, I discovered baths in Rome whose existence I had never
dreamed of, which offered pleasures that it seemed I had known
once, but in a dream. . . .

And now, still, I bathe nearly every day, as I imagine the soldier does, or the peasant, after his work is done, if there is a
stream nearby. My bathhouse is the sea, and the marble of the
pool is the black volcanic sand that gleams in the afternoon sun.
There is a guard who attends me—I suspect that he has been
ordered to prevent me from drowning myself—and stands impassively away from me, watching me incuriously as I let my
body into the water. He is a castrate. His presence does not disturb me.

On quiet afternoons, when the sea is calm, the water is like a
mirror; and I can see my face reflected there. It amazes me that
my hair is nearly white now, and that my face is becoming lined.
I was always vain about my hair, which began to go gray when I
was very young. I remember that my father came upon me once

when one of my maidservants was plucking out these gray hairs, and he asked me: "Do you look forward to becoming bald?" I replied that I did not. "Then," he said, "why do you allow your servant to hasten that condition?"

. . . The hair is nearly white, the face is lined—and as I lie in this shallow water, the body that I see seems to have nothing to do with that face. The flesh is as firm as it was twenty years ago, the stomach flat, the breasts full. In the chill water, the nipples harden, as once they did beneath the caress of a man; and in the buoyancy of the water, the body undulates, as once it did when it took its pleasure. It has served me well, this body, over the years—though it began its service later than it might have done. It began its service late, for it was told that it had no rights, and must by the nature of things be subservient to dictates other than its own. When I learned that the body had its rights, I had been twice married, and was the mother of three children. . . .

And yet that first knowledge was like a dream, and for many years I did not believe it. It was at Ilium, and I was worshiped as a goddess. Even now, it is like a dream; but I remember that at first I thought it all an amusing foolishness, a barbaric and charming foolishness.

I came to see that it was not. . . . That youth I chose that day in the sacred grove could not have been more than nineteen; he was virginal; and he was the most beautiful boy I have ever seen. I can close my eyes, and see his face, and almost feel the firm softness of his body. I believe that when I took him into the cave, I did not intend to fulfill the ritual. I did not have to; I was the Mother Goddess, and my power was absolute. But I did fulfill the ritual, and discovered the power of my body and the power of its needs. It was a power that I had been led to believe did not exist. . . . He was a sweet boy. I wonder what became of him, after he had entered the goddess and lain with her.

I believe that I must have lived in a kind of dream until the death of Marcus Agrippa. I could not believe what I had discovered, and yet its presence was with me always. I was faithful to Marcus Agrippa—I could not feel that the goddess who took her lover then at Ilium was wife to Agrippa; I was not faithful to Tiberius Claudius Nero.

It was after the death of that good man, Marcus Agrippa, that

Julia, daughter of Octavius Caesar, the August, discovered the power that had been hidden within her, and discovered the pleasure that she could take. And the pleasure she could take became her power, and it seemed to her that it was a power beyond that of her name and of her father. She became herself.

Yes, it has served me well, this body that is blurred by the water, that I can see as I lie supine in my pelagic bath. It has served me, while seeming to serve others. It has always served me. The hands that roamed upon these thighs roamed there for me, and the lover to whom I gave pleasure was a victim of my own desire.

Sometimes, bathing, I think of those who have given this body pleasure—Sempronius Gracchus, Demosthenes, Appius Pulcher, Cornelius Scipio—I cannot remember their names now, many of them. I think of them, and their faces and their bodies merge together, so that they are as one face and one body. It has been six years since I have known the touch of a man, six years since beneath my hand or my lips I have caressed the flesh of a man. I am forty-four years old; four years ago I entered my old age. And yet still at the thought of that flesh, I can feel my heartbeat quicken; I can almost feel myself to be alive, though I know that I am not.

For a while, I was the goddess to the mystery of all my pleasure; and then I became a priestess, and my lovers were the adepts. I served us well, I think.

And I think at last of the one from whom I had ultimate pleasure, one for whom all the others had been prelude, so that I might be prepared. I knew the taste and heft of his flesh more intimately than I have known anything else. I cannot believe that six years have gone. I think of Jullus. The tide rises gently, and the water moves over my body. If I do not move, I may think of him. I think of Jullus Antonius.

III. Letter: Gnaeus Calpurnius Piso to Tiberius Claudius Nero,
in Rhodes (3 B.C.)

I must say at the outset, my friend, that I am filled with apprehension; and I do not know whether it is justified or not. Let me give you a few causes, so that you may judge the soundness of my feeling.

Your wife, so far as I can determine, has been faithful to one man for more than a year. That man is, as you know, Jullus Antonius. She is seen constantly in his company; indeed, the liaison has become so widely recognized that no longer does either of them try to dissemble it. Julia receives guests in his home, and directs the activities of his servants. Her father *must* know of the affair by now, and yet he remains on friendly terms with his daughter, and with Jullus Antonius. Indeed, it is rumored that Julia intends to divorce you, and to take Jullus as her husband. In this rumor, however, I think we can put very little credence. Octavius Caesar would never allow it. Such an official alliance would simply destroy the delicate balance of power that he maintains, and he knows it. I mention the rumor only to indicate to you the extent to which the affair has grown.

Despite the scandal of his relationship with the Emperor's daughter—or perhaps because of it, for who can know the mind of the people?—Jullus Antonius's popularity continues to grow. He is at the moment, I should imagine, the second or third most powerful man in Rome; he has a very large following in the Senate, a following which, I must say, he uses most discreetly. Yet despite this discretion, I do not trust him. He has made no move to court those senators who have some influence with the military; he smiles upon all; he even conciliates his enemies. Yet I suspect that like his father he has ambitions; and unlike his father, he is able successfully to hide them from the world.

And, alas, your popularity among the masses seems to be suffering. It is in part because of your necessary absence; but that is not all. Libels and lampoons about you are being circulated widely; this, of course, is usual. Any distinguished figure is at the mercy of versifiers and hacks. But the distribution of these libels is far greater than any that I can remember in years; and they are particularly vicious. It seems almost that there is a campaign of sorts under way to discredit you. It does not do so, of course; no one who was your friend will become your enemy because of these libels, but it does seem to me symptomatic of something.

And the Emperor, I am sad to say, does not unbend in his dislike of you, despite the entreaties of your mother and your friends. So we can expect no comfort from that quarter.

Despite all this, you are well advised to remain in Rhodes. Let the lampooners invent their salacious poems; so long as you remain abroad, you will not be forced to act. The memories of men are short.

Jullus Antonius has gathered around him a band of poets—nothing so distinguished as those who were friends to the Emperor, of course; and I suspect that some of the libels and lampoons have been coming (anonymously, of course) from their pens. Some write poems in praise of Jullus himself; and he has let it be known that his maternal grandmother was a Julian. The man is ambitious; I am sure of that.

Do not forget that you have friends in Rome; and the absence of your self does not mean that you are not present in all our minds. It is a depressing strategy, but a necessary one, this waiting; do not become too impatient. I shall, as I have done, keep you informed of all that is pertinent here in the city.

IV. *The Journal of Julia*, Pandateria (*A.D. 4*)

Before Jullus Antonius and I became lovers, he used to tell me about his early years, and about his father, Marcus Antonius. Jullus had not been a favorite of his father—that distinction had fallen to his elder brother, Antyllus—and he remembered him as if he were almost a stranger. In his early years, Jullus had been raised by my Aunt Octavia, who, though a stepmother, was closer to him than had been his natural mother, Fulvia. Often, as I sat quietly with Jullus Antonius and Marcella and talked, it occurred to me that it was the most amazing thing that once, as small children, we had all played together at my Aunt Octavia's house. I could not then, and cannot now, recall those days with any precision; and when we tried to talk about childhoods and dredge up memories of them, it was as if we were inventing the characters and the events of a play, out of the conventions and necessities of an occasion in the past.

I remember one late evening, when the three of us lingered after the other few dinner guests had departed. It was a hot night, so we removed ourselves from the dining room and lounged in the courtyard. The stars glimmered through the soft air; the servants had gone; and our music was the mysterious chirp and whisper of the innumerable insects hidden in the darkness. We had been talking quietly, toward no particular end, of the accidents that befall us in our living.

"I have often wondered," Jullus said, "what would have happened to our country had my father been less impetuous and had managed to prevail over my friend Octavius Caesar."

"Octavius," I said, "is my father."

"Yes," Jullus said. "And he is my friend."

"There are those," I said, "who would have preferred such a victory over him."

Jullus turned to me and smiled. In the starlight, I could see the heavy head and the delicate features. He did not resemble the busts of his father that I had seen.

"They are wrong," he said. "Marcus Antonius had the inherent weakness of trusting too much the mere presence of himself. He would have erred, and he would have fallen, sooner or later. He did not have the tenacity that the Emperor has."

"You seem to admire my father," I said.

"I admire him more than I do Marcus Antonius," he said.

"Even though—" I said, and paused.

He smiled again. "Yes. Even though Octavius had my father and my elder brother put to death. . . . Antyllus was very much like Marcus Antonius. I believe Octavius saw that, and he did what was necessary. I was never fond of Antyllus, you know."

I believed I shivered, though the night was not cool.

"If you had been a few years older . . ." I said.

"It is quite likely that he would have put me to death also," Jullus said quietly. "It would have been the necessary thing to do."

And then Marcella said petulantly and somewhat sleepily, "Oh, let's not talk of unpleasant things."

Jullus turned to her. "We are not, my dear wife. We are talking of the world, and of the things that have happened in it."

Two weeks later, we became lovers.

We became lovers in a way that I could not have foreseen. I believe I determined that evening that we should become lovers, and I foresaw nothing in my conquest of Jullus Antonius that I had not seen before. Though I was fond of his wife, who was also my cousin, I knew her to be a trivial woman, as tiresome as I have found most women to be; and Jullus I took to be a man like all men—as eager for the power of conquest as for the pleasure of love.

To one who has not become adept at the game, the steps of a seduction may appear ludicrous; but they are no more so than the steps of a dance. The dancers dance, and their skill is their pleasure. All is ordained, from the first exchange of glances until the final coupling. And the mutual pretense of both participants is an important part of the elaborate game—each pretends helplessness beneath the weight of passion, and each advance and withdrawal, each consent and refusal, is necessary to the successful consummation of the game. And yet the woman in such a game is always the victor; and I believe she must have a little contempt for her antagonist; for he is conquered and used, as he believes that he is conqueror and user. There have been times in my life when, out of boredom, I have abandoned the game, and have attacked frontally, as a conquering soldier might attack a villager; and always the man, however sophisticated, and however he might dissemble, was extraordinarily shocked. The end was the same, but the victory was, for me, never quite complete; for I had no secret to hide from him and, therefore, no power over his person.

And so I planned the seduction of Jullus Antonius as carefully as a centurion might plan an advance upon the flank of an enemy, though in the ritual of this encounter, I thought, the enemy always wishes to be conquered. I gave him glances, and looked away hurriedly; I brushed against him, and drew away as if in confusion; and at last, one evening, I managed to arrange for us to be alone together at my house.

I languished on my couch; I said words that invited the hearer to offer comfort; I let my dress fall away from my legs a little, as if in distracted carelessness. Jullus Antonius moved across the room and sat beside me. I pretended confusion, and let my breath come a little faster. I waited for the touch, and prepared a little speech about how fond I was of Marcella.

"My dear Julia," Jullus said, "however attractive I find you, I must tell you at once that I do not intend to become another stallion in your stable of horses."

I believe that I was so startled that I sat upright on my couch. I must have been startled, for I said the most banal thing I can imagine: "What do you mean?"

Jullus smiled. "Sempronius Gracchus. Quinctius Crispinus. Appius Pulcher. Cornelius Scipio. Your stable."

"They are my friends," I said.

"They are my associates," Jullus said, "and they have been of service to me from time to time. But they are horses I would not run with. And they are unworthy of you."

"You are as disapproving," I said, "as my father."

"Do you hate your father so much, then, that you will not attend him?"

"No," I said quickly. "No. I do not hate him."

Then Jullus looked at me intently. His eyes were dark, almost black; my father's were a pale blue; but Jullus's eyes had that same intense and searching light, as if something were burning behind them.

He said: "If we become lovers, we shall do so in my own time and at terms more advantageous to us both."

And he touched me on the cheek, and he rose, and he left my room.

I sat where he left me for a long while, and I did not move.

I cannot remember my emotions at being so refused; it had not happened to me before. I must have been angry; and yet I believe that there must have been a part of me that was relieved, and grateful. I had, I suppose, begun to be bored.

For the next several days, I saw none of my friends. I refused invitations to parties, and once when Sempronius Gracchus called upon me unexpectedly, I had my maidservant, Phoebe, tell him that I was ill, and was receiving no visitors. And I did not see Jullus Antonius—whether out of shame or anger, I did not know.

I did not see him for nearly two weeks. Then, late one after-noon, after a leisurely bath, I called for Phoebe to bring my oils and fresh clothing. She did not answer. I drew a large towel about me, and stepped into the courtyard. It was deserted. I called again. After a moment, I crossed the courtyard and entered my bedroom.

Jullus Antonius stood in the room, his tunic bright in the shaft of late afternoon sunlight that slanted through the window, his face dark in the dimness above that light. For several moments neither of us moved. I shut the door behind me, and came a little into the room. Still Jullus did not speak.

Then, very slowly, he came toward me. He took the large towel that I had wrapped around me and slowly unwound it from my body. Very gently he toweled my body dry, as if he were a slave of the bath. Still I did not move, or speak.

Then he moved back from me, and looked at me where I stood, as if I were a statue. I believe I was trembling. Then he stepped forward, and touched me with his hands.

Before that afternoon, I had not known the pleasures of love, though I thought I had. And in the months that came that plea-sure fed upon itself, and multiplied; and I came to know the flesh of Jullus Antonius as I had known nothing else in my life.

Even now, after these many years, I can taste the bitter sweet-ness of that body, and feel beneath me the firm warmth. It is odd that I can do so, for I know that the flesh of Jullus Antonius now is smoke, and is dispersed into the air. That body is no more, and my body remains upon this earth. It is odd to know that.

No other man has touched me since that afternoon. No man shall touch me for as long as I shall live.

V. Letter: Paullus Fabius Maximus to Octavius Caesar (2 B.C.)

I do not know whether I write you now as a consular of Rome who is your friend, or as your friend who is consular. But write you I must, though we see each other almost daily; for I cannot bring myself to speak to you of this matter, and I cannot put what I have to say in one of the official reports that I give you regularly.

For what I must reveal to you touches upon both your public and your private self, and in such a way that I fear they cannot be separated, one from the other.

When at first you commissioned me to investigate those rumors which you judged to be so persistent as to be disturbing, I must confess that I thought you overly concerned; rumor has become a way of life in Rome, and if one spent his time investigating all that he hears, he would have not a moment for any other business that ought to occupy him.

So, as you know, I began the investigation with a great deal of skepticism. Now I am grieved to tell you that your apprehensions were right, and that my skepticism was mistaken. The matter is even more alarming than you initially suspected, or could imagine.

There is a conspiracy; it is a serious one; and it has gone a long way toward its completion.

I shall report my findings as impersonally as I can, though you must understand that my feelings protest against the coldness of my words.

Some seven or eight years ago—the year that he was consul—I relinquished to the service of Jullus Antonius, as a librarian, a slave whom I had some time earlier freed, one Alexas Athenaeus. Alexas was and is an intelligent man, and he has remained loyal to me through the years; he is, I am sure, a friend. When he learned of the investigation that I was conducting, he came to me in a highly distraught state, bringing with him certain documents removed from the secret files of Jullus Antonius, and a most disturbing series of revelations.

There is, incontrovertibly, a plot against the life of Tiberius. The conspirators have enlisted the support of certain factions around Tiberius in his retirement on Rhodes. He is to be murdered in the manner that Julius Caesar was murdered, and it is to be made to appear that it is an authentic uprising against the authority of Rome. Upon this pretext of danger it is planned that an army will be raised under the auspices of the senator and ex-consul Quinctius Crispinus, an army whose ostensible purpose is to protect Rome, but whose actual purpose is to assume power for that faction of conspirators. If you oppose the raising of this army, you will be made to seem either cowardly or indifferent;

if you do not oppose it, your position and your person may be in danger, to say nothing of the orderly future of Rome.

For there is strong evidence that a direct attempt will be made upon your life at the same time that the plan against Tiberius is carried out.

The conspirators are: Sempronius Gracchus, Quinctius Crispinus, Appius Pulcher, Cornelius Scipio—and Jullus Antonius. I know that the last name will cause you particular pain. I thought that Jullus was my friend, and I thought that he was yours. He is not.

But this is not the end of my report.

Alexas Athenaeus also informs me that, unknown to Jullus Antonius, there has been insinuated into his household a slave who is in actuality an agent of Tiberius. This agent is privy to the conspiracy; indeed, it was something that Tiberius's agent let drop that first aroused Alexas's suspicions. And the agent has been reporting directly to Tiberius about this affair. And from all that I can gather, Tiberius has a plan, too.

He apparently has as much proof of the conspiracy as I have; and he intends to use that proof. He intends to expose the plot in the Senate, using as his spokesman the senator and his former co-consul, Gnaeus Calpurnius Piso. Calpurnius will insist upon a trial for high treason; the Senate will be forced to accede; and Tiberius will then raise an army in Rhodes and return to Rome, ostensibly to protect you and the Republic. He will be a popular hero; and you will be made to seem a fool. Your power will be lessened; Tiberius's will be increased.

And there is yet one other thing—and this is the most painful—that I must report.

I am sure that for the past several years, since the absence of Tiberius Claudius Nero, you have not been wholly unaware of the activities of your daughter. I am sure that, out of pity for her condition and affection for her person, you have, as it were, looked the other way—as have most of your friends and even some of your enemies. But it becomes clear from the documents that I have in my possession that Julia has been intimate with each of the conspirators; and her lover of the past year has been Jullus Antonius.

If this matter becomes public, it will almost certainly be made to seem that Julia herself is a part of the conspiracy; and Tiberius may well have in his possession papers more damaging even than we imagine.

In any public disclosure of the plot, she will inevitably be implicated; and she is likely to be implicated so deeply that she will be found as guilty of treason as any of the conspirators. It is no secret that she hates Tiberius, and it is no secret that she loves Jullus Antonius.

The documents to which I have referred are safe in my possession. No eyes have seen them save mine and Alexas Athenaeus (and, of course, the conspirators), and no other eyes shall. They remain for you to use, however you may judge best.

Alexas Athenaeus is in hiding; the documents that he has taken from the household of Jullus Antonius are sure to be missed, and he is in fear of his life. He is a most remarkable man; I trust him. He has assured me that, despite his loyalty to Jullus Antonius, he reveres the Emperor and Rome more. He will testify, if need be. But I make a personal plea. If it is necessary to put him to torture to validate his testimony, please arrange it so that it is a ritual torture rather than an actual one. I trust the man implicitly, and he has lost nearly everything by his revelation.

My dear friend, I should have preferred to take my life than to be the one to impart this information. But I could not do so. The safety of your person and the safety of Rome must take precedence over what now seems would be the comfort of my own death.

I await whatever orders you may give me.

VI. *The Journal of Julia*, Pandateria (*A.D. 4*)

It is autumn in Pandateria. Soon the winds from the north will sweep down upon this bare place. They will whistle and moan among the rocks, and the house in which I live, though of this native stone, will tremble a little in the blast; and the sea will beat with a seasonal violence against the shores. . . . Nothing changes here except the seasons. My mother still shouts at our servant and directs her indefatigably—though it seems to me that in the last month or so she has become a bit more feeble. I wonder if she, too, will die upon this island. If so, it will be her choice; I have none.

I have not written in this journal for nearly two months; I had thought that I had no more to tell myself. But today I was allowed to receive another letter from Rome, and it contained news that reawakened memories of the days when I lived; and so I speak once more to the wind, which will carry my words away in the mindless force of its blowing.

When I wrote of Jullus Antonius, it occurred to me that it was an appropriate moment to cease these entries into a journal that sprawls itself out to no end. For if for a year or so Jullus Antonius brought me alive into the world, he also thrust me into this slow death of Pandateria, where I may observe my own decay. I wonder if he foresaw what might happen. It does not matter. I cannot hate him.

Even at the moment when I knew that he had destroyed us both, I could not hate him.

And so I must write of one more thing.

In the consulships of Octavius Caesar, the August, and Marcus Plautius Silvanus, I, Julia, daughter of the Emperor, was accused before the Senate convening in Rome of adultery, and hence of the abrogation of the marriage and adultery laws that my father had passed by edict some fifteen years before. My accuser was my father. He went into great detail about my transgressions; he named my lovers, my places of assignation, the dates. In the main, the details were correct, though there were a few unimportant names that he omitted. He named Sempronius Gracchus, Quinctius Crispinus, Appius Pulcher, Cornelius Scipio, and Jullus Antonius. He described drunken revels in the Forum and debaucheries upon the very rostrum from which he had first delivered his laws; he spoke of my frequentation of various houses of prostitution, implying that out of perversity I sold myself to anyone who would have me; and he described my visits to those unsavory bath establishments which permitted mixed bathing and encouraged all manner of licentiousness. These were exaggerated, but there was enough truth in them to make them persuasive. And at last he demanded that, in accordance with his Julian Laws, I be exiled forever from the precincts of Rome, and requested the Senate to order me placed on this Island of Pandateria, to live out the rest of my life in contemplation of my vices.

If history remembers me at all, history will remember me so. But history will not know the truth, if history ever can.

My father knew of my affairs. They may have pained him, but he knew of them, and understood the reasons, and did not upbraid me unduly. He knew of my love for Jullus Antonius; and I think, almost, he was happy for me.

In the consulships of Gaius Octavius Caesar and Marcus Plautius Silvanus, I was condemned to exile so that I would not be executed for high treason to the state of Rome.

It is autumn in Pandateria, and it was autumn that afternoon in Rome, six years ago, when my life ended. I had not heard from Jullus Antonius in three days. Messages that I sent to his house were returned unopened; servants that I sent were refused admittance, and came back to me puzzled. I tried to imagine those things that one in love is wont to imagine, but I could not; I knew that something else was amiss, something more serious than what a jealous lover can raise to beguile and torture one's lover.

But I swear I did not know what it was. I did not suspect; or perhaps I refused to suspect. I did not even suspect when, on the afternoon of the third day of silence, a messenger and four guards appeared at my door to take me to my father. I did not even recognize the significance of the guards; I imagined that they were there as a ritual protection of my safety.

I was carried by litter through the Forum and up the Via Sacra and past the Imperial Palace and up the little hill to my father's house on the Palatine. The house was almost deserted, and when the guards escorted me across the courtyard toward my father's study, the few servants who were around turned away from me, as if in fear. It was only then, I believe, that I began to suspect the seriousness of the matter.

When I was led into the room, my father was standing, as if awaiting me. He motioned the guards to leave; and he looked at me for a long while before speaking.

For some reason, I observed him very closely for those moments. Perhaps, after all, I did know. His face was lined, and there were wrinkles of weariness around those pale eyes; but in the dimness of the room, the face might have been that of him whom I remembered from my childhood. At last I said:

"What strangeness is this? Why have you brought me here?"

Then he came forward and very gently kissed me on the cheek.

"You must remember," he said, "that you are my daughter and that I have loved you."

I did not speak.

My father went to the little desk in the corner of the room and leaned on it for a moment, his back toward me. Then he straightened, and without turning said to me:

"You know one Sempronius Gracchus."

"You know that I do," I said. "You know him also."

"You have been intimate with him?"

"Father—" I said.

Then he turned to me. In his face there was such pain that I could not bear to look. He said: "You must answer me. Please, you must answer."

"Yes," I said.

"And Appius Pulcher."

"Yes."

"And Quinctius Crispinus and Cornelius Scipio?"

"Yes," I said.

"And Jullus Antonius."

"And Jullus Antonius," I said. "The others—" I said, "the others do not matter. That was a foolishness. But you know that I love Jullus Antonius."

My father sighed. "My child," he said, "this is a matter that has nothing to do with love." He turned away from me once again and picked up some papers from his desk. He handed them to me. I looked at them. My hands were shaking. I had not seen the papers before—some letters, some diagrams, some that appeared to be timetables—but now I saw names that I knew. My own. Tiberius's. Jullus Antonius's. Sempronius, Cornelius, Appius. And I knew then why I had been summoned before my father.

"Had you read those documents carefully," my father said, "you would know that there is a conspiracy against the government of Rome, and that the first step of that conspiracy is the murder of your husband, Tiberius Claudius Nero."

I did not speak.

"Did you know of this conspiracy?"

"Not a conspiracy," I said. "No. There was no conspiracy."

"Did you speak to any of these——friends of yours about Tiberius?"

"No," I said. "Perhaps in passing. It was no secret that—"

"That you hated him?"

I was silent for a moment. "That I hated him," I said.

"Did you speak of his death?"

"No," I said. "Not in the way you mean. Perhaps I said—"

"To Jullus Antonius?" my father asked. "What did you say to Jullus Antonius?"

I heard my voice tremble. I stiffened my body, and said as clearly as I could: "Jullus Antonius and I wish to marry. We have talked of marriage. It is possible that in talking of that I spoke wishfully of Tiberius's death. You would not have given your consent for a divorce."

"No," he said sadly, "I would not."

"Only that," I said. "I said only that."

"You are the Emperor's daughter," my father said; and he was silent for a moment. Then he said: "Sit down, my child," and motioned me toward the couch beside his desk.

"There is a conspiracy," he said. "There is no doubt of that. Your friends, whom I have named; and others. And you are involved. I do not know the extent and nature of your guilt, but you are involved."

"Jullus Antonius," I said. "Where is Jullus Antonius?"

"That will wait," he said. And then he said: "Did you know that there was also an attempt to be made on my life, after the death of Tiberius?"

"No," I said. "That cannot be true. It cannot be."

"It is true," my father said. "I should hope that they would not have let you know, that they would have made it appear an accident, or illness, or something of that sort. But it would have happened."

"I did not know," I said. "You must believe that I did not know."

He touched my hand. "I hope you never knew of that. You are my daughter."

"Jullus—" I said.

He raised his hand. "Wait. . . . If I were the only one who had this knowledge, the matter would be simple. I could suppress it, and take my own measures. But I am not the only one. Your husband—" He said the word as if it were an obscenity. "Your husband knows as much as I do—perhaps more. He has had a spy in the household of Jullus Antonius, and he has been kept informed. It is Tiberius's plan to expose the plot in the Senate, and to have his representatives there press for a trial. It will be a trial for high treason. And he plans to raise an army and return to Rome, to protect my person and the Roman government against its enemies. And you know what that would mean."

"It would mean the danger of your losing your authority," I said. "It would mean civil war again."

"Yes," my father said. "And it would mean more than that. It would mean your death. Almost certainly, it would mean your death. And I am not sure that even I would have the power to prevent that. It would be a matter for the Senate, and I could not interfere."

"Then I am lost," I said.

"Yes," my father said, "but you are not dead. I could not endure knowing that I had allowed you to die before your time. You will not be tried for treason. I have composed a letter which I shall read to the Senate. You will be charged under my law of the crime of adultery, and you will be exiled from the city and provinces of Rome. It is the only way. It is the only way to save you and Rome." He smiled a little, though I could see that his eyes were moist. "Do you remember, I used to call you my Little Rome?"

"Yes," I said.

"And now it seems that I was right. The fate of one may be the fate of the other."

"Jullus Antonius," I said. "What will become of Jullus Antonius?"

He touched my hand again. "My child," he said, "Jullus Antonius is dead. He took his life this morning, when he learned beyond doubt that the plot was discovered."

I could not speak. At last I said, "I had hoped . . . I had hoped . . ."

"I shall not see you again," my father said. "I shall not see you again."

"It does not matter," I said.

He looked at me once more. Tears came into his eyes, and he turned away. In a few moments the guards entered the room and took me away.

I have not seen my father since. I understand that he will not speak my name.

In the news that I received from Rome this morning was the information that after all these years Tiberius has returned from Rhodes and is now in Rome. He has been adopted by my father. If he does not die, he will succeed my father, and become the Emperor.

Tiberius has won.

I shall write no more.

BOOK THREE

Letter: Octavius Caesar to Nicolaus of Damascus (A.D. 14)

August 9

My dear Nicolaus, I send you affectionate greetings and my
thanks for the recent shipment of those dates of which I am so
fond, and which you have been kind enough to furnish me over
the years. They have become one of the most important of the
Palestinian imports, and they are known throughout Rome and
the Italian provinces by your name, which I have given them.
The *nicolai*, I call them; and the designation has persisted among
those who can afford their cost. I hope it amuses you to learn
that your name is known better to the world through this affectionate eponym than through your many books. We both must
have reached the age when we can take some ironic pleasure in
the knowledge of the triviality into which our lives have finally
descended.

I write you from aboard my yacht, the one upon which so
many years ago you and I used to float leisurely among the little
islands that dot our western coastline. I sit where we used to sit
—slightly forward of midship upon that canopied platform
which is raised so that the constant and slow movement of the sea

might be observed without hindrance. We set sail from Ostia this morning, in an unseasonably chill hour before dawn; and now we are drifting southward toward the Campanian coast. I have determined that this shall be a leisurely journey. We shall depend upon the wind to carry us; and if the wind refuses, we shall wait upon it, suspended by the vast buoyancy of the sea.

Our destination is Capri. Some months ago one of my Greek neighbors there asked me to be guest of honor at the yearly gymnastic competitions of the island youths; I demurred at the time, pleading the burden of my duties. But a short while ago, it became necessary for me to travel southward upon another mission, and I determined to give myself the pleasure of this holiday.

Last week my wife approached me with that rather stiff formality she has never lost, and requested that I accompany her and her son on a journey to Benevento, where Tiberius had to go on some business connected with his new authority. Livia explained to me what I already knew—that the people are not persuaded that I am fond of my adopted son, and that any display of affection or concern I might show will make more secure Tiberius's eventual succession to my power.

Livia did not put the matter so directly as she might have; despite her strength of character, she has always been a diplomatic woman. Like one of those Asian diplomats with whom I have dealt for much of my life, she wished to suggest to me without brutally stating the case that the days of my life are limited in number, and that I must prepare the world for that moment of chaos which will inevitably follow my death.

Of course Livia was in this matter, as she has been in most, quite reasonable and correct. I am in my seventy-sixth year; I have lived longer than I have wished to do, and such mortal boredom does not augment longevity. My teeth are nearly gone; my hand shakes with an occasional palsy that always surprises me; and the lassitude of age pulls at my limbs. When I walk I sometimes have the odd sensation that the earth is shifting under my feet, that the stone or brick or patch of earth upon which I step may suddenly move beneath me, and that I shall fall free of the earth to wherever one goes when time has done with one.

And so I acceded to her request, upon the condition that my accompaniment be a ceremonial one. I suggested that since sea travel makes Tiberius ill, he and his mother take the land route to Benevento, while I traveled in the same direction by sea; and that if either of them wished to make public the news that the husband or adoptive father traveled with them, I would not dispute it. It is a satisfactory arrangement, and I imagine that we all are more pleased by this subterfuge than we would have been by public honesty.

Yes, my wife is a remarkable woman; I suppose I have been more fortunate than most husbands. She was quite beautiful when she was a young woman, and she has remained handsome in her age. We loved each other for only a few years after our marriage, but we remained civil; and I believe that at last we have become something like friends. We understand each other. I know that deep within her Republican heart she has always felt that she married beneath her station, that she traded the dignity of an ancient title for the brute power of one whose authority was undeserved by his more humble name. I have come to believe that she did so for the sake of her first-born son, Tiberius, of whom she has always been inexplicably fond and for whom she has had the most tenacious ambition. It was this ambition that caused the first estrangement between us, an estrangement that grew so deep that at one period of our lives I spoke to my wife only of topics upon which I had made careful notes, so that we might not have to undergo the additional burden of misunderstanding, real or imagined.

And yet in the long run, despite the difficulties it caused between Livia and me, that ambition has worked for the benefit of my authority and Rome. Livia was always intelligent enough to know that her son's succession depended upon my undisputed retention of power, and that he would be crushed if he were not bequeathed a stable Empire. And if Livia is capable of contemplating my death with equanimity, I am sure that she will contemplate her own in a like manner; her real concern is for that order of which we both are mere instruments.

So in deference to that concern for order which I share, and in preparation for this voyage, three days ago I deposited at the Temple of the Vestal Virgins four documents, which are to be opened and read to the Senate only upon the occasion of my death.

The first of these was my will, which bequeaths to Tiberius two-thirds of my personal property and wealth. Though Tiberius does not need it, such a bequest is a necessary gesture to an adequate succession. The remaining portion—except for minor provisions for the citizens and various relatives and friends—goes to Livia, who will also by this document be adopted into the Julian family and be allowed to assume my titles. The name will not please her, but the titles will; for she will understand that her son will gain stature by her possession of the titles, and that her ambition will be that much more easily fulfilled.

The second was a set of directions for my funeral. Those who must put themselves in charge of that matter will no doubt exceed my instructions, which are lavish and vulgar enough to begin with; but such excesses invariably please the people, and thus are necessary. I comfort myself with the knowledge that I shall not have to be witness to this last display.

The third document was an account of the state of the Empire; the number of soldiers on active duty, the amount of money that is (or should be) in the treasury, the financial obligations of the government to provincial leaders and private citizens, the names of those administrators who are fiscally and otherwise responsible—all such matters that must be made public for the safety of order and the prevention of corruption. In addition, I appended to this account some rather strong suggestions to my successor. I advised against extending Roman citizenship so capriciously or widely as to weaken the center of the Empire; I advised that all men in high administrative positions be employed by the government at a fixed salary, so that temptation to undue power and corruption might be lessened; and at last I charged that under no circumstances should the frontiers of the Empire be extended, but that the military be employed solely to defend the established borders, especially against the German barbarians, who seem never to tire of their senseless adventures. I do not doubt that this advice will in the long run be ignored; but it will not be ignored for a few years, and I shall at least have left my country that poor legacy.

And finally I gave into the keeping of those estimable ladies in their temple a statement setting forth an account of all my acts and services to Rome and its Empire, with directions that this statement be engraved upon bronze tablets and attached to the columns that so ostentatiously rear themselves outside that even more ostentatious mausoleum that I have decreed will hold my ashes.

I have a copy of this document before me now, and from time to time I glance at it, as if it were written by someone else. During its composition, I found it necessary upon occasion to refer to a number of other works, so distant in time were some of the events that I had to record. It is remarkable to have grown so old that one must depend upon the work of others to search into one's own life.

Among the books that I consulted were that *Life* of me which you wrote when you first came to Rome, those portions of our friend Livy's history of the *Founding of the City* which concerns itself with my early activities, and my own *Notes for an Autobiography*—which, after all these years, seems also to be the work of someone other than myself.

If you will forgive me for saying so, my dear Nicolaus, all these works seem to me now to have one thing in common: they are lies. I trust that you will not too literally apply this remark to your own work; I believe you know what I mean. There are no untruths in any of them, and there are few errors of fact; but they are lies. I wonder if during your recent years of study and contemplation in the quiet of your far Damascus you have come to understand this also.

For it seems to me now that when I read those books and wrote my words, I read and wrote of a man who bore my name but a man whom I hardly know. Strain as I might, I can hardly see him now; and when I glimpse him, he recedes as in a mist, eluding my most searching gaze. I wonder, if he saw me, would he recognize what he has become? Would he recognize the caricature that all men become of themselves? I do not believe that he would.

In any event, my dear Nicolaus, the completion of these four documents and their deposition in the Temple of the Vestal Virgins may be the last official acts that I shall have to perform; I have in effect relinquished my power and my world, as I drift now southward toward Capri, and drift more slowly toward that place where so many of my friends have gone before me; and at last I may have a holiday that will not be disturbed by a sense of anything left undone. For the next few days at least, no messenger will rush to me with news of a new crisis or a new conspiracy; no senator will importune my support for a foolish and self-serving law; no lawyers will plead before me the cases of equally corrupt clients. My only duties are to this letter that I write, to the great sea that so effortlessly supports our frail craft, and to the blue Italian sky.

For I travel nearly alone. Only a few oarsmen are aboard, and I have given orders that they shall not work at their stations except in the event of a sudden squall; a few servants lounge at the stern of our craft and laugh lazily; and near the prow, always observing me carefully, is a new young physician that I have employed, one Philippus of Athens.

I have outlived all my physicians; it is some comfort to me to know that I shall not outlive Philippus. Moreover, I trust the boy. He seems to know very little; and he has not yet been a doctor long enough to have learned the easy hypocrisy that deludes his patients and at the same time fills his own purse. He offers no remedy for my disease of age, and does not subject me to those tortures for which so many so eagerly pay. He is a little nervous, I think, knowing himself to be in the presence of one whom he too solemnly considers the Emperor of the world; yet he is not obsequious, and he looks after my comfort rather than what another might think of as my health.

I tire, my dear Nicolaus. It is my age. The vision in my left eye is nearly gone; yet if I close it, I can see, to the east, the soft rise of the Italian coast that I have loved so well; and I can discern, even in the distance, the shapes of particular cottages and even make out the movement of figures upon the land. In my leisure I wonder at the mysterious lives that these simple folk must lead. All lives are mysterious, I suppose, even my own.

Philippus is stirring and looking at me apprehensively; it is clear that he wants me to cease what he takes to be work rather than pleasure. I shall forestall his ministrations, desist for a while, and pretend to rest.

At the age of nineteen, on my own initiative and at my own expense, I raised an army by means of which I restored liberty to the Republic, which had been oppressed by the tyranny of faction. For this service the Senate, with complimentary resolutions, enrolled me in its order, in the consulship of Gaius Pansa and Aulus Hirtius, and gave me at the same time consular precedence in voting and the authority to command soldiers. As propraetor it ordered me, along with the consuls, "to see that the Republic suffered no harm." In the same year, moreover, as both consuls had fallen in war, the people elected me consul and a triumvir for settling the constitution.

Those who slew my father I drove into exile, punishing their deed by due process of law; and afterward when they waged war upon the Republic I twice defeated them in battle. . . .

Thus begins that account of my acts and services to Rome of which I wrote you earlier this morning. During the hour or so that I lay on my couch and pretended to doze, thus affording Philippus some respite from his concern, I thought again of this account, and of the circumstances under which it was composed. It shall be engraved upon bronze tablets and attached to those columns that mark the entrance to my mausoleum. Upon those columns there will be sufficient space for six of these tablets, and each of the tablets may contain fifty lines of about sixty characters each. Thus the statement of my acts must be limited to about eighteen thousand characters.

It seems to me wholly appropriate that I should have been forced to write of myself under these conditions, arbitrary as they might be; for just as my words must be accommodated to such a public necessity, so has my life been. And just as the acts of my life have done, so these words must conceal at least as much truth as they display; the truth will lie somewhere beneath these graven words, in the dense stone which they will encircle. And this too is appropriate; for much of my life has been lived in such secrecy. It has never been politic for me to let another know my heart.

It is fortunate that youth never recognizes its ignorance, for if it did it would not find the courage to get the habit of endurance. It is perhaps an instinct of the blood and flesh which prevents this knowledge and allows the boy to become the man who will live to see the folly of his existence.

Certainly I was ignorant that spring when I was eighteen years of age, a student at Apollonia, and got the news of Julius Caesar's death. . . . Much has been made of my loyalty to Julius Caesar; but Nicolaus, I swear to you, I do not know whether I loved the man or not. The year before he was killed, I had been with him on his Spanish campaign; he was my uncle, and the most important man I had ever known; I was flattered at his trust in me; and I knew that he planned to adopt me and make me his heir.

Though it was nearly sixty years ago, I remember that afternoon on the training field when I got the news of my Uncle Julius's death. Maecenas was there, and Agrippa, and Salvidienus. One of my mother's servants brought me the message, and I remember that I cried out as if in pain after I read it.

But at that first moment, Nicolaus, I felt nothing; it was as if the cry of pain issued from another throat. Then a coldness came over me, and I walked away from my friends so that they could not see what I felt, and what I did not feel. And as I walked on that field alone, trying to rouse in myself the appropriate sense of grief and loss, I was suddenly elated, as one might be when riding a horse he feels the horse tense and bolt beneath him, knowing that he has the skill to control the poor spirited beast who in an excess of energy wishes to test his master. When I returned to my friends, I knew that I had changed, that I was someone other than I had been; I knew my destiny, and I could not speak to them of it. And yet they were my friends.

Though I probably could not have articulated it then, I knew that my destiny was simply this: to change the world. Julius Caesar had come to power in a world that was corrupt beyond your understanding. No more than six families ruled the world; towns, regions, and provinces under Roman authority were the currencies of bribery and reward; in the name of the Republic and in the guise of tradition, murder and civil war and merciless repression were the means toward the accepted ends of power, wealth, and glory. Any man who had sufficient money could raise an army, and thus augment that wealth, thereby gaining more power, and hence glory. So Roman killed Roman, and authority became simply the force of arms and riches. And in this strife and faction the ordinary citizen writhed as helplessly as the hare in the trap of the hunter.

Do not mistake me. I have never had that sentimental and rhe-
torical love for the common people that was in my youth (and is
even now) so fashionable. Mankind in the aggregate I have found
to be brutish, ignorant, and unkind, whether those qualities were
covered by the coarse tunic of the peasant or the white and purple toga of a senator. And yet in the weakest of men, in moments
when they are alone and themselves, I have found veins of
strength like gold in decaying rock; in the cruelest of men flashes
of tenderness and compassion; and in the vainest of men moments
of simplicity and grace. I remember Marcus Aemilius Lepidus at
Messina, an old man stripped of his titles, whom I made publicly
to ask forgiveness for his crimes and beg for his life; after he had
done so in front of the troops that he had once commanded, he
looked at me for a long moment without shame or regret or fear,
and smiled, and turned from me and strode erectly toward his
obscurity. And at Actium, I remember Marcus Antonius at the
prow of his ship looking at Cleopatra as her own fleet departed
leaving him to certain defeat, knowing at that moment that she
had never loved him; and yet upon his face was an expression almost womanly in its wise affection and forgiveness. And I
remember Cicero, when at last he knew that his foolish intrigues had failed, and when in secret I informed him that his life
was in danger. He smiled as if there had been no strife between
us and said, "Do not trouble yourself. I am an old man. Whatever mistakes I have made, I have loved my country." I am told
that he offered his neck to his executioner with that same grace.

Thus I did not determine to change the world out of an easy
idealism and selfish righteousness that are invariably the harbingers
of failure, nor did I determine to change the world so that my
wealth and power might be enhanced; wealth beyond one's comfort has always seemed to me the most boring of possessions,
and power beyond its usefulness has seemed the most contemptible. It was destiny that seized me that afternoon at Apollonia
nearly sixty years ago, and I chose not to avoid its embrace.

It was more nearly an instinct than knowledge, however, that
made me understand that if it is one's destiny to change the
world, it is his necessity first to change himself. If he is to obey
his destiny, he must find or invent within himself some hard and

secret part that is indifferent to himself, to others, and even to the world that he is destined to remake, not to his own desire, but to a nature that he will discover in the process of remaking.

And yet they were my friends, and dearest to me at the precise moment when in my heart I gave them up. How contrary an animal is man, who most treasures what he refuses or abandons! The soldier who has chosen war for his profession in the midst of battle longs for peace, and in the security of peace hungers for the clash of sword and the chaos of the bloody field; the slave who sets himself against his unchosen servitude and by his industry purchases his freedom, then binds himself to a patron more cruel and demanding than his master was; the lover who abandons his mistress lives thereafter in his dream of her imagined perfection.

Nor do I exempt myself from this contrariness. When I was young, I would have said that loneliness and secrecy were forced upon me. I would have been in error. As most men do, I chose my life then; I chose to enclose myself in the half-formed dream of a destiny no one could share, and thus abandoned the possibility of that kind of human friendship which is so ordinary that it is never spoken of, and thus is seldom cherished.

One does not deceive oneself about the consequences of one's acts; one deceives oneself about the ease with which one can live with those consequences. I knew the consequences of my decision to live within myself, but I could not have foreseen the heaviness of that loss. For my need of friendship increased to the degree that I refused it. And I believe that my friends—Maecenas, Agrippa, Salvidienus—never could fully understand that need.

Salvidienus Rufus, of course, died before he could have understood it; like myself, he was driven by energies of youth so remorseless that consequence itself became nothing, and the expense of energy became its own end.

The young man, who does not know the future, sees life as a kind of epic adventure, an Odyssey through strange seas and unknown islands, where he will test and prove his powers, and thereby discover his immortality. The man of middle years, who has lived the future that he once dreamed, sees life as a tragedy; for he has learned that his power, however great, will not prevail against those forces of accident and nature to which he gives the names of gods, and has learned that he is mortal. But the man of age, if he plays his assigned role properly, must see life as a comedy. For his triumphs and his failures merge, and one is no more the occasion for pride or shame than the other; and he is neither the hero who proves himself against those forces, nor the protagonist who is destroyed by them. Like any poor, pitiable shell of an actor, he comes to see that he has played so many parts that there no longer is himself.

I have played these roles in my life; and if now, when I come to the final one, I believe that I have escaped that awkward comedy by which I have been defined, it may be only the last illusion, the ironic device by which the play is ended.

When I was young, I played the role of scholar—which is to say, one who examines matters of which he has no knowledge. With Plato and the Pythagoreans, I floated through the mists where souls are supposed to wander in search of new bodies; and for a while, convinced of the brotherhood of man and beast, I refused to eat any flesh, and felt for my horse a kinship that I had not dreamed possible. At the same time, and without discomfort, I as fully adopted the opposing doctrines of Parmenides and Zeno, and felt at home in a world that was absolutely solid and motionless, without meaning beyond itself, and hence infinitely manipulatable, at least to the contemplative mind.

Nor when the course of events around me altered did it seem inappropriate that I assume the mask of a soldier and play out that appointed role. *Wars, both civil and foreign, I undertook throughout the world, on sea and land. . . . Twice I triumphed with an ovation, thrice I celebrated curule triumphs, and was saluted as Imperator twenty-one times.* Yet, as others have suggested, perhaps with more tact than I deserved, I was an indifferent soldier. Whatever successes I have claimed came from those more skillful in the art of battle than I—Marcus Agrippa first, and then those who inherited the skills of which he was author. Contrary to the libels and rumors spread during the early days of my military life, I was not more cowardly than another, nor did I lack the will to endure the hardships of campaign. I believe that I was then even more nearly indifferent to the fact of my existence than I am now, and the endurance of the rigors of warfare afforded me a curious pleasure that I have found elsewhere neither before nor since. But it always seemed to me that there was a peculiar childishness about the fact of war, however necessary it might have been.

It is said that in the ancient days of our history, human rather than animal sacrifices were offered to the gods; today we are proud to believe that such practices have so receded into the past that they are recorded only in the uncertainty of myth and legend. We shake our heads in wonderment at that time so far removed (we say) from the enlightenment and humanity of the Roman spirit, and we marvel at the brutality upon which our civilization is founded. I, too, have felt a distant and abstract pity for that ancient slave or peasant who suffered beneath the sacrificial knife upon the altar of a savage god; and yet I have always felt myself to be a little foolish to do so.

For sometimes in my sleep there parade before me the tens of thousands of bodies that will not walk again upon the earth, men no less innocent than those ancient victims whose deaths propitiated an earlier god; and it seems to me then, in the obscurity or clarity of the dream, that I am that priest who has emerged from the dark past of our race to speak the rite that causes the knife to fall. We tell ourselves that we have become a civilized race, and with a pious horror we speak of those times when a god of the crops demanded the body of a human being for his obscure function. But is not the god that so many Romans have served, in our memory and even in our time, as dark and fearsome as that ancient one? Even if to destroy him, I have been his priest; and even if to weaken his power, I have done his bidding. Yet I have not destroyed him, or weakened his power. He sleeps restlessly in the hearts of men, waiting to rouse himself or to be aroused. Between the brutality that would sacrifice a single innocent life to a fear without a name, and the enlightenment that would sacrifice thousands of lives to a fear that we have named, I have found little to choose.

I determined early, however, that it was disruptive of order for men to give honor to those gods who spring from the darkness of instinct. Thus I encouraged the Senate to declare the divinity of Julius Caesar, and I erected a temple in his honor in Rome so that the presence of his genius might be felt by all the people. And I am sure that after my death, the Senate will in like manner see fit

to declare my divinity also. As you know, I am already thought
to be divine in many of the towns and provinces of Italy, though
I have never allowed permission for this cult to be practiced in
Rome. It is a foolishness, but it is no doubt necessary. Nevertheless, of all the roles that I have had to play in my lifetime, this
one of being a mortal god has been the most uncomfortable. I am
a man, and as foolish and weak as most men; if I have had an advantage over my fellows, it is that I have known this of myself,
and have therefore known their weaknesses, and never presumed
to find much more strength and wisdom in myself than I found
in another. It was one of the sources of my power, that knowledge.

It is afternoon; the sun begins its slow descent to the west. A
calm has come upon the sea, so that the purple sails above me
hang slack against the pale sky; our boat sways gently upon the
waves, yet does not move forward to any perceptible degree. The
oarsmen, who all day have been taking their leisure, look at me
with a bored apprehension, expecting me to rouse them from
their ease and urge them to labor against the calm that has stilled
us. I shall not do so. In half an hour, or an hour, or two hours, a
breeze will rise; then we shall make for the coast and find safe
harbor and drop anchor. Now I am content to drift where the
sea will take me.

Of all the curses of age, this sleeplessness which increasingly I
must endure is the most troublesome. As you know, I have always been subject to insomnias; but when I was younger, I was
able to put that nocturnal restlessness of mind to purpose, and I
almost enjoyed those moments when it seemed to me that all the
world slept and I alone had leisure to observe its repose. Beyond
the urgings of those who would advise my policy in the terms of
their own vision of the world, which is to say in their visions of
themselves, I had the freedom of contemplation and silence; many
of my most important policies were determined as I lay awake
on my bed in the early hours before dawn. But the sleeplessness
that I have recently been undergoing is of a different kind. It is
no longer that restlessness of a mind so intent upon its play that it
is jealous of that slumber which would rob it of consciousness of
itself; it is, rather, a sleeplessness of waiting, a long moment in

which the soul prepares itself for a repose unlike any that mind or body has ever known before.

I have not slept this night. Near sunset, we harbored a hundred yards or so offshore in a little cove that protects the few fishing boats of some nameless village, the thatched huts of which are nestled on the slopes of a small hill perhaps half a mile inland. As evening came on, I watched the lamps and the fires glimmer against the dark, and watched until they flickered out. Now, once again, the world is asleep; a number of the crew has taken advantage of the night air, and chosen to sleep on deck; Philippus is below, next to the cabin in which he thinks I rest. Gently, invisibly, the little waves lap against the side of our ship; the night breeze whispers upon our furled sail; the lamp on my table glows fitfully, so that now and then I have to strain my eyes to see these words that I write to you.

During this long night, it has occurred to me that this letter does not serve the purpose for which it was intended. I wished at first, when I began writing to you, merely to thank you for the *nicolai*, to assure you of my friendship, and perhaps to give us both some comfort in our old age. But in the course of that friendly courtesy, I can see that it has become something else. It has become another journey, and one which I did not foresee. I go toward Capri for my holiday; but it seems to me now, in the quietness of this night, beneath the mysterious geometry of the stars, where nothing exists except this hand that forms the curious letters which by some other mysterious process you will understand, it seems to me that I go somewhere else, to a place as mysterious as any I have ever seen. I shall write further tomorrow. Perhaps we can discover that place toward which I travel.

August 10

There was a damp chill in the air when we embarked from Ostia yesterday, and rather foolishly I remained on deck so that I might see the Italian shore recede in the soft mist, and so that I could begin this letter to you—a letter which I intended at first simply to convey my thanks for the *nicolai*, and to assure you of my continuing affection, despite our long absence from each other. As you shall have understood by now, however, the letter has become more than that; and I beg the indulgence of an old friend to hear out what I shall discover to say. In any event, the chill brought on one of my colds, which has become a fever; and I became once again accustomed to an indisposition. I have not told Philippus of this new illness; I have, rather, reassured him of my well-being; for it appears that I am under some compulsion to complete the task of this letter, and I do not wish to be interrupted by Philippus's solicitudes.

The question of my health has always been less interesting to me than it has been to others. From my youth I have been frail, and subject to such a variety of maladies that more doctors than I like to imagine have been made wealthy. Their wealth has been largely unearned, I suspect; but I do not begrudge them what I have given them. So often has my body led me near death that, in my sixth consulship, when I was thirty-five years old, *the Senate decreed that every four years the consuls and the priests of the orders undertake vows and make sacrifices for the state of my health. To fulfill these vows, games were held so that the people might be made to remember their prayers, and all citizens, both individually and by municipalities, were encouraged to perform continued sacrifices for my health at the temples of the gods.* It was a foolishness, of course; but it did at least as much for my health as the various medications and treatments that my doctors subjected me to, and it let the people feel that they were participating in the fate of the Empire.

Six times during my life has this tomb of my soul led me to the brink of that eternal darkness into which all men sink at last, and six times it has stepped back, as if at the behest of a destiny it could not overmaster. And I have long outlived my friends, in whose lives I existed more fully than in my own. All are dead, those early friends. Julius Caesar died at fifty-eight, nearly twenty years younger than I am now; and I have always believed that his death came as much from that boredom which presages carelessness as from the assassins' daggers. Salvidienus Rufus died at the age of twenty-three, in his pride and by his own hand, because he thought he had betrayed our friendship. Poor Salvidienus. Of all my early friends, he was most like me. I wonder if he ever knew that the betrayal was my own, that he was the innocent victim of an infection that he caught from me. Vergil died at fifty-one, and I was at his bedside; in his delirium, he thought he died a failure, and made me promise to destroy his great poem on the founding of Rome. And then Marcus Agrippa, at the age of fifty, who had never had a day of illness in his life, died suddenly, at the height of his powers, before I could reach him to bid him farewell. And a few years later—in my memory, the years dissolve into one another, like the notes of tambour and lute and trumpet, to make a single sound—within a month of each other, Maecenas and Horace were dead. Except for you, my dear Nicolaus, they were the last of my old friends.

It seems to me now, as my own life is slowly trickling away, that there was a kind of symmetry in their lives that my own has not had. My friends died at the height of their powers, when they had accomplished their work and yet had further triumphs to look forward to; nor were they so unfortunate to come to believe that their lives had been lived for nothing. For nearly twenty years, it seems to me now, my life has been lived for nothing. Alexander was fortunate to have died so young, else he would have come to know that if to conquer a world is a small thing, to rule it is even less.

As you know, both my admirers and detractors have likened me to that ambitious young Macedonian; it is true that the Roman Empire is now constituted of many of the lands that Alexander first conquered, it is true that like him I came to my power as a young man, and it is true that I have traveled in many of the lands that he first subjugated to his rather barbaric will. But I have never wished to conquer the world, and I have been more nearly ruled than ruler.

The lands that I have added to our Empire, I have added to insure the safety of our frontiers; had Italy been safe without those additions, I should have been content to remain within our ancient borders. As it turned out, I have had to spend more of my life than I would have liked in foreign lands. From the mouth where the Bosporus spills into the Black Sea to the farthest shores of Spain I have traveled, and from the cold wastes of Pannonia where the German barbarians are contained to the burning deserts of Africa. Yet more often than not I did not go as conqueror, but as emissary, in peaceful negotiation with rulers that were more likely to resemble tribal chieftains than heads of state, and who often had neither Latin nor Greek. Unlike my uncle Julius Caesar, who found some odd renewal in such extended travels, I never felt at home in those distant lands, and always longed for the Italian countryside, and even Rome.

And yet I came to have respect and even some affection for these strange people, so unlike Romans, with whom I had to deal. The northern tribesman, his half-naked body swathed in the skins of animals he had killed with his own hands, staring at me through the smoke of a campfire, was not unlike the swarthy African who entertained me in a villa the opulence of which would dim that of many a Roman mansion; nor was the turbaned Persian chieftain with his carefully curled beard and his curious trousers and cloak embroidered with gold and silver thread, his eyes as watchful as those of a serpent, unlike the Numidian savage chieftain who stood before me with his javelin and his shield of elephant hide, his ebon body wrapped loosely with the skin of a leopard. At one time or another I have given power to such men; I have made them kings in their lands and given them the protection of Rome. I have even made them citizens, so that the stability of their kingdoms might have the name of Rome behind them. They were barbarians; I could not trust them; and yet more often than not I found as much to admire in them as I did to detest. And knowing them made me more fully understand my own countrymen, who have often seemed to me as strange as any people who inhabit the world.

Beneath the perfume and under the coiffure of the Roman dandy who minces about his carefully tended garden in his toga of forbidden silk, there is the rude peasant who walks behind his plough and is anointed by the dust of his labor; hidden by the marble façade of the most opulent Roman mansion there is the straw-thatched hut of the farmer; and within the priest who by solemn ritual dispatches the white heifer there is the laboring father who would provide meat for his family's table and clothing against the winter's chill.

At one time, when it was necessary for me to secure the favor and gratitude of the people, I was in the habit of arranging gladiatorial games. At that time, most of the contestants were criminals whose offenses would otherwise have been punishable by death or deportation. I gave them the choice of the arena or the legal consequences of their acts, and further stipulated that the defeated fighter might plead for mercy, and that he who survived three years, no matter what his offense might have been, would be set free. I had no surprise that the criminal condemned to death or relegated to the mines might choose the arena; but it always surprised me that a criminal who had been exiled from Rome more quickly chose the arena than the relatively safe hazards of a strange country. I never enjoyed these contests, yet I forced myself to attend them, so that the people might feel that I shared in their pleasure; and their pleasure in this carnage was extraordinary to behold. It was as if they took some strange sustenance into their lives by observing another less fortunate than they relinquish his own. More than once I have had to calm the lust of the mob by sparing the life of some poor wretch who had fought bravely; and I have observed, as if upon a single face, the sullen disappointment of unconsummated lust. At one time I suspended those games in which one or another of the contestants was intended to lose his life, and substituted boxing matches, in which Italian was pitted against barbarian; but this did not please the mob, and others who wished to buy the admiration of the people produced spectacles of such carnage and abandon that I was forced to give up my substitution and once again be guided by the desires of my countrymen, so that I might control them.

I have seen gladiators return to their quarters from the arena, covered with sweat and dust and blood, and weep like women over some small thing—the death of a pet falcon, an unkind note from a lover, the loss of a favorite cloak. And in the stands I have seen the most respectable of matrons, her face distorted as she shouted for the blood of a hapless fighter, later in the quietness of her home care for her children and her servants with the utmost gentleness and affection.

Thus if there runs in the blood of the most worldly Roman the rustic blood of his peasant ancestor, there runs also the wild blood of the most untamed northern barbarian; and both are ill-concealed behind the façade he has erected not so much to disguise himself from another as to mask himself against his own recognition.

It occurs to me, as we drift slowly southward, that without my having to tell them to do so, the crew, since they are under no compulsion to make haste, have instinctively kept always in sight of land, though as the wind has changed we have had to go to some trouble to make corrections to follow the irregular line of the coast. There is something deep within the Italian heart that does not like the sea, a dislike that has seemed to some so intense as to be nearly abnormal. It is more than fear, and it is more than the natural propensity of the peasant to husband his land, and to avoid that which is so unlike it. Thus the eagerness of your friend Strabo to sail blithely upon unknown seas, in search of strangeness, would bewilder the ordinary Roman, who ventures beyond the sight of land only upon the occasion of such a necessity as war. And yet under Marcus Agrippa the Roman navy has become the most powerful in the history of the world, and the battles that saved Rome from its enemies were fought upon the sea. Nevertheless, the dislike remains. It is a part of the Italian character.

It is a dislike of which the poets have been aware. You know that little poem of Horace's addressed to the ship that was bearing his friend Vergil to Athens? He advanced the conceit that the gods had separated land from land by the unimaginable depths of ocean so that the peoples in those lands might be distinct, and man in his foolhardiness launches his frail bark upon an element that ought not to be touched. And Vergil himself, in his great poem upon the founding of Rome, never speaks of the sea except in the most ominous of terms: Aeolus sends his thunder and winds upon the deep, waves are lifted so high that they obscure the stars, timbers are broken, and men see nothing. And even now, after so many years and so many readings of the poem, I am still moved nearly to tears by the thought of Palinurus, the helmsman, betrayed by the god of sleep into the depths of the ocean, where he drowns, and for whom Aeneas mourns, thinking of him as too trustful in the calm of sea and sky, lying naked on an unknown shore.

Of the many services that Maecenas performed for me, the most important seems to me now to be this: He allowed me to know the poets to whom he gave his friendship. They were

among the most remarkable men I have ever known; and if the
Roman, as he often did, treated them with as much disdain as he
dared, it was a disdain that masked a fear perhaps not wholly unlike that feeling he had about the sea. A few years ago it became
necessary for me to banish the poet Ovid from Rome because of
his involvement in an intrigue that threatened to disturb the
order of the state; since his part in the intrigue was more nearly
mischievous and social than malevolent and political, I made the
banishment as light as possible; I shall lift the banishment soon,
and allow him to return from the cold north to the more temper-
ate and pleasing climate of Rome. Yet even in his place of banishment, that half-barbaric little town of Tomis that huddles near
the mouth of the Danube, he continues to write his poems. We
correspond occasionally, and are on friendly enough terms; and
though he misses the pleasures of Rome, he does not despair of
his condition. But of the several poets that I have known, Ovid is
the only one whom I could not fully trust. And yet I was fond
of him, and remain so.

I could trust the poets because I was unable to give them what
they wanted. An Emperor may give to an ordinary man the
means to a wealth that would confound the most extraordinary
taste for luxury; he may bequeath such power that few men dare
to oppose it; he may confer such honor and glory upon a freedman that even a consul might feel constrained to behave toward
him with some deference. Once I offered to Horace the position
of my private secretary; it would have made him one of the most
influential men in Rome, and, had he been even discreetly corrupt, one of the richest. He replied that, alas, the state of his
health precluded his acceptance of a post fraught with such responsibilities. We both knew that the post was more nearly ceremonial than laborious, and that his health was excellent. I could
not be offended; he had the little farm that Maecenas had given
him, a few servants, his grape arbors, and enough income to import an excellent wine.

I suspect that I have admired the poets because they seemed to
me the freest and therefore the most affectionate of men, and I
have felt a closeness to them because I have seen in the tasks that
they set for themselves a certain similarity to the task that long
ago I set for myself.

The poet contemplates the chaos of experience, the confusion of accident, and the incomprehensible realms of possibility—which is to say the world in which we all so intimately live that few of us take the trouble to examine it. The fruits of that contemplation are the discovery, or the invention, of some small principle of harmony and order that may be isolated from that disorder which obscures it, and the subjection of that discovery to those poetic laws which at last make it possible. No general ever more carefully exercises his troops in their intricate formations than does the poet dispose his words to the rigorous necessity of meter; no consul more shrewdly aligns this faction against that in order to achieve his end than the poet who balances one line with another in order to display his truth; and no Emperor ever so carefully organizes the disparate parts of the world that he rules so that they will constitute a whole than does the poet dispose the details of his poem so that another world, perhaps more real than the one that we so precariously inhabit, will spin in the universe of men's minds.

It was my destiny to change the world, I said earlier. Perhaps I should have said that the world was my poem, that I undertook the task of ordering its parts into a whole, subordinating this faction to that, and adorning it with those graces appropriate to its worth. And yet if it is a poem that I have fashioned, it is one that will not for very long outlive its time. When Vergil died, he earnestly beseeched me to destroy his great poem; it was not complete, he said, and imperfect. Like a general who sees a legion destroyed and does not know that two others have triumphed, he thought himself to be a failure; and yet his poem upon the founding of Rome will no doubt outlast Rome itself, and certainly it will outlast the poor thing that I have put together. I did not destroy the poem; I do not believe that Vergil thought I would. Time will destroy Rome.

My fever has not abated. An hour ago, I had a sudden attack of dizziness and a sharp pain in my left side, followed by a numbness. I discover that my left leg, always a little weak, is now hardly capable of movement. It will still support my weight, but it drags beneath me uselessly; and when I prick it with my stylus, there is the merest ghost of a pain.

I still have not informed Philippus of my condition; there is nothing that he can do to relieve my condition, and I should prefer not to humiliate him by forcing him to perform vain solicitudes upon a body whose deterioration is far beyond the reach of any ministrations he might attempt. After all these years, I cannot be angry at a body that fails; despite its weakness, it has served me well; and it is perhaps appropriate that I should attend its demise, as I might attend the death of an old friend, remembering as the soul slips away into whatever immortality it might find, the mortal soul which could not in life separate itself from the animal that was its guest. I am able now, and have been for some months, almost to detach myself from the body that contains me and observe this semblance of myself. It is not an ability altogether new, and yet it seems to me now that it is more natural than it has been before.

And so, detached from a failing body, almost oblivious to the pain that now is its habitation, I float above the unimaginable sea southward toward Capri. The high sun glints upon the water that parts before our prow, the white foam hisses as it spreads and disperses upon the waves. I shall rest from my task, and perhaps some of my strength will return. This evening we harbor at Puteoli. And tomorrow we shall land at Capri, where I shall perform what might be the last of my public functions.

We are at harbor. It is early afternoon, and the mists have not yet blurred the coastal lands from the sight of the sea voyager. I remain at my table, and occupy my leisure with this letter. I believe that Philippus, who continues to watch me from his station at the prow of our ship, has begun to suspect that the condition of my health has sharply worsened. A look of doubt has settled upon his fine young face, and his hazel eyes beneath the brows that are straight and delicate as a woman's glance at me from time to time. I do not know how much longer I shall be able to conceal my condition from him.

We have dropped anchor at a little cove just north of Puteoli; and farther north is Naples, where some years ago Marcus Agrippa constructed a causeway between the sea and the Lucrine Lake, so that the Roman fleet might conduct its maneuvers safe from the vicissitudes of weather and the pirate fleets of Sextus

Pompeius. At one time, as many as two hundred war ships trained upon that inland harbor, and thus became capable of defeating Sextus Pompeius and saving Rome. But during these years of peace, silt has been allowed to clog the entrance to this training ground; and now I understand that it has been turned into an oyster bed so that the Roman rich might have the pleasures of their new existences enhanced. From where we are anchored, I cannot see this harbor, and I am just as pleased that I cannot.

In recent years the possibility has occurred to me that the proper condition of man, which is to say that condition in which he is most admirable, may not be that prosperity, peace, and harmony which I labored to give to Rome. In the early years of my authority, I found much to admire in my countryman; in the midst of privation he was uncomplaining and sometimes almost gay, in the midst of war he had more care for the life of a comrade than he did for his own, and in the midst of disorder he was resolute and loyal to the authority of Rome, wherever he thought that authority might lie. For more than forty years we have lived the Roman peace. No Roman has fought Roman, no barbarian foot has trod in unchallenged enmity upon Italian soil, no soldier has been forced to bear arms against his will. We have lived the Roman prosperity. No person in Rome, however lowly, has gone without his daily ration of grain; the provincial citizen is no longer at the mercy of famine or natural disaster, but may be sure of aid in any extremity; and any citizen, whatever his birth, may become as rich as his endeavor and the accidents of the world allow him. And we have lived the Roman harmony. I organized the courts of Rome so that each man might go before a magistrate with some assurance of receiving at least a modicum of justice; I codified the laws of the Empire, so that even the provincial might live in some security from the tyranny of power or the corruption of greed; and I made the state secure against the brutal force of ambitious power by instituting and enforcing those laws against treason that Julius Caesar had promulgated before his death.

And yet there is now upon the Roman face a look which I fear augurs badly for his future. Dissatisfied with honest comfort, he strains back toward the old corruption which nearly robbed the state of its existence. Though I gave the people freedom from tyranny and power and family, and freedom to speak without fear of punishment, nevertheless *the dictatorship of Rome was offered to me by both the people and the Roman Senate, first when I was absent in the East,* following the defeat of Marcus Antonius at Actium, *and later during the consulship of Marcus Marcellus and Lucius Arruntius, after I had saved Italy, at my own expense, from that famine which destroyed the grain supply of Italy. Upon neither occasion did I accept,* though I incurred the displeasure of the people. And now the sons of senators, who might be expected to serve their fellow men or even themselves with some honor, clamor to hazard their lives in the arena, pitting themselves against common gladiators, for what they imagine to be the sport of danger. So has Roman bravery descended into the common dust.

Marcus Agrippa's harbor now furnishes oysters for the Sybarite of Rome, the bodies of honest Roman soldiers fertilize his luxuriant garden of clipped box and cypress, and the tears of their widows make his artificial streams flow merrily in the Italian sunlight. And in the north the barbarian waits.

The barbarian waits. Five years ago, on that part of the German frontier that is marked by the Upper Rhine, a disaster befell Rome from which she has not yet recovered; it is perhaps a portent of her fate.

From the northern shore of the Black Sea to the lower coast of the German Ocean, from Moesia to Belgium, a distance of more than a thousand miles, Italy lies unprotected by any natural barrier from the Germanic tribes. They cannot be defeated, and they cannot be persuaded from their habits of pillage and murder. My uncle was not able to do so, nor could I during the years of my authority. Therefore it was necessary to fortify that frontier, to protect at once the northern provinces of Rome and at last to protect Rome itself. The most difficult part of that frontier, since it protected land that was particularly rich and fertile, was the area in the northwest, below the Rhine. Thus, of the twenty-five legions of some one hundred and fifty thousand soldiers that protected the Empire of Rome, five legions of the most experienced veterans I had assigned to that small region. They were under the

command of Publius Quintilius Varus, who had successfully
served as proconsul of Africa and governor of Syria.

I suppose that I must hold myself responsible for that disaster,
for I allowed myself to be persuaded to give the German command to Varus. He was a distant relative of my wife, and he had
been of some service to Tiberius in the past. It was one of the
most serious mistakes I ever made, and the only time in my memory that I placed a man of whom I knew so little in such a high
position.

For on the rude and primitive border of that northern province, Varus imagined that he might still live in the luxury and
ease of Syria; he remained aloof from his own soldiers, and began
to trust those German provincials who were adept at flattery and
able to offer him some semblance of the sensual life to which he
had become accustomed in Syria. Chief among these sycophants
was one Arminius of the Cherusci, who had once served in the
Roman army and had been rewarded by the gift of citizenship.
Arminius, who spoke fluent Latin despite his barbaric origin,
gained the confidence of Varus, so that he might further his own
ambitions of power over the scattered German tribes; and when
he was sufficiently sure of Varus's credulity and vanity, he falsely
informed him that the distant tribes of the Chauci and the Bruc-
teri were in revolt and sweeping southward to threaten the security of the provincial border. Varus, in his arrogance and recklessness, would not listen to the counsel of others; and he
withdrew three legions from the summer camp on the Weser and
marched northward. Arminius had laid his plans well; for as
Varus led his legions through the forest and marshland toward
Lemgo, the barbarian tribes that had been forewarned and prepared by Arminius, fell upon the laboring legions. Confused by
the suddenness of the attack, unable to maintain an orderly resistance, bewildered by the thick forest and rain and marshy
ground, they were annihilated. Within three days, fifteen thousand soldiers were slain or captured; some of the captured were
buried alive by the barbarians, some were crucified, and some
were offered to the northern gods by the barbaric priests, who
decapitated them and secured the heads to trees in the sacred
groves. Fewer than a hundred soldiers managed to escape the am-

bush, and they reported the disaster. Varus was either slain or took his own life; no one could be sure which. In any event, his severed head was returned to me in Rome by a tribal chieftain named Maroboduus, whether out of an anxious piety or an exultant mockery I do not know. I gave the poor remnant of Varus a decent burial, not so much for the sake of his soul as for the sake of the soldiers who had been led to disaster by his authority. And still in the north the barbarian waits.

After his victory on the Rhine, Arminius did not have the wit to pursue his advantage; the north lay open to him—from the mouth of the Rhine nearly to its confluence with the Elbe— and yet he was content merely to plunder his neighbors. The following year, I put the German armies under the command of Tiberius, since it was he who had persuaded me to appoint Varus. He recognized his own part in the disaster, and knew that his future depended upon his success in subduing the Germans and restoring order in those troubled northern provinces. In this endeavor he was successful, largely because he relied upon the experience of the veteran centurions and tribunes of the legions rather than upon his own initiative. And so now there is an uneasy peace in the north, though Arminius remains free, somewhere in that wilderness beyond the border he disturbed.

Far to the east, beyond even India, in a part of that unknown world where no Roman has been known to set foot, there is said to be a land whose kings, over unnumbered successive reigns, have erected a great fortress wall that extends hundreds of miles across the entirety of their northern frontier, so that their kingdom might be protected against the encroachments of their barbaric neighbors. It may be that this tale is a fantasy of an adventurer; it may even be that there is no such land as this. Nevertheless, I will confess that the possibility of such a project has occurred to me when I have had to think of our northern neighbors who will be neither conquered nor appeased. And yet I know that it is useless. The winds and rains of time will at last crumble the most solid stone, and there is no wall that can be built to protect the human heart from its own weakness.

For it was not Arminius and his horde; it was Varus in his weakness who slaughtered fifteen thousand Roman soldiers, as it is the Roman Sybarite in his life of shade who invites the slaughter of thousands more. The barbarian waits, and we grow weaker in the security of our ease and pleasure.

Again it is night, the second night of this voyage which, it becomes clearer and clearer to me, may be my last. I do not believe that my mind fails with my body, but I must confess that the darkness came over me before I even noticed its encroachment; and I found myself staring sightlessly to the west. It was then that Philippus could no longer avoid his anxiety and approached me with that slightly rude manner of his that so transparently reveals his shyness and uncertainty. I allowed him to place his hand upon my forehead so that he could judge the extent of my fever, and I answered a few of his questions—untruthfully, I might add. But when he tried to insist that I retire to my room below deck, so that I might be protected from the night air, I assumed the role of the willful and crotchety old man and pretended to lose my temper. I did so with such energy that Philippus was convinced of my strength, and was content to send below for some blankets with which I promised to wrap myself. Philippus elected to stay on deck, so that he could keep an eye on me; but soon he nodded, and now, curled on the bare deck, his head cradled in his folded arms, with that touching faith and completeness of the young, he sleeps, certain that he will awake in the morning.

I cannot see it now, but earlier, before the late afternoon mists rose from the sea to shroud the western horizon, I thought I could make out its contours, a dark smudge against the vast circle of the sea. I believe that I saw the Island of Pandateria, where for so many years my daughter suffered to live in her exile. She is no longer on Pandateria. Ten years ago, I judged that it was possible to allow her to return in safety to the mainland of Italy; now she abides in the Calabrian village of Reggio, at the very toe of the Italian boot. For more than fifteen years, I have not seen her, or spoken her name, or allowed the fact of her existence to be mentioned in my presence. It was too painful for me. And that silence merely defined another of the many roles that contained me in my life.

My enemies have found an understandable pleasure in contemplating the ironic use to which I finally had to put those marriage laws that I promulgated and had enacted by the Senate some thirty years ago; and even my friends have found occasion to be displeased by their existence. Horace once told me that laws were powerless against the private passions of the human heart, and only he who has no power over it, such as the poet or the philosopher, may persuade the human spirit to virtue. Perhaps in this instance both my friends and enemies were right; the laws did not move the people toward virtue, and the political advantage I achieved by pleasing the older and more staid segments of the aristocracy was momentary.

I was never so foolish as to believe that my laws of marriage and adultery would be obeyed; I did not obey them, nor did my friends. Vergil, when he invoked the Muse to assist him in the writing of *The Aeneid*, did not in any substantial way believe in her whom he invoked; it was a way that he had learned to begin the poem, a way to announce his intention. Thus those laws which I initiated were not intended so much to be obeyed as to be followed; I believed that there was no possibility of virtue without the idea of virtue, and no effective idea of virtue that was not encoded in the law itself.

I was mistaken, of course; the world is not poem; and the laws did not accomplish the purpose for which they were intended. But in the end they were of use to me, though I could not have foreseen that use; and I have not been able to regret since then that I allowed them. For they saved the life of my daughter.

As one grows older, and as the world becomes less and less to him, one wonders increasingly about those forces that propelled him through time. Certainly the gods are indifferent to the poor creature who struggles toward his fate; and they speak to him so obliquely that at last he must determine for himself the meanings they portend. Thus in my role of priest, I have examined the entrails and livers of a hundred beasts, and with the aid of the augurs have discovered or invented whatever portents seemed to me appropriate to my intention; and concluded that the gods, if they do exist, do not matter. And if I encouraged the people to follow these ancient Roman gods, I did so out of necessity rather than any religious conviction that those forces rest very securely in their supposed persons. . . . Perhaps you were right after all, my dear Nicolaus; perhaps there is but one god. But if that is true, you have misnamed him. He is Accident, and his priest is man, and that priest's only victim must be at last himself, his poor divided self.

As they have known so many things, the poets have known this better than most, though they have put the knowledge in terms that may seem trivial to some. I agreed with you in the past that they spoke too much of love, and gave too much value to what at best was a pleasant pastime; but I am no longer sure that that agreement was well advised. *I hate and I love,* Catullus said, speaking of that Clodia Pulcher whose family caused so much difficulty in Rome, even in our time and long after her death. It is not enough; but what better way might we begin to discover that self which is never wholly pleased or displeased with what the world offers?

You must forgive me, Nicolaus; I know that you will disagree, and that you have no way to voice your disagreement; but I have in late years sometimes thought that it might be possible to construct a system of theology or even a religion around the idea of love, if that idea were extended somewhat beyond its usual application, and approached in a certain way. Now that I am no longer capable of it, I have been examining that mysterious power that in its many varieties existed within me for so many years. Perhaps the name that we give to the power is inadequate; but if it is, so are the names, spoken and unspoken, that we give to all the simpler gods.

I have come to believe that in the life of every man, late or soon, there is a moment when he knows beyond whatever else he might understand, and whether he can articulate the knowledge or not, the terrifying fact that he is alone, and separate, and that he can be no other than the poor thing that is himself. I look now at my thin shanks, the withered skin upon my hand, the sagging flesh that is blotched with age; and it is difficult for me to realize that once this body sought release from itself in that of another; and that another sought the same from it. To that instant of pleasure some dedicate all their lives, and become embittered and empty when the body fails, as the body must. They are embittered and empty because they have known only the pleasure, and do not know what that pleasure has meant. For contrary to what we may believe, erotic love is the most unselfish of all the varieties; it seeks to become one with another, and hence to escape the self. This kind of love is the first to die, of course, failing as the body that carries it fails; and for that reason, no doubt, it has been thought by many to be the basest of the varieties. But the fact that it will die, and that we know it will die, makes it more precious; and once we have known it, we are no longer irretrievably trapped and exiled within the self.

Yet it alone is not enough. I have loved many men, but never as I have loved women; the love of a man for a boy is a fashion in Rome that you have observed with some wonder and I believe repulsion, and you have been puzzled by my tolerance of such practices, and more puzzled perhaps because despite my tolerance I have not engaged in them myself. But that kind of love which is friendship has seemed to me best disengaged from the pleasures of the flesh; for to caress that body which is of one's own sex is to caress one's self, and thus is not an escape of the self but an imprisonment within it. For if one loves a friend, he does not become that other; he remains himself, and contemplates the mystery of one that he can never be, of selves that he has never been. To love a child may be the purest form of this mystery; for within the child are potentialities that he can hardly imagine, that self which is at the furthest remove from the observer. My love for my adopted children and for my grandchildren has been the object of some amusement among those who have known me, and has been seen as an indulgence of an otherwise rational man, as a sentimentality of an otherwise responsible father. I have not seen it so.

One morning some years ago, as I walked down the Via Sacra toward the Senate House, where I was to give that address which would condemn my daughter to a life of exile, I met one whom I had known when I was a child. It was Hirtia, the daughter of my old nurse. Hirtia had cared for me as if I were her own child, and had been given her freedom for her faithful service. I had not seen her for fifty years, and would not have known her had not a name I once was known by slipped from her lips. We spoke of the times of our childhoods, and for a moment the years slipped away from me; and in my grief I almost told Hirtia of what I had to do. But as she spoke of her own children, and her life, and as I saw the serenity with which she had returned to the place of her birth so that she might meet her death in the pleasant memory of that lost youth, I could not speak. For the sake of Rome and my authority, I was to condemn my own daughter; and it occurred to me that had Hirtia had the power to make the choice, Rome would have fallen and the child would have survived. I could not speak, for I knew that Hirtia would not understand my necessity, and would be troubled for the little time that remained in her life. For a moment, I was a child again, and mute before what I took to be a wisdom that I could not fathom.

It has occurred to me since that meeting with Hirtia that there is a variety of love more powerful and lasting than that union with the other which beguiles us with its sensual pleasure, and more powerful and lasting than that platonic variety in which we contemplate the mystery of the other and thus become ourselves; mistresses grow old or pass beyond us; the flesh weakens; friends die; and children fulfill, and thus betray, that potentiality in which we first beheld them. It is a variety of love in which you, my dear Nicolaus, have found yourself for much of your life, and it is one in which our poets were happiest; it is the love of the scholar for his text, the philosopher for his idea, the poet for his word. Thus Ovid is not alone in his northern exile at Tomis, nor are you alone in your far Damascus, where you have chosen to devote your remaining years to your books. No living object is necessary for such pure love; and thus it is universally agreed that this is the highest form of love, since it is for an object that approaches the absolute.

And yet in some ways it may be the basest form of love. For if we strip away the high rhetoric that so often surrounds this notion, it is revealed simply as a love of power. (Forgive me, my dear Nicolaus; let us pretend that once again we are engaging in one of those quibbles with which we used to amuse ourselves.) It is the power that the philosopher has over the disembodied mind of his reader, the power that the poet has over the living mind and heart of his listener. And if the minds and hearts and spirits of those who come under the spell of that appointed power are lifted, that is an accident which is not essential to the love, or even its purpose.

I have begun to see that it is this kind of love that has impelled me through the years, though it has been necessary for me to conceal the fact from myself as well as from others. Forty years ago, when I was in my thirty-sixth year, the Senate and people of Rome accorded me the title of Augustus; twenty-five years later, when I was in my sixty-first year, and in the same year that I exiled my daughter from Rome, the Senate and people gave me the title of Father of my Country. It was quite simple and appropriate; I exchanged one daughter for another, and the adoptive daughter acknowledged that exchange.

To the west, in the darkness, lies the Island of Pandateria. The little villa where Julia lived for five years is uninhabited now and by my orders uncared for. It is open to the weather and the slow erosion of time; in a few years it will begin to crumble, and time will take it, as it takes all things. I hope that Julia has forgiven me my sparing her life, as I have forgiven her for having thought to take mine.

For the rumors that you must have heard are true. My daughter was a member of the conspiracy that had as its end the assassination of her husband, and the murder of myself. And I invoked those marriage laws that had so long lain unused and condemned her to a life of exile, so that she might not be condemned to death by the secret effort of her husband, Tiberius, who would have made her endure a trial for treason.

I have often wondered whether my daughter has ever admitted to herself the extent of her own guilt. I know that the last time I saw her, in her confusion and grief at the death of Jullus Antonius, she was not able to do so. I hope that she will never be able to do so, but will live out her life in the belief that she was the victim of a passion which led to her disgrace, rather than a participant in a conspiracy that would certainly have led to her father's death, and almost certainly would have destroyed Rome. The first I might have allowed; the second I could not.

I have relinquished whatever rancor I might have had against my daughter, for I have come to understand that despite her part in the conspiracy there was always a part of Julia that remained the child who loved the father who was perhaps too doting; a part of her that must have recoiled in horror from what she felt she was at last driven to do; a part of her that still, in the loneliness of Reggio, remembers the daughter that once she was. I have come to understand that one can wish for the death of another and yet love that victim without appreciable diminution. At one time I was in the habit of calling her my Little Rome, an appellation that has been widely misunderstood; it was that I wished my Rome to become the potentiality that I saw in her. In the end, they both betrayed me; but I cannot love them the less for that.

To the south of our anchorage, the Lucrine Lake, dredged once by honest Italian hands so that the Roman fleet might protect the people, furnishes oysters for the tables of the Roman rich; Julia languishes on the barren Calabrian coast at Reggio; and Tiberius will rule the world.

I have lived too long. All those who might have succeeded me and striven for the survival of Rome are dead. Marcellus, to whom I first betrothed my daughter, died at the age of nineteen; Marcus Agrippa died; and my grandsons, the sons of Agrippa and Julia, Gaius and Lucius, died in the service of Rome; and Tiberius's brother, Drusus, who was both more able and equable than his brother, and whom I raised as my own son, died in Germany. Now only Tiberius remains.

I have no doubt that more than any other Tiberius was responsible for the fate of my daughter. He would not have hesitated to implicate her in the conspiracy against his life and my own, and he would have been pleased to see the Senate pass the sentence of death upon her, while he assumed the demeanor of sorrow and regret. I cannot bring myself to do other than despise Tiberius. At the center of his soul there is a bitterness that no one has fathomed, and in his person there is an essential cruelty that has no particular object. Nevertheless he is not a weak man, and he is not a fool; and cruelty in an Emperor is a lesser fault than weakness or foolishness. Therefore I have relinquished Rome to the mercies of Tiberius and to the accidents of time. I could do no other.

August 11

During the night, I did not move from my couch but kept a vigil on the stars that move slowly in their eternal voyage across the great dome of the sky. Toward dawn, for the first time in days, I dozed a little; and I had a dream. I was in that curious state where one dreams and knows that one dreams, yet finds there a reality which mocks that of one's waking life; I wished to remember the contours of that other world; but when I was awakened, the memory of the dream fled into the brightness of the morning.

I was awakened by the stirring of the crew, and by the sound of a distant singing; for a moment, in my confusion, I thought of those Sirens of whom Homer wrote so beautifully, and imagined myself to be bound to the mast of my ship, helpless against the call of an unimaginable beauty. But it was not the Sirens; it was a grain-ship from Alexandria that sailed slowly toward us from the south, and the Egyptian crew, dressed in white robes with garlands on their heads, stood on deck singing in their native tongue as they approached us; and the musky odor of burning incense was borne to us on the morning breeze.

We watched their approach with some puzzlement, until at last the huge ship which dwarfed our own came so close that we could make out the smiling swarthy faces of the men; and then the captain stepped forward and hailed me by name.

With some difficulty, which I trust I concealed even from Philippus, I rose from my couch and went to the deck rail, upon which I leaned while I returned the greeting of this captain. It appeared that the ship had unloaded a cargo of goods at the harbor between Puteoli and Naples, and had been informed of my presence nearby; and the crew had wished, before they made their way back to their far Egyptian homeland, to greet me and to give me thanks. The ship was so close that I did not have to shout, and I could see clearly the dark face of the captain. I inquired his name; it was Pothelios. And as the crew continued its low singing, Pothelios said to me:

"You have given us the liberty to sail the seas and thus furnish Rome with the bountiful goods of Egypt; you have rid the seas of those pirates and brigands that in the past would have made that liberty empty. Thus the Egyptian Roman may prosper, and may return to his homeland secure in the knowledge that only the accidents of wind and wave threaten his safety. For all this we give thanks to you, and pray that the gods will allow you good fortune for the rest of your days."

For a moment I could not speak. Pothelios had addressed me in a stiff but passable Latin; and it occurred to me that thirty years ago he would have spoken in that demotic Egyptian Greek and that I would have been hard put to understand him. I returned the captain's thanks and said a few words to the crew, and directed Philippus to see that each member of that crew be given some coins of gold. Then I returned to my couch, from where I watched the huge freighter turn slowly away from us and move southward, its sails bulging in the wind, its crew waving and laughing, happy in their safety and homeward voyage.

And so now we too move southward, and our less bulky ship dances upon the waves. The sunlight catches the flecks of white foam that top the little waves, the waves slap gently and whisper against the sides of our ship, the blue-green depth of the sea seems almost playful; and I can persuade myself now that after all there has been some symmetry to my life, some point; and that my existence has been of more benefit than harm to this world that I am content to leave.

Now throughout this world the Roman order prevails. The German barbarian may wait in the North, the Parthian in the East, and others beyond frontiers that we have not yet conceived; and if Rome does not fall to them, it will at last fall to that barbarian from which none escape—Time. Yet now, for a few years, the Roman order prevails. It prevails in every Italian town of consequence, in every colony, in every province—from the Rhine and the Danube to the border of Ethiopia; from the Atlantic shores of Spain and Gaul to the Arabian sands, and the Black Sea. Throughout the world I have established schools so that the Latin tongue and the Roman way may be known, and have seen to it that those schools will prosper; Roman law tempers the disordered cruelty of provincial custom, just as provincial custom modifies Roman law; and the world looks in awe upon that Rome that I found built of crumbling clay and that now is made of marble.

The despair that I have voiced seems to me now unworthy of what I have done. Rome is not eternal; it does not matter. Rome will fall; it does not matter. The barbarian will conquer; it does not matter. There was a moment of Rome, and it will not wholly die; the barbarian will become the Rome he conquers; the language will smooth his rough tongue; the vision of what he destroys will flow in his blood. And in time that is ceaseless as this salt sea upon which I am so frailly suspended, the cost is nothing, is less than nothing.

We approach the Island of Capri. It shines like a jewel in the morning sun, a dark emerald rising out of the blue sea. The wind has almost died, and we float as if upon the air toward that quiet and leisurely place where I have spent so many happy hours. Already the island inhabitants, who are my neighbors and my friends, have begun to gather at the harbor; they wave, and I can hear their voices calling. Gaily, gaily they call to me. In a moment I shall rise and answer them.

The dream, Nicolaus; I remember the dream I had last night. I dreamed I was again at Perusia, during the time of Lucius Antonius's uprising against the authority of Rome. All winter we had blockaded the town, hoping to effect Lucius's surrender and thus avoid the shedding of Roman blood. My men were weary and disheartened by the long waiting, and threatened revolt. To give them hope, I ordered that an altar be constructed outside the city walls and that sacrifice be offered to Jupiter. And this is the dream:

A white ox, never yoked to the plough, was led to the altar by the attendants; its horns were gilded, and its head was garlanded by a wreath of laurel. The rope was slack; the ox came forward willingly, its head raised. Its eyes were blue, and they seemed to be looking at me, as if the beast recognized who was to be its executioner. The attendant crumbled the salt cake on its head; it did not move; the attendant tasted the wine, and then poured the libation between its horns. Still the ox did not move. The attendant said: "Shall it be done?"

I raised my ax; the blue eyes were upon me; they did not waver. I struck, and said: "It is done." The ox quivered and sank slowly to its knees; still its head was upraised, and its eyes were upon me. The attendant drew his dagger and slit the throat, catching the blood in his goblet. And even as the blood flowed the blue eyes seemed to look into mine, until at last they glazed and the body toppled to one side.

That was more than fifty years ago; I was in my twenty-third year. It is curious that I should dream of that after so long a time.

EPILOGUE

Letter: Philippus of Athens to Lucius Annaeus Seneca,
from Naples *(A.D. 55)*

I was surprised and pleased, my dear Seneca, to receive your letter; I trust that you will forgive my delay in replying. Your inquiry reached me in Rome on the very day that I was leaving the city, and I have only just begun to get settled in my new home. You will be pleased to learn that at last I have taken the advice you have given me, both to my face and in your writings, and have retired from the bustle and confusion of my practice, so that I might devote myself to the quiet dignity of learning, and pass on to others what little knowledge I have gained through the years. I write these words from my villa outside Naples; the sunlight, dispersed by the budding grapevines that arch over my terrace, dances over the paper upon which these words appear; and I am as happy as you promised I would be in my retirement. For that assurance and the truth of it, I wish to thank you.

Over the years our friendship has, indeed, been too sporadic; I am only grateful to you for remembering me, and for overlooking the fact that I did not speak out on your behalf during that unfortunate time that you were forced to spend on the barren waste of Corsica; you have understood better than most, I suspect, that a poor physician without worldly power, nor even a hundred like him, could have prevailed against the will of one so erratic as our late Emperor Claudius. All of us who have admired you, even in our silence, are elated that once again your genius may brighten the Rome that you have loved.

You ask me to write about that matter of which we have spoken upon those too infrequent occasions that we have had to converse—my brief acquaintance with the Emperor Caesar Augustus. I am happy to accede to your request, but you must know that I am consumed with a friendly curiosity: may we expect a new essay? an Epistle? or perhaps, even, a tragedy? I shall wait eagerly to learn the use to which you intend to put my few memories.

When we have spoken of the Emperor before, perhaps desiring a friendship which I imagined might be enhanced by your continued curiosity, I have been somewhat too mysterious and selfish with the information I would impart. But now I am in my sixty-sixth year—ten years younger than Octavius Caesar when he died. And I believe that I have at last gone beyond that vanity against which you have so often inveighed, yet have been kind enough to except me. I shall tell you what I remember.

As you know, I was physician to Octavius Caesar for only a few months; but in those few months, I was always near him, more often than not within a distance from which I could hear him call; and I was with him when he died. I do not know even now why he chose me to attend him during those months that he knew were to be his last; there were many others more famous and more experienced than I; and I was only in my twenty-sixth year at the time. Nevertheless, he did choose me; and though I could not conceive it in my youth, I suspect now that he was fond of me, in that curious detached way that he seemed to have. And though I was able to do nothing for him in his last days, he saw to it that I was a rich man after his death.

After a leisurely voyage of several days south from Ostia, we debarked at Capri; and though it was clear that his health was failing, he would not be so impolite as to ignore the throng that awaited him. He chatted with many of them, calling them by name, though upon occasion in his weakness he had to lean on my arm. Since most of the inhabitants of Capri are Greek, he spoke to them in that language, apologizing from time to time for his rather strange accent. At last he was content to bid his neighbors farewell, and we made our way to the Emperor's villa, which commanded a remarkable view of the Bay of Naples, not many miles away. I persuaded him to rest, and he seemed content to do so.

He had promised the island youths to observe the gymnastic competition that had been arranged to select those who would represent the island in the games at Naples the following week; and despite my protestations, he insisted upon fulfilling that promise; and again despite my wishes, he invited them all to his villa that evening for a banquet in their honor.

He was extraordinarily gay at the banquet. He invented licentious epigrams in Greek, and encouraged the young men to groan at their badness; he joined them in their boyish games of throwing crusts of bread at each other; and in the face of their strenuous activities of the afternoon, he jokingly insisted upon calling them the "Idle-landers" rather than the "Islanders," because of the leisurely life that they ordinarily led. He promised to attend the games in Naples, in which they were to compete; and insisted that he was gambling his entire fortune on their success.

We remained at Capri for four days. Most of the time the Emperor sat quietly, gazing at the sea, or at the Italian coast line to the east. There was a quiet smile on his face, and every once in a while he would nod slightly, as if he were remembering something.

On the fifth day we crossed to Naples. By this time the Emperor was so weak that he could not walk unassisted. Nevertheless, he insisted that he be taken to the games at which he had promised the young athletes he would be present; and I confess that, though I knew his end was near, I could not but assent to his going. It was clear that it would have made the difference of only a few days, at the most. He sat all afternoon in the blazing sun, cheering the Caprian Greeks to their victories; and when the contests were over, he found himself unable to rise from his chair.

We carried him from the stadium on a litter, and he let it be known that he wished to go at once to one of his childhood homes, at Nola. Since it was a journey of only eighteen miles, I consented; and we arrived at his old home in the early hours of the morning.

Knowing that the end was near, I had word sent to Benevento where Livia and her son Tiberius had been staying for several days. According to the Emperor's instructions, I made it clear that he did not wish to see Tiberius, though he would allow the information to be spread that Tiberius had indeed attended him during his last hours.

On the morning of the day he died, he said to me:

"Philippus, it is near, is it not?"

There was something in his manner that forbade me to dissemble with him.

"One cannot be sure," I said. "But it is near. Yes."

He nodded tranquilly. "Then I must fulfill the last of my obligations."

A number of his acquaintances—I believe he had no one then whom he would have called a friend—had heard of his illness in Rome, and had made haste to Nola. He received them, bade them farewell, and admonished them to assist in the orderly transference of his power, and obliged them to support Tiberius in his accession to authority. When one of them made a show of weeping, he became displeased, and said:

"It is unkind of you to weep upon the occasion of my contentment."

He wished to see Livia alone, then. But when I made a movement to leave the room, he beckoned me to stay.

When he spoke to Livia, I could tell that he was weakening rapidly. He made a gesture to her; she knelt and kissed him on the cheek.

"Your son—" he said. "Your son—"

He breathed hoarsely for a moment; his jaw went slack; and then, by an apparent effort of his will, he regained a little of his strength.

"We need not forgive ourselves," he said. "It has been a marriage. It has been better than most."

He fell back upon his bed; I rushed to his side; he still breathed. Livia touched his cheek. She lingered beside him for a moment, and left the room.

Some moments later, he opened his eyes suddenly and said to me:

"Philippus, my memories. . . . They are of no use to me now."

For a moment, then, it seemed that his mind wandered, for he suddenly cried out: "The young! The young will carry it before them!"

I put my hand upon his brow; he looked at me again, raised himself upon one elbow, and smiled; then those remarkable blue eyes glazed; his body twitched once; and he toppled on his side.

Thus died Gaius Octavius Caesar, the August; it was at three o'clock in the afternoon, on the nineteenth day of August, in the consulships of Sextus Pompeius and Sextus Appuleius. He died in the same room that his natural father, the elder Octavius, had died in seventy-two years before.

Of that long letter which Octavius wrote to his friend Nicolaus in Damascus, I must say one thing. It was entrusted to my care for delivery; but in Naples, I received word that Nicolaus himself had died two weeks before. I did not inform the Emperor of this, for it seemed to me at the time that he was happy in the thought that his old friend would read his last words.

Within a few weeks after his death, his daughter Julia died in her confinement at Reggio; it was whispered by some that her former husband, the Emperor Tiberius, allowed her to starve. Of that rumor I do not know the truth, nor I suspect does anyone who is now alive.

It is the fashion of the day, and it has been the fashion for more than thirty years, for many of the younger citizens to speak with some condescension of the long reign of Octavius Caesar. And he himself, toward the end of his life, thought that all of his work had been for nothing.

Yet the Empire of Rome that he created has endured the harshness of a Tiberius, the monstrous cruelty of a Caligula, and the ineptness of a Claudius. And now our new Emperor is one whom you tutored as a boy, and to whom you remain close in his new authority; let us be thankful for the fact that he will rule in the light of your wisdom and virtue, and let us pray to the gods that, under Nero, Rome will at last fulfill the dream of Octavius Caesar.

Rome, Northampton, Denver, 1967–1972

TITLES IN SERIES

For a complete list of titles, visit www.nyrb.com or write to:
Catalog Requests, NYRB, 435 Hudson Street, New York, NY 10014

J.R. ACKERLEY Hindoo Holiday*
J.R. ACKERLEY My Dog Tulip*
J.R. ACKERLEY My Father and Myself*
J.R. ACKERLEY We Think the World of You*
HENRY ADAMS The Jeffersonian Transformation
RENATA ADLER Pitch Dark*
RENATA ADLER Speedboat*
CÉLESTE ALBARET Monsieur Proust
DANTE ALIGHIERI The Inferno
DANTE ALIGHIERI The New Life
KINGSLEY AMIS The Alteration*
KINGSLEY AMIS Girl, 20*
KINGSLEY AMIS The Green Man*
KINGSLEY AMIS Lucky Jim*
KINGSLEY AMIS The Old Devils*
KINGSLEY AMIS One Fat Englishman*
WILLIAM ATTAWAY Blood on the Forge
W.H. AUDEN (EDITOR) The Living Thoughts of Kierkegaard
W.H. AUDEN W.H. Auden's Book of Light Verse
ERICH AUERBACH Dante: Poet of the Secular World
DOROTHY BAKER Cassandra at the Wedding*
DOROTHY BAKER Young Man with a Horn*
J.A. BAKER The Peregrine
S. JOSEPHINE BAKER Fighting for Life*
HONORÉ DE BALZAC The Human Comedy: Selected Stories*
HONORÉ DE BALZAC The Unknown Masterpiece *and* Gambara*
MAX BEERBOHM Seven Men
STEPHEN BENATAR Wish Her Safe at Home*
FRANS G. BENGTSSON The Long Ships*
ALEXANDER BERKMAN Prison Memoirs of an Anarchist
GEORGES BERNANOS Mouchette
ADOLFO BIOY CASARES Asleep in the Sun
ADOLFO BIOY CASARES The Invention of Morel
CAROLINE BLACKWOOD Corrigan*
CAROLINE BLACKWOOD Great Granny Webster*
NICOLAS BOUVIER The Way of the World
MALCOLM BRALY On the Yard*
MILLEN BRAND The Outward Room*
SIR THOMAS BROWNE Religio Medici and Urne-Buriall*
JOHN HORNE BURNS The Gallery
ROBERT BURTON The Anatomy of Melancholy
CAMARA LAYE The Radiance of the King
GIROLAMO CARDANO The Book of My Life
DON CARPENTER Hard Rain Falling*
J.L. CARR A Month in the Country*
BLAISE CENDRARS Moravagine
EILEEN CHANG Love in a Fallen City
JOAN CHASE During the Reign of the Queen of Persia*

* *Also available as an electronic book.*

UPAMANYU CHATTERJEE English, August: An Indian Story
NIRAD C. CHAUDHURI The Autobiography of an Unknown Indian
ANTON CHEKHOV Peasants and Other Stories
GABRIEL CHEVALLIER Fear: A Novel of World War I*
RICHARD COBB Paris and Elsewhere
COLETTE The Pure and the Impure
JOHN COLLIER Fancies and Goodnights
CARLO COLLODI The Adventures of Pinocchio*
IVY COMPTON-BURNETT A House and Its Head
IVY COMPTON-BURNETT Manservant and Maidservant
BARBARA COMYNS The Vet's Daughter
EVAN S. CONNELL The Diary of a Rapist
ALBERT COSSERY The Jokers*
ALBERT COSSERY Proud Beggars*
HAROLD CRUSE The Crisis of the Negro Intellectual
ASTOLPHE DE CUSTINE Letters from Russia*
LORENZO DA PONTE Memoirs
ELIZABETH DAVID A Book of Mediterranean Food
ELIZABETH DAVID Summer Cooking
L.J. DAVIS A Meaningful Life*
VIVANT DENON No Tomorrow/Point de lendemain
MARIA DERMOÛT The Ten Thousand Things
DER NISTER The Family Mashber
TIBOR DÉRY Niki: The Story of a Dog
ARTHUR CONAN DOYLE The Exploits and Adventures of Brigadier Gerard
CHARLES DUFF A Handbook on Hanging
BRUCE DUFFY The World As I Found It*
DAPHNE DU MAURIER Don't Look Now: Stories
ELAINE DUNDY The Dud Avocado*
ELAINE DUNDY The Old Man and Me*
G.B. EDWARDS The Book of Ebenezer Le Page
MARCELLUS EMANTS A Posthumous Confession
EURIPIDES Grief Lessons: Four Plays; translated by Anne Carson
J.G. FARRELL Troubles*
J.G. FARRELL The Siege of Krishnapur*
J.G. FARRELL The Singapore Grip*
ELIZA FAY Original Letters from India
KENNETH FEARING The Big Clock
KENNETH FEARING Clark Gifford's Body
FÉLIX FÉNÉON Novels in Three Lines*
M.I. FINLEY The World of Odysseus
THOMAS FLANAGAN The Year of the French*
EDWIN FRANK (EDITOR) Unknown Masterpieces
MASANOBU FUKUOKA The One-Straw Revolution*
MARC FUMAROLI When the World Spoke French
CARLO EMILIO GADDA That Awful Mess on the Via Merulana
MAVIS GALLANT The Cost of Living: Early and Uncollected Stories*
MAVIS GALLANT Paris Stories*
MAVIS GALLANT Varieties of Exile*
GABRIEL GARCÍA MÁRQUEZ Clandestine in Chile: The Adventures of Miguel Littín
ALAN GARNER Red Shift*
WILLIAM H. GASS On Being Blue: A Philosophical Inquiry*